About the Author

Born and raised in Malta to a Maltese father and British mother, Moyra Sammut had an idyllic childhood, with both cultures instilled in her and her siblings. The blend of the two cultures, together with a fascination for World War II, were thus deeply rooted, as real-life events were passed on to her from both grandfathers, who actively participated in the war; one as an air raid recruit based in Malta and the other fighting in Anzio with the British Army.

Ms Sammut travelled extensively during her employment as a travel journalist, where she would document far-to-reach destinations in such vivid descriptions that it earned her a middle page weekly spread in local newspapers, which is where her love for writing became apparent as her popularity spread.

In her first book, 'A Map of Scars', she conveys the memoires passed on to her with intense and historic realism, which the reader is invited to delve into.

To Debbie, I hope you enjoy reading this book as much as I enjoyed writing it.

A Map of Scars

Moyra Sammut

A Map of Scars

Olympia Publishers
London

www.olympiapublishers.com
OLYMPIA PAPERBACK EDITION

First Published in 2021

Olympia Publishers
Tallis House
2 Tallis Street
London
EC4Y 0AB

Printed in Great Britain

Dedication

To my mother, Pauline, my rock, my father, Aurelio, who taught me how to be strong and independent and my sisters, Romina and Yvette, who accepted me as I am

Acknowledgements

I have to start with Josephine Gauci who supported me; making this book possible, Vanessa Pace — who patiently read and reread my book helping me proofread it, Colleen Figg, who guided me throughout, Stefan Varga, for the amazing portrait, Julia Azzopardi for the design of the cover and last but not least, Simon Cusens, who advised on many factual aspects to the story.

Chapter 1
Malta — May 1939

The balmy and salty air permeated George's nose; she inhaled deeply from the balcony window whilst listening to the waves. She loved the view — the mighty bastions of the 'Three Cities' rising majestically from the Grand Harbour, a reminder of centuries of history. She admired the speckles of light from the houses and the light of a waning moon reflecting on a beautifully calm sea.

A *dghajsa* was making its way across, ferrying the odd passenger. She lit a cigarette, exhaling the smoke out of the window. It was early, her parents had not gone to sleep yet; she waited patiently for the lights downstairs to go out.

George crept out of the small cellar door onto St Barbara Bastions. Pulling down the soft brown trilby to cover her face or rather, throw it into shadow. She walked towards *Strada Stretta* feeling the usual excitement which enveloped her every time she planned an illicit night out down at the 'Cairo'.

Adjusting her tie and jacket as she passed "Blackley's", the baker's shop in *Strada Reale* quickly glancing in the shop window to appraise her appearance as she passed by. Satisfied with what she saw, carried on with her gait towards the bar. She loved Valletta, she loved the island for that matter but Valletta especially, there was something about the people, they were all very close knit and looked out for one another. *Strada Stretta* was, as usual, a hub of activity.

'Aaaah, there you are George; I was waiting for you; I wondered when you were coming.' Marlene owner of the Cairo bar said, watching her walk up to the bar counter.

'Hmm, I am a bit late. My parents went to bed later than usual, so it was difficult for me to slip out', she said, smiling at her old friend.

The Cairo Bar or 'the Camel' as she affectionately referred to it, was situated in the middle of *Strada Stretta,* a narrow dingy street in Valletta with a notorious reputation for drunken sailors, prostitutes and misfits; a bohemian area chock-full of drinking bars, cabaret halls, Jazz bars, restaurants and residents, all co-existing harmoniously. To George, *Strada Stretta* was a safe haven among its debauchery for her to live her double life. In the dark she hid under the cloak of her disguise; hat, shirt, trousers, jacket, tie and shoes. It had not been easy to put together her 'look'. The shoes were the hardest to find because most shoe makers she had approached raised an eyebrow when she said the shoes were for her ten-year old non-existent brother and could not produce him in reality. Finally, she found Fredu, tucked away at the bottom of *Strada San Paolo*, who did not turn a hair at this young shorthaired woman's request for a pair of boy's shoes. He had measured her feet and produced the most elegant pair of fashionable soft brown leather brogues within a week. The rest of the clothes she acquired by craftily duping shopkeepers. Her hair she kept cut at the barbers' across from the Cairo bar, for most hairdressers refused to cut her hair in the short bob she liked. Giuseppi was always pleased to see her and never asked intrusive questions.

Of course, George was extra careful and guarded to never let her parents find out about her unconventional habits. They would never understand, she didn't quite understand herself; just that she was different to other women, she felt more comfortable in men's clothing; she supposed she was a bit like Bobby and young Guzi who was already showing he was heading down the same path. Bobby worked the bars of *Strada Stretta* dressed as a woman — he was an outrageous transvestite and the sailors loved him.

Her mother spent every moment she could telling her only daughter to stop cutting her hair so short and that she should settle down and find a nice boy and get married. George cringed imagining her mother's voice say the very words, as if standing next to her. How could she, George, say anything? How could she tell her mother that finding a boy and getting married was the last thing in the world she wanted? In desperate moments she had entertained the thought of running away and writing to her Aunt Marie Louise in England asking her if she could go and stay with her for a while. But how would she find the courage to abscond and leave her mother and her father, both of whom she adored? She tried to imagine her father reading a letter telling him that she had run away to

England; she knew it would destroy him and devastate her mother. But the feeling of wanting to escape grew stronger every day; she wanted to be somewhere anonymous, somewhere she could live freely, away from the restrictions of not being able to live as she wanted.

George broke her train of thought whilst she sipped on the glass of gin and tonic that Marlene had placed in front of her. The Cairo had the pyramids of Giza painted on its walls complete with a couple of sphinxes and camels roaming a desert. It was a dimly lit bar, Marlene preferred it that way, citing that its darkness provided the right atmosphere for drawing custom from outside. There was one bulb profusely dotted with fly excrement that shone over the bar and a couple of kerosene lamps hanging on the nicotine-stained walls that gave the paintings — which had seen better days — a yellowish hue. The lights outside from the New Life Musical Hall next door lit Cairo Bar's entrance and part of the inside to show the decor— once one's eyes became accustomed — of local beer *Farsons'* plaques and a couple of stained mirrors.

There was a lot of noise outside; white uniformed sailors with prostitutes feigning enthusiasm clinging onto their arm, passed by in small groups, laughing loudly. There were others in the bar. The regulars, Toni and Felich, huddled over a glass of wine always discussing politics, Carmenu and Giovanni laughing and making lewd remarks about the voluptuous bar girls standing in the doorway. George loved it all, she felt safe because if anybody noticed she dressed differently they didn't care and why should they? Besides, Bobby had paved the way for her, with his gaudy and elaborate dresses and exaggerated wigs, the sailors fell head over heels for his flamboyancy. The residents of the street had gotten used to seeing George frequent the Cairo, they never questioned her presence, but rather, they turned a blind eye, because all sorts of strange things happened in the street. Tonight, was no exception, albeit quieter than usual, though more navy ships were expected in the Grand Harbour later that night.

A young man with dark slicked-back wavy hair neatly dressed in a brown double-breasted suit and wearing round wire-rimmed glasses with thick lenses, looked very serious as he walked in. He appeared out of place, yet he wasn't awkward at all, instead he calmly sauntered up to the counter and stood next to George. He turned to her and nodded briefly as was customary, since the Maltese were known to be very friendly. Marlene asked the young man what he wanted to drink. He ordered a tumbler of red wine.

'You are not from around here, are you?' Marlene asked the man in a friendly yet inquisitive manner.

'No, I'm not, I'm from Senglea, I had to meet a friend but he didn't turn up.'

'What is your name my friend?' Marlene asked.

'My name is Carmelo' he said.

'So, what do you think happened to your friend, Carmelo?' Marlene quizzed him, busying herself wiping down the grey marble counter.

'I don't know but it doesn't matter; I will get in touch with him tomorrow,' Carmelo replied politely.

He sat on a vacant stool next to George, who was quietly drinking and at the same time eavesdropping on the conversation. She did not want to draw any unsolicited attention from the newcomer. Carmelo turned to her and offered her a drink. She declined with a shake of her head. She noticed he was carrying a wooden case with him which he had placed at the foot of his stool. He saw her looking at the case.

'That's my paint box; I'm an artist,' Carmelo offered, smiling.

George nodded in acknowledgement. If Carmelo noticed that she was a woman dressed in men's clothing, he didn't show it and that made George feel at ease.

'So, are you an established artist?'

'Well, no, I wouldn't say that, I'm still studying,' he said laughingly and carried on, 'I used to attend the Umberto Primo Art Lyceum here in Valletta, but now I study and live in Rome,' a sense of pride in his voice.

At that particular moment a group of sailors passed by raucously laughing and Carmelo swore under his breath, *'Haqq l'inglizi!'* (Damned British!)

'I take it you are not fond of them!' George said nodding towards the source of the disturbance.

'Not particularly,' he replied, grimacing.

George chose to ignore Carmelo's obvious irritation and instead carried on questioning him.

'So where is it you study in Rome?'

'I study at the *Regia Accademia Di Belle Arti*,

'How long have you been studying there then?'

'You ask a lot of questions,' Carmelo said, as a matter of fact.

'I suppose I do' she replied.

'I'd been trying for a couple of years, it took me a while to get in too, I tried for a scholarship with some financial backing by the Italian General Consulate a couple of times. It was the only way a working-class man like myself would ever get into such a prestigious art school like *The Accademia*, this is now my last year there.'

'Do you miss Malta?'

'Yes, I do very much, but as things stand, I don't agree with British colonization; we should not be dictated to, we are better off being part of Italy, so at the moment I prefer to live in Italy till things change.'

'So, in fact what you're saying is you are a supporter of Fascism!'

'The fact of the matter remains that Malta voluntarily accepted to become a British colony in 1813; I mean we were horribly abused by the French so the British protectorate was the best thing that happened to us.'

'It's not the point, the British were clever because making Malta a crown colony meant that their fleet had the perfect naval base. Maltese citizens are decent folk and should be treated with dignity and equal living conditions and not forced to submit to this absurd social divide! That's why I'm an avid Italian irredentist, we were treated with much more dignity when we were under the Sicilian protectorate.'

'And what on earth is an irredentist?'

'I'm part of a nationalist movement which promotes the unification of geographic areas like Malta, Italian-speaking persons such as myself, who want to form a majority of the population and yes I'm a fascist if that's what it makes me, I support Mussolini and his ideals, if you truly understood his politics you would also see why I'm one of his most avid supporters,' Carmelo was short of foaming at the mouth when he finished.

'Gosh that's a mouthful; I can see you are very passionate about the subject of irredentism which in all honesty I don't fully understand.'

'Yes, I apologise, I didn't mean to sound so harsh, but people fail to see that under the colonial rule we are in fact suffering, suffering because there is a great social divide, we are treated like scum, it's our island, we should be treated with respect.

George said nothing more on the subject of colonial rule, not wanting the situation to get out of hand.

There followed an awkward silence before Carmelo's mood changed.

'Do you have an interest in art?' he asked, changing the subject.

'Yes, I do, especially Michelangelo's work; I mean I would love to see the Sistine Chapel one day.'

'Aaah, an admirer of the *Rinascimento*!' he exclaimed, pleased with the Italian connection.

'I don't paint of course but I read as much as I can about art and yes, I do love the Renaissance period, but I also love classic French art, especially the impressionists, you know Renoir, Manet, Degas, Monet, Cezanne… I'm fascinated by the style.'

'Well then since you love art so much it would be nice if we could meet up and see the wonderful Parish Church of Senglea, dedicated to the nativity of the Virgin Mary.'

'I wouldn't mind though you might not recognise me during the daytime,' she stated boldly, recklessly even.

'I'm sure I will, let us say a week next Saturday; today is the tenth so a week on Saturday will be the twentieth, I will meet you at the front of the Royal Opera House at ten a.m. and I will take you to Senglea. I have to leave now but I look forward to seeing you again, and it was a pleasure meeting you.'

George nodded in agreement and smiled, not even giving a second thought that this man was a complete stranger.

'I hope you find your friend,' she said as an afterthought.

'I'm sure I will.'

With that Carmelo finished his wine in one gulp and left, disappearing into the melee of raucous sailors outside. The street was picking up momentum as it got later and George looked at her watch which told her it was one thirty in the morning. Meanwhile young Guzi, Marlene's son had by this time donned a gaudy sequinned dress and equally gaudy wig to complete his transformation. He was immediately surrounded and drowned in wolf whistles. The barmaids were having a good night, their tin tokens were piling up whilst the boys drunk themselves to a stupor.

It was time for her to leave, she took a right turn out of the door. The New Life Music Hall was on a roll, it was bristling with dancers and revellers. George had to elbow her way through the crowd till the end of the street before she found a clear way out. There wasn't a soul in sight and she thanked her lucky stars under her breath, the last thing she wanted was to be seen slipping through the small cellar door which, as far as her parents were concerned, had not been opened in donkeys' years. It was her good fortune to have found the other entrance door in the internal courtyard that led to the cellar. The door had been obscured by thick ivy and it was only George's inquisitive nature that led her to it some years ago. Since then, she had used it to her advantage, hiding her clothes down there.

The door opened easily; the lock was well oiled; George had taken care of that with some cooking oil. She ascended the stairs in complete darkness and felt her way to the first room where she quickly shed her clothes and put on a nightdress. The rest was easy; She was used to it by now, making it unnecessary to use any kind of light to show her the way. She pushed the yard door very gently and squeezed herself through between door and ivy and closed it quietly behind her. There was a kerosene lamp which her father left alight all night long hanging in the hallway. The cold solid flagstone steps to the upstairs made no sound; she padded barefoot to her bedroom. All was quiet; her parents were sound asleep and she slipped into bed. Her thoughts drifted to the extraordinary meeting with Carmelo. He was rather an odd fellow, yet she did not doubt his intelligence because he seemed to be a well-educated young man. She resolved to tell her best friend Connie about her encounter with Carmelo.

Chapter 2

George and Connie had finished their shift at Arnolds' Glove Factory in Birkirkara which meant they had to catch two busses to get to Sliema.

It was a glorious afternoon; colourful Maltese boats bobbed gracefully, their reflections stretching the length of the sheltered harbour of Sliema Creek. It was exceptionally hot for May, but as the afternoon wore on it had started to become somewhat cooler. George sat on a bench next to *Bonello's Kiosk* in St Anne's Piazza sipping lemonade with her best friend.

'What time does the film start? Because I need to pop into Victor's Pharmacy before we leave', directing her question at Connie who had suggested they see *Kate Plus Ten* at the Manoel Theatre in Valletta.

'George *hanini* (dear), I already told you, it starts at seven-fifteen p.m. which incidentally leaves you just an hour and a half; where's your mind these days?'

'Sorry, yes I am a bit absent-minded lately; I've got a lot going on in there; thing is, I've been getting the urge to leave the island; if truth be known I really want to go to London, do something more towards the war effort, do you know what I mean?'

Connie nodded silently in acknowledgement. The war was a foreboding subject that hung threateningly in the air and they were well aware of the implications. She was not likely to have the opportunity to do what George had in mind. She had very strict Catholic parents, but Connie was as independent as George, even though her circumstances were very different.

'*Insomma*' (anyway) Connie carried on, 'we should make a move; I don't want to miss the film because Jack Hulbert and Genevieve Tobin are starring in it!'

'Oh, OK then, we mustn't miss it must we?' George replied laughing.

George headed to Victor's Pharmacy across the road from where they were sitting, to buy some aspirin. As soon as she got back, they left to catch the bus from The Strand.

They made it to Valletta in the nick of time. They passed by the Opera House and walked down *Strada Reale* to *Strada San Giovanni* chattering away till they arrived. There were people milling around the entrance queuing to get tickets; the girls joined the queue and were soon seated in the grand auditorium to watch the show.

After the film finished, they decided to go for a drink at the King's Own Band Club in *Strada Reale*. The place was packed and they struggled to find a table.

'Look George, there's one over there in the corner, that couple are getting up from their seats.' Connie indicated to a table in the far corner of the room.

They wove their way in between the chequered cloth tables and sat down. The waiter, seeing two women on their own, flattened his hair with his hands, put on his most charming smile and made his way to their table. 'What will you have ladies?' he asked.

Connie piped up and said, 'Two lemonades please.'

'Eeh, yes of course, I bring for you.' The waiter left and soon returned with the drinks.

'George, you know earlier on you said you wanted to leave Malta and go to work in London? Tell me how on earth are you going to persuade your mother to let you do that? I mean I know your father is a bit more lenient and likes you to be independent, but somehow I don't see your mother giving in so easily; it's practically unheard of for a woman to go off unchaperoned and do something like that on her own, can you imagine *my* mother if I told her I wanted to work abroad, she would have a fainting fit?' Connie laughed at the thought.

'To be honest Con, I don't think for one minute it's going to be plain sailing, in fact it's probably going to be the opposite; I'm not sure I should say anything to them', pulling a face as she said this.

'What? Not say anything to them? You mean run away?'

'Well yes, that's exactly what I've been thinking of doing!'

'You're being very brave, but I don't know how you would go about it for sure and I don't think that it's going to solve your situation if you know what I mean!'

I can't see any other way, can you?'

'I can't imagine being without you, I'll miss you George, it will be very strange; we've been friends for all these years, not to see you would be very hard for me, because I'm guessing that it would be a very long time before you came back, if ever.'

George was taken aback. In all the time she had known Connie, she had never heard her express herself in this way.

'Come on Con, it's not that bad and of course I'll be back eventually, besides you can't keep me away from you for too long.' 'I will miss you too and anyway, we don't know for sure there is going to be a war, with a bit of luck this Hitler business will blow over and I haven't left yet.' George finished this last sentence with a smile hoping it was reassuring, if not to herself, to her best friend sitting at the table with her.

'I'm not so sure this war is going to blow over, Hitler has risen to phenomenal heights in Germany; according to my father he is sort of a dictator just like Mussolini and he is up to no good,' Connie responded.

'Oh, bugger Hitler! Anyway, I wanted to tell you I met this extraordinary fellow, his name is Carmelo and he is an art student, very passionate about art, he has asked me to meet him a week on Saturday.'

'Hmm never heard of him but where did you meet him? Don't tell me it was at the Cairo? Surely not!' Connie said incredulously, watching her friend nod her head.

'Yes, I did, I thought it a bit odd myself but I think he just came into the first place he found, as a friend he was meeting let him down.'

'Oh, then you must be careful, he is a complete stranger and you never know, he might be after something!'

Connie chuckled as she said that, to which George retorted, 'Not in a million years and you know that!'

They left the band club walking at a leisurely pace, looking at the shops and the latest fashions to which George feigned interest in as they went along. Because both of them lived in Valletta it was of course convenient not to have to worry about catching a bus. They parted at the corner of Wembley Stores on *Strada Levante.*

George headed home. The old but elegant house her father had rented was meant to be for a duration of a couple of years but his posting got extended indefinitely. He was the only qualified Royal Engineer who had the experience to carry out the tunnelling works that were needed in the event of a war. Her father Harry didn't mind because it was a good place to bring up children and Georgina—or George, as she liked being called, had grown up into a fine young woman, who spoke three languages, was wise to the local culture and very independent. George was his only child. Not for want of his wife Frances and himself trying, because Frances, being Maltese, wanted a large family just like the one she had come from. But for some reason, which they never spoke about, George remained their only one. It worried Harry sometimes, that George had no siblings. He worried that if anything happened to Frances or himself, how George would cope. They were a close-knit family, Frances saw to that. His wife was a staunch Catholic and never missed a service on Sunday. It was her day of worship and he respected her.

He had made sure his family would be taken care of; Harry had eventually bought the house on St Barbara Bastions, it had a solid cellar to go with it and he was now glad it did, because of the way things were going. It was the best investment he had ever made. It was a big place, all the rooms had high ceilings with thick wooden beams and vast windows overlooking the Grand Harbour. The kitchen had a balcony which was George's favourite place to read whilst Frances prepared the daily meals. There were the bedrooms, all four of them, one of which Harry had converted into a library—one of his greatest passions was collecting books. There was a large mahogany desk beneath the window littered with model aircraft; George frequently sat with him for hours helping him put the models together whilst discussing great events in history and art. George was an intelligent child who had an insatiable appetite for knowledge and was forever plying him with questions which he didn't always have the answers to, so he started to introduce her to his collection of books, which she read, absorbing everything like a sponge. After finishing her studies in the French language and literature she landed a job at Arnolds' and for all things she seemed happy. These days Harry sensed her discord, there was something occupying her mind, she was constantly distracted.

'Papa I'm home' George called out twiddling with the knob on the Rediffusion in the sitting room till it sprung to life to the *BBC World Service*.

'I'm in here George, put the kettle on love; I'm dying for a cuppa.' Her father's voice resonated from the library where he was fiddling about with a model aircraft. 'How was the film then?'

'It was quite exciting actually, a rather unusual subject for a change, the main character, which Genevieve Tobin played, was a woman who was the leader of a criminal gang, you don't see that often in films, you know, being given the lead role. It had me gripping the seat a couple of times I must say,' she replied from the kitchen whilst lighting the Primus stove.

'Pa, I need to talk to you about something but I'm a bit apprehensive about telling you,'

'Hmm what is it you want to talk about?'

She set the tea tray on her father's desk and watched him as he patiently attached a wing to the body of the model aircraft.

He stirred the teapot and poured the tea through the tea strainer in a cup, added some sugar and milk and stirred pensively. George waited anxiously whilst he calmly took a sip of tea.

'Well dad, I know it's not the usual thing to ask, but I've been thinking for a long time that I should go to England.'

'I see, you've been very quiet lately and I wondered if there was something wrong with you.

Harry went quiet absorbing his daughter's words.

'I'm not happy for you to go alone; I mean you are still quite young George and you know your mother is going to find every reason under the sun for you not to leave, don't you?'

'I know mum is going to dig her heels in over this, but the thing is Dad, I've been feeling restless of late. I feel somewhat useless when I know I can be doing more with myself other than sewing gloves. Both mum and you have given me a decent education, I just feel wasted and I want to do something more worthwhile; if you know what I mean!'

'I think at this point it's best to let me discuss it with your mother, sort of pave the way. You are a lucky young lady with the way things are looking at the moment; your mother might be persuaded that it's safer for you to be as far away from the island as possible.'

'Dad, I can stay with Aunt Marlu and Uncle Ted; I mean, when they write, they always ask when I am going to visit them and your mind would be at rest!'

'Yes, I suppose that's true and they would love to have you, in fact they said so in their last letter to us the other day.'

'I really think that would work, Aunt is fun and Uncle Ted is such a sweetheart, do you think you could pull it off with Mama?'

'Hmm,' he said rubbing his black stubble, 'I don't know, but put it this way, the threat of war is your best trump card and the fact you are going to stay with my sister and her husband is to your advantage. Mind not a word to your mother till I have spoken to her.'

'No, I won't breathe a word and thank you Dad I appreciate it.' George hugged her father.

He looked at her with pure affection, she was all they had; sometimes it was hard to accept how fast she had grown. He knew it was time to let her go; she had grown into a wonderful woman; she was a credit to them both.

Harry returned to his model aircraft pensively. Frances was not going to give in without a fight; he knew his wife's Maltese temperament only too well.

A well-educated and strong woman, Frances Abela fell in love with Harry Parker the first time she saw him near a shop in Valletta. She saw him with a map in his hands looking perplexed and somewhat vulnerable… and lost. He was a handsome man with a thatch of black hair and smiling blue eyes, smart in his uniform sporting the Royal Engineer's badge.

She had stopped to help him and it was love at first sight for both of them. He had asked her to join him for a drink and they didn't stop talking the entire time. They had met the next three nights till it was time for Harry to get back to England. But they had written to each other for a number of months before Harry asked her to marry him, as soon as he knew he was being posted back to Malta. They had married and honeymooned in Gozo and as he always put it — it was the best time of his life. George followed ten months later.

Chapter 3

It was one of those days when George found herself irritated by a humid Sirocco, the kind that clung to one like a second skin.

Bugger this heat she thought as she fanned herself for the umpteenth time, hanging halfway out of her bedroom balcony window, trying hopelessly to cool down.

'Georgina,' her mother suddenly called, 'Come and put the Rediffusion on please.'

'Coming Mama.'

It was six o'clock in the evening; her father was usually home by that time but he hadn't arrived yet.

'Mama, Papa's late today, did he say anything before he left this morning?'

'No *qalbi (sweetheart)* he didn't but I'm sure he will be home soon,' Frances concluded.

No sooner had Frances finished her sentence than they heard the front door open.

Harry walked in; he looked exhausted and worried at the same time. 'Hello you two,' he smiled heading straight for the Rediffusion.

'I was just going to turn it on Papa.' George said. The Rediffusion sparked to life.

'*This is the BBC World Service at six o'clock with the news headlines; Apprehension is running high as Hitler's rise to power could spell war...*'

Frances and George looked at Harry, alarmed. Harry met their worried gaze steadily.

Whilst the news still went on Harry said, 'We all knew this was coming, that's why I was late coming home, we had word from headquarters that Hitler is intending to invade Poland and I'm pretty sure it won't be long before he declares war on England, especially with that spineless twit Chamberlain in government. The last thing I heard was that he is going to try and negotiate some sort of peace treaty to keep Britain from being involved in the war, but I can't see that happening.'

Frances looked at George and George anticipated her mother's look.

'Mama it still doesn't make a difference I still want to go; besides I've already sent a letter to Aunt Marlu.'

Frances looked towards Harry for support, they had spent countless nights talking into the small hours of the morning about George, and both knew deep down, it was futile to object; they knew George was adamant about leaving.

'George,' her father looked at her,' you can't blame us for worrying, you've not been exposed to the real world out there, living here on this island is not the same as being abroad, you've led an insulated life here, it's not going to be easy for you. Life in an institution means discipline and hard work and I just want to make sure you know what you are in for or up against,' he finished with a look of resignation in his eyes.

George knew the look well, because it wasn't the first time she had made a decision to do something, and her father had conceded. But her mother was another thing.

'Georgina I still think it will be far too dangerous for you to leave here now; what if war is declared on England? That will mean that Malta will be at war too.'

'Exactly Mama, which is why I will be much safer in the countryside with Aunt Marlu and Uncle Ted,' George retorted exasperated.

An uncomfortable quiet had settled in the Parker household, the kind that follows an unresolved issue.

George, not wishing to argue with either of her parents, went to her room to change since she was due to meet Connie at seven p.m. She could hear her parents talking in hushed and worried undertones downstairs. She went to the kitchen where there was a kettle of hot water simmering on the Primus stove. Her mother was now sitting quietly at the kitchen table darning a sock. 'I'm just going for a wash Mama; do you need any of the hot water?'

'No, you go ahead *hanini (dear)*, I will boil some more if need be.'

George carried the kettle upstairs to the bathroom and filled the sink with the hot water and then opened the cold tap to adjust the temperature. She lathered her flannel with a new bar of Lux soap her mother had placed on the sink and washed herself. After she had towelled herself dry, she walked to her room and opened her wardrobe pulling out a pair of beige slacks she knew she looked good in and a pale blue blouse and appraised herself in the mirror. Slim with a tight waist; her legs were slender and her straight black hair framed her face in a neat short bob. She was an attractive-looking woman, she resembled her father and had his fine chiselled features. She knew that men glanced furtively at her whenever she passed them by, however for some odd reason they never openly admired her, as if they were a little afraid of her. She smiled, amused at the thought, *'yes, she could be a little indifferent sometimes and probably seemed unapproachable, but she liked it that way, she was not interested in men giving her attention.'*

Glancing one last time in the mirror and inspecting herself, she left her room and went to say goodbye to her mother before she left.

'I won't be long Mama, Connie and I are just going to grab a drink from Tony's Bar in *Strada Mercanti.*'

Her mother looked up pursing her lips 'Oh Georgina you are wearing trousers again? You have that lovely dress you never wear, I just don't understand your obsession with trousers!'

'Maaa I'm more comfortable this way!'

Frances sighed, 'Ok *qalbi (sweetheart)* be careful and don't be too late please.'

'No Ma I won't, where's Papa by the way?'

'Need you ask?'

'I suppose not; he's in the study, I guess. See you later then.'

With that George left the house shutting the door behind her and turned right to walk up to where she was meeting Connie.

Connie was waiting for her at the top of the street. Both of them hugged and started walking in the direction of the bar.

'I wonder what Tony's will be like this evening!' Connie commented.

'I don't know, I suppose there'll be a few of the boys from the RMA and some officers from the Navy, I could do with a laugh, a bit of cheering up, you know.'

'I was thinking, since we're off tomorrow I don't suppose you fancy going for a swim, do you? I thought we could walk down to St Elmo's

Bay, what do you think?'

Connie turned to her, 'That's a brilliant plan, I was just thinking to myself that we can easily get down there for one thirty. I'll get Mammina to make us a packed lunch.'

They arrived at Tony's bar and found it full of the military, and all were drinking and chatting at the top of their voices, in fact it was deafening as they came closer.

'Blimey!' exclaimed George, 'there's a right party going on here.'

'Yes, there is,' Connie's eyes were sparkling, she loved a party.

'I guess I had better get the drinks in then, what would you like?'

'I will have me a brandy with lemonade please.'

George pushed her way to the front of the bar and waved to get the attention of the barman.

'Tell me *sinjorina* what can I get you?

'A brandy with lemonade and a gin and tonic please.'

The barman fixed the drinks and gave them to George who gave him a two shilling and waited for the change and made her way back to where she had left Connie, who had in the meantime wasted no time in striking up a conversation with a handsome chap.

'George come and meet Joseph, and this is his friend Carmelo.'

'Hello again Carmelo, I see you found your friend then?' George said as she shook hands with both of them in turn.

'You know Carmelo?' Joseph asked directing his question at George.

Connie in the meantime looked at George lifting an eyebrow questioningly as if to say *'is this the same Carmelo you told me about!'* *To which George acknowledged with a discreet wink.*

'Well yes sort of, we met briefly' George said guardedly and continued by asking what Joseph did for a living, seeing as he and Carmelo were the only Maltese there.

'I've just been accepted to sit for an entrance exam at the *Regia Accademia Delle Belle Arti,*' Joseph said proudly. 'I will be travelling to Rome with Carmelo next Sunday,' he continued.

George noticed Carmelo wasn't saying much.

'I'm surprised to see you here Carmelo after our last conversation!'

'Yes, well, I had no choice really because this is Joseph's local haunt and where I was supposed to meet him last time.'

'Well never mind now, have you been painting today?' she asked him.

'Yes, I have, I promised to finish off a portrait for someone so I've been concentrating on it.'

'Will you finish it before you leave?' George asked.

'Certo! Yes, I will.'

Connie interrupted the conversation by asking both men if they wanted to join them for a swim. Joseph declined saying he had things to do but Carmelo said he would join them and with that the conversation turned to lighter subjects throughout the evening, though the subject of war cropped up, there was no escaping it and they all agreed that it would inevitably reach the island.

The sun shone from a cloudless sky; the Mediterranean Sea was beautiful at this time of year; crystal clear and inviting Maltese families gathered on the flat globigerina rocks beneath St Elmo's. It was a favourite haunt and a harbinger to the beginning of summer.

George and Connie walked to Fort St Elmo where Carmelo was waiting for them, they carried on together towards the shoreline. They came to their favourite spot and lay down their towels. The sea was shimmering invitingly and it wasn't long before they all dove in to cool off after their walk.

'Aaah that was lovely, I can't remember the last time I went swimming this early in the year,' Carmelo exclaimed laying contentedly on his towel soaking up the sun.

'Tell me Carmelo, don't you get lonely living on your own in Rome?' assuming that he lived alone.

'Not really George, first of all most of my time is taken up at the Accademia, and I also have my friends Emvin and Esprit as well as a few others; we spend a lot of time together because we also study and live in the Italian government-funded *Casa della Redenzione Maltese*,' Carmelo explained, saying his friends' names as if he expected George to know who he was talking about.

'I've never heard of them,' George said feeling a bit stupid that she didn't recognise any of them.

'They are great artists alongside Anton Inglott and Freddie Apap, they are already making a name for themselves,' he said proudly.

'Well now it's your turn,' George said, teasing him.

'One day, who knows if I will become famous?'

George turned to Connie. 'Con, I'm famished, shall we tuck into your Mammina's feast?' Connie's mother was an amazing cook and the occasions when she went to their house, she was constantly plying her with delicious traditional Maltese titbits like home-made sheep's cheeslets called ġbejniet or a generous dollop of *Bigilla,* a pate made from Djerba beans. She never resisted of course and more often than not consumed the lot.

'Hmmm OK, let's see what she has packed' Connie rummaged around in the cane basket.

'Oh, yum what a feast! My word, look at this! Egg sandwiches, tuna ftiras (Maltese flat bread), bread pudding, peaches, loquats, plums, as well as homemade lemonade, your mum's done us proud Con!' George exclaimed inspecting the food that Connie laid out on a flat piece of rock next to them. They all happily munched away on the food and afterwards lay down, sated.

'I swear it Con, your Mammina is really quite exaggerated when it comes to food, one will never starve whilst she is around.' They laughed at George's statement which was in fact quite correct. Mrs Bonello was the perfect housewife the neighbours waxed lyrical about her prowess in cooking, she threw herself into her culinary skills. But not many knew that behind closed doors she was unhappy, her kitchen was her sanctuary a place where she could escape a dark family secret that outside of the family only George knew about.

They lapped up the sun dozing contentedly.

'Carmelo, I am assuming we are still meeting next Saturday, right?' George asked.

'Yes of course and I will show you what I have been working on too if you like.'

'Yes, I would love that, thank you,'

The afternoon wore on and by four p.m. the happy youngsters left.

George said good bye to Connie and Carmelo and they parted ways. The walk back to St Barbara Bastions seemed longer than usual in the late afternoon sunshine. George opened the front door and let herself in. It was quiet and cool; a respite she appreciated after her searing walk. She went over to the kitchen sink and helped herself to a glass of water.

Though it was difficult to get fresh chicken; when she did, her mother, like today, had left a pot of broth simmering away on the kerosene stove, sending wafts of delicious aromas throughout the house.

'George is that you?' George heard her father calling out and she followed the sound of his voice to his usual refuge and his favourite spot in the house.

'Papa, everything OK?' she finally replied when she arrived at his study.

'George love, I've got some good news; there's a ship called the *RMS Stratheden* leaving Malta for London on the 22nd of August; I've booked you a passage on it. She's a lovely ship, only two years old and you'll be sharing a twin cabin. It's a second-class passage but you should be comfortable enough. So that gives you a couple of months or so to get everything in order!'

George beamed. She hugged her father and said, 'I suppose we had better write to Aunt Marlu and let her know then.'

'Yes, I will do that later on.' He smiled at his daughter's evident pleasure and enthusiasm.

In the evening, George made haste and went to find Connie at her house to tell her the news. There was still so much to do; she still had to get her passport issued at the British High Commission.

Chapter 4

At supper George gathered at the dining table with her parents and the three of them discussed her future journey. As soon as her parents went to bed George slipped out to go to the Cairo. It was as busy as usual when she got there, Marlene was occupied serving a group of sailors who were rowdily singing a rendition of *Tommy Dorsey's The Dipsy Doodle*. George smiled and went over to the bar waiting for Marlene to acknowledge her.

'Hello George! It's busy tonight isn't it?'

'Yes, I can see that Marlene, just give me my usual please.' laughing at Marlene's enthusiasm. Guzi, Marlene's son was in full swing, dressed in a gaudy green dress, acting the part of the dame of the bar for the night, sailors and soldiers encouraging his cheeky banter. Business was good most nights but the weekend was the best. *Strada Stretta* was a cacophony of every possible character imaginable and George embraced it with gusto. Tonight, was no exception; Guzi was doing a rip-roaring trade. The bar was full to bursting with the barmaids pocketing tin tokens to be exchanged for money at the end of the night.

George in her trousers, white shirt and waistcoat with a cap on, blended in with the crowd. She happily drank with the sailors, the soldiers, the prostitutes, the bar maids Stella and Maria, whom Marlene employed on the weekend and of course the transvestites, who entertained them all with their garish costumes, exaggerated make-up and shrill voices. There was always some skirmish going on; that odd uniformed bloke who drank too much or perhaps bestowed unwanted attention on the barmaids, but they were tough and thick-skinned and most of the time could take care of themselves. Tonight, was no exception. Stella planted a boot up the arse of a drunken sailor who could barely stand up and ended up flat on his face outside the bar. This brought on raucous laughter from his mates who just carried on without him.

For George these small nightly escapades added spice to her life and she felt a certain 'joie de vivre' which reminded her of the books she'd read about the gay nightlife of Paris and had longed to go there. This had only enhanced her passion for the language and anything French. At school her choice to learn French and not Italian had led to her being ostracised by most in class, except by her best friend Connie who had attended *St Dorothy's Convent* in Mdina with George. She did not care; it mattered little to her because she was a solitary kind of person anyway; Connie was her only friend.

There was a terrific din from the *New Life Music Hall* next door and George went to the entrance of the *Cairo* to have a look at what all the commotion was about. The dancing had spilled onto the street and women in the balconies overlooking the street were clapping to the happy tunes that were being played by a three-piece band of guitar, accordion and drums. George watched them with a smile on her face; and thought, *'this is where she belonged but it was never going to be possible to live this way of life permanently.'*

The wings of change were flapping around her heart, constantly making her feel restless; the time had come, she could feel it, there was more to her mundane existence on this tiny island. She was going to make a difference, she knew it.

George paid Marlene and left the cacophony behind. It grew quiet approaching St Barbara Bastions. She slipped in behind the small cellar door into complete darkness. She was about to start changing when she saw a very faint light from a kerosene lamp in the far corner of the room. Startled, she froze; her immediate thoughts were that the house was being burgled, but then, the light suddenly grew brighter and the shape of her father loomed out of the shadows.

'What's this George? What's going on lass?' he asked her in a quiet but angry voice.

George, caught off-guard stammered, 'Papa, I, I...' she couldn't carry on.

Her father looked at her taking in what she was wearing and said, 'Get changed and come to the study and don't make a sound either, your mother is asleep.'

She started to shake uncontrollably; hurriedly changing out of her clothes, which she left in the usual place. She was grateful she had left her dressing gown in the cellar because although it was warm, she shivered as she pulled open the door and dropped the ivy back in place to hide it. She climbed the stairs barefoot to her father's study. He was standing facing the window with his hands clasped behind him. He heard her come in and turned around. His face took on a look disbelief combined with a plethora of emotions.

'George, I'm not going to pretend I understand because I don't, I cannot comprehend what's been happening, because it's very obvious that this is not the first time it's happened, judging by the stack of clothes you left in the cellar,' he ended.

'Papa I'm sorry you had to find out this way, I don't quite understand it myself, I just like dressing in men's clothing, I didn't know what to say to you, let alone to Mama; please don't tell her Papa, she just wouldn't understand, it would destroy her!'

'Oh what! And *I* understand, do I?' The anger in his voice was raw.

'I don't know Papa, I don't know what to say to you, I know you are disappointed in me.' Tears welled up turning her father into a watery vision.

'Disappointed is an understatement George, I'm livid, I can't believe what you have been up to behind our backs, I've obviously given you too much liberty and you have abused it completely… perhaps it's just as well you are going to England, it will knock some sense into you!' He was visibly choked and distressed not knowing quite how to handle this bizarre discovery.

'I'm sorry Papa,' George said quietly.

'We will not discuss this again George, I am trusting you to see some sense and stop this nonsense; it would kill your mother if she found out!'

'Yes Papa, good night,' George, walked meekly out of the room.

Harry felt his heart breaking, he had heard of people like George but never in a million years would he have believed that his own daughter was like 'that'. He paced the floor rubbing his chin and running his hand through his hair trying to figure out if there was some solution to the problem. He certainly couldn't tell Frances; she would never understand. He would just have to leave things as they were and hope that George would find her own way out of this, for he certainly couldn't seek the help of a priest, who would most certainly condemn her to a life in hell.

George crept up the stairs to her room, subdued, wanting to curl up and disappear somewhere for a hundred years and wake up to find everything was fine and that her confrontation with her father was just a nightmare. But that wasn't going to happen. It was a point of no return. She was mortified that her father had found her out, and heartbroken that she had hurt him so badly. She was now determined more than ever to start a new life where nobody knew her except for her aunt and uncle; she would be anonymous. She hoped her father would not say anything to them about the incident.

When she recounted what happened to Connie the next day, Connie immediately put her arm around friend's shoulder and tried to comfort her.

'Oh lord George that was so unfortunate, your father probably found out quite by accident you know, he probably went looking for something in the cellar. I don't suppose you will be going to *Strada Stretta* again?'

'Well at this point I had better lay low, but I'd like a favour from you Con, I need you to go to the *Cairo* and tell Marlene what's happened and that I won't be going there again, at least not for a while.'

'Hmm George I will try to, but I have to be careful because of my mother, you know how many questions she asks before I go anywhere.'

'Well, if you don't manage it, I will just have to write a note to Marlene and maybe you can at least post it through the door.'

It felt strange for George not to go on her nightly jaunts, but she could no longer take the risk. Instead, she filled her evenings looking forward to leaving the island and the life she anticipated living, even though it felt like she was running away.

She made it a point to tell her mother that she was meeting a nice young chap called Carmelo. She knew her mother would relate everything to her father.

When Saturday the twentieth came, George made her way to the magnificent building of the Opera House. It was an imposing piece of architecture with immense columns and the city's pride and joy, it was also a favourite landmark to meet at.

Carmelo was waiting for her sitting on the Opera steps, and next to him a shiny dark green motorcycle and sidecar sporting a polished Norton badge was parked near the pavement. George smiled with pleasure; she had never ridden on a motorcycle before let alone one with a sidecar.

'This is a lovely surprise, Carmelo,' she said, smiling at him.

'I borrowed it from a friend, I thought you might enjoy the journey much more than in a bus,' he laughed.

They drove from Valletta through Floriana, past Marsa and then Paola before eventually arriving in Senglea.

'Shall we get a drink before I start bombarding you?'

'I wouldn't mind, I'm quite thirsty and a bit windswept.'

They drove through St Michael's Gate towards a small bar in a side street, where they parked and sat down outside on stools at a table. Carmelo went inside and got them both a lemonade.

'I've never been to Senglea, I didn't realise just how pretty it is with its narrow streets.'

'It's got quite a history you know, it was a hunting ground for the Knights Of The Order of St John before it was turned into a fortified city complete with bastions by Grand Master Claude de la Sengle; the city went through hell when the Ottoman Empire invaded during the Great Siege in 1565, and if that wasn't enough it was also taken over by the French and then by the British.' The last few words he said with pursed lips.

'I think I should brush up on the history of Malta a bit more, I mean a bit more than what I learnt at school that is.' Feeling embarrassed, regretting she hadn't done so before meeting Carmelo. History hadn't been one of her strong points at St Dorothy's School.

'Perhaps you should, Malta is steeped in history, for such a tiny island we have much to boast about; she is a very strategically situated island in the Mediterranean and her harbours are priceless, that's why so many have tried to conquer her!' George picked up on his insinuation towards the British.

'Carmelo, I cannot really appease you politically when it comes to our island, we both have different opinions about it and who should rule but I don't want to spoil the day arguing about it' George said, sensing Carmelo's indignation.

'You're right George, let's finish up and walk to the Basilica of the Maria Bambina, it's magnificent and I can't wait till you see the statue

'No, I'm an only child, I think Mum and Dad tried but no more children came along and I never really asked them about it to be honest' George replied.

'What about you?'

I have a brother who is in America, another one who is a priest and a sister who is married. My father works at the dockyard and my mother is always at home keeping house and cooking, she's a great cook and I miss her cooking,' Carmelo said wistfully.

'That's a large family!' George said.

'Not really, when you consider that the average family has between seven to ten children!'

'I suppose you are right; Joseph, our handyman, has six children!'

'Hmm you are very British in your ways,' Carmelo said, not in an offensive way.

'Well yes, I suppose I am, with Papa being British, it's always been that way, but I've tried to educate myself beyond school, and I constantly read when I'm not working at Arnolds' or going out'

'Tell me George why do you dress the way you do at night?' he asked her, looking serious.

George was caught off guard for a moment by the question and pondered for a few seconds before giving her answer.

'I like dressing that way, it gives me a certain kind of freedom which as you know women do not have, but obviously I can't do it all the time, it's not acceptable is it?'

'It makes no difference to me, I like you the way you are, George,'

'Thank you, Carmelo, you won't say anything to anyone will you?'

'No, no I won't, your secret is safe with me.'

'I'm leaving for England in August you know, for some reason I will feel safer knowing I'm going there. I want to join the WAAFS, at least that is my intention, I haven't told anyone yet over here, just my best friend Connie, my parents and my aunt and uncle know obviously because I am staying with them for a short while,' George said.

'Well, I have written my address for you if would like to write to me,' he said as he handed her a folded piece of paper.

'Yes, I will, though I'm not very good at writing regularly but I will definitely keep in touch with you. I will send you my address as soon as

I am settled,' she said whilst carefully placing the folded piece of paper in her handbag.

'Let's take a short walk to my house, my mother will be overwhelmed with excitement at meeting you; she doesn't get to see many new people, I don't think she has ever ventured farther than Valletta in her lifetime.'

'I can't wait.'

Carmelo's mother was in the kitchen. That's where she always was, in the kitchen preparing the traditional *Minestra* soup and some other delicious roast or stew.

'Mama this is my friend Miss Parker' Carmelo announced walking into the kitchen with George in tow.

'Carmelo don't do this to me, I'm not dressed right, Madonna Santissima dear boy — this she said in Maltese with the intent of hiding her embarrassment.'

'Please don't worry, I'm very glad to meet you.'

'Carmelo, where are your manners? Offer Miss Parker some tea and also fetch some biskuttini and the honey ring, I just bought them from the baker' she fussed.

Carmelo went over to where the kerosene stove kept a small *stanjata* (a metal kettle) of hot water gently simmering.

They all sat at a kitchen table large enough to seat four persons. The table itself was an informal place that was mainly used by the family. So George was not surprised when she found herself being ushered into the family sitting room, which, to George's surprise, was beautifully furnished with eighteenth century pieces of furniture. A three-piece red velvet damask and oak settee with two armchairs was the centre piece and observed, to her amusement, that it was covered in plastic to preserve it. Two cabinets and a chest of ornate inlayed draws complimented the rest of the room.

They had tea and George was made to taste both the lovely sweets whilst Carmelo's mother dominated the conversation waxing lyrical about Carmelo's prowess as an artist with a few tears thrown in at his impending departure. Carmelo came to George's rescue by insisting he show George his finished painting. George sighed in relief, she was charmed by this sweet and simple woman but she was more curious to see Carmelo's work.

His bedroom was a simple whitewashed room with an olivewood table complete with a grey marble slab which had the box of paints and the portrait he had obviously just finished. The paint was still wet, she could smell the linseed oil and turpentine.

'Carmelo it's marvellous, I just love your style, it's so fluid and yet it has so much depth.'

'Thank you, I'm flattered, but I have a long way to go yet, though I'm not sure what's going to happen!'

'What do you mean? You said you are going back to Rome tomorrow to carry on, aren't you?'

'Yes, I am but George you know what's brewing, you know there is a war coming and I know who's side I'm going to be on, we may never see each other again,' he studied her intently.

'Don't be silly Carmelo, of course we will see each other again, everything will probably blow over before you even know it.'

He looked at George, his hooded eyes obscured by the thick lenses he wore. He was a handsome man, tall and soft spoken. He often liked to observe people as he was doing now with George. She waited for him to say something and he did.'

'Let's make a promise that when this is over, I will take you to Rome to see the Sistine Chapel.'

'I would love that.'

For the first time in her life George felt an unfamiliar warmth towards this quiet and tall handsome man. It felt strange but not unpleasant. She was aware he was gazing at her and it made her blush which did not go unnoticed by Carmelo. He gently picked up her hand and held it firmly.

'I wish we had more time, I will remember this day forever, I'm glad I met you.'

She felt a little sad that it would probably be a very long time till she saw him again. She felt comfortable with him. She squeezed his hand. He bent towards her and kissed her on the cheeks. She caught a whiff of cologne as he did so.

They drove back to Valletta where Carmelo dropped George off and left again to go back.

Chapter 5

'Ok George, this is it now,' Harry told his daughter.

'Papa there is no turning back, I really want to go and you know I don't have a choice. I have to make an appointment to get my passport so I would appreciate your help.'

'Yes, love that won't be a problem, both Mama and I will have to sign but it won't take long. I'll also get Uncle Ted to open an account at Barclays Bank in London for you; both your mother and I agreed that we will deposit two hundred pounds in it; that will be enough to tide you over for a while till you get settled.'

'Gosh Papa, Mama, that's really too much, besides I have my own savings, but thank you both so much,' she looked at both of them with affection.

'Just look at it as emergency money, just in case, you know if something happens,' they both said.

'Nothing is going to happen, please don't worry, I will be fine,' she smiled, wanting to reassure them or maybe herself. She was suddenly enveloped with a feeling of apprehension. George had packed and repacked her suitcase a dozen times in the past two weeks. She had packed her secret stash of men's clothes at the bottom, making sure her mother would not see them.

On the eve of her departure on the twenty-first August her mother came up to her room with an assortment of personal hygiene and basic First Aid articles.

'Mum I haven't got any room in my case for all that!' she exclaimed, exasperated.

'Georgina you are going to take these with you, you've got a week at sea and you are going to need them,' Frances said dumping a box of aspirin, cough mixture, a bar of soap and a tube of toothpaste in the suitcase. George sighed in resignation; there was no point in arguing with her mother.

'I also want you to take this with you,' handing her daughter a miniature Bible which was worn with frequent use, 'I've had it since I was a child, keep it safe,' tears welled up in her eyes.

'Oh Mama, please don't cry.' George gathered her mother in her arms and hugged her tightly, her own eyes welling up causing a lump in her throat. She felt vulnerable and for an instant questioned herself if she was making the right move. The two women remained quietly hugging, both acknowledging the grief of parting for the first time.

'Mama thanks for the Bible, I will treasure it and I promise you I will go to church on Sundays where possible and when not, any other day I can.'

George, not having been able to sleep the night before, woke up early before the sun had risen. She double checked her suitcase for the hundredth time and eyed the clothes she was going to wear.

George brought her suitcase down and her father loaded it into the trunk of the services car he had borrowed. He drove them all to the Grand Harbour where the *Stratheden* was moored. There was a crowd of people boarding with various travel apparel and stevedores loading last-minute crates and boxes. The *Stratheden*, with her large steaming funnel in the centre, looked grand; her white presence imposing in the brilliant August sunshine. The ship was due to depart in half an hour, leaving plenty of time for their good-byes. Connie came rushing towards her, 'George… 'I thought I had missed you,' she said embracing her best friend.

'Connie I'm so glad you came,' she said returning the embrace, reluctantly letting go to turn to her parents.

'Mama, Papa, thank you so much for everything, I love you, I know it's not going to be easy for you both being without me, but in a way, you prepared me for this for a long time, you knew that one day I would want to make my own way.'

'That's true enough, it's just that it's crept up faster than we expected; anyway, Mum and I will get used to it.' His voice lacked the conviction of his words.

'Please be careful Georgina, we have brought you up well; the world out there is different to Malta. I will pray for you every day and please send us a telegram as soon as you arrive, I've only agreed to this because your father assures me it's safer for you,' Frances said with tears rolling down her face. Harry put his arm around his wife's shoulders both watching George making her way up the gangplank. The *Stratheden* engines churned the water to a furious froth and the funnel belched a cloud of smoke which drifted on the early morning breeze.

George turned round to wave at her parents and Connie with a lump in her throat and a tightness in her chest. Tears slid down her face; she was glad her mother couldn't see them.

Frances Parker was beside herself with grief, watching her only child climb the gangplank, her slight form seemingly lost against the gargantuan size of the liner.

'Frances, love she'll be fine, look there are other women on board and she'll soon have plenty of company along the way,' Harry held his wife trying to comfort her, knowing what effect the absence of George would have on them.

With all the tearful goodbyes done, George made her way onto the ship and stood on the top deck at the rails. The dock was now packed with families and well-wishers. Her parents looked somewhat small and despondent from where she was standing.

She wondered if she would see either of them or Connie again. Her thoughts turned to watching merchant seamen pulling the ship's mooring ropes in from the waiting dockworkers as they released them. The huge engines churned water to turbulent froth as tugboats pulled the ship away from the dock. The ship moved out in the direction of the breakwater, already the two specks of her parents waving frantically disappeared from sight.

'Your family?' a strong voice enquired next to her.

She turned her face around to reply to the voice, expecting a man, but instead found a woman with a shocking thatch of red hair and freckles peppering her face.

'Yes, it's hard for them, we are a close-knit family and I'm their only child.'

The woman standing next to her had one of those faces that made you want to smile all the time. 'I'm Gracie, Gracie Miller, how do you do?' She introduced herself to George with a firm handshake.

'Pleased to meet you too, Georgina Parker, but call me George, everyone else does.' The two women made light conversation whilst watching the Grand Harbour and the island of Malta disappear over the horizon.

'I suppose we ought to go and find our respective cabins,' Gracie said as she rummaged in her handbag for her ticket. 'What's your cabin number?'

'Oh, hang on let me just find the ticket, hmm yes here it is, number 224.'

'Well, I'll be damned, that's my cabin number too!' Gracie exclaimed. Both women giggled like a couple of schoolgirls at the coincidence.

The cabin was adequate; two single beds with a bedside cupboard for each person. The cabin was small and they kept bumping into each other, it made both women laugh at the space they were meant to share for the next seven days. They set about unpacking their luggage and when they finally finished, went in search of a much-needed cup of tea. They found the tourist class veranda cafe and ordered a pot of tea and some cheese sandwiches. George was famished; she didn't have any breakfast before she left, the fact of the matter was she had been too excited to eat and had only managed a cup of tea.

After they had finished, George suggested they go and find the ship's notice board to peruse the entertainment. They found it with the help of an obliging steward called Mr Potter.

'Oh, great look, there's a fancy-dress dance on tomorrow night, and a singing competition on Monday twenty fifth and that's the day we pass the Straits of Gibraltar, according to this map, I don't want to miss that!' George said enthusiastically. 'We can go to the ship's library and look up some costumes we can make.'

'Great idea, I fancy the singing myself.'

They went for a walk on the top deck for some air. It had grown fresh out at sea, a respite from the heat George left behind. Her head was full of conflicting thoughts, wondering what was in store for her.

'Hey George, come out of la-la land will you? It's a bit too breezy, let's go and meet the ship's captain,' Gracie's voice boomed over the ship's engines, breaking her out of her thoughts.

George followed Gracie, who led them to the dining room, which looked smart with its white-clothed tables decorated with small vases of flowers and sparkling cutlery. Captain Hughes had a crowd of people around him as he introduced himself and explained the dining etiquette, followed by the ships' entertainment and activities, which both women had an inkling of anyway.

Their first lunch experience came in the form of a creamy pea soup followed by grilled mutton chops with baked potatoes and broccoli and if the food was anything to go by, both of them agreed that it was going to make the trip all the more pleasurable. With lunch over, they went to the Veranda Lounge to have coffee and relax for a while to let their lunch go down.

'I bet we'll find all we need in the Encyclopaedia Britannica in the library,'

'What's that? What are you talking about Gracie?'

'Sorry I was just voicing my thoughts, I was thinking about the fancy dress tomorrow.'

'Oh, right yes, I'm pretty much sure we will, let's go then and have a look.'

The library was a decent size with a collection of the sort of books expected from the latest tomes to classics, but the two women went in search of the encyclopaedia section, which dealt with anthropology.

'Found it, let's look at something from Asia.'

'Like what for example?' Gracie questioned.

'Well let's look up India, look here it is, see it says here that the women wear something called a Saree, it looks easy enough, this seems to be a collarless blouse she's wearing and then it looks like a long swathe of cloth wrapped around her several times and then she has the coloured dot on her forehead called a bindi.'

Gracie looked doubtful 'George, where on earth are we going to find material as long as that?'

'Simple, let's find a steward and see if they have any spare sheets in the laundry bay, maybe a couple of old ones we can sew together,'

'OK and what about a sewing machine? What are we going to do about that? And what am I going to wear?'

'Well look the Indian man is wearing something called a Salwar Kameez and a turban.'

'A what?' Gracie asked.

'Look at the picture… and it's white too, so I bet we can persuade a steward to lend you a white shirt and a pair of white trousers too.' George, by this time was laughing hysterically.

'George you're barking mad, we won't get away with it you know, especially the trouser part!'

'You leave it to me, go back to our room, here's the key, just give me half an hour.'

With that, George left Gracie in the library studying the pictures. She went in search of Mr Potter the Steward. After finding him and explaining what she had in mind, he directed her to the laundry room where the housekeeper was counting sheets. With that Mr Potter left George with the promise of lending her his spare white shirt and a pair of trousers. The laundry *wallah* called Mr Mukherjee was more than obliging, he found two sheets and helped George sew the two ends together on a hand operated Singer machine to make one long piece of material. For a turban Mr Mukherjee rummaged around in the ample sewing cupboard and found an old sheet from which he cut a wide strip.

'All OK miss, you will make a fine Indian Rajah for tomorrow night, good luck miss.'

'Thanks Mr Mukherjee' trotting off to find Gracie, her arms laden with the material.

She burst through the cabin door making Gracie jump.

'Oh lord George you weren't joking were you!'

'Nope, now all we have to do is figure out how to darken our faces to look like natives,' she said giggling.

There was a knock on the cabin door.

'Oh, hello Mr Potter,' George greeted the Steward whilst he handed her the rest of the outfit for the fancy dress costume. 'Lovely, thank you, I promise to deliver this safe and sound and clean.'

'Thank you, miss, and have fun tomorrow,' he said.

'Thank you, Mr Potter,' George gave him the most gratifying smile she could muster in appreciation. He left closing the cabin door behind him.

'Well Gracie what do you reckon?'

'You've certainly done us proud, but who is going to wear what? We've both got short hair!' exclaimed Gracie.

'Tell you what, let's each try putting the costumes on and see what fits,'

Gracie was the first to try on Mr Potter's shirt but the buttons wouldn't do up across her bust and they both burst out laughing while Gracie scratched her head in frustration.

'Well, that's that then, looks like I'll have to wear the saree *thingamajig*' she said as she undid the shirt and proceeded to rummage in the wardrobe to find a blouse that would go under the saree. In the meantime, George had undressed and put Mr Potter's shirt on; it was a perfect fit. She put on the trousers — which were a bit baggy — but at least they fitted, held up by a belt. Next came the turban and having never worn one, she struggled to wrap the cloth around her head. Eventually she managed to assemble it in a haphazard manner and looking somewhat dishevelled, turned to her friend for approval.

'Oh my God, George you look the ticket, you look just like a bloke, unbelievable!' Gracie exclaimed, incredulous, 'all you need now is a dark face, a moustache and beard,' she laughed infectiously.

'Gracie don't exaggerate will you!' she said turning to inspect herself in the small mirror hanging over the bathroom sink. She really did look like a handsome bloke with all her hair tucked inside the turban. She smiled with satisfaction.

'Blimey you don't look half bad yourself Gracie, all you need now is that *bindi* dot they put in the middle of the forehead, we are going to look great, aren't we?'

'I reckon we can definitely pull this off!'

They undressed again and put the clothes neatly away in the wardrobe till the following day.

'OK well that's sorted now, how about a game of shuffleboard?'

'Never played it and I've never heard of it either, so you will have to show me or fill me in.'

'Right, let's go to the top deck and have a look to see if anybody else is playing,' Gracie said leaving the cabin explaining to George the rules of the game.

The weather was pleasant, they hadn't left the Mediterranean yet so it was still relatively warm and most of the passengers were on deck, either reading a book or playing shuffleboard. There was a group of young men standing by the railings watching the ongoing game and they were laughing at a joke they had just shared. One of them turned after he spotted the two women walking in their direction, the rest of them very quickly sobered up too. There weren't that many single women on board, George and Gracie were two of them and they attracted the young men's attention.

The women stopped at a table with four chairs and sat down.

'Hello ladies, fancy a bit of company? The lads and I were wondering if you would have a game of shuffleboard with us, what do you say?' the young man asked.

'Sure, why not?' piped up Gracie catching George's look of irritation.

Gracie leaned closer to her friend, 'Let's have some fun!'

'I'm Bert by the way and this here is Charlie,'

'Oh, very well then. Let's give them a run for their money,' George retorted and laughed.

They split into teams of two. George and Gracie started first. George grabbed the shuffle cue stick and stood in the shooting area and aimed for the area with the highest points at the end and pushed a yellow disc. With a satisfied grin on her face, she moved back to allow Bert to have his shot. He tried his hardest to knock George's yellow disc with his black one but to his chagrin failed miserably. It was Gracie's turn to push a disc, hers landed just short of Bert's. The other lads howled with pleasure and egged their team on. It was Charlie's turn and he managed to shove his disc close to George's.

'Damn,' George said under her breath with a determined look on her face. She took her last disc and gave it a mighty shove sending Charlie's disc flying out of the playing area. The lads whistled and all looked at Charlie for his reaction, but he just smiled good humouredly. Gracie fared better with her last shot and came up close to George's disc, then, it was Bert's turn with the last disc of the match and he aimed with his cue stick and tried to knock George's disc out, but only managed to knock Gracie's out of the way.

Both women whooped with pleasure and laughed and so did the lads. They carried on playing shuffleboard till it was time for dinner. Before each of them left, Bert and Charlie asked the women if they would meet them at the fancy dress dance the next evening. Gracie looked at George and raised an eyebrow and shrugged as if to say, 'why not' and she nodded at Bert, 'OK lads we'll see you tomorrow then, shall we say eight o'clock in the dining room?'

Bert and Charlie bade them a good evening and went off in search of their friends, whilst the two women went to their cabin to freshen up for dinner.

Chapter 6

'So, what do you think of Bert and Charlie then?' Gracie asked tucking into her pork chop.

'What is there to think, they're just a couple of blokes, I mean I enjoyed their company and all that… why are you asking, did you by any chance fancy one of them?'

'Are you serious? Don't be soft! We're on this boat for the next six days so we've got to keep ourselves amused.'

'I suppose you're right,' George said twirling the stem of her wine glass between her fingers. 'I wonder what the lads will be dressing up as, I want to make sure they don't recognise us, remind me to take the wine cork with us to blacken our faces with,' she finished off smugly.

The steward cleared their table which was a signal for them to move into the Cafe Lounge. George remembered to pick up the cork and put it in her purse. When they got back to their cabin, the room *wallah* had already been in to turn down their beds. George peeped out of the porthole and saw the sky was crystal clear, it was a beautiful night and she contemplated going for a walk on deck since Gracie had already fallen asleep. But a yawn put paid to her plans and she decided to call it a night.

Saturday dawned bright with a brisk wind and after a short walk on deck, George and Gracie went to the dining room for breakfast. They sat on a table next to a couple who were talking about the impending fancy dress and how little they had to create something for the evening with. Both women looked at each other knowingly but said nothing, feeling that they had the perfect costume for the evening. The fancy dress dance was turning into a competition, because the table behind them were also discussing what to wear. Breakfast was underway in minutes, for as soon as the passengers were seated, stewards in crisp white uniforms were all a hustle and bustle carrying trays of coffee and teapots to the seated patrons.

'What would madams like for breakfast?' asked Mr Potter, their steward.

'Oh, hello Mr Potter, how lovely to see you, I'll have some porridge and toast please.'

'Definitely the English breakfast for me please with an extra sausage, oh and some toast too,' Gracie grinned, she loved her food!

'You must have hollow legs; I don't know where you put it all'

'I'll have you know I have quite an appetite,'

'Anyway, changing the subject, I'm getting really excited about tonight, I'm dying to see the look on Bert and Charlie's faces.'

'I bet they won't recognise you,' Gracie said smugly.

'Well, that should be a laugh then.'

They spent most of the day in the library because although it dawned bright, by the time lunchtime came around, the weather had changed dramatically. It became cloudy and dull with a drizzle that left no option but for most to stay inside and occupy themselves as best they could. They played Whist all afternoon, drinking copious amounts of tea until Gracie decided she was tired and wanted a nap, to which George agreed would be a good idea.

By the time they both woke up it was time for the evening's event.

They dressed up in their costumes and stood back to survey each other's efforts.

'Gracie you look amazing, and that blouse will do just as well as a *choli* and you've managed to wrap the *sari* round you like a true native!'

'As you well know I spent enough time in the library perusing books, not that there were many of them, but that dated copy of *National Geographic* had some decent photos in it so that helped, now then what about you? That shirt looks OK and so do the trousers, but we still have to blacken your chops,' Gracie said.

'I just thought about that, we need a candle, I'm sure I saw one somewhere and a box of matches.'

'They are in my bedside cabinet, let me get them,' 'Here we are, now where's that cork you brought back with you?' Gracie asked.

'I put it in my handbag, let me just rummage around, hmm here it is,' she produced the cork and gave it to Gracie who proceeded to burn the end of it over the candle flame.

'There that should do it, wait just a few seconds to let it cool down,' she said, waving the cork in her hand, 'let's try it now' applying the cork to George's face, smudging it as she went along, 'Hmm that looks good enough,' admiring George. George got up and looked at herself in the mirror, she hardly recognised herself.

'Right, last thing is the moustache and beard; I'll do that with my eye pencil,' and proceeded to apply short strokes to her upper lip, followed by longer ones on her chin. 'Not bad.'

'Hang on, you left a bit out, let me touch it up for you, 'you'll need some help with the turban, I know just how it's supposed to go on,' she winked secretly winding the cloth around George's head, completely covering her hair.

'How did you figure that out, don't tell me you saw it in the National Geographic, because I saw the magazine too and there weren't any instructions,' George chuckled to herself.

'Actually, it didn't occur to me straight away till I saw the room *wallah,* and on account of him being Indian, I just asked him and he explained and Bob's your uncle,' she elucidated, feeling chuffed with herself.

'You clever thing you, well I shall look quite the part!' George looked pleased with herself.

The fancy dress dance was to be held in the dining room. The transformation was swift, all tables and chairs had been removed just after dinner and now it was clear to welcome all the absurdly dressed passengers who were participating. A small podium had been erected at the far end of the room and a five-piece band was already playing a George Formby number. Sure enough, Bert and Charlie were already there with their friends milling around, each with a glass of ale in their hands, joking and laughing. They hardly noticed George and Gracie walk in. They were unrecognisable, they looked like a couple of scruffy natives.

'Look they haven't even noticed us,' George whispered and giggled at the same time. They walked over to a makeshift bar and ordered a couple of gins and tonic. They remained with their backs towards the lads. The band was playing a foxtrot and couples dressed in all sorts of fancy apparel drifted to the dancefloor. George finished her drink first,

'Come on then Gracie let's give it a whirl on the dance floor.' Another lively foxtrot came on. Bert and Charlie went over to them. Charlie was the first to wolf whistle Gracie once he realised who she was, 'Crikey Gracie I hardly recognised you' he said with a smile, 'Bert, look who it is, it's George!' Bert looked dumfounded and said, 'Well I don't know how I like you best, I think it's both, fancy a dance then?'

They spent the rest of the evening with the lads who entertained them with stories whilst they drank. At around eleven the captain climbed onto the podium to announce the winners of the fancy dress. The fancy dresses were varied, but apart from their costumes there were another two passengers who were in with a chance, one was wearing a Greek style toga and the other was dressed like an American Indian. Where they managed to find feathers mystified the girls, but still they waited in anticipation. 'And the winners for the best overall costume are Miss Georgina Parker for her Indian Rajah Costume and Mr Peter Banks for his Greek toga costume!' the captain finished off to rapturous applause.

'Gosh George you won!' Gracie stated excitedly as her friend walked off the podium with a bottle of *Brut Champagne*. It was around one in the morning when the dance eventually petered out. Bert and Charlie wanted to carry on entertaining them, but they bid them a polite good night and went to their cabin.

They didn't wake till late and had missed breakfast altogether. After washing and dressing they ventured into the lounge and ordered a pot of coffee. Mr Potter their usual steward served them their coffee and said, 'There you go Miss George and Miss Gracie, your coffee! And just to let you know, we will be passing through the Straits of Gibraltar in about an hour, so that's the only land you will see close up before we carry on the journey, and we will be sailing into the Bay of Biscay, so I hope you are good sailors because it's always a bit choppy going through it,' he finished with a smile.

'Oh lord! I hope I don't get queasy,' George grimaced.

'You'll be fine, just suck on a piece of lemon, that will stop your stomach from getting upset.'

They drank their coffee in silence feeling somewhat worse for wear from the night before, though Gracie seemed to be perking up much faster than George.

'I'm actually starving,' Gracie piped up.

'Hmm I'm definitely not thinking about food right now…'

'Lunch is in one hour so I can hold on till then.'

'Let's get some fresh air; I'm sure I'll feel better,'

They finished their coffee and walked up several stairs till they came to the top deck. There was no sign of the lads and both of them were relieved as they did not feel like any boisterous company. The *Stratheden* sailed at a steady pace of fifteen knots, in the distance the head of Gibraltar was just about visible. It lay in a blue haze and gradually turned to a murky brown till the Rock came into view. They watched the ship sail into the Atlantic Ocean.

'Shall we go down to the dining room, it's about lunchtime and I really can't hold on much longer, my stomach is grumbling.'

They were quick to get used to the routine of life on board and the seven days at sea were coming to an end. They were looking forward to *terra firma*.

'I can't wait to get off now, I've had enough,' George suddenly said, lifting her head up from reading a dated magazine which she had found at the ship's lounge. 'My Aunt Marlu will be waiting for me at Tilbury, what about you then?'

'Oh, I will make my own way, I found a bedsit advertised in the *Woman's Illustrated*. I wrote to the landlady, a certain Mrs Peggy Matthews, I sent her a deposit, it's somewhere in Peckham. Apparently its quite a large place, according to her there is another lodger besides myself.'

'Well, that will be all right for you then, don't forget to give me your address so we can at least meet up; my Aunt and Uncle live in this charming house in Bramley that backs onto a stream, but I suppose I'm going to have to get my own place later on. Papa got me an application sorted for the WAAFS,' George ended.

'You know I never asked you but it's just clicked; your dad isn't Eng. Harry Parker by any chance, is he?' Gracie asked her.

'Well yes, he's in the Royal Engineers, how did you know?'

'Because I finally realised that I've seen you somewhere before, you were at the officer's mess at Kalafrana about two months ago, you were standing next to your dad; there was a bunch of the cabaret dancers whom

I came over with, on the opposite side of the room.'

'Well, it's a small world, though I must confess, I don't remember you, though I do remember the troupe of cabaret dancers, I mean the blokes were all over them,' she ended, chuckling.

'Well, they were friends of mine that's why I was sitting by the bar getting a drink though I didn't stay long, but that's when I noticed you. Anyway, I'm hoping that my Uncle Norbert who's in the RAF can pull a few strings for me and help me get a posting as a pilot to fly transport planes, because that's what I really want to do.'

George imagined Gracie would fit perfectly into the job of a pilot, she had a no nonsense look about her with her stocky stature and cropped hair, she was rather like a mischievous boy.

'I'm feeling sleepy George,' she settled into her bed, 'see you in the morning then.'

'See you in the morning... good night!'

It was heavy and overcast when Gracie woke up, the *Stratheden* had started to pitch and roll on entering the English Channel. She rolled out of her bed with a thud on the floor. Stunned and half asleep she stood up feeling a bit wobbly and steadied herself. She went over to George and shook her, 'George, George, for God's sake wake up,' Gracie laughed shaking George who woke up confused and groggy.

'Wha...' what's the matter?'

Finally coming to, she sat up and noticed that the cabin seemed to roll from left to right and then heave.

'Hurry up and get dressed will you, we must have hit some choppy weather again!'

They hurried out their cabin and headed to the upper deck. The corridors were teeming with passengers in various state of animation and stewards were trying to calm them down, announcing they had encountered a bit of a swell since they were sailing into the English Channel. They were hit by a howling wind and could just make out Calais on the portside. There were very few passengers on the top deck, only those that came out for a smoke and most sheltered in between the lifeboats.

'Well at least we will be home soon!' She shouted above the wind. George gesticulated towards the stairs to the Veranda Cafe for breakfast.

She felt a little queasy and settled for a pot of tea, but Gracie went for a full breakfast instead of the toast.

'Aren't you going to eat something, you will feel a lot better if your stomach has something to work on you know,' she said with her mouth full of bacon and egg.

'Oh God how can you eat, it's ghastly, my stomach is churning!'

George swallowed a mouthful of hot tea but it made her feel worse. Thankfully after a while the boat seemed to steady itself. A voice over the ships' tannoy informed passengers that they were an hour away from Dover, which meant that the rest of the journey up to London Tilbury Docks would be relatively calm since the wind was blowing from the starboard side.

Chapter 7

By four in the afternoon the *Stratheden* crept into Tilbury Docks and was assisted by tug boats to berth. The ships' rails were double lined with passengers wanting to be the first to get a glimpse of the dock. Passports were inspected and passengers descended the gangplank, which had finally been lowered. They followed the queue and immediately got swallowed up in a crowd of people, some going, some coming to pick up others. George craned her neck hoping to catch a glimpse of Aunt Marlu. Gracie pulled at George's sleeve. 'I guess we'd better say goodbye here else we're just going to get lost in this lot.' They hugged and parted ways. Once the dock started to clear, she saw her aunt waiting and she waved.

'Oh, my dear, dear, Georgina how lovely to see you finally, you must be tired, let's put your trunk on the back seat of the car, it's just over here,' she pointed towards a shiny red Austin Sixteen.

'Oh, my word what a beauty, Aunt!' George exclaimed.

'Yes, she is rather lovely, isn't she? Uncle Ted bought her for me a few months ago, drives like a dream.'

'Where's Uncle Ted by the way?'

'He's been called to the Ministry of Defence, not a good sign, it's something to do with new developments within the German camp, I'm sure you heard about the grumblings and griping going on,' her aunt carried on.

'Well yes of course I've heard nothing but! You know what it's like at the moment, everything is speculation, you hear so much but nothing is quite for certain is it?'

'Well dear, I don't think Chamberlain is prepared for what's to come, it seems like he's burying his head in the sand, at least that is what most of the nation believes; I can feel that there will be a change in power and Winston Churchill is a strong contender.'

Hearing her aunt talk made George feel a bit unworldly at that moment because she obviously wasn't in touch with the British politics and current affairs.

'Anyway, dear it's about sixty miles to Bramley, it will take us about an hour and a half but when we get home you can rest while I prepare dinner, it won't take me long.'

It was still light and the air felt warm whilst driving out of London. When they hit the countryside, they passed fields of grazing cows and sheep and hills and copses of woods and everywhere was so green. George had forgotten just how beautiful the English countryside was; she had been ten years old when she had last visited her father's home county of Yorkshire with her parents. When they approached Guildford, her aunt switched the headlights on. Twilight was setting in; skirting the town, they headed towards Bramley, passing a couple of public houses all lit up and cosy on the way. The final approach to the village was the treelined Horsham Road with pretty cottages and terraced houses. They passed the Jolly Farmer and Wheatsheaf pubs before they arrived.

'When Uncle Ted gets back, we'll go to the Wheatsheaf for a drink, it's such a lovely little pub, we know the owners really well, Louie and Susan, they do a lovely roast dinner on Sundays,' Aunt Marlu said nodding in the direction of the Wheatsheaf.

They turned into Foxburrow Hill Road and pulled up in front of an adorable cottage with a pretty front garden.

'Home sweet home Georgina,' her aunt smiled.

'How lovely, Aunt; in the last rays of light the garden looks heavenly,' George said following her inside.

After a cup of tea Aunt Marlu showed George to her room, which was upstairs. It had a window framed with chintz curtains that overlooked the garden. A brass bed, a bedside table, a chest of drawers and a double door wardrobe completed the decor.

'This is lovely, Aunt, thank you, I'll just unpack and come downstairs and keep you company till Uncle Ted gets back.'

She unpacked and came across her mother's Bible. She rubbed her thumb across the front cover feeling the embossed words. She was overwhelmed with homesickness and thought, *'Have I done the right thing to come all this way, what if I don't make it and the war starts…?'* She had been OK on the journey across the sea, but now in the quiet of her room, she felt a lump form in her throat and wished she could hug her mother or hear her father's voice. She would write to them tomorrow she decided, but before she did, she would ask Aunt Marlu if she could call them to let them know she had arrived safe and sound.

George walked down the stairs and found her aunt in the kitchen preparing supper.

'Hmm that smells good, I didn't realise how hungry I was till the smell wafted out of the kitchen,' George laughed poking her nose in the air and closing her eyes to concentrate on the delicious smell.

At that moment there was the sound of a key in the door and Uncle Ted walked in.

'Uncle Ted! Oh, I'm so pleased to see you!' George ran to her uncle and wrapped her arms round his neck giving him a tight hug.

'Hello young lady, crikey you've grown up since the last time we saw you, it's only been a few years, why you are practically a young woman, she's stunning isn't she Marlu?'

'Of course I'm a young woman now Uncle,' George blushed.

'Ted you're embarrassing the poor girl, go and wash up, supper will be ready in five minutes.'

After supper they retired to the cosy sitting room. Uncle Ted lit his pipe and sat in his favourite armchair; Aunt Marlu sat next to George on the settee.

'Georgina, I hear you've set your heart on the WAAFS then?' Uncle Ted stated.

'Yes, that's what I'm hoping to do, my application is in and I received a date for an interview but there is no confirmation yet of my engagement and obviously as to when the training will begin, it's all up in the air at the moment from what I gather.'

'Hmm yes I had a word with HQ about the current situation of the WAAFS, though they have been going since June, they still haven't quite organised themselves yet, so you might have a bit of a wait on your hands for the time being, but I will keep you updated, in the meantime we can keep a lookout for other opportunities for you.'

She hid her disappointment, not wanting to seem ungrateful. She planned to write to Gracie knowing that her friend would invite her to London for a few days, which she intended to take full advantage of.

'Thanks Uncle maybe you could recommend me for a secretarial post at the MOD,' she said jokingly.

'Well actually that wouldn't be such a bad idea, but it would probably mean moving to London, I'm not sure if your parents would approve of you being on your own so soon.'

Aunt Marlu piped up and said, 'Oh I'm sure Georgina would be all right, she's a sensible woman and besides she would have to live in shared accommodation so she won't quite be alone.'

'I'm going back to London in the morning, it's going to be this way for the next few weeks but I will investigate and see what I can come up with,' Uncle Ted added, puffing on his pipe.

After they had been to the Wheatsheaf for a quick drink they returned home and at around ten o'clock George bade good night to her aunt and uncle and climbed the stairs to her bedroom. She gazed out of the window, the sky was dense, there were no stars out; lit windows from houses opposite shed soft shadows. It was so quiet she could hear her heartbeat on her breath. She wondered if she would sleep if she lay down on the bed, because her mind was churning with all sorts of thoughts. She was thinking about her parents, Connie, Malta jumbled up with what was to happen in the next few days. She tried to calm herself but to no avail so she grasped the little Bible and flicked through the pages randomly and started to read...

'My God, my God, why have you forsaken me?
Why are you so far from saving me, so far from my cries of anguish?
My God I cry out by day, but you do not answer, by night, but I find no rest...'

She had fallen asleep with the Bible laying across her heart and the bedside light still on. She was still fully clothed when at seven thirty in the morning she woke up; she undressed and put her dressing gown on. She tiptoed down the stairs thinking everyone was still asleep but found her aunt brewing a fresh pot of tea... her uncle had already left for London.

'Good morning dear, would you like a cup of tea?'

'Hmm yes please, would love one.'

'Did you sleep well?'

'Well, I thought I wouldn't at first because my mind was going nineteen to the dozen, but then I woke up this morning with my clothes still on, so I must have dozed off.'

'Never mind, you must have been exhausted, well a bit of breakfast will do you good. I'm making some scrambled eggs on toast, would you like some?' Aunt Marlu asked.

George nodded.

'So how have mum and dad been?' Aunt Marlu asked George as she was buttering a piece of toast.

'Well Mama has been worried sick about me coming here and I will have to make sure I write to them often and hopefully she will feel a bit more confident about me living an independent life. I suppose it doesn't really help that I'm their only child, as for Papa,' she shrugged her shoulders, 'he's a chip off the old block, he worries but he knows I can take care of myself, that's the way he brought me up, he made sure that should I ever find myself alone I can fend for myself,' George knew this to be true about herself, her father had made sure she was independent in every way.

'Yes, I can imagine how worried mum must be, but I'm sure she will get used to the idea sooner or later; I was thinking we should pop over to the post office to send a telegram to them just to let them know you've arrived safely.'

'Well yes that's a good idea because I want to send one to my best friend Connie too,'

'All right so let's get ourselves spruced up and we can leave in about three quarters of an hour.'

They walked towards the post office and sent the telegrams, after which they made their way to Bramley High Street.

'Let's have a quick drink at the Wheatsheaf before lunch,' Aunt Marlu said. They walked in through the pub that was all dark polished wood and settled themselves at a table by the window with their drinks. George took a sip of her gin and tonic whilst her Aunt drank from her half pint of stout.

'George, I hope you don't mind me asking you, but you haven't mentioned anybody special back home.'

George shifted uncomfortably in her seat as she always did when this question arose.

'No Aunty, there's nobody special, I'm not really interested in getting involved, I want a career and the two don't seem to go together.'

'I see, so you don't think of getting married and having children?'

'I don't really think about it much, it's not that I don't love children, because I do, but the thought of being a housewife just doesn't appeal to me right now.'

'What do Frances and Dad think about this?'

'Oh lord, I haven't ever said anything like this to them, never discussed it, it's just not the done thing, is it? Mum expects me to get married I suppose, but it's not what I want,' George finished off.

'Well maybe later on you will change your mind, you never know dear.'

'Maybe, we shall see.'

That evening she thought about the conversation she had had with her aunt. It was funny how Aunt Marlu should ask about her love life… it seemed a bit odd to her, she wondered if her father had written and mentioned the cellar incident. *Surely not*, she thought. It wasn't for lack of opportunities, because there were plenty of young men who had tried to take her out, but she always felt indifferent towards them. She pushed the thoughts out of her head and fell into bed hoping to sleep; she had a long day tomorrow; she was off to London with her Uncle Ted. Thankfully she drifted off to sleep without her thoughts badgering her.

CHAPTER 8

Uncle Ted loved pushing his car on the open road and George revelled in the wind blowing her hair back. Aunt Marlu had offered her a scarf but she declined and now sitting next to her uncle in his two-seater shiny green *Triumph Dolomite* on their way to London, she absorbed the lovely countryside whizzing past. It took them just under two hours to arrive in central London. They passed Trafalgar Square and headed to Whitehall where they parked the car in front of the War Office. She followed him up the vast staircase, climbing to the left till they came on to the first floor where she was introduced to some officers who were waiting to be seen by Lt Gen. Henry Pownall. She stared at the beautiful architecture, admiring the domed ceiling above.

'Its impressive isn't it?' said a voice next to her.

George looked up into the bluest eyes she had ever seen and all of a sudden, she blushed.

'Yes, yes, it is, was it so obvious that I was staring at it?' she had a mischievous grin on her face.

'Well yes nobody looks at it most of the time because they are too preoccupied with other things,' he paused for a second 'Sorry I haven't introduced myself, I'm Peter, Lt Peter Crawley,' lifting his eyebrow, as he said this and waiting for her to introduce herself.

'Georgina Parker, I'm here with my uncle, Ted Pickering.'

'Oh, I know Ted Pickering, a very amiable fellow, he's in the Royal Engineers, isn't he?'

'Yes, he is and he's just coming now,' she carried on sweetly

'Hello Pickering, how are you, old fellow?'

'It's Peter Crawley isn't it? How the devil have you been?'

'I'm up for a debriefing so I'm just kicking my heels till they call me in, but your niece has been keeping me company.'

'Is that so Georgina, well how about you join us for a spot of lunch Crawley, when you've finished from here? It's eleven thirty, so let's say in an hour from now, there's a small cafe just round the corner. We can meet there.'

George was about to protest, but it was too late, her uncle had seen to that. She put on her best smile and nodded her head in Crawley's direction before following her uncle into an office that had twelve secretaries tapping away furiously at their typewriters.

Her uncle gestured George to stop and said, 'They're looking for a typist, they're one short, what do you think?'

George was never one to shy from an opportunity; she was the sort to try something at least once. 'Yes, I will give it a try, Uncle and I appreciate the opportunity.'

'OK let me see if I can pull a few strings.'

At twelve thirty on the dot Lt. Crawley was standing outside the cafe waiting for them to turn up. He shook hands with Uncle Ted and with George in turn. George could only guess why Uncle Ted had invited Peter Crawley to lunch and she felt annoyed. She did not want to be lumbered with him and she had a feeling it would only be a matter of time before he invited her out.

Sure enough, towards the end of a lunch of cheese sandwiches and a slice of Victoria Sponge, Peter invited her to a dance at his officer's mess. George thanked him and told him she would think about it, but she had no intention of accepting his invitation.

In the afternoon George travelled by train to Finsbury where she had to meet the Commandant Dame Katherine Jane Trefusis Forbes for an interview at Adastral House. The interview was nerve wracking and it took forever. Some of the questions she was asked had her a bit apprehensive until she was asked how good her mathematics and French were, to which she replied in perfect French: *'Mes mathématiques sont très bonnes'*.

She left the interview unsure of her progress simply because the commandant didn't once give any positive reaction to her responses; she could only pray and hope. She was asked to wait another hour before she was given a letter of acceptance and was offered a position as Clerk Special Duties, which meant nothing to George, but she was happy to have made it into the WAAFS. she now had to wait to be called up.

With that she caught the train back and met her Uncle.

'How did it go?' he asked.

'It was fine, the Commandant, with a rather long name, Dame Katherine Jane Trefusis Forbes, grilled me something rotten especially about my grasp of the French language; she also hammered me about mathematical calculations. I waited an hour and I was informed I was needed as a clerk and I accepted; at least I got a foot in, she also said that the Company was affiliated to the six hundred City of London RAF Auxiliary Squadron, who have their training base at Hendon. She recommended that I go out there on Sundays on a voluntary basis, to get experience in their canteen till my position was official. Also, on Friday evenings they will be holding meetings in the hut on the grounds here of the HAC (Honourable Artillery Company) to learn more about the RAF, as well as marching, saluting etc., well at the moment it's all double Dutch to me!' she exclaimed, pulling a face. 'So, you needn't worry so much about the job at the war office Uncle, because I have a feeling, they will send for me soon.'

On the drive home she was quiet and thoughtful and had already made up her mind to send Gracie a letter suggesting that she visits. Though she had only been at the Pickerings for a few days she was already beginning to feel edgy, however she did not want to hurt her aunt and uncle's feelings; they had been so good to her.

'Aaaah, there you are both of you, just in time for tea, I've boiled the kettle.'

They both walked through the door, George looking a bit windswept.

'How was your day Georgina, did your interview at Finsbury Barracks go well?' Aunt Marlu questioned her.

'I actually had a super day, the interview went well, I signed up, so it's looking promising,' she helped herself to a cup of tea, 'and I have a feeling they will call me up soon.'

'Marlu my darling, I imagine we will have to start looking for a bedsit in London for Georgina with the way things are going. It won't be feasible for her to travel from Guildford, plus I'm not always making the journey into London.'

'Well Uncle and Aunty, I have a friend who lives in London, I thought I would drop her a line or two and see if there's anything going in the house she's lodging at.'

Friday first September was a day nobody would ever forget, especially the Pickering's and George who woke with a jolt. She wasn't quite sure why. Her watch said six a.m. *'I wonder what all that noise is downstairs.'* she thought.

She switched on her bedside lamp; it was still dark outside. She crept downstairs, the light in the sitting room was on.

Her Aunt looked ashen and Uncle Ted had his arms around her comforting her.

'What's happened...?' George instantly became worried.

'Hitler invaded Poland about an hour ago, he attacked the Polish garrison in Danzig on the coast; the MoD just called to tell me; I have to leave immediately, take care of Aunt Marlu and I will get in touch as soon as possible. The telephone will be jam packed with calls so don't panic if you don't hear from me right away.' Uncle Ted literally ran out to his car and drove away.

'This is not good Georgina.' Her Aunt who was normally the calm and collected one looked at George her bottom lip trembling.

She sat next to her Aunt comforting her. They spent most of the day waiting for a phone call — which never came — and listening out for the sound of her uncles' car parking outside. He arrived Saturday morning at three a.m. Her Aunt had stayed up waiting for him unable to sleep. Saturday was spent listening to Uncle Ted relating all the events. The Luftwaffe had launched an invasion supporting some sixty-two divisions of the Wehrmacht which included tank divisions, artillery and infantry commencing an all-out onslaught of Poland. George listened absorbing every word in horror. He spoke of the terrible atrocities the Nazi death squads were inflicting on Jewish communities, concentration camps were cropping up at an alarming rate; all to incarcerate any asocials.

'But Uncle, where did all this hatred come from? It's madness, wasn't the last world war enough!'

'The problem is George, the German people felt betrayed by the signing of the Armistice on November 11th 1918, most felt that Germany had not surrendered unconditionally but rather came to a compromise with the Allies to end the war and the actual Treaty of Versailles took longer to negotiate because it was meant to end the war of all wars; the German population didn't see it that way, they did not take kindly to the 'reparations' it fired great resentment.'

'But how did the war start in the first place? I mean it's all so senseless...'

'There are many things that are senseless in life my dear, but believe it or not it all started with the assassination of the Archduke of Austria, Franz Ferdinand by a Serbian nationalist, the rest is as they say, history!'

George shook her head in silence mulling over her uncle's words. It was just too sad to imagine what could possibly justify the cost of human life for the sake of a pointless war.

Sunday morning at eleven fifteen, whilst all of them were sitting in the lounge having tea, the wireless abruptly stopped broadcasting its music to allow Neville Chamberlain to confirm what everyone had been dreading for the past 48 hours.

They listened intently to the Prime Minister's message:

'This morning the British Ambassador in Berlin handed the German Government a final Note stating that, unless we heard from them by 11 o'clock, that they were prepared at once to withdraw their troops from Poland, a state of war would exist between us. I have to tell you now that no such undertaking has been received and that consequently this country is at war with Germany. You can imagine what a bitter blow it is to me that all my long struggle to win peace has failed. Yet I cannot believe that there is anything more or anything different that I could have done and that would have been more successful...'

'Well, that's that then,' Uncle Ted said as a matter of fact.

They listened to the rest of the speech sombrely and when it finished, they sat contemplating what it all meant.

Uncle Ted turned to George and said, 'I'm not sure it's a good idea you going to live in London now; it's the first place that will be attacked!'

'Uncle, I have no choice, I will have to live there to get on with my career in the WAAFS, whatever happens I am going, it's what I have always wanted to do,' she said defiantly.

Uncle Ted looked doubtful and directed his gaze to his wife for support.

'Let's just wait and see what happens before we all come to any hasty decisions.'

After the initial panic of the declaration of war, life seemed to carry on as normal and the Pickering's relented to George going to London, at least for a weekend; George had received word from Gracie, who had invited her to stay for a few days to find her feet, so to speak. She was of course relieved and made arrangements with her uncle who was off to the War Office the following Friday. It worked out perfectly because Gracie had told her she was off all that weekend.

The platform at Waterloo Station was packed, a melee of passengers got off trains and others got on. George made her way to the exit and descended the tube station to catch an underground train to the Oval. She was on the bus heading in the direction of Peckham High Street within ten minutes of waiting at the bus stop. The bus trundled through Camberwell and finally arrived some half an hour later in the high street, where George got off, lugging her case and walking the few minutes to the house where Gracie lived. She knocked on the door. A window on the first floor opened and Gracie's tousled red head popped out.

'Geooorge, you made it, I'll be down in a couple of ticks,' she said disappearing from the window.

The door opened and Gracie flung her arms around George, giving her a strong hug, which George returned wholeheartedly, because she was sincerely happy to see her friend.

'Come on in mate, kettle's boiling in the kitchen, Mrs Matthews is out shopping for our supper at the moment, so we have a few minutes of peace to catch up on things, so tell me how has it been, staying with your aunt and uncle?'

'Well, you know what it's like, it was a massive change from being home in Malta to coming here; I mean I had a certain amount of freedom and independence, Mum made sure I went to church every Sunday but she left me pretty much to my own devices, which most girls back home couldn't do, so all in all I haven't really had a chance to really test my liberty here,' George ended with a smile.

'You will be just fine and I have a bit of good news too, the other lodger is leaving for Scotland so her room is to become vacant, and it's right next to mine, so what do you reckon?' Gracie asked her.

'But that's fantastic, when can I move in do you think?' she asked.

'Daisy is supposed to be leaving Friday the 22nd September so I guess it's best to speak to Peggy, that is, Mrs Matthews, I'm sure she will be pleased to have you,' Gracie ended with a smile.

With her mind racing whilst chatting to Gracie she had already made up her mind to take the room, she would let her aunt and uncle know as soon as she got back to Guildford. In the meantime, she had a whole weekend to look forward to. At that moment Peggy Matthews walked in.

'Mrs Matthews this is George, the lady who I told you was visiting for the weekend.'

'Hello dear so lovely to meet you, Gracie has told me all about you and how you travelled together from Malta, how lovely to live on such a warm island. I went there you know, it was in July 1937 with my husband Peter, though he's gone now, God rest his soul,' glancing at a photo of her late husband on the sideboard.

'Oh, I'm sorry about your husband Mrs Matthews, I'm glad you enjoyed Malta with him, it's a lovely island and the people are so sweet and friendly and not to mention extremely helpful,' she concluded, looking at Mrs Matthews to allow her to carry on what she was saying.

'That's quite all right dear, anyway enough of that; Gracie tells me you are looking for lodging. As it happens, Daisy is leaving for Scotland, so the room will be vacant from Saturday 22nd. The rent is eight shillings a week which includes your laundry, breakfast and evening meal. I will require one week's deposit; how does that sound to you?'

'That's sounds fine Mrs Matthews, will it be all right to give you everything when I next come down?'

'Yes of course dear, and call me Peggy, everybody else does.'

'Will you be OK with your luggage?' Peggy asked her.

'I've got just one suitcase so it won't be a problem, I will ask my Uncle Ted if he can drive me here; he will want to know where I'm staying anyway.'

'Right,' said Peggy, 'I will let you girls get on with it.' And with that Peggy proceeded to the kitchen.

Gracie, who had been sitting quietly observing what was going on said, 'why don't we go up to my room and you can get changed if you want or just leave your suitcase there then we can go off to the High Street?'

'That's a great idea, OK let's be off then, by the way, I just wanted to ask, is there a telephone in the house? I need to give the number to my aunt and uncle and also let the WAAFS office know where I am.'

'Yes, there is, it's in the hallway just as you come in, I will show you on the way out.

Peckham High Street was teeming with people, they walked along chatting and browsing the shops until they came to a little cafe where they entered and ordered a pot of tea and two buns.

'You know, it's going to be so much fun having you stay right next to me.'

'Yes, it's going to be grand, but I'm worried it's going to be short-lived since I'm waiting for my call up. It was made quite clear to me that I would be spending an awful lot of time training at the barracks, it's a bit daunting actually.'

'Well, I'm sort of expecting the same, because you know I've applied for the RAF transport section, there have been rumblings that we will get called up soon too,' Gracie said ruefully.

'It's all exciting stuff at the moment but I doubt it will remain that way if the Germans decide to bomb us, I mean this Hitler is evil and means business, his meteoric rise to power in the last few years has been downright scary, he seems to want to swallow up the world.'

'Let him try to come here I say, us pommies will show him a thing or two,' Gracie said animatedly, bunching her hands threateningly and laughing at the same time. George did not share her enthusiasm, this war business was sure to have some terrible consequences.

'Hmm the government must be worried though Gracie because I heard from Uncle Ted that they have started to evacuate children to the countryside as a precaution.'

'Yes, I heard that and I saw it happening yesterday at the train station at the Oval, it was packed, I thought it was a mass picnic for children until I saw their little faces, most of them were crying their eyes out with their distraught mothers, poor mites.'

They finished up their tea and buns and headed back to the house.

'So, you can use my bed whilst you're here, I can sleep on the sofa, it's quite comfortable.'

'Are you sure Gracie, I don't mind the sofa, honestly!'

'Yes, really, I'll be fine, anyway that's settled, so I was wondering how much nightlife you've experienced?'.

'Just the odd bar in Valletta with my friend Connie and then there have been the Officers' Mess soirees and the Chalet dances on the esplanade in Sliema, nothing too exciting really; of course, there's the cinema but a lot of the movies were old because they took ages to come to the island,' George pursed her lips.

'Great, then we can head over to the West End and watch a film, there's *Clouds Over Europe* and some big names acting, Laurence Olivier for one, then there's Ralph Richardson and of course my favourite, Valerie Hobson,' Gracie ended with a big grin.

'Hmm I've heard of Lawrence Olivier but not the other two.'

'Really? Not even Valerie Hobson? She's an absolute stunner!'

'I'm sure she is!' George laughed at her friend's enthusiasm for the actress. Later in the afternoon they caught a bus and an underground train to the West End.

They went to a pub close to the Ritz Cinema in Leicester Square till the show started.

'George can I ask you something personal?'

'Sure, ask away.'

'Well, the thing is, you've never mentioned having any boyfriends, I mean you must have had many admirers back in Malta?'

'Oh Lord, what is it with people around me asking about my personal life! Yes, there have been admirers but none have made an impact on me, I don't seem to have any interest in that kind of thing right now, the one time I did accept a man's attentions it made me feel very uncomfortable, they always want more don't they?' George replied feeling a bit annoyed.

'Oh mate, I'm sorry, I didn't mean to pry, but I know what you mean, I feel very much the same, they tend to paw at you like a dog that wants affection,' Gracie guffawed.

'You don't think there's something wrong with me do you Gracie? Thing is I've never really spoken about it to anyone?'

'Don't be daft lass there's nothing wrong with you, besides you might just be happier with female company you know, close friends and all that.'

'Yes, maybe you're right, I just feel so awkward in a man's presence,

I mean I notice them looking at me all the time and I don't dislike them or anything, but it doesn't do anything for me, I don't understand women who go all soft and gooey over a bloke,' George sighed in exasperation.

'Oh lord is that the time?' Gracie changed the subject as she looked at her watch, 'we'd better leg it because the show starts in five minutes.'

They drained their glasses and left in a rush.

Chapter 9

'That was a damned good film don't you think?' She asked George whilst walking towards Leicester Square underground station and descending the stairs to the platforms to catch a southbound Northern Line train to the Oval.

'I have to admit I thoroughly enjoyed it and you're right, that Valerie *whatshername* IS a stunner, but most of the time these actresses are stunning anyway, aren't they?'

They didn't have to wait long before the familiar rumble of the train wheels whipping on the tracks was heard before it appeared out of the tunnel. With a hiss of pneumatic brakes, the train came to a halt and the guard at the back opened the doors to people pouring out and getting in. 'Mind the gap! Stand clear of the doors!' the guard yelled before he shut the doors again.

They were just passing through Charing Cross when Gracie asked George if she fancied going to a club, she knew in the Kings Road in Chelsea. George nodded in agreement not giving it another thought remaining quiet for the rest of the journey to the Oval, mostly because it was a bit noisy on the train.

It was around ten thirty p.m. when they arrived at the Oval, and they were in the process of contemplating taking a taxi when the bus appeared.

Once back at the house George called her aunt and uncle reassuring them she was all right, and also letting them know of her plans to take up accommodation in London.

'OK Aunty, please don't worry I will catch the three o'clock train from Waterloo on Sunday, see you at Guildford station then, give my love to Uncle Ted, bye, bye.' George replaced the phone in its cradle.

'Well, that's done and I'm about ready for bed,' she said as she yawned. Both women climbed the stairs in silence, both with their minds full of uncertainties.

They got up late and spent the day listening to the wireless as reports came through of Hitler's advance into Poland.

'We definitely need cheering up George, so are you up for the club then?'

'Well, I don't know, I've never been to a club before, what's it all about?'

'Right then we will soon change things; you will have to wait and see, let's say we aim for going out at six o'clock, we will get a taxi back tonight,' Gracie winked mysteriously.

She dressed carefully that evening, dark brown slacks with a pink blouse and a dark brown sweater. In the kitchen Gracie eyed her up and down and said, 'I think we should visit Marks and Spencer's mate!' George felt self-conscious and realised Gracie was right, she needed to change her wardrobe.

On the bus George shifted in her seat, it felt a bit uncomfortable and lumpy.

'What's up with you? You're fidgeting like mad!' Gracie laughed at her friend.

'I know, it's the seat, it feels lumpy, I'm trying to find a comfortable position,' George grumbled.

'Well, we'll soon be in the West End, look we're just coming up to Trafalgar Square, we can get off at the next stop and walk from there if you like.'

'Oh bother, let's get off then and get a drink in a pub somewhere!'

'That's more like it, I'm gagging for a pint.'

'Really? A whole pint? Crikey I've never even had a beer, just gin and tonic or red wine!' George giggled.

'We'll have to change that mate, come on, we get off here!'

They went down the stairs of the double decker and got off at the stop both laughing at Gracie's last remark.

'Let's walk to Oxford Street then and grab another bus into the Kings Road in Chelsea, we should get there by about 6.15 p.m. we can have a drink in the club, no point in wasting any time.' They walked briskly in the direction of the street.

They arrived on the Kings Road and only had a short way to walk before they reached an obscure green door and descended a steep staircase. Gracie knocked on the door and they were ushered in by a masculine looking woman. The stairs led down to a windowless cellar bar that was small with a very smoky atmosphere. The bar was located at one end of the room, with the toilets and a cloakroom at the other.

George looked around perplexed at what the place could be.

'Gracie what on earth is this place you've brought me to?' looking at her questioningly.

There was a sudden moment of uncertainty as Gracie found herself wondering whether she had made the right decision to bring George to the *Gateways* Club.

'It's a place where women like you and me can feel safe in,' Gracie replied

'I've no idea what you're talking about… feel safe, what do you mean?'

'Take a look around you properly.'

'There are a lot of women and men and it's a bar,' feeling a bit stupid because she couldn't fathom what Gracie was trying to tell her.

'George looked closer, they are *all* women, every one of them. This place is a haven for women who like women.'

George's jaw dropped in astonishment and shock, she backed up against a dark corner that offered some respite from what she had just been told. She wanted to run in fear as if her secret was out, but instead she remained rooted to the spot till Gracie pulled her to a table and chairs and made her sit down.

'George I'm sorry I didn't mean to shock you, I just thought you were like me, I just sort of got a feeling, but if I'm wrong, if I've misunderstood you, we can leave right now.'

George remained speechless, still in shock, she scrutinised the women properly, some were dressed like her, but there were others who were wearing suits and had short hair and looked very manly. It was very confusing as she had never expected to see women who dressed like she did when going to the Cairo.

'George for God's sake say something, you're worrying me now,'

'Gracie, just get me a drink, make it a double gin and tonic, just give me a minute or two to let this all sink in and you had better explain things a bit more when you come back.'

From a gramophone somewhere the dulcet tones of Anita Boyer

singing *Darn That Dream* drifted as if on the smoky atmosphere itself and suddenly couples came together to the limited dance space. George watched incredulously, she had no idea these places existed and tried to adjust to the scene before her. Gracie returned from the bar with the drinks and placed them on the table. They sat quietly watching the coupled women on the floor swaying gently.

'Thing is, you never mentioned any blokes you were dating you didn't mention anything for that fact and I just got the impression you just weren't interested, I took a risk bringing you here, am I wrong about you?' Gracie asked her directly.

George struggled to find words to say, 'I'm not sure, I'm feeling very confused right now, you've just plonked this on my lap and I'm trying to find the words to say; I just never thought about it, is all, how could I? I've never come across anything like this so I've never really had the opportunity to form an opinion or emotions for that matter, I've never felt really comfortable in the company of a man, but then again I haven't had anything like this to compare with,' she ended, all in one breath.

'So, I'm not wrong then?'

'Gracie I can't answer that because I've never developed feelings for a woman, at least I don't think so. My only attachment has been to my friend Connie back home, I mean we were always close but that's about it.'

They were silent for a while as they sipped their drinks. A couple in the opposite side of the bar were kissing; George lowered her eyes. Gracie did not miss the reaction; she placed a reassuring hand on George's.

'George it's fine, it just takes getting used to, I felt the same way as you but after the initial shock I felt a sense of relief that I found somewhere I belonged, it's not something you can blow your trumpet about because it's very taboo but at least you know you are not going mad and you're not alone, if you know what I mean.'

'This has been a real eye opener, it's something I have to think carefully about, I have to search myself and figure things out for myself, but what you've done has made me face myself and deal with something that I didn't realise was there. I mean I've always felt different but I just didn't know what it meant or means.'

'So, you'll come here again with me? We can come back next Saturday if you like, the second time round is always much easier.'

'Maybe, just give me some time to adjust and we shall see,'

They left *The Gateways* at eleven thirty and hailed a black cab.

Gracie accepted the lack of conversation from George's part as a contemplative remnant from *The Gateways*.

The next day George woke up in a very distracted state of mind. When she sat down at the dining table with a cup of tea, Gracie put the wireless on to listen to the news, it was eleven o'clock. Both women were listening absentmindedly to some music when George said, 'I'd better get myself sorted, I have to leave to catch my train from Waterloo at one thirty,' gulping down the last mouthful of tea as she said this.

'Look George do you want me to come with you to the station?'

'No, I'll be fine, I just need to pack my suitcase then I will be off, I'll grab a sandwich from the café on the concourse.'

So much had happened of late, Hitler, the declaration of war and that blessed club *Gateways*, scenes of which she could not push from her mind. She was glad when the time came for her to go back to Guildford even though she knew she would be back the following week.

She bade goodbye to Gracie and set off. Once on the platform she waited for her train which had not come in yet. She overheard passengers talking anxiously about the state of things. She admitted to herself she was a bit anxious and homesick herself being so far away from her parents and wondered how they were coping with the news, for they must have heard by now that England was at war and she knew they would be out of their minds with worry because the whole idea of her coming to England was for her safety's sake and now safe was the last thing she was feeling.

Her train finally hissed and blew into the platform. Once most of the passengers got off the train, she chose a second-class carriage towards the middle and settled in her seat. She was alone for the first few minutes but then more passengers joined. Halfway into the journey she felt peckish and devoured the cheese and tomato sandwich which looked sad in its paper bag and she suddenly longed for the smell of her mother's cooking wafting from the kitchen. Her eyes blurred and a tear slid down her cheek, imagining her dad in his study forever tinkering with his model planes. She would write them a long letter and the thought made her feel better. Both Uncle Ted and Aunt Marlu were waiting at Guildford Station. They hugged her warmly and once in the car and on their way to Bramley, Aunt Marlu plied her with questions about her weekend.

'It was a strange sort of weekend to be honest, so much went on, most of the time we were all preoccupied with the events that happened, when I say all, I mean Mrs Matthews, that is Peggy, Gracie and myself. We went to the pictures on Friday evening, that was enjoyable enough. Saturday was a lovely day, we went shopping and then into the West End again, and today we just got up late, had some tea and I made my way here,' George ended.

'Yes Georgina, we are all rather worried, the War Office has been on the end of the phone constantly, in fact I have to be in London early tomorrow and I'm not sure when I'm coming back to Guildford at this point and moment, but I can take you on next Friday for sure because I will be back for some fresh clothes. I can see, your mind's made up,' Uncle Ted said.

Aunt Marlu interrupted and said, 'There's an official letter waiting for you on the table in the hallway, I think it might be from the WAAFS,' she finished off with a smile.

'I'm suddenly feeling very tired, I'm looking forward to a cup of tea and then bed.'

Which is exactly what she did but not before opening the brown envelope. It *was* from the WAAFS ordering her to report for a week's training course at Hendon RAF barracks on Monday second of October. She put the letter on her bedside table, switched off the light and fell asleep instantly.

George arranged to travel to London on Friday the fifteenth. She had just enough time for a wash and a cup of tea before she found herself sitting next to her uncle for the second time. She felt a bit guilty at the hurried goodbye with her Aunt but there was no turning back now, this was what she had come to England for. The journey into London was quicker than usual, there didn't seem to be that many cars on the road, so that before she knew it her uncle was pulling up in front of her new address in Peckham.

'Uncle thank you both so very much for everything, I will come and visit again as soon as I'm settled,' George said to her uncle as he helped her with her suitcase.

'Georgina, I feel your stay with us was far too short and sweet but I understand you want to lead your own life; do call us at least once a week and don't forget to let your father and mother know what you're up to. By the way, before I forget, here's your Barclays Bank book, take care of it dear,' he said leaning over and kissing her on her cheek.

'Thank you once again, and I will call you later on this week.' She got out of the car and took the suitcase her uncle handed her. Her uncle pulled away from the kerb and drove off leaving her standing by the door. She knocked, but nobody answered so she sat on the doorstep till someone came along, and that was Peggy, weighed down by two shopping bags.

'Oh hello, Peggy, let me help you with those,' grabbing one of the bags walking into the kitchen. She returned to drag her suitcase in and left it in the hallway.

'Thanks, dear, let's make a cup of tea before anything else, because I've got to go out again in a little bit.'

The kettle boiled and Peggy made them a pot of tea. It was a homely kitchen, everybody congregated there even though there was the sitting room to retire to; the kitchen just seemed the right place to be.

'So George, till Daisy leaves I've made up the sofa for you to use. You will have to take it in turns to use the bathroom, of course I'll leave you to sort that with Gracie when she gets back,'

'That's lovely Peggy, thank you, and here's my deposit, I'm giving you the rent right up till the end of October so that way I'm all sorted, because I have to report to Hendon Barracks Monday 2nd October, I'm assuming they will want me to start training so I might be away for some time,' George advised her.

'Don't worry dear, all your belongings will be safe and the door to your room has a lock so you can lock it before you have to go,' Peggy replied. 'I'll also give you a receipt for the deposit and the rent, but if you don't mind, I'll write that out later.'

With that, after finishing her tea, George went upstairs to leave her case in Gracie's room.

A few minutes later a voice from downstairs called out to her.

'George, are you here? Come down and have a cup of tea, will you?'

George smiled affectionately at the sound of her friend's voice and went downstairs.

'Well Gracie, looks like I'm home now, not that I have much to make it home, but I feel good about being on my own, seeing as it's the first time,' she concluded.

'You're not really alone are you; you've got me and Peggy too, anyway you will soon get used to it.'

'I suppose I will soon enough, I'm going to have to anyway because I've been summoned to Hendon RAF Barracks so I'm bound to make new friends when I get there and I suppose I will get to know more of what's to happen.'

'Of course you will, I suppose the same is going to happen to me, though I've started, I'm expecting a posting soon to the RAF transport, at least that's what I keep being told, but hey, in the meantime let's have a good time, God knows we are going to need it.'

'Oh lord what have you got in mind?' George asked.

'Weeeeell, I have been invited to a house party next Wednesday and I'm dragging you along with me.'

'What kind of house party?' George narrowed her eyes at Gracie.

'Um you know, a house party with booze and music and all sorts of things going on.'

'I suppose it's too much to ask you to be a bit more specific?' George asked her.

'Yes, it is too much because I want it to be a surprise,' Gracie replied cheekily.

'Hmm just like the last surprise I suppose!' George exclaimed.

'Oh, come on George it wasn't that bad after you had gotten over the shock.'

'I haven't thought about it much to be honest, I think I'm avoiding the subject or I don't want to face it, it's one or the other or both,' she laughed nervously.

'Loosen up Georgie girl, you will be just fine mate, you'll see, either way you will discover your true path,' Gracie was trying to be philosophical.

'When is this house party again then?'

'It's next Wednesday the twentieth at a good friend of mine's house and when she gets a party going it *really* gets going, so just come with an open mind,' she warned her jokingly.

'Gracie you're scaring me! It's just a party for goodness' sake,' George retorted somewhat cross with her friend.

'Yep, it's just a party.'

'I suppose we ought to go shopping tomorrow, I haven't a decent thing to wear, I could do with a pair of slacks and a blouse and maybe a jacket, because it's getting chilly in the evenings.'

'Well, I'm free in the afternoon, we could pop down to the High Street and have a mosey around, what do you say?' Gracie asked her.

'Great, I was dreading going on my own, incidentally I'm starving, is there anything I can nibble on till lunch, it's just I hate going through Peggy's larder when she isn't here.'

'Oh, don't worry about that, Peggy always leaves some bread, butter and jam just in case, there's also some Digestives in the biscuit jar on the window sill over there,' Gracie pointed in the direction of the kitchen sink window.

'Hmm OK I think I'll just help myself to a biscuit, do you know where the tea plates are?' she asked.

Yes, in the cupboard on the left-hand side, over there,' she pointed again just to the left of where George was sitting.

She helped herself to a biscuit and nibbled at it pensively, while Gracie browsed a magazine. The phone rang in the hallway, Gracie went and answered it.

'George it's for you, it's your mum,' Gracie yelled.

George ran to the phone, 'Mama? oh Mama how lovely to hear from you, how is everyone? Yes, I'm fine, just getting settled in my new lodgings, Mama please don't start worrying, I'm doing really well, yes, I'm taking good care of myself and Aunty and Uncle are well too. Where's Papa? Can I speak to him...? Hello Papa, yes, I'm fine, pardon? Yes, I'm reporting to Hendon on Monday second October, yes, I will take care of myself, please don't worry, can you tell Connie I sent her my best regards, I love you both... byeee!' The line went dead and George placed the phone in its cradle.

Back in the kitchen Gracie had made another pot of tea. She refilled

George's cup.

'Gracie, you don't talk much about your family, I mean do you have a family?'

'I don't talk much about my family because I haven't got one, I was put in an orphanage when I was a baby, I have no idea who me Ma or me Da are and I'm not likely to find out either,' Gracie replied guardedly.

'I'm sorry, I didn't mean to pry; I can be so tactless sometimes.'

'Don't worry about it mate I'm used to it now, that is, being on my own, I have been since the age of sixteen. Anyway, I've been working at the Peek Frean Biscuit factory in Bermondsey since I left the orphanage. I can't stand the smell of biscuits, but that's why I applied for the Air Transport Auxiliary so for me I feel it's a step in the right direction, I start training at the White Waltham Airfield in a week's time, so that won't be long after you really.'

'Where on earth's White Waltham doo-da then?

Gracie laughed and said, 'It's in Berkshire somewhere, obviously I have to get there by train and then we are supposed to be picked up from the station.'

'So, what exactly is it that you are *supposed* to be doing?'

'Well as far as I know we have to learn how to fly aircraft that are either new or have been repaired and deliver them to other Air Force bases, but eventually I'm hoping to fly them further afield, we shall see,' Gracie said with a grin and a wink.

'Hmm sounds much more exciting than what I'll be doing, that's for sure.'

'So, what brought you to Malta then, I never asked you, because I'm sure you hadn't planned on going there!'

'Hah! You'll laugh if I tell you! One of my friends is a Variety Hall dancer and there were six of them going over to entertain the troops, and I was asked if I wanted to go and help them with their wardrobe, well you can imagine I'd never been anywhere except the orphanages and the bloody biscuit factory and I thought why not! The rest is history as they say.'

'Good for you; what's for lunch by the way?' she said, changing the subject.

'I think Peggy said we are having pork chops and boiled potatoes.'

No sooner had Gracie finished her sentence when Peggy walked in the door.

'Hello girls,' Peggy said placing her laden shopping bags on the dining table.

'I suppose you're hungry!'

Both of them nodded in unison. By the time they sat down to lunch it was just after one o'clock, but as far as they were concerned it was well worth the wait, the pork chops tasted heavenly with Peggy's home-made gravy.

'Peggy, that was delumptious,' Gracie said with a satisfied smile.

George laughed heartily at her friend's coined word, 'OK Gracie, let me guess... delicious and scrumptious right?'

'Spot on mate, spot on!'

Even Peggy laughed at Gracie's enthusiastic description of lunch. After they had helped Peggy wash up the dishes, both women retired to Gracie's room for a rest, before going on the planned shopping spree.

They enjoyed a leisurely walk towards the British Home Stores.

'Right, let's head up to the women's section, we're bound to find a pair of slacks; what colour did you say you wanted?'

'Well, I was thinking of getting two pairs, one in cream and the other in dark blue,' George replied.

'Hmm yes they're sensible colours and you'll need a couple of blouses to go with them, and of course a jacket.'

'I need a pair of shoes too and some stout ones because I'm not sure what to expect, so I'm thinking they have to be sturdy.'

'There're the slacks over there, let's have a look.' Gracie indicated to a row of slacks next to a mannequin dressed in an outfit of blouse and trousers.

They spent some time choosing George's clothes before she went to the changing room to try them on.

'What do you think? Does it look all right?' George gave an exaggerated twirl in a pair of navy-blue trousers and a plain light blue blouse.

'You know what? You're going to turn a few heads; I'm going to enjoy introducing you!' Gracie grinned with satisfaction.

'Oh, don't be daft, you'll embarrass me, so please go easy on the introductions, will you?'

'I won't have to do anything because they will be all over you; you look stunning!'

'Stop it, you are incorrigible Gracie Miller! Let's find my jacket and grab a cup of tea at the Lyon's café,' she ended, changing the subject with a blush on her face.

They sat by the window and ordered tea and crumpets from the 'nippy' waitress who swiftly went off to place their order. The café was packed, everyone was in an animated conversation and the hum of voices rose above the two of them.

'My word it's busy in here isn't it?'

Gracie nodded in agreement, reluctant to pause from eating her crumpet which was covered in butter, some of which had dribbled down her chin. George placed a napkin in front of Gracie indicating with her head to the dribbling butter with amusement. After Gracie had wolfed down both her crumpets, she gulped her first cup of tea and then proceeded to pour her second. After adding sugar and milk she took a gentler approach to her second cup and sipped at it.

'So, what exactly am I to expect from this party then?'

'George mate, there's nothing to worry about really, it's just a party, there will be a lot of my friends and we are all the same, if you get my drift, there will be a few women whom you will get to meet and well the rest we will have to wait and see.'

'I'm feeling a bit nervous about the whole affair, but then again I'm also sort of excited too; do we have to take any booze with us?' George asked.

'Aah yes now you mention it, that's a good point, we will have to take something with us; how about a bottle of Gordon's?' Gracie asked.

'Sure, that's fine by me, we can go halves, what do you think?'

'Yep, let's do that.'

Armed with the bottle of gin and laden with George's bags they made their way back to the house. In Gracie's room they sorted out the various bits of clothing items and folded them neatly. Gracie had made room in her chest of drawers till George could move into Daisy's room. George was still to meet Daisy, she expected she would at tea time since that was when Daisy got in from work. George sat on the sofa whilst Gracie boiled the kettle to make tea. Peggy was out at her knitting circle and it was just the two of them lounging around. It left time for George to gather her thoughts and mull over how her mum and dad were coping without her, especially since the declaration of war. So far war had not hit the Maltese islands, but in their last telephone conversation, George had sensed the anxiety in her mother's voice.

'Penny for your thoughts?' Gracie interrupted.

'I was just thinking about Mama and Papa, it seems like I've been away ages rather than just a few weeks, time goes by so fast here, Mama's really worried about me being in London, especially since the declaration of war and no amount of reassurance is pacifying her,' George said pulling a face.

'Your parents are bound to worry; of course, I never had that problem and I can't say it bothered me because I have never known otherwise, so in a way I'm lucky or at least I think I am,' Gracie said ruefully.

'Hmm, I suppose I'm lucky because I come from a very loving environment but being an only child has had its drawbacks, because my parents have been a lot more attached to me. What I mean is though, I'm fairly independent and that's thanks to papa, but Mama has always tried to insulate me from the 'world outside.'

'Yeah well, I've had none of that, it's more like being shoved from one orphanage to another, you kind of grow up tough and streetwise because the matrons I've had have been a nightmare and the punishments were awful and there was never enough food, which is probably why I like it so much.'

'Well, you still turned out all right, for all the bad things you went through, you've got a great personality, you're funny and you're great company; it feels like I've known you forever!'

'Aww thanks mate, I'm certainly glad we met up and you're not so bad yourself!'

At that moment the front door opened and Daisy walked through.

'Oh hello, you must be George the Malteser, how do you do?' Daisy said smiling, directing her outstretched hand at George who took it and shook it warmly.

'Yes, that's me and of course you must be none other than Daisy?'

Daisy nodded and sat down at the kitchen table, which always seemed the place everyone sat at in Peggy's house.

'Oh, good you've made some tea, is there enough for me?' Daisy asked.

'Of course, there is mate, let me get the cups and saucers and stuff and we can all have one,' Gracie said.

'I bet you can't wait to move into my room!'

'I think I'm more excited at just moving here, but it would be nice to get my own room yes, but I'm still not in any particular hurry because I don't really have much to move, just a suitcase, and Gracie doesn't mind putting up with me sharing hers, its only for a couple of days,' George said good humouredly.

'I'm off to Scotland next Saturday, it feels so strange because I've been here almost a year, so it's been home for me here, but my Ma hasn't been feeling too well so I decided to go back and take care of her for a while.'

'Yes, Peggy and Gracie mentioned you were leaving and I guess it happened at the right time for me but I'm sorry about your Ma.'

'Well, there's nothing can be done about it except to go, so it's all sorted.' Daisy smiled.

Peggy turned up half an hour later from her women's knitting circle and set about preparing supper. The girls lent a hand, it was to be a cold meal with sliced boiled ham, tomatoes, cucumber, lettuce and hardboiled eggs. They sat down and each of them talked about their day as they ate. The conversation then turned to Daisy.

'What will you do once you get to Aberdeen; I mean will you find work or are you going to take care of mum full time?'

'I think I will have to look after her constantly for a while and then see if I can find something that allows me to do both,' Daisy replied.

'I've never been to Scotland though I've been to Paris, Papa took us there for a week a couple of years ago, it was more for my sake really, to practice my French,' George added.

'Ooooh la, la, how come you never mentioned that you could speak French, George?'

'I don't know really, I just never thought about mentioning it, not much call for it here is there?' she laughed.

'Oh, I don't know, you could have tried for a job teaching it instead of getting yourself in the WAAFS.'

'Crikey you've applied with the WAAFS, I was thinking about that myself before this business of Ma cropped up!' Daisy was envious.

'Actually, I've enrolled already, I'm due to start my initiation on the 2nd October though I have no idea what to expect, I'm guessing it will be lots of marching and drill practice, but beyond that, I've no idea except that I'm supposed to be assigned as the special duties clerk whatever that means.'

'Living here must be so different for you George, I mean leaving such a lovely place with all that sunshine and blue sea.'

'Yes, it is a bit, but I'm getting used to it, life here is a far cry from Malta, everyone is so laid back there and it's a little bit backward too, I mean it's a very insular island as it goes, it would never be approved that a young woman like me live on my own… it's unheard of, the only good thing is that my Papa's English, so, he sort of rubbed off on Mama a bit and she wasn't as strict as other mothers over there.'

'Oh Lord, that would drive me absolutely potty, though when I was there, I didn't really notice the restrictions,' Gracie interjected.

'Mind you it's a bit like that in Aberdeen, that's why I left in the first place, everyone gossips and knows everyone's business,' Daisy clucked in disgust.

Peggy had been listening quietly to the three of them talking and then she said, 'The thing is I never had children but I suppose it's only natural to want to protect them isn't it?'

'Can't answer that Peggy and not likely I ever will, can't see me being a housewife, don't get me wrong though I do like em, it's just'; children are not for me, I don't want to be tied down,' Gracie laughed.
'Nope I somehow can't imagine you being a housewife with half a dozen kids either!'

'Neither can I,' Daisy chipped in.

'Never mind ay, who's for a bit of Dundee cake? I'll put a pot of tea on,' Peggy said.

They all said yes in unison and were soon tucking into the decadent cake. After they finished eating and washed the dishes, they all lounged around in the sitting room. Gracie concentrated on listening to the wireless, Peggy knitted, Daisy went to her room and George settled down to write to her parents. Peggy got up to draw the curtains and offered to make tea for everyone.

George finished her letter and sipped her tea as she perused the Radio Times programmes.

'It's three o'clock, this is the BBC World Service, Good afternoon, these are the news headlines: Hitler's troops have surrounded Warsaw…'

'Bloody hell,' Gracie exclaimed, 'this Hitler is just not going to stop, is he?' directing her outburst at George.

'It doesn't look like it, does it? And you know what that means, I bet it won't be long before he turns his attention to us,' George stated.

'I fancy a drink… how about it, George? Daisy? We can go to the local for an hour,' Gracie asked.

'I'll go with you,' Daisy offered, who had since joined them.

'I'll stay in I think, I want to write home, so If you don't mind you two go and drown your sorrows and enjoy yourselves, God knows you should before things change.

By the time Gracie and Daisy returned, George was dozing on the couch, oblivious to the two girls' inebriated giggles.

'So what time are we going back to the club this evening?' George asked Gracie before she went upstairs.

'I was thinking we should set out in about an hour, you are OK about it aren't you?' Gracie asked.

'Yes, I am, but I'm still a bit nervous about the whole thing, I'm still a bit confused but I will give it another try,' George replied.

There wasn't much said after that, they set about preparing for the evening. George arranged the new clothes she was going to wear and Gracie went to the bathroom to wash. They were both ready within an hour and headed out to the bus stop. The red double-decker appeared in the distance and gradually made its way to where they were waiting alongside a small queue. The bus conductor ushered them on board; they climbed to the upper deck and settled halfway down the aisle. The conductor made his way towards them to take their fare and then returned to his position holding onto the bar at the side of the bus entrance. George gazed at the scenery whizzing past: shops, houses, people, trees, all seemed to merge into one blurry picture. They arrived at Oxford Street and changed onto another bus that took them all the way to Chelsea.

George recognised the stop coming up where they had to get off. Gracie rang the bell and the double decker came to a shuddering halt, almost throwing them off balance. She swore under her breath, which made George laugh. They got off the bus and it trundled away, leaving them to walk the rest of the way down the Kings Road, to where the *Gateways* Club was (or 'The Gates' as it was affectionately known) on the corner of Bramerton Street. The familiar green door loomed before them, at least it loomed before George, whose mouth suddenly went dry. Gracie knocked on the door, which was opened by the same woman as last time who smiled at them and pointed them down the steep stairs. George felt she was walking into a lion's den, it was one thing to dress up back home, but this was different; she had a sudden desire to turn tail and run. She didn't; instead, she bit her lower lip and descended the stairs behind Gracie. The place was dark and smelt of beer and cigarettes; for one brief moment George thought they were alone, but as her eyes adjusted to the darkness, she noticed that there were couples tucked away in the corners and the bar was lined with women. George took a deep breath in the hope it would ease her beating heart to a steady rhythm. Gracie went up to the bar and ordered them some drinks, she started chatting to a couple of women who seemed to know her. At one-point Gracie nodded her head in George's direction and when she made her way to their table the other women followed suit.

'George, meet Penny and Marge, good friends of mine, I invited them to sit down with us,' Gracie said rather too sweetly. George blushed red to the roots of her hair and it didn't go unnoticed by the two women.

'Gracie you're a bad lot, you've gone and made the poor girl blush!' Penny said, amused.

'I'm sorry, I'm just not used to this, I'm not even sure I should be here!'

'Don't worry love; we don't bite, just put yourself at ease, you will eventually get used to it,' Marge winked knowingly.

Gracie, Penny and Marge started to talk about the machinations of war, almost ignoring George, who was grateful and quietly sipping her gin and tonic, furtively observing what was going on around her. It was then she realised that a tall woman with short dark hair was staring intently at her. She caught George's eye, and flashed a bright smile at her.

This made George blush once again and she quickly looked at her shoes. But not to be put off, the woman walked up to George and said, 'Come and dance with me.'

George tried to refuse but the woman was insistent and she gently led her onto the small space that served as a dance floor. Gracie only gave her a glance as she passed by her and she smiled smugly.

The woman pulled George to her and held her firmly as they swayed gently to Glenn Miller's *Stairway to the Stars*. She looked up at the woman who had striking green eyes framed by a delicate oval face with a cleft chin; she felt something totally unfamiliar stir inside of her. She caught her breath as the woman leant her face close to her ear and whispered, 'My name is Griff; what's yours?'

George could barely expel her name as her heart thudded and hoped that Griff couldn't feel what was going on.

'My goodness, how your heart beats,' Griff commented, mischievously.

'Hmm,' George mumbled.

They danced for a few more minutes and George made an excuse of needing the bathroom, before escaping to her table and begged Gracie to go with her. They made their way to the tiny bathroom, where George stood shaking.

'Oh my God that was strange,' she mumbled, in the process of trying to calm herself.

'Strange, but not unpleasant,' Gracie remarked, amused.

'I don't know what I felt or what I was supposed to feel; well I didn't *not* like it, it felt kind of nice being held and she is rather good looking too.'

'Yes, that's our Griff, never a shortage of women with her, she's nice enough but doesn't entertain long relationships, can't blame her really with her looks; just keep a tight hold of that heart of yours,' Gracie warned.

'Oh, don't be silly Gracie I probably won't see her again after tonight and she is not my type anyway.'

In fact, Griff took a shine to George and kept trying to dance with her throughout the evening, going as far as to ask to see her again, but George refused her saying that she wouldn't be around that long. If Griff was disappointed, she didn't show it, even though not many refused Griff Harrington!

Marge and Penny had left the table and gone off to another one where more of their friends were sitting. Gracie looked up questioningly at George as she sat down next to her.

'Well?' asked Gracie.

'Well, what? Nothing is going to happen and I'm not likely to see her again anyway, and I'm not attracted to her!' George retorted defiantly.

Gracie said nothing but had a smug look on her face and continued to enjoy the music and sip her drink. She lit a cigarette and drew on it, letting the acrid smoke plunge deep into her lungs and slowly let it out again. Her eyes drifted to the bar where a slim brunette dressed in a white flowing dress and scarf around her neck was ordering a drink. Gracie hadn't noticed her coming in. She decided to go up to her and introduce herself. George watched her saunter over to the bar next to the woman. After a few minutes they disappeared onto the dance floor. She suddenly felt very alone and vulnerable. She was still unsure of this latest episode in her life as she had never thought of dating a woman. She *did* actually feel more comfortable in their presence and she admitted she *had* felt something when dancing with Griff, something she had never felt when embraced by a man. But she had been speaking the truth when she said she didn't have the time to pursue attachments of any kind, she was dedicated to her career and somehow did not foresee anything else.

Gracie had reappeared just as suddenly as she had disappeared and asked George if she wanted one for the road. She declined and felt relieved that the end of the evening was in sight. She was dying for some fresh air as the smoky atmosphere had started to irritate her eyes. Gracie got up as if to go and George was about to follow suit when she found Griff by her side.

'Going so soon?' Griff asked.

'Yes,' the word came out almost rudely.

'I hope we meet again,' flashing her brilliant smile.

George mumbled something inaudible and made her way to the doorway, climbing the steep stairs as fast as she could.

'Steady on George what's all the hurry?' Gracie said catching hold of George's arm.

'Nothing, I just wanted to get out of there before that Griff woman got her claws into me.'

'Oh Lord, I'm starving, shall we stop for some fish and chips?'

'Oh, all right then, you and your hollow legs' George giggled, 'where can we get some then?'

'There's one up the road just before we get to the bus stop.'

They stopped at the fish and chip shop for battered cod and chips and walked the short distance to the bus stop, eating their food till the bus came. They were halfway through when the bus arrived. The bus was half empty so they got a seat at the front and carried on eating till they finished. George rolled up both their newspapers into a ball and held onto them till they eventually got home. Peggy was still up and asked them if they wanted a cup of tea. Both of them were gasping for a cup so they sat down at the kitchen table.

'There's a letter arrived for you George, it's next to the phone,' Peggy said.

'Oh lovely, I wonder who it's from,' George murmured getting up from the table and walking to the hallway to retrieve the letter. It had a Malta two-penny stamp and George assumed it was from her parents. When back in the kitchen George opened the letter and found that it was from her friend Connie. George read it briefly and put it away in her handbag resolving to read it again later. In the meantime, the hot cup of tea in front of her sat invitingly, and she took a sip.

'Aah that's lovely Peggy, it just hits the spot, those fish and chips really made me thirsty, I think I overdid it on the salt,' George chuckled.

'I was just going to ask you girls, I'm bringing out the washtub tomorrow so if you want to wash any of your clothes, I will leave it out in the back garden, it's meant to be a nice day tomorrow according to the weather report on the wireless,' Peggy said with a smile.

Gracie, who had been quiet all this time, piped up with a groan and said, 'Thanks for reminding me Peggy, I've got a load to do, my worst nightmare!' she ended, pulling a face.

Peggy and George laughed.

'It's OK Gracie, you're not on your own, I need to wash some clothes too,' Hoping to comfort her friend.

'Well ladies, it's past my bed time, so I bid you both good night and see you in the morning; it's Sunday, so you won't have to wake up early,' Peggy ended with a smile.

The next day dawned bright and sunny and after they had breakfast, George and Gracie went out into the back garden and sat on the grass lapping up the sun and watching Peggy rub and bash her clothes in the bath tub, suds and water flying over the side.

Gracie lit a cigarette and lay flat on her back watching the smoke curl up and disappear into nothing. George lay prostrate, breathing in the smell of the grass and watching tiny insects crawl their way through what must have seemed to them like a jungle, at least that's what her imagination told her.

'I don't suppose any of you girls could give me a hand to put the sheets through the wringer, could you?'

George promptly got up, leaving her daydreaming behind and went over to where the wringer was and started to turn the handle vigorously, whilst Peggy pushed the sheets through. This was repeated several times after rinsing the sheets. George then helped Peggy hang the sheets on the washing line.

'I think some lemonade is in order, I made a fresh batch this morning, go help yourselves and I will leave the washing stuff out for you; I need to go and visit Mrs Bates down the road.'

Gracie let out a long groan, 'Damn it, the last thing I feel like doing is washing my clothes, but I suppose I'm going to have to,' she got up and went to get her dirty laundry from her room.

George grinned at Gracie's predicament and sipped her lemonade whilst she sat back on the grass.

'Never mind, it's my turn next, though I don't have half of what you've got to wash,' George said laughing. With that, she went into the house and up the stairs to get a book to read, one that Gracie had offered to lend her, it was a story by Virginia Woolf called *Three Guineas*. She returned to the back garden to find Gracie huffing and puffing away.

'Go for it, Gracie!' George laughed watching her scrubbing away at a pair of slacks.

George settled back onto the grass and read her book, getting so totally immersed that she did not notice Gracie creeping up from behind and slapping her head with a wet towel. George yelled in surprise and got up to run after Gracie, who by that time, had skedaddled behind the shed, waiting for her revenge. When George didn't turn up, she peered round the corner but couldn't see her so she came out of hiding, only to find George waiting on the other side of the shed, she sped off running round the garden with George in hot pursuit. They were, by this time, giggling hysterically, when Daisy, hearing all the commotion, came out to the garden to see what was happening. Clocking on to what was going on, she joined in the kerfuffle and all three of them were now running in circles, each trying to dodge the other, till they dropped on the grass, out of breath and laughing.

'Where did you come from anyway Daisy, I didn't see you in the house today?' Gracie asked.

'I went out for a walk down the High Street, I was supposed to meet a friend but he never turned up, so I came back to you lot giving chase.'

'I suppose you're all packed now, aren't you?' George asked her.

'Yes, most of it, I will shove my last few bits and pieces in, on Saturday before I leave. My train leaves at eleven thirty a.m, so I will still have a bit of time before I go. We can at least have a last cup of tea together aye?' she asked both of them.

'Of course we will Daisy, you never know, we might even visit you in Scotland too!'

'George why don't you move your stuff into my room anyway, because all my things are packed, so you may as well,' Daisy said.

'Are you sure you don't mind?'

'Not at all, I'll let Peggy know, I'm sure she'll be OK about it.' George did her washing and hung it out to dry. Daisy finished off her last-minute packing and Gracie went out to the pub for a quick half.

It was whilst laying peacefully on the grass reading her book that George felt time was rushing by. It seemed like she had barely arrived when so much had happened. Her mind was constantly thinking about her parents, her new life here, she wasn't sure of the kind of life that Gracie had introduced her to, but if she was honest, it no longer scared her and she was getting used to the idea that perhaps what had been missing was female company. Still, it made her nervous but she decided that from now on she would take things in her stride; she wanted to learn things and not seem so unworldly and inexperienced. She also felt safe from prying eyes and questioning looks because she was far away from home. Strange that the word 'home' also meant London with its busy streets, huge shopping malls, pubs and cinemas. Then of course there were the 'hidden' places like *Gateways*. Her thoughts turned to Griff— she was of course charming but too fast; George chuckled to herself at the thought of Griff coming on to her, at least she had refused her advances, but more than anything it was the imminent war that lay hovering like a dark cloud over everyone, that bothered her the most. She had to admit she was afraid of the unknown. She was still to collect her gas mask from the local air raid warden but it pushed home the reality of war which she was reluctant to acknowledge and she supposed the other girls felt the same. Gracie kept putting off picking up hers, saying it was too cumbersome to carry around and Daisy insisted she would not be needing it 'up north'. Peggy had hers already since she was out and about constantly. The telephone rang at least four or five times a day from some expectant mother needing her services. She admired Peggy; she never tired of being a midwife and running the guesthouse too but George supposed she had to survive somehow after losing her husband.

CHAPTER 10

'How was your day, Peggy? You look a bit tired!'

'I'm exhausted, Mrs Jarvis's confinement was a hard one; she had a breech birth so we had to wait for an ambulance to take her to hospital and then I had to rush off to Mrs Fowler who was delivering twins and straight after that I had to check up on Mrs Garter, poor woman, she has six children to look after with another on the way!'

'Phew that's one hell of a day you've had… well you needn't worry about supper because Gracie and I will get some fish and chips and your usual pie and chips.'

'Bless you dear, I'm sorry you've both had to look after yourselves these last couple of days, I don't know what's got into those women they weren't due for another week!' Peggy exclaimed.

George remained silent for a short while to give Peggy time to come to her senses after her tough day.

'Peggy, would you know if there is a church nearby? Because I haven't come across one yet since I've been here,' George asked her.

'Why yes of course there is, there's St James's church on Elm Grove not very far from here actually, about a twenty-minute walk. It's a lovely church, very peaceful during the day and there's a lovely Sunday service too,' Peggy ended with a smile.

By Wednesday morning George was a bag of nerves but she was determined to grin and bear it just for her friend's sake and also, she knew that there would be little time to partake of these events once she started work. She had pressed a crisp pale blue blouse and a plain pair of black trousers that made her look very svelte, complemented by a pair of soft leather lace-ups; she felt she would brush up quite well. Gracie stood in the doorway appraising her.

'Bloody hell George you look stunning, I'd better keep an eye on you tonight.'

'Gracie, stop it, you are incorrigible, if this is meant to give me courage you are having the completely opposite effect on me.'

'Oh, come on George, you love it, you should be feeling chuffed.'

George threw a pillow at Gracie in protest and ran out of her room to the bathroom to brush her teeth.

'Geooorge do hurry up will you, we're running late,' Gracie yelled from downstairs.

She took one last look in the mirror above her chest of drawers and grabbed her jacket and handbag from where she had left them on the bed. She literally ran down the stairs to where Gracie was waiting for her with the front door open.

'Have fun girls!' Peggy called out from the sitting room.

'Thanks Peggy!' both of them replied in unison.

They walked to the bus stop a few minutes up the road and waited till the bus turned up. They crossed the Vauxhall Bridge Road and stopped off at Warwick Way, taking them into Pimlico, where a twenty-minute walk brought them to a house tucked away in Ecclestone Square Mews. The lights were all on and there was music blaring out of one of the open windows upstairs. The front door was ajar and the minute they set foot inside, George realised that the owner was obviously rich. Thick Persian carpets started from the door leading to every room downstairs, which was packed with women. They both took their jackets off and hung them on the crowded coat rack. Climbing the wide staircase George couldn't help but gawp at the expensive art adorning the walls.

'Gracie who on earth is the person who owns this house?' George asked incredulously.

'It belongs to Lady Virginia Davenport-West, but we call her Ginny for short; she's a chip off the old block, her old man's loaded, and is away most of the time, this is one of those times,' Gracie replied, enjoying George's expressions of awe.

There was a cloud of smoke floating in the air with a small group of women sitting around a table rolling cigarettes. The smoke smelled different, sort of pungent rather than acrid.

'What's that smell Gracie?' George asked screwing up her nose.

'Hmm it's called marijuana, it makes you feel very calm and peaceful and smiley too.'

'Oh, you mean it's a narcotic?'

'Well yes sort of,' Gracie replied, surprised that George even knew what the word narcotic meant.

'Have you tried it?'

'Yes, loads of times, but I wouldn't try it if I were you, because you will choke on it for sure, apart from going green around the gills,' Gracie chuckled.

They wandered from the huge sitting room where most of the party was gathered and coincidentally where the music was coming from and into the kitchen where all the drinks were. The kitchen table was groaning under the weight of beer bottles, glasses and bottle upon bottle of branded whiskies, brandies and gins. Bottles of tonic water as well as a spritzer bottle of soda water were on either side. A bowl of sliced lemons complemented the selection. George had never seen so much booze in all her life! Sure enough, she expected it in a bar or in the officer's mess back home, but nothing like this.

They helped themselves to a drink and wandered into the equally spacious dining room, where their hostess Ginny was in an animated conversation with no other than Griff! George stood stock still in shock.

'Gracie, you never told me that Griff would be here,' George hissed from between her teeth.

'So what, just ignore her and if you don't want her attentions then just tell her, besides she hasn't even come over yet!' Gracie all but growled at her.

George realised that she had annoyed her friend so she remained quiet, sipping her drink. Gracie wandered off and left George to her own devices. It wasn't long before she attracted the attentions of Ginny.

'Hello there, I'm Ginny and you are?'

'George, George Parker, very pleased to meet you, quite a party you've got going here!'

'That's a positive comment I take it, come and sit over here with me and tell me all about yourself' Ginny said, monopolising George and leading her to a beautiful gilded *chaise longue* next to a huge and imposing marble fireplace. George was mortified for a few seconds and her mouth went dry.

Ginny laughed and said, 'I can see you are new to all this, don't worry dear I don't bite, you are so sweet and innocent, unlike this lot of heathens.'

George plucked up the courage to talk and surprisingly, after a few minutes, she felt at ease and found herself telling Ginny all about her life in Malta, till the conversation turned to the current affairs of the situation in Europe, both of them were so engrossed that they didn't notice Griff resting her elbow on the fireplace mantle listening in on the conversation.

'Ginny you're boring the poor girl half to death,' Griff interrupted.

'Actually, I'm not bored at all, I'm enjoying every moment… now, if you don't mind…' George turned back to Ginny, who was taken aback and flattered at the same time.

'Oops OK, I'll bugger off then, shall I?' Griff said. George gave her a look that didn't even merit an answer.

Ginny suggested to George she show her around and tell her a little about the history of the Davenport-West family. They drifted from one room to another, whilst Ginny explained the opulently framed paintings, till they came to one of the closed rooms. Ginny opened the door and led her in, closing it behind them. George came face to face with an enormous four-poster bed made of solid mahogany and beautiful red damask drapes. There were two bedside tables, one on either side, a dressing table to the right-hand side of the room next to a tall window, of which the curtains were drawn. For a moment George felt a little out of her depth… She thought, *'Why has she brought me into this room?'*

Ginny moved to the dressing table and pulled out a small silver box and opened it. George watched fascinated whilst she took out some white powder and placed it on the shiny surface of a small pocket mirror. With a razor blade she proceeded to pulverise the powder in a chopping motion. When Ginny had finished, she had separated the powder into four short lines. She turned to George and said, 'Do you know what this is, George?'

'No, I have absolutely no idea,' she said truthfully.

'It's called cocaine; it makes you feel pretty wonderful. Would you like to try it?' Ginny asked her with a sweet smile.

George, nodded and moved over to the dressing table. She looked questioningly at Ginny, who put a small silver tube to her nose and snorted a line up each nostril. She sniffed delicately a couple of times to make sure that none of the powder came out and pinched her nose a couple of times.

'Take a couple of breaths and be careful not to breathe out or all the powder will just spread all over the place; put the silver tube to one nostril and close the other with your finger,' Ginny explained.

George did as she was told and snorted the powder up both her nostrils and copied Ginny perfectly.

'There, how do you feel? isn't it amazing?'

George nodded; the cocaine numbed her nose and throat leaving a bitter taste at the back of her tongue. The effect was sudden, the drug took hold of her, she relaxed to the point of not having a care in the world, and smiled at Ginny, who pulled her slowly towards the bed. She sat George down and began to stroke her hair and her face. The cocaine took George to another dimension, she melted at the touch of Ginny's caressing hands. Encouraged by her reaction, Ginny gently placed her lips on George's. George's heart thudded ferociously in her breast. Ginny looked into her eyes and for a moment was held captive by her intense stare, then she drowned in the kisses that covered her mouth, her face, her eyes, her neck… George succumbed to waves of euphoria enveloping every inch of her body. This woman was an expert and she knew it. It was her *pièce de résistance,* taking a woman for the first time to the heights of ecstasy. She was a willing candidate; letting Ginny lay her head on the pillow and going to work on her, teasing her body skilfully. She ran her hands over her smooth skin feeling George quiver, stroking her, kissing her breasts; running her tongue over her belly; George ran her hand through her hair pulling her towards her, arching her back, wanting more. Ginny obliged and entered her; she was lost, responding only to this skilful woman's lovemaking, not wanting the pleasure that was rocketing through her to stop. Then it happened, an explosion of total fulfilment, tingling nerve-endings, gasping for breath and trying to control her pounding heart. She lay trembling in wonder at what had just happened. Ginny held her in her arms, murmuring in her ear softly till she quietened down. They lay that way for about half an hour. George wanted to reciprocate but Ginny stopped her gently. And just like that it was over!

Ginny kissed her on her nose saying, 'I'll leave you to get dressed and join the party.' She left without so much as a glance backward and walked out of the door shutting it behind her.

Somewhat confused by her rather cold and abrupt exit, she wondered if she had been naïve and had succumbed too readily to her advances... It was certainly obvious that this was not the first time she had taken advantage of new blood in her circle of friends and partygoers. She supposed that there was always going to be a victim in these circumstances... In this case George had no reason to complain... quite the opposite. This was her first experience with a woman... She certainly did not anticipate it being her last.

George stayed as she was for a few minutes and then got dressed standing in front of the dressing table mirror to fix up her dishevelled hair. Her face stared back at her looking soft; a woman who had experienced lovemaking for the first time. There was a definite glow in her eyes and she smiled knowingly at herself. *So, this is what it's all about* she thought to herself. She left the bedroom and walked into the outside atmosphere which was in full swing. There were women sitting on the stairs, others leaning against anything that took their elbows, all drinking and laughing. She searched around for Gracie going from one room to the other until she came to the kitchen and finally found her, her arms around the waist of a short brunette and another three women Gracie was talking to, who hung on to every word she was saying. George smiled, amused at Gracie's prowess with women, which she hadn't really noticed before. Gracie suddenly turned round as if anticipating her.

'Oh, hello you! Where have you been?' raising an eyebrow in the process of asking her.

George mumbled something about being with Ginny.

'Oh lord, really? Seriously? No way!'

George nodded looking very satisfied with herself that the big question had finally been settled. She was more than satisfied, because she knew which direction she wanted her life to go. Before she had met Gracie, she had no idea these things existed. She had never even thought of it. At least back home it never occurred to her that it was possible to be with another woman; it was out of the question. Here it seemed just a little easier to accept her kind. It was at least possible to pursue it in a clandestine manner, though it was still something she had to get used to. Gracie broke her train of thought.

'Fancy a bit of fresh air then?'

They went outside to the enormous landscaped garden and sat on a pretty white bench. Gracie lit a cigarette and inhaled deeply.

'Come on, spill the beans then, how the hell did *that* happen?' George related all, telling her about the strange white powder Ginny called cocaine and the rest of the story up until Ginny walked out of the room.

'Bloody hell, she didn't waste any time did she! And are you feeling OK?'

'Yes, I am, actually I feel very alive, but I suppose it's the effect of the cocaine.'

'Gosh, cocaine, ay! George, really?

'Yes really,' she replied grinning from ear to ear.

'Well, it's getting late, so I think we should head home anyway,' not entirely happy that Ginny had literally taken advantage of her friend.

They hailed a taxi to take them back to Peckham and on the way, they talked about the evening's events, or more to the point George's escapade.

CHAPTER 11

The week passed relatively fast thanks to Gracie. George had certainly taken a lot on board and her life in Malta was now a far cry from the short time she had been in London. Things were so different here, she had to unlearn everything she had learnt; she realised that she had to become a bit wiser to life in order to survive, especially now with the outbreak of war and all the preparations occupying everyone's time. So far there was no sign of a German invasion and people settled back to a normal life again. Newspaper sales doubled as everyone wanted to keep abreast of what was happening.

Come Sunday evening, George felt an excitement grow in the pit of her stomach. She was to start a new life in the WAAFS and had no idea what to expect. George had hardly been able to sleep a wink, she opened her bedroom window which looked out over the garden, and took in a deep breath. She could smell the dewy grass and she spotted the odd sparrow flying briskly in search of food. The sky was a deep pink with scattered grey clouds, making the scene look like a Constable painting. She smiled. Her small suitcase was packed with what she thought would be necessary, trousers, blouses and some stout shoes, her Bible and toiletries. She crept downstairs and was hoping that Peggy was already awake as she was spitting feathers and gasping for a cup of tea. Thankfully Peggy was, and in her dressing gown, making a pot.

'Ah there you are, good morning, I thought you might like a cuppa, seeing as you are leaving so early.'

'Thanks Peggy I really appreciate it, there won't be anywhere open till I get to the train station.'

They drank their tea enjoying the early morning quiet before the rest of the world woke up. George had said goodbye to Gracie the night before and had agreed to call her later in the week when she had settled into the new barracks. She hugged Peggy and left to make her journey to Innsworth in Gloucester. It took her almost four hours to get there and when she arrived, she met up with an unlikely bunch of women who seemed to come from all walks of life. There were debutantes, prostitutes, a vicar's daughter and academics, but when the driver came to pick them up it didn't really matter where they came from or who they were as they were now all equals.

They arrived at Innsworth barracks and were allocated to Nissen huts, heated up by an antique boiler in the middle of the room. In the first week of training of regimented life, George learnt all about how to salute officers, recognise different ranks, how to march, and what the word ablutions meant and how to pass a kit inspection. There were myriad Air Force rules and requirements and the training was going to last weeks. At the end of the first week, George realised just how much of a safe and sheltered life she had led. Spending time with these women meant getting to know them up close and personal. They shared humour, understood what tolerance was all about and learnt to respect each other. After the first week had passed, they were kitted out in their two sets of uniforms, complete with sensible black shoes, an overcoat and hat and the hilariously unfashionable 'blackouts', official thick black knickers which George found scratchy and uncomfortable. One week passed into the next, all of them went from one drill to another and before they knew it a whole month had gone by, leading to their passing-out parade. George was given a weekend pass before she was to go on to her first posting. She was more than pleased, because although she had kept in touch with Gracie, she was looking forward to seeing her friend and calling her family to let them know of her progress in the WAAFs, she imagined her Mama and Papa would be dying to know, because she had only got the chance to write a couple of letters to them. The train journey from Gloucester to London seemed to take forever but nevertheless it gave her time to think and watch the idyllic scenery till they approached the outskirts of London. George noted how most chimneys had palls of smoke drifting up. The sky was grey well and truly heralding autumn. Soon the weather would change dramatically to ground frosts, rain and whipping winds. George loved the winter weather, after the heat of summer on the island; it was a welcome respite. Every day she wondered how her parents were coping without her. She felt that her life was changing so fast she could hardly keep up with it and yet it only seemed like yesterday when she left Malta — her second home. Her thoughts were interrupted by the hiss of the brakes being applied to the train making it crawl into Paddington. The train doors opened and passengers poured out like scurrying ants. George took her time to allow most of the crowds to disperse. She lugged her suitcase to the exit and decided to get a taxi to Peckham even though it would cost an arm and a leg, but she didn't fancy going round the houses to get there. The taxi sped over the Vauxhall Bridge and George was relieved that she was halfway there. The weekend was going to be a short one since she had to be back in Gloucester on Monday 6th November, but at least she would get to see Gracie and they would catch up on all the gossip, George smiled at this and realised how much she had missed her friend. The taxi parked by the kerb in front of the house. George paid the taxi driver and he touched his cap before driving off. She let herself in and was instantly overwhelmed by the smell of homeliness. Peggy popped her head round the door of the kitchen and came out to greet George with a hug. Gracie in her usual fashion of gracelessness came bounding down the stairs two at time, grabbed and swung George around making her giggle.

'George me mate, I'm so glad you're home, come into the sitting room and tell me what's been going on.'

Gracie settled into the armchair by the bay window. Peggy was in the throes of making a pot of tea in the kitchen. George sat in the other armchair opposite her friend.

'Well, the first day we were shown to our huts and then a sergeant came in and told us to stand next to our beds and to listen to all the rules, Christ there were tons of them! Most of the time it's been drills and more drills, waking up really early in the morning, we had to be up, bed made and standing to attention outside by eight o'clock to do a quick march to the mess. We've been living in these basic Nissen huts and the heating is simply awful, it's this ancient stove in the middle of the room and we're all huddled around it to get warm before we jump into our cots as fast as possible to keep from freezing half to death. Lights out is at ten at night. The food is diabolical and as you can see the uniform is nothing to write home about,' pulling a face making Gracie laugh.

'What about the other women? What are they like?' Gracie asked.

'Well, they are an odd mixed bunch; they've come from all walks of life. For God's sake one of them, Maggie, is a prostitute or rather was, but, funnily enough, once you get to know them, the differences stop there. We all wear the same uniform so everyone is equal and the saluting, oh Lord! It never stops. All we do is march, put our left foot forward, it's knackering I can tell you and the blisters I'm nursing, thank God my mum packed some plasters for me!' George ended with a laugh and paused to light a cigarette.

'George since when do you smoke?' Gracie asked her with a gobsmacked look on her face.

'Want one?' George asked laughing.

She took a cigarette out of the offered pack and lit up.

'I used to smoke the odd one back in Malta, but now I'm smoking every day.

Peggy walked in with tray of tea, sandwiches and biscuits, which they both eyed hungrily. After the grub they had been served at the barracks canteen, Peggy's sandwiches tasted heavenly. They poured tea and tucked in like they had never eaten and Peggy laughed at them.

'I shall miss you girls when you are gone, because, I'm assuming George, that you won't be staying long will you?'

'Well Peggy I would like to keep the room for the next couple of months, at least till I find out where I'm going to be posted, but I will give you plenty of notice.'

'And I will do the same because I'm in the same boat really, so I'll leave things as they are because this is my proper home for the time being,' Gracie added.

'All right then girls just let me know so as I don't end up without any lodgers,' Peggy said, looking at them affectionately.

'That won't happen for sure Peggy,' George said, both of them nodding in agreement.

'Right then girls, I've got to go out and check on one of my patients who is about to drop her bairn any time, so I will hopefully see you at some point; and, we have lamb chops tomorrow,' Peggy ended with a smile knowing full well how much they appreciated her cooking.

The rest of the afternoon was spent talking about their various trainings and where they hoped they were to be posted. At around six in the evening, they decided to treat themselves to a fish and chip supper.

They walked to Sid's fish and chip shop and ordered equal portions of cod and chips. By the time they were ready, they were salivating with the smell of salt and vinegar filling their noses. They walked back with their warm packages and sat in the kitchen devouring their food with relish straight from the newspaper.

'Oh Lord! I needed that!' exclaimed Gracie, wiping her mouth with a napkin she had pulled out from a drawer in the Welsh dresser.

'Excuse me, what about mine then?' George chided jokingly.

'Oops here you are.'

George wiped her mouth on the napkin and picked up the greasy newspapers and threw them in the bin, washing her hands in the kitchen sink.

'Fancy sharing an orangeade with me mate? Only, I have to get rid of the fishy taste in my mouth now.'

'Hmm go on then,' George said as she watched Gracie pop the top off a Corona bottle. She measured out the orangeade equally into two glasses.

'That was just the ticket, I can hardly move,' Gracie said after she had polished off the whole glass and ended with a large burp.

'Oops excuse me!' she said laughing.

'George rolled her eyes, 'Your manners are atrocious!'

'Yes! Yes! I know, tell me something new! Now tell me, what exactly will you be doing in this posting of yours?'

'I really don't know much about it except I'm to be a filter plotter, something to do with radars, nothing to do with what I was originally given to believe I would be doing, you know, that stupid clerk's job,' George replied.

'Sounds much more exciting than mine, all I've been doing is cleaning and repairing aircraft parts, getting all greasy and oily!'

'But that's not so bad, it's better than working in a biscuit factory, which I'm sure is very tedious, apart from the fact that the smell must have driven you round the bend,' George replied.

'I suppose you're right.'

'Gracie I was thinking, I quite fancy going to watch a film tomorrow, what do you think?'

'Hmm we could do, or we could take a trip to *The Gateways*?'

'No definitely not Gracie, I don't want to go anywhere near there, I need to concentrate and I can't risk anything happening, please don't be offended,' George replied adamantly.

'OK mate, we'll just go and watch a film, I will have a look what's on in the *Daily Mirror*, what do you fancy watching then?'

'Oh, I dunno, what's on?'

'Well, there's *The Four Feathers* with John Clements and that's on at the *Odeon* or there's *The Sun Never Sets* with Douglas Fairbanks at The Leicester Square Theatre, so we can choose either one.'

'Let's go and see *The Four Feathers*.'

'Right then, that's settled, I don't know about you, but I'm ready for bed, I'm feeling tired all of a sudden.'

'I'm about the same, I'm just going to write a quick letter to Mama and Papa and I'll follow suit. Good night, I will see you in the morning then.'

The wireless was on when George came downstairs for some breakfast; Peggy had already left and Gracie was in the sitting room listening to it and reading the newspaper.

'God almighty, those bloody bastard Germans have sunk the *Royal Oak*; eight hundred and thirty-three lives lost and that flippin' Chamberlain does nothing about it!' Gracie exploded almost foaming at the mouth.

'Oh no, that's awful, what a terrible loss of life!'

'Retaliation will come soon Gracie and we are doing our bit for the war effort, although to be honest, it doesn't feel like we're doing enough.'

'I want to get out there and up in the air but it's not going to bloody happen any time soon is it? Because they won't allow women to fly planes yet!' Gracie grumbled and lit a cigarette, puffing away at it furiously.

'I bet that will all change; men are being conscripted in large numbers, who's going to do their jobs in the meantime?'

'I suppose you're right, mate.'

'So, what are you up to today before we watch the film this evening?'

'I'm not doing much today, simply because I don't know when I will be back on my next leave, so I mean to enjoy my time off doing bugger all!' Gracie replied.

'I've got some shopping to do, I need some soap and talcum powder and toothpaste. I keep hearing rumours that these things are going to be hard to come by soon, I even heard that some sort of rationing is being considered by the government; apparently supply ships are not getting through, they're being sabotaged by German U-Boats,' George said a bit subdued.

'Bloody bastards, I suppose I ought to get up off my arse and go shopping with you for the same things, I didn't even give it a thought, damn it!'

'Well let's get that sorted out and then I have a proposal to put to you, but I want to talk about it over lunch, so we can stop at Mildred's tea house, I really like their food.'

They left the house just after ten thirty a.m. and walked up the Peckham High Street to Brown's Chemist, not more than ten minutes' walk. At the chemist's George bought all she needed and added a bottle of aspirin to her list and paid, at the same time waiting for Gracie to finish her shopping. The day had turned grey and chilly. Leaving the chemist, they walked briskly to the tea house. It was warm and cosy inside Mildred's and they did not waste any time ordering a meat pie and boiled potatoes with gravy for each of them.

'So, what is it that you wanted to propose to me?'

'Well, I was thinking, we are going to be away a lot and I think it's daft for us both to keep our rooms, so why don't we share a room at least, so we can keep our belongings in one place and have somewhere to stay when we are on leave; we can take it in turns to pay the rent, what do you think?' she waited for Gracie's reaction.

'Actually, that's a damned brilliant idea mate and that will save us some money for sure, because the wages we will both be earning aren't going to be much.'

'Well, that's that then, we'll tell Peggy when we get back, I'm sure she will be OK with the arrangements.'

They returned home and Gracie settled on the sofa to carry on reading her paper and listening to the wireless whilst George sat on the armchair by the fireplace, first writing to her parents, and then proceeded to write a letter to Connie, whom she had not written to for some time. She often thought about Connie and she missed her. There were thoughts crossing her mind of how Connie never seemed to talk about that special man in her life; in fact, she had seen Connie show interest many times but never seemed to act on it., She had plenty of male friends but none that she could call close, but perhaps that didn't really mean anything. She asked Connie if she could call in on George's parents once in a while. If truth be known, she was worried. Malta was defenceless; in a letter she had received recently from her them, they had mentioned that their only aerial defence were three dilapidated bi-planes to defend the whole of the island, although more troops from England were being mobilized to be posted over there. Still, it wasn't any sort of consolation and she prayed that they would remain safe. She portrayed her thoughts to Connie and she explained to her that letters would not be that forthcoming in the near future because she doubted that there would be a regular ship or plane leaving the shores of England to deliver the post.

Hitler had already proven that no ship was safe. She told Connie that should anything happen to her, she would find most of her personal belongings at the address she was living in. She did not want to alarm her parents, so she abstained from telling them any extra information, apart from the day-to-day life she was leading. She also sent a short note to Carmelo hoping that he would somehow receive her letter in Rome.

She would post the letters later on the way when going to watch the film. In the meantime, George went to get a couple of envelopes and stamps, which she had bought a stash of, since she wrote frequently to her parents. It was one of the things she made sure always she had enough of.

She lay on her bed hoping to get a rest for an hour or so, but sleep eluded her, there was too much going on in her mind to even contemplate shutting her eyelids. Her thoughts were on her next posting. She had not been told what it was going to be, only that she had to be back at Innsworth Barracks on Monday at lunchtime sharp. She was apprehensive; asking herself *if she was capable of whatever they were going to train her in. There had been a mention of something called radar training but she hadn't a clue what it meant, still it couldn't be any worse than her stint at Innsworth.* She must have been lying on her bed for ages, because she heard Gracie calling her from downstairs asking her if she wanted a cup of tea. Since she couldn't sleep, she joined her.

'Are you OK mate, you're looking a bit dazed?'

'Yes, I'm all right just got a lot on my mind that's all.'

To which Gracie uttered an 'Hmm' and carried on listening to the wireless.

At that moment Peggy walked in and after George poured her a much-needed cup of tea, she put forward the proposal that she and Gracie had talked about.

'Well, I don't have a problem with that, all I have to do is get you a spare key, I imagined that you would have to come to some sort of arrangement, so all you girls have to do is to let me know which room you will be keeping so I can obviously rent out the other one.'

'We haven't decided which one to keep yet, but we will certainly let you know by tomorrow,' George replied, looking at Gracie, who just nodded in agreement. It seemed that she also was deep in thought and far away. So many things to contend with, so many changes so fast, it was no wonder that they were both so preoccupied. Still the pictures would be an ideal evening's entertainment for them both.

'That was a great film, I loved it.'

'Yes, that was definitely brilliant, it had a great story to it, shall we go for a swift half before we catch the bus back?'

'Yes, because I'm parched,' Gracie replied, laughing.

They walked to Greek Street in Soho and found *The Three Greyhounds Pub*, which was so full; they had to squeeze their way to the bar to order two half pints of bitter. They found a bit of space next to the bay window looking out onto the street.

'So, what are you up to tomorrow?'.

'To be honest I was going to do nothing but now I'm thinking of going over to Bramley to see my aunt and uncle, because God knows when I will see them next, but I have to call them first and it's a bit short notice; if we get home by ten o'clock it should be OK though.'

'Hmm we should make it by then; incidentally what are we going to do about our rooms?' Gracie asked.

'I think it's best we keep your room because it's larger, I'll move my stuff in this evening after I've made the telephone call and we'll tell Peggy too.'

'Well, we had better drink up and get going then because time's getting on a bit.'

They made it home by ten thirty. George took a chance and called her aunt and uncle. They were more than pleased to see her Sunday and her aunt suggested she come ready with her suitcase so she could get a lift with her Uncle Ted who would then drop her off at Paddington station on the Monday morning.

When she had finished her phone call, George packed what she needed into her kitbag and moved the rest of her things to Gracie's room as they had agreed. George told Peggy of the arrangement between them and Peggy told her to take Gracie's key and she would get another one cut on Monday for her.

George looked around her room to make sure she had removed everything. She left and shut the door behind her and went and knocked on Gracie's door.

'Come in mate,' Gracie called out. Gracie was sitting on her bed with her back resting against the head board. 'You're off then?' getting up to hug her friend.

'Yes, I'm off, take care of yourself Gracie and hopefully I will get another weekend pass next month.'

'You take care too, you watch yourself, right!'

George nodded, left the room and went downstairs. She had said her goodbyes to Peggy the night before so she went straight to the door and walked out, shutting it behind her. Nostalgia enveloped her; the little grocery shop, the pharmacy, Mildred's tea shop, Sid's fish and chip shop… places that had become part of her life. She took mental pictures of them as she passed, somehow they gave her comfort. The bus arrived, she hopped on climbing up the stairs to the top finding a seat at the front. Being so early there weren't many passengers; she sat quietly observing the buildings whizzing by. The grey swirling waters of the Thames flowed dull and dismal, broken only by the odd barge whilst crossing the Vauxhall Bridge. She got off taking the usual route on the underground before finding herself on a train to Guildford. She enjoyed the journey. The sprawls of houses turned to expanses of green fields sometimes with herds of cows, sometimes with sheep. It was a beautiful crisp and cold sunny morning. It made her think of home, her little island and how the sun shone most of the year, though she did miss the greenery that England afforded. Still there was no beating the closeness of the sea, the sweet fruits of summer, the smell of fresh Maltese bread in the morning, the goat herder shouting out for whoever wanted fresh milk and the general hubbub of what went on in the streets of Valletta. Yes, she missed it and missed Connie and her parents but it was a sacrifice she was prepared to make to get to where she wanted to be in life and counted her lucky stars that they had agreed to allow her to join the WAAFS. She thought of her dear friend Connie, who so envied George; poor thing was stuck in a rut because her mother expected her to get married and have children. Connie had confided in her once not so long ago and had told her that she wanted children and all that but she wasn't sure about living with the same person for the rest of her life, it was such a huge commitment. The church made the sanctity of marriage seem like a dream, but her parents' marriage was far from the truth and had made her sceptical. George had felt sorry for her, having to live up to the family's traditions and expectations especially knowing what Connie's family was really like. Though they were best friends and they shared much of their personal thoughts and feelings, she knew that all was not right.

CHAPTER 11

The train jolted and came to a gradual halt, so much so that George thought they had arrived, but that was impossible because there were at least another five stops till Guildford. The guard came into her carriage followed by two people from the home guard as well as two policemen. The guard asked passengers for their tickets, closely scrutinised by the others. They were almost upon George when one of the policemen started questioning a young man sitting two seats in front of her. The man got up as if to run away when he was apprehended and handcuffed. Whilst escorting him off the train in George's direction she caught his eye and he smiled at her shrugging his shoulders at the same time. The incident was over and done with within a matter of minutes and the train carried on with its journey, but George couldn't help wondering about the young man and what he could possibly have done to merit his arrest. She supposed one couldn't be too careful with the current situation. It left her feeling insecure and was relieved when she finally arrived at Guildford Station. Uncle Ted was waiting for her; he hugged her and opened the car door for her. It was only a short drive to Bramley and they soon arrived at the Pickerings' modest little cottage. Aunt Marlu had just popped a joint of beef into the oven.

'Oh, hello dear, you've arrived, I'm so happy you're here.'

'I'm glad I came too Aunty, because the way things are going with my training and posting, I just have no idea when I would see you both next.'

'No, things aren't looking good George, in fact we were wondering how you have been coping. The MoD has called me to London permanently from next week and there has been a huge amount of movement from Hitler's armies across Poland and the lowlands,' Uncle Ted said.

'Yes, I have been following what's been happening from the papers, it's awful. I've also heard of the persecution of the Jews in Germany,'

George added.

'It's worse than that, information leaking through is that they are euthanising the sick and the disabled in a programme that Hitler is calling 'mercy killings'; any person who shows any kind of disability, mental retardation or physical deformity is earmarked, it's damned out of order!' Uncle Ted exclaimed angrily.

'Oh, I know Uncle and that's awful, can't anything be done?'

'At this point in time no, we don't have enough accurate information or military resources and also because they aren't ready yet, we are just not prepared enough, though God knows, we will be drawn into this war sooner rather than later, this is just the calm before the storm; we will be physically engaged after Christmas for sure.'

'Does that mean to you will have to fight?'

'Yes, it most certainly does,' he said ruefully.

George looked at her aunt who had been silently listening to their conversation. She could see she was worried.

'Ted dear, let's just enjoy our day with George; all this talk about war is disconcerting, it will come soon enough, why don't we go across to the Wheatsheaf and have a drink till lunch is ready?' Aunt Marlu suggested.

'Super idea darling, yes let's go,' he said smiling.

The pub was quite busy and the atmosphere was jolly, with lots of remarks about showing Hitler what for. So as much as Aunt Marlu wanted to avoid the subject of war, it was impossible at the Wheatsheaf, but at least it was jovial. They sat by the bay window looking out at the front. A young man in uniform walked in to loud cheering and much slapping on the back and half the pub wanted to buy him a drink.

'That's young Toby Lewis, he's just recently signed up with the army,' Aunt Marlu volunteered sipping her gin and tonic. Uncle Ted was already at the bar wanting to buy Toby a drink too. George smiled, amused that the young man was all smiles, lapping up the attention, especially from a couple of young local girls.

She thought about the incident on the train and proceeded to tell her aunt about it.

'Well, I suppose there will be a few more of these incidences; I had heard that they were rounding up the foreigners who are being treated as aliens,' Aunt Marlu said.

'But surely not all foreigners are a threat to this country Aunty?' she murmured.

'No, I don't suppose they are, but it's best to be on the safe side than risk one of them being a spy and jeopardising our national security.'

George thought about it; the implications were indeed dangerous for England, she supposed that there were spies already operating and it was a case of them being caught before the damage was done. She wondered what role she would be playing in the war; all was to be revealed tomorrow. In the meantime, she meant to enjoy her day and was looking forward to her Sunday roast with all the trimmings that Aunt Marlu was so good at preparing. They stayed at the pub for another hour and then took a walk to the Holy Trinity Church because Aunt Marlu said she wanted to invite the vicar, Mr Dashwood, to tea. George stepped through the church doors; it was quiet and peaceful with Sunday service over. She took a seat on a pew in the middle of the church and stared at the altar. She felt a sudden urge to pray; to ask God to take care of her and her family; to give her the strength to cope with whatever was in store for her. A solitary candle flickered, she watched it mesmerised, her mind drifting in the quiescent environment. She heard the door open and someone walked down the aisle, their every step echoing. She half expected to see her aunt or uncle but as she turned her head, she saw it was Toby, the young soldier from the Wheatsheaf. He came up to the pew she was sitting at and smiled at her and asked with a nod raising his eyebrows if he could sit next to her. She acknowledged with a wave of her hand.

The two sat quietly for a while and then Toby whispered, 'I like coming here to get a bit of peace and quiet and gather me thoughts like, the pub got a bit noisy for me.'

'Yes, I know what you mean, it seems to be the right place to gather your thoughts doesn't it?'

'It is, but you're not from around here, are you?'

'No, I'm a real mixture actually, the last place I lived in was Malta, my Papa's English, my Mama's Maltese and I'm here because I joined the WAAFs. In fact, I'm going to my first posting tomorrow.'

'Oh right… I never heard of Malta, where is it?'

'Well, it's sort of at the end of Italy if you've ever seen a map, it's at the toe end since Italy is shaped like a boot.'

'Hmm that gives me some idea,' Toby said vaguely.

George looked at her watch and said, 'I think I had better go outside because my aunt and uncle will be wondering where I am.'

'Righty ho then.'

He followed her down the aisle till they reached the outside. Aunt Marlu who was standing in the shade of a cypress tree talking to the vicar beckoned to them to go near her.

'Hello Toby, how are you dear and how's your mother?'

'I'm fine Mrs Pickering, but me mam is a bit upset I've joined up, me being her only son 'n all that,' he replied politely.

'Don't worry dear, your mother will get used to it, but it's understandable, nearly all the youngsters in the village are signing up.'

'Hello Toby, how are you doing young fellow?' Uncle Ted just joined them.

'I'm right as rain Mr Pickering sir, just rarin' to go now, me regiment moves out tomorrow.'

'And what regiment is that then?'

'Infantry sir, Royal Fusiliers,' he replied proudly.

'Good for you Toby, glad to see you're doing your bit for King and country; give our regards to your mother.'

'I will sir, thank you sir.'

'Well, good luck Toby and take care,' George told him as they shook hands. The Pickerings' bade Toby good bye and they walked back to the cottage, where the smell wafting from the opened front door had George's mouth-watering. After lunch they sat in the cosy living room listening to the BBC's men's chorus on the wireless. Uncle Ted was smoking his pipe and Aunt Marlu was reading a copy of *Vogue* tapping her foot to Sweet Kitty Clover. George was happily sitting in the armchair feeling full and sated.

'Uncle, you've not said much about your involvement in the war effort, I mean I know you're down at the MoD in London all the time, but what is it exactly that you are doing?' George asked.

'Well, most of it is pretty much classified, but it looks like I will be seeing action in France soon. I'm going to be sent off with the 170th

Tunnelling Company, or so I understand, the MoD wants me over there because of my experience as a mining geologist. They know about my stint in Africa; I shan't be alone of course, there are others like me you know, mining geologists, surveyors, and we will be tunnelling on some parts of the French coast, but we will be a non-combatant unit.'

'Aren't you afraid of what might happen?' she asked.

'Well, there is some concern of course, it's only natural, but one just wants to get the job done, if you know what I mean.'

'So when are you officially being called up then Uncle?'

'I'm off to Chatham depot tomorrow but I have to pass by the MoD first, so we can drop you off at Paddington, then afterwards Aunt Marlu will return here with the car. I will catch a train to Chatham later. Do you know where you are off to?'

'I haven't a clue, Uncle, all I know is I have to report back to Innsworth and then all of us are going to our new posts.'

'I would rather face the bush of Africa than this blessed war,' Aunt Marlu grumbled.

'Hmm, I can imagine, Africa must have been such a wonderful experience for you!'

'It was all terribly exciting of course, especially for me, because I hadn't been anywhere abroad before; in Ghana everything was so very basic and of course one had to get used to the change in climate, it was very hot, but so beautiful and lush,' Aunt Marlu explained animatedly.

'Where did you live? I mean did you have to live in a hut?'

'Well to start off with Uncle Ted went to Ghana, in West Africa, before me, because they were still surveying the ground between well-established gold mines namely Ashanti and Ariston. Ashanti was in Obuasi and Ariston in Prestea, so Uncle Ted was kept very busy travelling between the two. At that time conditions in the bush were somewhat primitive and it meant that Uncle Ted and the other geologist lived in tents in a clearing within dense jungle forests, which is why I did not go with him straight away. I set off in November 1934 on a ship called the *Accra* and of course I had never been abroad before so you can imagine what an adventure it was for me getting there. The *Accra* stopped at Las Palmas and Madeira and then finally Freetown in Sierra Leone. I was met by this lady doctor who was in charge of the maternity section in the local hospital. I was escorted to her quarters and after she poured me a sherry, she excused herself on account of her being needed in the theatre. She returned half an hour later with this beautiful newly born black baby that was dusted in talcum powder and it resembled an enormous plum… I just wanted to hold it forever.' This last sentence was a little heart-breaking since Aunt Marlu was never able to have children.

'Oh my gosh aunt how absolutely lovely…'

'Eventually Uncle turned up and we made our way to a place called Ensu, and then we drove seven hours to our house which was on top of a hill overlooking the Ashanti Mine. I soon settled in and took care of keeping house and making sure all our houseboys did their routine jobs, you know, one would do the cooking, the other the laundry and ironing and so on.'

'So how long did you end up staying there in the end?'

'Oh, we were there from 1934 to 1938 so that's four years, before we returned home.'

'You must have seen so much wildlife; I suppose you were sad to leave Africa?'

This time it was Uncle Ted who replied, 'Yes, we were, to be honest, life in the bush isn't easy but you learn to appreciate the simple things in life; unfortunately, we had to return because of rumours that were filtering through to us that there might be a war and we couldn't stay after that, because I knew I was needed back in England. We came back late December in 1938 and by then things had already been escalating…' He gazed pensively into the fire reliving memories of Africa whilst Aunt Marlu recounted stories well into the evening of the stunning bush they lived in; George lost herself dreaming she was hunting herds of antelope and elephants roaming along rivers infested with crocodiles…

CHAPTER 12

They set off early the next day in Aunt Marlu's car. They sped off to London and were in front of Paddington Station by nine thirty. She kissed and hugged her aunt and uncle goodbye and left them to enter the station concourse.

She had put on her uniform because that was all she had now, the rest of her civilian clothes she left in Peckham, besides she had no real need for them where she was going; she just had her kitbag. The station was busy, there were soldiers everywhere waiting to board a train to their barracks. There were civilians, all carrying the obligatory gas mask and children being evacuated lining the platform. George felt sorry for them, it must be so hard for them, poor little mites being separated from their parents; the scene made her think of hers and brought a lump to her throat.

The Great Western train chugged into the platform billowing plumes of steam. When it came to a halt, the doors opened, with passengers spilling on to the platform and others taking their place. George walked halfway down the platform and boarded the train, finding a vacant seat. She placed her kitbag and gas mask on the overhead rack and then sat down. The compartment was full with three men and two women passengers including herself. Ten minutes later the guard outside checked that everyone was safely on board and whistled for the train to leave. She settled down to read an old copy of *Vogue* which her aunt had given her. She noticed that they had already pulled out of London leaving the peripheral housing and reaching the first throes of the Reading countryside which was dotted with farms. The day was a grey one but she hardly noticed it; the greenery made up for the lack of sun and the greyness; it was November after all and to be expected, she supposed. The train made stops at Swindon and Stroud before arriving at Gloucester Station. The journey took just under three and a half hours. She was glad to get off the train, which at least had not been so crowded once most of the passengers had got off at Swindon. There were the other girls from her unit waiting outside the station. An RAF lorry was meant to be sent to collect them. George went over to them and greeted them. They were all laughing and joking, enjoying their last bit of freedom before their postings. The lorry turned up about twenty minutes later and George climbed the tailboard to get a decent seat, since the last time she clambered on board one of these trucks, she had ended up in the middle, which was dreadfully uncomfortable, the other girls followed suit for the short journey to Innsworth Barracks.

When they arrived, most of them groaned at the dreary appearance of the long rows of huts. There were other women who had arrived before them with their NCO's barking orders to get in line to be marched to their respective hut. George was assigned to hut number 13 and was soon ordered, together with the others, to the cabbage-smelling kitchen quarters, where everyone queued up with their irons for a ghastly lunch. George wrinkled her nose up but said nothing, instead she juggled her tin plate and cup for the offering that was slopped in with weak tea in her cup. She sat with the rest on the long trestle table and ate her food, more out of hunger than relish.

After about twenty minutes an NCO came into the dining area and shouted out the names of those whom she wanted to follow her and George was one of them. They marched back to their hut.

'Right, you lot, gather your belongings, you are being transferred to Leighton Buzzard, you'll start your training as plotters with a bit of luck. You'll all receive further orders once you arrive,' the NCO barked. George found herself back at Gloucester Train Station. They boarded a train to Leighton Buzzard. Th army truck was waiting to transport them to the Plotter's School; *It looks like a prison* she thought gloomily. They were billeted in a work house on the first floor, which had an iron staircase leading to the dormitory. The ablutions were somewhat primitive in the form of lead sinks lined up and chained to the wall and there was no privacy in the lavatories, something George was not used to. The whole building was covered in camouflage netting with trees and bushes stuck in it. At supper time they went to the mess with their 'irons' and were treated to a watery stew with bread and butter. It left her feeling dismal and longing for a plate her mother's wonderful food.

At lights out George hoped that sleep would envelope her, but it was the last thing that happened, because she just tossed and turned till the small hours of the morning, finally succumbing at around three. She was in shock when she heard the roll call to wake up at six a.m. Bleary eyed, she almost fell out of her cot following the rest of the women to the ablutions. It was freezing! The cold water shook her wide awake. By the time George was kitted out and had made her cot up, she was ready for breakfast, no matter how awful it was. She was grateful for the stodgy porridge and weak tea, it warmed her up. That first morning they were shown into a large room which was full of maps and telephones. They all took an oath hand on the Bible swearing in accordance to the Official Secrets Acts. This alarmed George and she hoped she would remember everything; it made her feel a little insecure although she guessed that the other women were in the same predicament.

The training was intense and went on for two weeks. Each night, lying in bed, George and the other women tested each other to make sure that they had learnt all the details of becoming a plotter. Finally, a list of stations needed for plotters was presented to them and they had to choose which fighter command station they wanted to go to. George wanted to be close to London so she chose Colerne in Wiltshire and sure enough that's where she was sent. On the day of departure, they said their farewells to each other. George had become friendly with a woman called Edna who had also chosen Colerne, so they travelled together and took a train to Bath where they were met by the usual lorry. With their kitbags in tow, they climbed the tailboard, and to their surprise, found they were the only ones on it.

Colerne was a large station built out of concrete blocks. They were taken into 'B' block. Outside their window was a runway that led to a hangar. The noise was terrific and they quickly learned to put cotton wool in their ears to lessen the noise the Spitfires, Hurricanes and Mosquitoes were making whilst taxiing by the hangar every day.

They were placed on 'A' watch working side by side and were soon referred to as Parker and Bowles, the gruesome twosome. The operations room was underground. They had to give their code number before entering, and this was changed daily. They collected a headset and took over from the next shift of plotters. A routine was established and George soon got used to the work. Then without any warning, they were posted to Exeter. The toing and froing was tiresome; they were looking forward to finally being stationed in one place and staying. It seemed that they were not alone this time round; there were several others on board. They drove around seven miles to a quaint village called Pinhoe, and passed two pubs: The *Poltimore Arms* used by the Army and *Hearth of Oak* which was frequented by the RAF. They carried on to a large house on an equally large park. This was to be their home for a while. There were a few huts nestling among the trees. Each hut had twenty beds in it, ten either side of the room. They quickly settled in and since they had no shift that day George decided to write to everyone home and abroad. When she had finished, she suggested to Edna they go to the *Hearth of Oak.*

They sat on a seat in the bay window sipping a cider each. A friendly cat wound its way in between the table legs and settled on George's lap purring instantly. George stroked the feline and made firm friends with it, so much so, that when they went to the pub after their shift it would always be there, as if waiting for her. George's birthday was a few days away. She had been discussing with Edna if they should organise a bit of a knees-up at the pub. Edna was not one to pass up an opportunity for a party. Not much in the way of entertainment had presented itself since she had joined up, so she jumped at the chance and went over to the publican Mr Crudd.

'So, what do you think, Mr Crudd, can you put something together for us next Sunday, the 26th it being my pal's birthday?' she asked.

'Well young ladies, I'm sure we can come up with something, we can lay on some sandwiches and other tidbits,' Mr Crudd said, tapping the side of his nose.

'That's super, so let's spread the word when we get back, it's the 22nd today so that gives us four days; Lord knows, I'm in need of some entertainment!' George said.

Word did indeed spread about the impending birthday celebrations; when Sunday came, the pub was packed to bursting. George was trying to talk above the raucous crowd but it was well-nigh impossible. She had drinks lined up in front of her at the bar she was never going to be able to drink!! She smiled to herself enjoying every minute, feeling sorry for the night shift, who obviously were not able to make it. Edna had taken full advantage of all the attention and drinks and was looking the worse for wear. George was about to try and coax her friend into leaving since they were on an early morning shift. But that didn't look like it was going to happen! The pub doors opened and a bunch of army lads walked in, shouting, 'There's a party on lads, we love a party, don't we?' The two military groups looked at each other menacingly and all of a sudden, all hell broke loose and fists flew, as both army and pilots laid into each other.

'Oh Lord, Edna, let's get out of here!' George shouted above the noise. They just about managed to make it to the front door without getting clobbered by the rowdy fighters, before six burly military police turned up to break up the fight. George and Edna hurriedly walked towards their billet, George steadying Edna, who was walking in an alarmingly haphazard way.

'Ooooh, I don't feel so good George, I think I drank too much,' suddenly doubling up and vomiting violently in a nearby bush.

'Oh dear, Edna, you are a silly goose, come on, let's get you back!' She helped Edna the rest of the way. A group of the RAF boys passed them by, wolf whistling and making lewd remarks laughing loudly. George decided to ignore them, she just wanted to get Edna to her cot and hope that they would both be fit for their shift. Edna had already recuperated enough to giggle hysterically and cling on to George's neck whilst George lowered her into her cot. At that moment Edna pulled George to her and kissed her soundly on the lips. George, taken unawares, was about to pull away when Edna whispered, 'I've been wanting to do that for ages!'

George was not sure how to react so she said 'thank you' which made both of them laugh at the awkwardness of her answer.

Edna conked out without a further word and George laughed at the night's adventure, tucking herself into her own cot before falling asleep.

At five o'clock in the morning, George woke up and went to the ablutions ahead of Edna who was still fast asleep. She decided to let her be and would wake her when she was ready, which was just as well, since Edna was nursing a prize hangover and looked very pale and the worse for wear. At six thirty a.m., after having gulped down a mug of hot sweet tea, they marched the short distance from their billet to the 'Ops' room. The atmosphere in the 'Ops' room was in full swing when they entered and took over from their respective plotters.

The plotting table was full of coloured arrows, plotting incoming an imaginary enemy from France, for at this time, the Germans had not started any engagement across the waters yet, although their advances into Poland had reached a critical point. They had to be ready in the event of an aerial invasion, which, according to reports from their meagre sources in France, was imminent. How they managed to get through their shift, God only knew because Edna had to keep going out for 'fresh air' frequently, but finally it ended and they headed straight to their billet.

'Oh God, my head is still pounding,' Edna groaned.

George opened her kit bag and pulled out a bottle of Aspro. There were a few still left and she mentally thanked her sense in buying some before she left Peckham.

'Here Edna get these aspirin down you, you'll feel better soon with a good night's sleep.'

At that moment the door to their billet opened and the staff sergeant walked in with letters in his hand.

'ACW2 Parker?'

'Sir?' As George got up off her cot, stood to attention and saluted.

'Here's your mail, nothing for ACW2 Bowles,' the staff sergeant barked.

'Thank you, Sir,' she saluted smartly.

The staff sergeant left the billet, leaving the women on their own again. George left Edna to sleep off the rest of her hangover and went over to the large window sill and looked out before opening the first of her letters, one of which was from Gracie.

From her words it seemed like Gracie's wish had come true as part of the ATA, she was now well on her way to being a Ferry Pilot for the Air Transport Auxiliary. The letter went on to say that she was due some leave in December and wondered whether George was going to be on leave too. There was news about Peggy asking if they still wanted to keep the room. George had meant to tell Gracie that she still wanted to keep it, there was no point in her sending her belongings home, unless of course she left them at Aunt Marlu. She would ask Gracie what they should do when they next met. The second letter was from home, she recognised her mother's handwriting. She opened it and started to read it. Her mother wrote about how Malta was preparing for war and that food was already in short supply. Her father was constantly at the coast preparing the island's shore defences and there was an uneasy calm settling over its people.

Mussolini, Italy's dictator, was favouring Hitler and with Malta being so close to Italy, the Maltese were becoming anxious, for they were aware of their strategic position in the Mediterranean. Her mother went on to say that most were insecure because the only air defence they had were the three bi-planes, so something had to be done and Malta was awaiting expectantly for Britain to come to their aid and send a batch of spitfires. A lump in her throat grew with each word she read; she could tell from her mother's words that she was frightened at what was imminent. She felt guilty for having left her, but there was nothing she could do now. She put the letter back inside the envelope and placed it in her kitbag along with Gracie's. She would get time later to reply to them and send them off with the Force's postal system.

They had been at Exeter Ops for nearly three weeks and Christmas was fast approaching. There was talk of a small panto for the Army and RAF, the one time the forces got together and buried their differences. George was approached by one of her staff officers asking if she wanted to be part of the cast. She had never acted before and was somewhat reluctant, but could see from the look in the staff sergeant's eyes that he wasn't going to take no for an answer.

Rehearsals started in the next couple of days and they were using the canteen out of hours for practice. George got the part of an amorous Frenchman whilst Edna, who got roped in too, was a navy sailor. There were another four, all men from the RAF and they all had the part of dames. In true panto fashion, at the dress rehearsal, all had to find their own costumes, so George and Edna badgered the boys for theirs but the boys had a harder time finding clothes that fit. The day of the panto was set for the sixteenth of December. It was to be a big thing with their NCOs and Staff sergeants attending, as well as most of the Ops team and most of the RAF personnel. The canteen was turned into a makeshift theatre with a low platform acting as the stage. A couple of floodlights were found and erected onto the ceilings and the rest of the props were soon found and placed on stage. George had disguised herself well and chuckled inwardly at her prowess. It took her back to her covert days in Malta and the fancy dress on the ship and how she won first prize. The panto was set in Paris with a couple of young British girls on holiday sitting at a café and were to be accosted by an amorous Frenchman. The innuendos flowed and raucous laughing was followed by whistles and catcalls. George's interpretation of a Frenchman drew the most applause; her French accent was impeccable. After the show the 'cast' changed and removed their makeup so they could join the crowd that remained in the canteen for drinks. There was an air of festivity, it being so close to Christmas. Most would be away from their families and made the best of whatever parties were going on. George was still awaiting confirmation of her leave, but as yet she had heard nothing. She was hoping she could meet up with Gracie.

'Phew, I'm glad that's over!' George commented to Edna.

'Yes, me too, it was fun but it's back to the grindstone tomorrow; at least we're on a late shift so we can sleep in and then maybe we can go for a swift half down the pub, what do you reckon?' Edna suggested to George.

'Sounds good to me.'

The next day, at the start of her afternoon shift, George was told that her leave was approved. She had five days off from the 22nd December, so she decided to stay till Christmas Eve with Gracie and spend Christmas Day and Boxing Day with her Aunt Marlu. She made a mental note to call both her aunt and Gracie later on. George left Edna and went to her billet. Her NCO was waiting by the door.

'It looks like you've made quite an impression on someone Parker!'

'Sir?'

'Maj. Le Petite was at the panto quite by chance and has asked to see you.'

'Now Sir?'

'Yes, *now* Parker, at the double!'

'Very well Sir!'

With that George followed the NCO to the offices.

'Major Le Petite, Sir, ACW2 Parker.'

The major dismissed the NCO, who smartly saluted, clicked his heels and left.

George stiffened and remained ramrod straight and at attention.

'At ease Parker, that was quite a performance you put on.'

'Thank you, sir, I'm glad you liked it.'

'More to the point, I was impressed by your ability to disguise yourself and by your command of the French language,' Maj Le Petite said and carried on, 'tell me, where did you learn to speak French that way?'

'I studied at St Dorothy's School in Malta Sir; I read books and listened to French radio on the wireless.'

'Surely one of your parents is French?' The major continued.

'No Sir, my father is British and my mother is Maltese but she's also a teacher of French.'

'Hmm, right that makes sense, well I would like you to consider something, but I cannot give you any information at this moment.'

'Sir?' George said raising her eyebrows, wondering what the major was on about.

'How would you feel about doing a service to this country?'

'It's what I'm here for Sir, anything I can do towards the war effort.'

'Very well, I'm returning to London this evening but I will be in contact.'

'Yes Sir, thank you Sir,' totally mystified, she saluted and took what she understood as being dismissed and left the major's office, none the wiser than when she walked in and agog with what just happened. She wondered what it was that the major had in mind; her brain was going nineteen to the dozen. She almost ran to her billet with the intention of telling Edna of her meeting with the major, but then decided against mentioning the incident after all. Her instinct seemed to caution her that it was not wise to talk to Edna about something the major himself was reluctant to tell her. She slowed her pace. Her thoughts turned to her father; he would have guided her in the right direction. She missed him badly and thought of the unfortunate episode of when he found her in men's clothing in the cellar. She remembered the confused and pained look in his eyes when he confronted her. She had thought of lying to him but she couldn't. Instead, he had quietly told her to never mention it to

128

her mother, whatever the 'it' meant, for at the time, even she had no idea. It was after meeting Gracie that everything had fallen into place. She thought of Ginny and felt a rush of pleasure through her body and tried to recover quickly before entering the door to her billet. Edna was napping and George sat on her cot and wrote a letter to her mother. It was just after six in the evening when she went to bed, her mind still working its cogwheels, mulling over events of the day.

'Hi Peggy, it's George, is Gracie at home? Oh, good she is!' There was a pause while George waited for Gracie to come to the receiver, 'Gracie, good news I've got my leave approved and I will be coming down on the 22nd of December, yes I should be leaving right away, first thing in the morning on the twenty second, but don't forget I have to come all the way from Exeter so I would imagine I will be in Peckham at around two in the afternoon. Yes, I'm looking forward to seeing you too. Take care, bye!' George placed the phone in its cradle and nodded a grateful thank you to her staff sergeant for allowing her to call.

On the Thursday which was the day before she was due to go on leave, George received instructions that she was to report to Baker Street Offices on the 27th December. George was more than happy; it meant she could travel there straight from her aunt and uncle's house.

It was whilst they were on a five-minute cigarette break, that she decided to tell Edna that she was being transferred.

'Edna, I've got some news, I'm being transferred to a different section. I don't really know much; it all seems pretty hush-hush.'

'Gosh what's going on George, do you have absolutely no idea where they are sending you?'

'Nothing more than what I've already told you, I just have to report to the Baker Street office in London.'

They lit a cigarette and smoked, wondering what was to become of them.

'Well, we may as well have a Christmas drink together, seeing as this is your last day here then,' Edna sighed.

'Yes, let's and I don't want anyone to know, so please keep it quiet.'

The walk to the pub was a quiet affair. Strangely enough the pub was empty, even the cat had disappeared. They didn't stay long, the atmosphere felt too sombre.

When they got back there was no one in their billet. Edna watched George pack her kit bag. She got up from her cot and stood next to her. Without any warning she cupped George's face in her hands and kissed her soundly on the lips. This time George did not hesitate and reciprocated ardently. She pulled Edna to an obscured corner by the ablutions and carried on kissing her, letting her hands explore her soft curves. The scent of Edna's warm skin made George delirious. Her lips trailed her neck, her breasts, her soft belly down even further to her mound of Venus. She smelt her sex enticing her to go further to a place she had never been before and yet as if she knew what she already had to do, she delved her tongue into the soft moist folds which beckoned her to taste her womanly sweetness. Pushing against her rhythmic playful tongue, Edna threw her head back in ecstasy, George felt her urgency and entered her swiftly bringing her to climax.

She collapsed against George. She pulled her skirt down whilst embracing her. She shyly looked into George's face, searching for some remorse — there was none. George smiled at her, kissed her forehead, her eyes, her lips and held her with tenderness.

'I never knew women could do '*that*'.'

George smiled and said, 'Neither did I, but it seemed the most natural thing in the world to do; I'm happy to have met you Edna…'

They hugged briefly.

After having a quick cup of tea in the mess canteen, George walked in the direction of the truck that was going to drop her off at Exeter Station. Her shoes crunched on the frosted path and her breath clung in white puffs, it was colder than she had ever experienced. The driver, didn't say much, just smiled, started the truck to life and drove out of the grounds. George waved goodbye at Edna who was standing at the billet door.

The trees lining the road were bare of leaves and grey, making a stark contrast against a clouded sky. Sheep huddled together for warmth on the frost-covered hills. They passed a horse and cart laden with bales of hay on its way to feed the cows in the field next door to the sheep. George blew on her cold hands to try and warm up. She fished around her kitbag to look for a pair of course woollen issue gloves that she had been given;

she put them on, grateful for the protection they offered against the cold.

Exeter Station came into view and the driver stopped the truck and waited for George to climb down. There was a good twenty minutes before the train to London Waterloo was due. She got herself some tea, wrapping her hands around the cup. There were other passengers waiting for the same train who were all queuing up for a hot drink. Soldiers were everywhere on the platforms. Some had their sweethearts clinging on to their arm, hoping it wasn't the last time they were to see each other.

George wondered the same thing. *Was she going to suffer some awful fate? And what was it that they wanted her to do?* She sighed, knowing full well that she had to wait till the following week to find out; meanwhile she was determined to enjoy herself with Gracie and have a peaceful Christmas with her aunt and uncle.

The train to London finally arrived into the platform and George meandered over to it. She found an empty second-class carriage and put her kitbag on the overhead rack. She settled in the corner of the seat, wiping a clear patch on the steamed-up window with her gloves. As soon as all passengers were on board, the guard whistled its departure and the train pulled out. She must have fallen asleep because she felt someone shaking her.

'Miss, Miss, the train has arrived.' It was the conductor who woke her up.

'Thank you,' George uttered and gathered her kitbag and got off the train, walking along the platform with the last few remaining passengers. She went over to the tobacconist to get herself a packet of cigarettes, a habit which became worse since taking part in the panto where she was required to smoke a *Gitane* a number of times. Her journey to Peckham was relatively painless and without any delays; frankly, she was surprised, she had expected trains and busses to be overloaded with troops making their way home.

George let herself into the house, it was quiet, nobody was home. She went upstairs to the room she shared with Gracie, and dumped her kitbag on the floor next to the wardrobe. She then went downstairs again and put the kettle on. She prepared three cups and saucers, assuming that Peggy and Gracie would soon be there. George's thoughts turned to how very anglicised she had become in the past few months and was amused at how much tea she drank; she had never touched the stuff in Malta, she smiled at the thought, how different things were now! She lit a cigarette and drew on it with gusto, examining the packet of *Craven A* nonchalantly whilst waiting for the kettle to boil. The front door opened and Gracie walked in. She knew it was her because Gracie always said 'whoops a daisy' as she came in. George laughed fondly and called out to her.

'I'm in here!'

'Oh Lord, George I meant to be here before you got in, sorry mate!' she said walking over to her friend and giving her a hug.

'Kettle's boiling, I thought you might like a cuppa.'

'Thanks, I'm just about gagging for one,' Gracie laughed.

George measured three teaspoons of tea leaves and poured hot water into the teapot, whorls of steam rising as she did so. Gracie sat unceremoniously at the kitchen table and lit a cigarette offering one to George.

'No thanks, hon, I've just put one out.'

'So, tell me what you've been up to because it's been ages, and your letters don't give all the details,' she said grinning cheekily.

George related what had been happening in the last few months, including the arduous shifts she had had to work and how she celebrated her birthday and what an eye opener all the training was. She didn't mention her little escapade with Edna or the mysterious transfer and thought that maybe she would tell her later on when she knew more. Gracie in turn related her side of things, how she had finished her training and was soon to start ferrying planes from one airfield to another. She waxed lyrical about a female pilot she had met called Amy Johnson and how she had flown halfway around the world from England to Australia.

'She is a fine pilot,' Gracie said, 'still I would love to fly a plane someday to France or to Italy, you can come with me George,' she said chuckling.

'Just learn to fly first then we will see.'

'George, I was thinking we should go to the *Gateways* again, because the way things are going it won't be open for much longer.'

'Hmm I suppose we could go there tomorrow evening,'

'Blimey! You've changed your tune!' Gracie exclaimed laughing her head off.

'All right! All right! don't rub it in, I suppose my curiosity is now getting the better of me and last time we went, I was too mortified to have a good look around.'

'OK then, we should aim to leave at around six tomorrow evening.'

'Righto!'

Saturday evening was bitterly cold and both women had to swaddle themselves in coats and scarves; they were thankful when the bus came so they could get out of the biting wind. The bus windows were all misted and George occasionally cleaned a patch of glass with her scarf so they could see where they were going. They crossed the Vauxhall Bridge: the Thames looking inky black and hardly visible. The blackout rules since September had left London in complete darkness; it was all very surreal. By the time they arrived in Chelsea, they had to make their way to *The Gateways* cautiously, especially since Gracie had two left feet and tripped over nothing and everything! The green door to the club was shut and Gracie knocked on it soundly. It was opened by a burly butch with a shock of orange curly hair.

'Freezin out tonight innit?' the woman said in a typical East End voice.

They nodded politely, taking off their coats and scarves and hanging them in the small cloak room. Somewhere in the background, the sound of '*Kiss Me Goodnight Sergeant Major*' played and couples danced close to each other. They found a table, this time at the back of the club, where other women in various states of animated conversations sat as well. George was relieved that there was no sign of Griff. Gracie looked at her friend and anticipated her thoughts.

'It doesn't look like she's here tonight mate so I think you can relax and tell me what you want to drink.'

'Thank God for that! I think I'll stick to gin and tonic for the evening.'

The bar was busy, not surprisingly, since there was talk of it closing down for the duration of the war, however short or long it would be. It was the only place where women felt safe and could be themselves and not invite strange looks about their attire. George was still not comfortable dressing in her men's clothes since she arrived in London, but tonight she did feel confident enough to wear blue trousers, a pale blue shirt with a wine-coloured pullover. She did not look masculine but she didn't look feminine either; she liked it that way. There were four women standing by the bar, one of them looked at George curiously.

Gracie came back with the drinks chuckling, 'Oh Lord, George you're being given the eye!'

'Stop it, I can see that, what am I supposed to do?' she nervously fished a cigarette out from her pack and lit it with a trembling hand.

'Well, under normal circumstances, you would go up to her and offer her a drink; that is, if you want to,' Gracie replied cheekily.

'Bloody hell, I'm not ready for this!' She swallowed her drink in one gulp and almost choked, making Gracie laugh hysterically. She steadied her nerves and drew on her cigarette a bit more calmly.

The woman was very pretty and did not stop looking at George, so she stubbed her cigarette out in the ashtray on the table and plucked up the courage to walk over to her. When she got there, she became tongue tied, her confidence flying out of the window and almost scuttled back to whence she came; of course, Gracie was watching her with total amusement.

'You're new at this aren't you?' the woman asked George before she could turn away.

'Erm! yes I am, is it so obvious?' she asked shyly.

'Yes, I'm afraid it is, but I don't bite! My name's Evangeline, but you can call me Evie.' She held out her hand to George, who took it immediately and shook it.

'I'm George, pleased to meet you.'

'Your accent's a bit funny, you're not from around, here are you?'

'Umm no I'm a bit of a mixture really, I'm half Maltese and half British, but what do you mean my accent is funny?'

'Well, it's definitely not a London accent; it's a bit sort of King's English, you know… a bit posh.' Evangeline laughed.

'Is it? I've never really thought about it' she replied, feeling a bit self-conscious.

'I like what you're wearing, even *that* is a bit different to what everybody else is wearing; I mean the butch girls always wear a suit. I don't quite know what to make of you, but I like you,' Evangeline told her candidly.

George blushed to the roots of her hair; nobody had ever complimented her this way.

'Thank you, can I get you a drink?'

'Yes please, I'll have whatever you're having,' Evangeline replied.

George ordered the drinks and whilst she was waiting, Evie slipped her arm through George's. George felt a warm sensation in the pit of her stomach and looked at Evie and noticed what lovely brown eyes she had. Evie caught her looking at her and gave her a flirty smile, making George blush again. The bartender handed George the drinks and she gave one of them to Evangeline.

'So, what do you do George I mean you are an awfully long way from home aren't you?'

'It's a long story, but I can tell you right now I'm with the *WAAFS* and I'm on five days' leave.'

'I'm not in a hurry, are you? So, when did you realise... you know?' Evangeline asked looking at George intensely.

'I've always felt a bit different. I wasn't really sure what it was till I met Gracie — that's my friend over there,' George said pointing at Gracie and carried on, 'she brought me here and everything sort of started to fall into place; I was of course shocked to see women like me, I didn't think there were others who felt the same, in fact I was so terrified I just wanted to run away, I couldn't seem to face my demons.'

'I can quite understand how you felt because I went through pretty much the same thing, but oh what a relief it was when I finally accepted who I am,' reflecting George's predicament.

'But what is it exactly that you are?'

'Why, a lesbian of course!' she replied.

'A lesbian! I've never heard that word before!'

'Well, that is what *we* are called and it's often used derogatorily as an insult by ignorant bastards,' Evangeline said pursing her lips.

George laughed at her comical facial expression.

'So anyway, I kind of grew up in an insulated environment; my Mama, who is the Maltese one, is very Catholic and it was a case of church every Sunday and she constantly indoctrinated me to getting married someday and having children; it's not that I don't like children, because I do, but I don't want to have them myself; it all sounds so very complicated doesn't it?'

'Well yes and no because I understand your dilemma, I love children but I don't know how much that's going to happen because like you, I don't want to get married, at least not to a man.'

'My father… he caught me with my men's clothes on not so long ago, I had just entered the cellar and I found him there just waiting. I felt I wanted to die, I looked at him, I could see confusion and then hurt in his eyes and I just didn't know what to say, I didn't have to say anything in actual fact because he just told me to make sure Mama never found out and he just walked away and the only confrontation was literally ten minutes in his study,' George lamented with a lump in her throat.

'Gosh! What an awkward situation!'

'Yes, it was; we never spoke about it again.'

They went quiet for a few minutes, George pondering over what she had just told Evie.

'Let's have a dance,' Evie extended her hand to George in invitation, wanting to take her away from a memory that was obviously distressing her.

'What?' George asked breaking her train of thought and seeing Evie's outstretched hand.

She took her hand and walked to the dance floor pulling her gently towards her. It felt wonderful; inhaling Evie's perfume; she felt dizzy swaying gently to the music. Evie pressed herself into George almost melting into her. She held Evie tightly and pushed her nose through her hair. They kissed in what felt like the most natural thing in the world; George nearly fainted with the pleasure of tasting her lips. Not once did Evie show any sign of concern about George's lack of experience. This was a completely different feeling, her encounter with Ginny; she now realised, had been a cold and unemotional affair and at least the encounter with Edna had managed to restore her self-esteem.

She thought she had died and gone to heaven; she could feel her heart beat on every breath she took. Evangeline was also aware of the intense feeling that was passing between them, the chemistry was undeniable. She guided George to a dark corner of the room and they kissed like they were never going to see each other again. The passion of their embrace left George breathless… she had to pull away for just a second before continuing. Somewhere in the background a bell rang in the bar announcing last orders. George looked up almost annoyed. *Had so much time passed by?* Evidently it had, because Gracie, who had herself been occupied for most of the evening, was signalling George to come over to her.

'Evie come with me over to my friend's table, will you?'

'Yes of course' Evangeline said composing herself and adjusting her clothing.

'Gracie, this is Evangeline, Evie for short.'

'Hello Evie, you've been keeping George busy all night, haven't you?' she winked mischievously.

'GRACIE!' George chided.

'It's all right George; she's just pulling your leg,' Evie said good humouredly.

'Why don't we get a drink for the road?' George suggested trying to cover up her embarrassment.

Evie waited at the table while they went to get the drinks.

'What happens now?' George hissed under her breath.

'Dunno mate, if you had a room, I guess you would ask her over, but seeing as we are sharing one, that's going to be a problem, maybe she'll ask you over to hers, that would solve everything.'

'Oh Lord, let's just go over and have our drinks and see what happens then.'

They sat around the table sipping their drinks, Evie held George's hand under the table; the gesture did not go unmissed by Gracie, who suddenly piped up and said, 'Evie, George and I share the room we are staying in because we are away most of the time, so if you want to spend the night with her, she will have to go back to yours.' She got a resounding kick on her ankle from George, who at that point wanted the ground to swallow her up with embarrassment and would have gladly throttled her friend.

'Well, that's settled then, because I *do* have a place of my own, it's a very small flat though *and* I don't live too far from here, so George if you feel comfortable with that, I would love you to come over,' Evie invited her, smiling sweetly.

George was overcome with shyness, fear and every emotion that could be mustered up in her mind and only managed a nod in Evie's direction. They finished their drinks and walked over to the cloakroom, where they retrieved their coats and scarves. Once outside, Grace walked to the end of the road and waited for a taxi and George and Evie walked in the opposite direction and managed to hail a taxi almost immediately. The cabbie asked for the address, 'Where to miss?'

'The Fulham Road corner with Epple Road please,' Evie replied.

'Right you are, Miss,' he responded.

They were quiet the entire journey, however in the darkness of the taxi, they held hands, each giving a squeeze now and then. The taxi stopped in front of a brown door next to a tobacco shop. They got out and Evie paid the fare. The taxi drove off and Evie turned to George and looked at her eyes to see if there was any sign of apprehension or perhaps, she might have even considered changing her mind, but there wasn't, and she didn't. She opened the door that led up to a short flight of stairs. At the top, Evie guided George to a small but cosy sitting room and switched on a lampshade. It was tastefully furnished with chintz curtains, a brown leather sofa, a book case, an oak sideboard as well as a coffee table. There were also a few paintings hanging on the wall. Evie went over to the window to make sure the curtains were closed properly. George stood self-consciously by the door.

'Come and sit down, George, make yourself comfortable, would you like something to drink?' Evie asked her.

'Yes please, what have you got?'

'I have some beer and I also have some whisky.'

'In that case I'll have a whisky and water please.'

Whilst Evie disappeared into what must have been the kitchen, since she could hear cupboard doors being opened, George was about to sit down on the sofa, when she spotted the gramophone. She had only ever seen one once before and that was at her aunt and uncle's place, so she assumed that Evie must be well off to be able to afford such a luxury.

Evie came through with the drinks and placed them on the coffee table. She noticed George by the gramophone.

'You can put something on if you like.'

'I'm afraid I don't know how to work it,' George replied feeling somewhat embarrassed.

'Oh, that's all right, here, let me do it.'

George went and sat down on the sofa and picked up her drink. Evie looked through a small collection of records and chose one to put on; she placed it on the gramophone and lowered the stylus. Within seconds Glenn Miller's 'Moon Love' filled the room. She sauntered over to George and held out her hand to her.

'Dance with me!' smiling seductively knowing full well what effect she was having on her.

George stood up and took Evie in her arms and started to dance gently. They remained that way, not saying anything, just moving and enjoying the closeness of their bodies. George relaxed and felt confident enough to nuzzle Evie's neck, where the smell of her perfume was making her feel almost dizzy; the same dizziness she felt back at the club. Evie succumbed to her caresses encouraging her to go further. George sought her lips and kissed her passionately, locked in an embrace neither of the two wanted to be freed from. Evie sighed with pleasure and could not bear the ache she felt between her legs any longer; she led George to the bedroom. George was in total wonderment at the new emotions happening inside of her. Her stomach had butterflies flitting uncontrollably whilst watching Evie take her clothes off; she had put on a small side lamp that was throwing glorious light over her body, making it glow. Evie looked like a goddess. She moved over to George languidly and started to undress her; she thrilled at the flitting movement of Evie's fingers when she unbuttoned her blouse. It fell to the floor as did her trousers and everything else. George felt nervous. She had been semi naked with Ginny and had not a care in the world aided by the cocaine; she needed none of that to realise that this was a beautiful and raw emotion she was feeling, like parts of her were being peeled back, being completely sensitive to the growing feeling within, standing before Evie; every part of her being literally exposed and yet she was unafraid. Evie sensed George's vulnerability and very tenderly pulled her towards her and kissed her reassuringly. They lay together on the bed. George touched Evie's face, her neck, growing more confident stroking Evie's breasts feeling her nipples harden, sending ripples of pleasure throughout her own body. Evie moulded herself into George so they could both feel their nakedness. They made love not once or twice but many times till the small hours of the morning. George was in awe and totally smitten; Evie was an amazing lover and had explored every possible part of her body. George in turn, was a fast learner and swooned with pleasure when Evie climaxed over and over again. They lay quiescently in each other's arms savouring what had just happened between them…

George lit two cigarettes and gave one to Evie.

After taking a drag from hers George said, 'You have obviously done this before.'

'A few times yes; does it bother you?'

'No, it doesn't, I'm with you now and that's all that matters,'

'There's never been anyone special so far.'

'Me neither, I mean I love Connie but she is my best friend back home, that's as close as I have come to loving another woman apart from Mama of course but that's different,' George explained smiling.

George leant over to the ashtray on the bedside cabinet and stubbed both their cigarettes out.

When she turned back Evie laid her head on George's shoulder.

'Evie, you never said what you do, for a living, that is.'

'No, I didn't, but you never asked,' Evie replied, seeming reluctant to talk about it.

'What is it that you do then?'

Not one to mince her words Evie replied, 'I'm an escort.'

'An escort? What's that?'

'I'm hired to escort high-class gentlemen to parties and stuff like that.'

'What is it exactly that you do then?' By this time George sat up propping herself with a pillow.

'I dress up in expensive clothes and jewellery and attend functions with a gentleman who requires someone by his side to look attractive. It's pretty boring really as I have nothing in common with these people. They're a bunch of pompous arses, who speak like they have a plum stuck in their throats, they waffle all night long, drink too much and they're as boring as fuck — please excuse my French! At the end of the night, the gentleman usually escorts me home by taxi and pays me, and that's that, but there are times when I'm required to go a little further.'

Evie said the last sentence rather quietly feeling she was about to deal with a rather precarious reaction from George.

George felt her stomach lurch at the last bit. 'You mean you are a prostitute?'

Evie cringed at George's words, 'Yes, sort of.'

'But I don't understand, you like women, don't you?' George uttered, feeling confused and dismayed.

'Yes, I do, I dislike men intensely, but the work pays very well, better than some factory or office job; it affords me certain luxuries like having my own flat and other things, does this mean you don't want to see me anymore?'

'I… I don't know, Evie, don't get me wrong I like you a lot, I'm just trying to get my head around this.'

'You're the first person I've told about what I do, normally I lie, but I don't want to lie to you.'

Now that Evie had told her about her work, the flat and its décor made sense.

There were a few seconds of uncomfortable silence as if waiting for an invisible crisis to be averted…

'You know what? It shouldn't make any difference, I would like to see more of you and I need to go beyond this, I don't want it to be an obstacle between us. I need to tell you though, I don't know how much we are going to be able to do that; I'm being posted to a secret location next Monday, I can try and keep in touch with you if you have a telephone.'

'I'm glad I met you George and yes I have a telephone, it's one of the trappings of my success, it's not one of the best jobs in the world I know, I won't let things go further if it bothers you, honestly I won't, it's just a job George, nothing more,' Evie said earnestly.

George smiled and hugged her and said, 'It would definitely make your job more tolerable.'

'Right,' Evie said as she got out of bed and opened the curtains, 'so now we have sorted that out, how about some breakfast on this grey and dull Sunday morning?' winking, and carried on, 'my own little ray of sunshine!'

George beamed, 'Yes please!' She couldn't remember when she'd felt this happy.

'We can have bacon and eggs with bread and butter, how does that tickle your fancy?'

'Hmm that sounds super!'

Evie went to the kitchen and busied herself putting the breakfast together. George got out of the bed and shivered looking for her clothing that was scattered all over the floorboards. She looked out of the window whilst she was dressing and saw the weather outside, glad she was inside with the smell of frying bacon, it felt homely. She stood at the kitchen door watching Evie in her dressing gown, sleeves rolled up, pouring hot water into the teapot.

'Why don't you put a record on George? You know how to now,'

George put on the first record she found and went back to the kitchen. There was a cup of tea waiting for her and she picked it up and sipped at it. Evie was busy dishing out the bacon and eggs on to the plates, but not busy enough to keep looking at George every few seconds and smiling. There was a small table in the kitchen, Evie placed the plates on it and fished around in a drawer for cutlery and set them on the table.

'Evie, can I ask you something personal?'

'Yes of course.'

'How did you get into this job of yours?'

Evie furrowed her eyebrows. She had half anticipated George asking. It had to come around sooner or later and she had already mentally prepared herself to be completely honest, she liked George and was falling for her.

'Well, it started as a joke really; one of my friends said she was doing it and when she told me about the amount of ridiculous money she was making, I decided to give it a go, I never meant it to progress beyond the occasional event, to sort of supplement my earnings, but then it became more frequent. The other stuff in fact has only happened twice,' Evie said with distaste.

'I'm happy you've been honest with me, but I can't say I approve of what you do, maybe I'm a little jealous.'

'George, darling it's just a job and I won't be doing any of the other 'thing', I promise you; I like you and I want to see more of you and I certainly don't want you getting upset over this.'

'I'm not upset, honestly, I just feel a little bit insecure because I've never been exposed to this kind of thing, but it makes me feel easier now that you've told me you're not doing that 'thing' anymore; I like you too and I would like to see as much of you as I can.' George said.

'Right, well let's enjoy breakfast then!'

After breakfast they sat in the sitting room enjoying another cup of tea and listening to the gramophone. Evie loved *Tommy Dorsey* and George watched her tap her foot to the music.

She leant over and kissed her on the lips. Evie responded and they were soon locked in an embrace and made love on the sofa.

'I can't get enough of you my darling George.'

She thrilled to the word 'darling' and looked at her shyly, 'I feel exactly the same, I don't know how I'm going to leave here!' Agonizing over her departure.

'Don't go then! It's Christmas Eve today just in case you hadn't noticed! Spend the rest of the weekend with me!' Evangeline proposed.

'God, I would like nothing more, but I've committed myself to spending Christmas with my aunt and uncle in Bramley. I could try and get out of it I suppose; Gracie wouldn't mind for sure, may I use your telephone?'

'Please do darling.'

George went to the hallway and called Gracie first and told her very briefly that she was OK and of her plans. Then she called her aunt.

'Hello Aunty, it's George, yes I'm fine, well I wanted to talk to you about that, would you be terribly disappointed if I didn't make it for Christmas? Yes I understand Aunty Marlu, it's just there's this lovely party I would like to go to because God knows when I will be able to go to another one, I'm being transferred to a secret location on Wednesday; no nothing to worry about, I will write and tell you both about it, yes Aunty and thank so much for understanding, Yes I will call Mama and Papa on Christmas Day if I can get through, Happy Christmas, give my love to Uncle Ted, thank you, good bye.'

George returned to the sitting room grinning like a Cheshire cat. Evie, seeing George's face, stood up and flung herself at her. They hugged in delight at the prospect of spending more time together. George was in awe at how things could just change overnight. It's not to say that

143

she didn't miss home, for she did, and was feeling a bit homesick now, she wished she could share her happiness with her parents; in fact, she wanted to climb to the top of a mountain and tell the whole world about Evie, but she knew it wasn't going to be possible.

'So now we have three whole days together, what shall we do?' Evangeline asked with a mischievous look in her eyes.

'Oh, I haven't the foggiest idea, but we can start by getting some groceries in so at least we can have a Christmas lunch, our very first one together,' George replied chuckling. They eventually went out and went to Peckham to pick up George's kitbag, as she needed a change of clothes; she also needed a clean uniform for the following Wednesday since she had to report to HQ in Baker Street, it was all very hush-hush as no more information was given to her other than what was deemed necessary. They were soon on their way and didn't notice the journey to Peckham; they were too busy looking at each other with new secret sensations.

Thankfully Gracie was at home when George and Evie arrived. Gracie raised an eyebrow at both of them and they all burst out laughing, knowing full well what that implied. Gracie and Evie settled down to a cup of tea whilst George went upstairs to pack. She still had her suitcase but decided to leave it with Gracie as she had her men's clothes safely stashed inside. With her kitbag packed, George went downstairs to join the other two in the sitting room.

'All sorted then mate?' Gracie asked with a wink.

'Yes thanks, I've left you three months' rent money on the cupboard and I've left my trunk under your bed, like that it's out of the way, oh and just in case anything should happen, you have my aunt's address and my address in Malta too.'

'What on earth could possibly happen mate? I mean that's being a bit dramatic isn't it?' Gracie asked whilst Evie looked on bewildered, but saying nothing.

'Well, you never know; they want to see me at Bakers Street HQ and they are being very enigmatic, so I'm not sure what to expect!' George replied.

'George sweetheart you're scaring me, I've only just met you and you are acting as if you are going to disappear!' Evie exclaimed somewhat distressed.

'I'm sorry darling, I didn't mean to upset you, I'm just preparing myself that's all,' she said sombrely.

'Lighten up you two, it's Christmas Eve, you can at least enjoy the next couple of days together, I know I will, Christmas lunch with Peggy and then down to the pub!' Gracie chuckled.

'All right, well we had better be off then, because we still need to get some groceries in! Gracie, thanks for being such a great pal, give Peggy my best regards and wish her a Merry Christmas from me!' George said, happy to be spending time with Evie albeit feeling a bit guilty leaving Gracie to spend the festive season with just Peggy.

They said their goodbyes with George promising to either call or write to her.

Despite a war going on, the people in the High Street went about their way preparing for Christmas day, the butcher had a couple turkeys hanging in his window, there were baskets of potatoes, carrots, cabbages and parsnips outside the vegetable shop, with housewives lining up, and business went on as usual. This, George observed as they walked to the bus stop. She felt very homesick and Evie, as if reading her mind, linked her arm through hers in comfort. They were sitting on the bus to the Oval Station when Evie turned to her; who had gone very quiet.

'Penny for your thoughts?'

'I was thinking of Mama and Papa actually, it's the first time I've been away from them for Christmas, they must be really missing me.'

'Why don't you place a call to Malta tonight?'

'I could but I'm worried about the cost, it's so expensive!' George said ruefully.

'George, I want you to call your family up, don't worry about the cost, I will take care of it.'

George's face brightened up. 'That's really sweet of you darling, I appreciate it and I know my parents will be thrilled to hear from me, though I don't know how they are going to take the fact that I shan't be spending Christmas with my aunt and uncle!'

'That's settled then, let's sort out the groceries.'

It took them half an hour to get to the Fulham Road, and laden with kitbag and groceries they climbed the stairs to the apartment. The day was coming to a close and was turning to dusk. Evie automatically went to close the curtains. Ever since the blackout laws, she was careful to observe them, although she lamented how much she missed watching the sunset from her sitting room window.

'I can actually imagine how warm and cosy it must look in here...'

'Well, we don't get much sun here in the winter as you probably well know, it must be so different on Malta...' emptying the grocery bag and putting things into the larder as she spoke.

'Well yes, sunsets on the island are magnificent, especially in the summer; most Maltese families are out and about enjoying walking along the seafront, or taking a swim and tucking into what we call a 'hobza' which is our crusty loaf of bread that's stuffed with tinned tuna, olives and pickles, but it's a bit different in the winter time because we tend to gather at home in the kitchen surrounded by visiting aunts, uncles, cousins, you name it, and a big pot of vegetable soup called *minestra* — a traditional vegetable soup — which is placed on the table and everyone tucks in and eats together with chunks of crusty bread; it's totally delicious!' she finished off enthusiastically.

'It sounds wonderful, no wonder you miss home so much, I would love to go there one day and share a part of your life.'

'I would love for you to come; I would show you some beautiful places on the island!'

'All that talking has made me thirsty, I'm gasping for a cup of tea; would you like one hon?'

'Hmm yes please!' George replied, whilst rifling through Evie's collection of records.

'George you can put on the wireless if you like.'

She found the 'on' button for the wireless and the set jumped to life, she fiddled with the tuning knob till she found the BBC station.

'This is Lance B Todd coming to you from Odsal Stadium bringing you the latest in the England versus Wales match...'.

'Oh God that's the rugby, change the station George, you'll find The Radio Times on the coffee table, there's all the programmes.'

'I haven't heard much about rugby because we only get the *BBC World Service* in Malta and it's transmitted through something called a Rediffusion, which is similar to a wireless set, but it serves its purpose, mostly news and religious programmes, with the odd drama thrown in, I used to listen to Radio Luxembourg a lot, they had a lot of French programmes on,' George said, amused.

'Well, you can't expect an island so small and cut off to be up to date with the times I suppose.

'Right,' she said, 'I've managed to find Radio Luxembourg...' which was playing *Putting on The Ritz*.

'Come and sit beside me darling,' she patted the empty space next to her.

George moved her tea over to where Evie was sitting and plonked herself next to her.

'Who would have known, George, that we would meet each other?'

'I certainly would never have believed that I would be here, let alone meet such a gorgeous woman!' kissing her on the lips.

She returned the kiss and murmured, 'Tell me George, were you always this way inclined?'

'Well, I've always felt different but it wasn't till I was about sixteen that I started dressing up in my father's clothes when there was no one in the house. I had no idea what it meant, just that it felt right to me. But I could never divulge such a thing to my parents, although as I told you, dad caught me in our cellar one night as I was changing from one of my nightly jaunts.'

'Oh George, you poor thing!' Evie sympathised and pulled George to her, hugging her.

'But what about you? What's your story?'

'There's not much to tell really; my mother died when I was quite young, I have a brother whom I haven't seen in a few years; my father disowned me when he found out I had been carrying on with another woman in an 'unnatural manner.' I haven't seen him in years either and I had to fend for myself since the age of sixteen.

'Gosh it must have been hard for you to survive; I've been spoilt rotten compared to you!'

'I was very scared in the beginning but then you get used to it and you get on with it as best you can.'

George brushed an imaginary object from Evie's hair and touched her face tenderly and then pulled her right hand to her lips and kissed it.

The two stared at each other as if in a cocoon, shutting out the world and all its strife, both aware that their time together was so limited and wanting it to last forever.

They spent the evening preparing dinner and later just sat next to one another, listening to the wireless, dancing, embracing and kissing. Christmas came and went and Boxing Day passed in a whirl of lovemaking and promises, which each knew was going to be difficult to fulfil or maintain because of the unknown, because of what their destinies held.

George prepared to make her way to Baker Street with a heavy heart, not wanting to let go. With her kitbag on her shoulder and her gas mask on the other, she left Evie, both of them crying. she kept looking back at her standing in the doorway; it was early morning and only very few people about, who were still lulled by the aftermath of Christmas festivities. George made her way to the bus stop and waited for the bus to arrive. Once on, all the way to *Baker Street*, her only thoughts were of Evie, her soft skin, her sweet kisses, the smell of her hair and the wonderful intimate moments they had shared, which made her smile and yearn for her.

She walked into a couple of buildings before entering the right one where she was to meet Major Le Petite again. There were military personnel everywhere, some walking with batches of papers in their hands and others deep in conversation. George approached the reception where she was asked to sign a register before being directed to Major Le Petite's office on the first floor. She knocked and opened the door.

'Yes, can I help you?' a smart man in uniform asked.

'I'm here to see Major Le Petite, Sir.'

'Do you have an appointment?' he asked.

'Yes sir, Major Le Petite is expecting me,' she replied.

'One moment please,' the man said picking up the phone. 'Major Le Petite will be with you shortly, please take a seat.'

George sat on one of the chairs in the room and placed her gas mask and kitbag by her feet. She had been there about fifteen minutes before she was ushered into the major's office. She saluted.

'At ease Miss Parker, do come in, won't you sit down?' the major said kindly.

'Thank you, Sir,' George replied. The tall man before her never failed to impress her… she sat opposite him.

The major offered her a cigarette. George took one and the major lit her up.

'Miss Parker, I'm well aware that you have no idea why you have been called here,' the major began.

'No Sir, I don't,' George replied honestly.

'Very well, let me enlighten you, we are in dire need of persons to take on undercover activities for our secret service… MI6 to be precise, are proposing starting a division of counter espionage, this is of course top secret and you cannot reveal any information to anyone, not even your family or friends, you will be bound by the Official Secrets Act.'

'Sorry Sir I don't quite understand what you are trying to tell me.'

'How would you feel about going on a mission which could mean a fifty percent or even a hundred percent chance of not returning alive from it?' the major looked at her sombrely.

'I don't know Sir, but if it meant doing something to stop that heinous dictator in his tracks, then yes, I would most certainly consider it!'

'Very well then,'

'Thank you, Sir… may I ask, why me?' George asked.

'Let's just say, as I had commented to you on the day of the panto, your command of French and your ability for disguise made you the perfect candidate.'

'Whatever it is, I'll do it, Sir!'

'Very well Miss Parker, if you are sure, I see you are ready to ship out, so you will stay the night in London and tomorrow you will join another four personnel who are all males, for an interview. You are to report at 07:00 hrs at the St Ermin's Hotel in Westminster and you will be briefed there. Are there any questions you would like to ask?'

'No Sir, thank you, Sir.'

With that, she saluted smartly, picked up her belongings and walked out of the building. She saw a telephone kiosk about three hundred yards in the direction of Marylebone Road and walked towards it with Evie on her mind; she would at least have one more night with her. She put two pence in the coin box and dialled Evie's number, hoping she was still at home. Evie *was* still at home, pushing her nose into the pillow that George had slept on, breathing in her scent.

The phone rang three times before she answered.

'Evie darling, I have one last night in London before I'm off again.'

'Sweetheart that's wonderful, will you make your way to me straight away?'

'Yes, yes, I'm leaving now...' almost breathlessly, putting the telephone back in its cradle. She stepped out of the telephone kiosk and made her way to Baker Street underground. The station was packed: she made her way through the melee until she reached the entrance for the platform going southbound. She wanted to get to West Brompton and then catch a bus the rest of the way. The District Line train trundled out of the tunnel bringing with it a rush of warm air. All who were waiting in the platform surged forward squeezing in through the already crowded car.

'Mind the gap, mind the gap!' the guard shouted.

And like the rest of the crowd George pushed her way onto the train. She had to stand up for most of the journey until Earls Court, then it got considerably better and after that she was able to get off the train easily. She changed onto another District Line train for the short journey to West Brompton. When she exited the station, a light drizzle had started; she decided to hail a taxi. She gave the driver the address and arrived on the Fulham Road in fifteen minutes.

Evie opened the door. George ran inside and lifted her up in an embrace, as if she hadn't seen her in a long time.

'I could kiss you forever...'

'I think I'm in love with you George!'

'I feel exactly the same way darling.'

There was this intense moment... their eyes locked and they kissed... it felt like their souls were communicating... there were words bounding in their head wanting to get out, but there were too many of them to say all in one go...

George felt her heart soar, she felt dizzy; a euphoric happiness had settled in her soul and she could have never been happier, her only thoughts now were of Evangeline and the one night they had left together.

They bathed and then went to the bedroom, there was no time to waste; they wanted to make love for as long as they could, stopping only to smoke a cigarette. They did not eat, for they were full of each other, and when George looked at the small alarm clock on Evie's bedside table, she sighed, knowing full well that their time together was coming to an end. A heavy sadness had already started to weight her heart as she clung onto Evie, who had dozed off sweetly in her arms. She kissed the tip of her nose, waking her up. Evie looked into George's eyes and there read love, desire, sadness and acknowledged that it was time for George to go. It was four thirty and black as the ace of spades outside. There would be no sign of light till six. Evie dragged herself out of bed, switched on the bedroom light and went to put the kettle on, it was chilly and she shivered, drawing her dressing gown tight around her. George went to the bathroom to have a wash and quickly towelled herself dry. Her uniform was laid neatly on the chair beneath the window in the bedroom. She thanked God for the large woollen overcoat, at least it would keep her warm till she got to Westminster.

Evie had laid out the table with tea and some bread and jam, seeing this, George realised just how hungry she was. They drank and ate in silence, each not wanting to believe that it would probably be a very long time before they saw each other again.

It was time to leave. George pulled Evie towards her, holding her tight, pushing her nose through her hair, breathing in her scent. Evie did not want to let go of George, clinging on a few more minutes.

'Sweetheart I have to go, I can't be late; I'll try and call as soon as I can.'

'My darling, it's going to be like hell without you, it's only been a few days but it feels like years!' tears were rolling down her face.

'My love; my Evie, please don't cry, I will think of you every day and night and I promise I will call you as often as possible and write too.' George tried to mollify her, knowing how hard it was going to be for both of them.

They walked together to the front door and before opening it they kissed deeply one last time. It was still dark outside when they said goodbye; George didn't look back.

She shivered, pulling her coat tighter around her; puffs of condensed breaths formed in the air blowing into her gloved hands and stamping her feet at the same time to keep them warm. The bus seemed to take forever. Finally, when it came, like a great shadow, it appeared with its headlights dimmed.

'Hop on luv,' the conductor said kindly.

George climbed to the top deck, there were only two passengers seated at the front. She chose a seat in the middle of the double-decker and immediately became engrossed with her thoughts of the past few days with Evie. Never in a million years did she ever imagine that she could live this kind of life, be with someone like Evie and be intimate. It was unimaginable in Malta, but here in London, it was a haven of anonymity. No one knew your business, especially not now with a war on; everyone was absorbed with their own business. It suited George just fine, because of her cloak and dagger past, now she felt free to be whom she really was. A degree of apprehension was building up inside her, not knowing where she was going or what her new role would precisely entail, only that all was to be revealed later that day. The bus reached the underground station and George got off. She must have smoked a quarter of a pack of cigarettes before she arrived at St James's Park. By six forty-five a.m. she walked till she came to the imposing entrance of the St Ermin's Hotel. There was a large Victorian wrought iron gate with the name of the hotel emblazoned across the top arch.

George passed through the gate with buildings on either side as if heralding the approach to the columned front door. She went straight to the concierge who, looking at her uniform, immediately directed her to the first floor. The décor was magnificent, with paintings and ornate furniture everywhere. George preferred to climb the stairs rather than take the lift. She was in awe of the beautiful undulating balcony, admiring it whilst climbing the left side of the double staircase. Everything was pristine, with rich plasterwork adorning all the walls… the ceilings were lit by the enormous chandeliers. George turned right at the top and followed the concierge's directions till she came to an anteroom, where five men were sitting, all dressed in civilian clothes, chatting and smoking. They hardly gave her a second glance. She sat on a vacant chair next to one of them. She pulled out a cigarette and lit up, inhaling deeply; it calmed her down somewhat. George leafed through a brochure on the hotel; the hotel had been built on the grounds of the former Chapel which had been built in the fifteenth century and dedicated to St Ermine.

They waited there for at least twenty minutes before a door opened and a suited gentleman greeted them, ushering them into what looked like a classroom; there were a number of desks, chairs and even a blackboard.

'Good morning Miss Parker and gentlemen, my name is Mr. Phillip Waring. I suppose you are all wondering what in actual fact you are doing here, so to put it simply, you are here because your country needs you and you have been selected to undergo intense interviews to ascertain your skills, after which, whoever is chosen will undergo specialised training! Any questions so far?'

Nobody said a word.

'Good so we will carry on; you will be trained in all manner of warfare which you will attain in the coming months; you are the first recruits to undergo such training and will be the blueprint for others,' he concluded.

There was more information imparted, but not enough to enlighten them as to what was to happen, and by lunchtime, all of the recruit's minds were in a whirl. At twelve thirty, Mr. Waring informed them that they had a lunch break of one hour. After which they would each be interviewed and then sent to their respective training ground.

Lunch was a superb affair; a hot buffet of soup, roast beef or lamb or halibut meuniere with all the trimmings followed by a decadent charlotte russe. George was famished and ate with relish from the beautiful fare that was laid on for them. During the course of lunch, she drank a couple of glasses of perfectly chilled *St Emilion Bordeaux* which was of course something she had never tasted before. She had already befriended the men, whom she hoped would be her colleagues for the next few months. At a quarter to two they were directed to an office on the opposite side of the grand stairs. They had all been interviewed and assessed by five p.m.

They then waited outside the room until an officer came out and called the names of those who had been selected to complete the training. Four out of the five men as well as George were chosen. They were directed to the front of the building where an army truck was waiting. They all climbed in with their various pieces of luggage and kitbags in tow and in minutes the truck drove off. They still had no idea where their final destination would be, but the close proximity of them all sitting together, gave them the ideal situation to start bonding.

There was Algernon Trelawney, a banking clerk with Barclays, Hamish McBride, originally from Edinburgh but now living in London teaching French, Reginald Grenfield, a Sandhurst Graduate and last but not least Adam Shilling who did not have a job but had other questionable skills. They were an amiable bunch and George took to most of them, except for Algernon… who was a bit full of himself and professed to know everything and wouldn't stop talking; this annoyed not only George but the rest of the lads on board too; they ignored him.

At long last Algernon took the hint and sat quietly whilst everyone else lit a cigarette, which George had offered. They chatted to one another, this being the first real opportunity to introduce themselves properly and get to know each other, asking where they were from. When it was George's turn, they all plied her with questions about Malta and she happily obliged. The truck had rumbled out of London and took to the country roads heading north. They tried reading sign posts but most had been obscured to deter the enemy so they all took it in turns to try guessing their destination, which was still a mystery to them.

The truck slowed down and headed out to what looked like an airfield. It finally came to a halt and there, waiting on the ground, was a *De Havilland* aircraft, its propellers whining and spluttering whilst its engines warmed up. There was an officer waiting for them. They all climbed out. None of them had been on a plane before and George became nervous.

'Good afternoon Miss Parker, gentlemen, you are about to board this aircraft, which is taking you to Inverness-shire, Scotland. You will be met and transferred to a further destination when you arrive; good luck and safe journey.' And that was that! No more information was imparted.

They boarded the plane one at a time, putting their luggage in first. They sat down, their backs to the rib-cage of the plane, they strapped up waiting for it to take off. The pilot pulled off the brakes and the *De Havilland* moved forward, slowly at first and then at full throttle, gaining ground till it finally lifted up from the runway and into the air, shuddering in the process. In fact, the plane's wooden body shuddered all the way to

Inverness-shire, making a couple of the passengers queasy. They were on the aircraft for what seemed like hours on end. When they finally landed, it was dark. The whining propellers stopped turning and the group disembarked the aircraft, feeling somewhat cramped, but happy to stretch their legs. It was freezing and every one of them drew their coats tighter to their body. The transport was waiting for them. They quickly clambered onboard with their luggage and were on their way within minutes. They were unable to see anything outside as it was pitch black, so they resorted to smoking and small talk. The road they were on became bumpy and the truck went slower. It was a few minutes past eight o'clock, Reggie banged on the window separating them from the driver and shouted out 'How much further?' The driver shouted back with what sounded like half an hour. Reggie sighed and so did George, who was feeling exhausted by this time.

'Cigarette anyone?' Adam asked.

Everyone except Algie took one and lit up. The mixture of smoke and breath hung in the air and it seemed to get worse as they went along. They had no idea where they were with little or no information given to them, their wild guesses were just that — wild!

Eventually the truck came to a halt outside a huge complex looming like a monstrous shadow in the dark. They were led to the front of it. George followed the truck driver inside and the others followed. They were greeted by a smart officer who held a clipboard in his hands. 'Welcome to all of you, my name is Lt. James Kerrigan.'

'I'm sure you are all tired and hungry. If you leave your luggage here and proceed to the dining room, there is food waiting to be served.' This last statement put a smile on all their faces and they followed the lieutenant to the dining room. There was a roaring log fire burning that did much to alleviate the cold and they were grateful. They sat at the dining table and as if by secret code, the housekeeper, Mrs Ferguson, a robust woman in her fifties, appeared with plates of Scottish highland salmon. The combination of food and wine put them all in good spirits. They were plied with an abundance of whisky; after all the New Year was soon upon them, it was the 28th of December, so they used it as an excuse to start celebrations early and were soon on the brink of inebriation, except for George, who not being much of a drinker, had

155

refrained from taking one of many for the road. George decided to retire and left the men to it. They had been informed that they had to be ready for their first induction at nine thirty the next morning.

She crept up the stairs to her room. She didn't put the light on but walked over to the window. It overlooked a wooded area lit by a waning moon and for the first time she saw the snow. It was deep with mounds among the trees. The room was cold so she placed some newspapers and twigs into the fireplace and lit them. They caught fire instantly; she then placed a couple of thick logs and soon a small fire blazed, taking the chill out of the room. George undressed hurriedly, thanking her good sense to pack two pairs of trousers in her kitbag. There had been no mention of any additional kit to be issued. She slipped into the narrow bed and fell instantly to sleep, dreaming of Evie.

The alarm went off at six. George woke up with a start, wondering for a moment where she was. She knew she was in Scotland but where exactly was she? After bathing, she dressed hurriedly in trousers, shirt and pullover plus her overcoat and went downstairs to the dining room to find that only Adam had come down.

'You all right George? Heavy night last night wasn't it?' Adam asked chuckling.

'Yes, I'm fine Adam, what time did you all go up then?' George asked.

'Oh, it must have been after one in the morning, but I bet those three will be nursing a prize hangover,' Adam replied chuckling again.

'Adam, do you have any idea where we are?'

'Well according to my sources, we are in the middle of nowhere, a place called Arisaig in the Scottish Highlands and we are to be billeted at Garramore, a cottage very close to here, apparently it's a shooting lodge built for the son of a local laird,' Adam finished with a satisfied smile.

'Crikey you've done your homework haven't you?'

He tapped the side of his nose with his index finger and said, 'Aaaah lass the whiskey did its job yesterday!' He smiled conspiratorially. George laughed.

The dining room door opened and the other three walked in. Reggie looked a bit worse for wear but Hamish and Algie went straight to where breakfast was keeping warm on the sideboard under silver cloches. Adam, Algie and Reggie helped themselves to eggs, kippers and bacon, but George and Hamish settled for a steaming bowl of porridge with jam. There was tea and coffee on the table brought in by Mrs Ferguson. Throughout breakfast they chatted about their prospective training and were about to get up, when Lieutenant Kerrigan walked in and sat down with them.

'Right then lads, Miss Parker, when we finish here, collect your kitbag and other belongings and meet outside at 09:00 hours. You will be transferred to your billet and then you will start your training. You will come back to Arisaig House and receive your kits and Staff Sergeant Dougal Mc Donald will instruct you in physical training and give you your programme for the next week.' Lieutenant Kerrigan advised them.

There was a scraping of chairs as they all got up to leave. At nine sharp they were outside where last night's truck was waiting for them, the engine ticking over. The truck belched a cloud of grey exhaust and it took off rumbling towards Garramore, which was not more than four miles away. They smoked and chatted and laughed all the way, for them this was the start of an adventure there was no turning back from. They arrived at the cottage; George thought it wasn't so much as a cottage but more like a lodge. It was grey stone and complemented the sky outside which was also grey, and George, at that precise moment, pictured her island with its glorious blue skies and felt a great nostalgia descend on her briefly before her thoughts were interrupted by the voice of Kerrigan ushering them inside the lodge. George and the lads quickly dumped their belongings and went back out again for the journey to Arisaig. At nine thirty a.m., Dougal Mc Donald was waiting for them and took them inside to the now familiar surroundings. They were issued with two thick short wool jackets and trousers, two shirts and two pullovers. Adam joked 'what about underwear', but he quickly quieted down; Dougal cut him short with a stern look. They were given time to change their clothes before Dougal took them out into the field and started their exercise drill to warm them up. From then on it was a gruelling four-hour programme of walking, running and bodily manoeuvres. They stopped for a well-earned lunch of roast venison and potatoes. With their spirits revived, they carried on with the second part of the afternoon, which involved even more gruelling training, where they had to walk on a log six feet up in the air, keeping their balance, climbing rope ladders, nettings and crawling on their bellies through mud tunnels. By the evening they were all dirty, bruised and exhausted, so much so, that by the time they had washed and changed, they could hardly eat the magnificent Angus beef stew served to them at their lodge.

Later when she was alone, George's thoughts turned to Evie; she had hardly been left with any time for thought after the rigours of the day, she missed her and wondered what she was up to and how she would be celebrating the New Year.

The next two days were tough bouts of training and at the end of it, Dougal came in to the lodge, his boots clomping on the floorboards.

'Right lads, George, seeing as its New Year's Eve, we will be celebrating with a supper of roast lamb and drinks afterwards, and tomorrow you have the day off,' Dougal informed them.

They all cheered and sat at the dining table to start their feasting; there was no worrying about hangovers. They tucked into a supper of steaming mulligatawny, followed by the roast with heaps of potatoes and buttery steamed carrots. George stuck to a bottle of port and let the others get on with the whisky. The company became bawdy and there was much jesting and laughter, but she took it all in her stride and she could see that they treated her as one of them, which gave her much pleasure, since she did not want to be treated any different to them. The training was tough; but she was strong and though not as much as the lads, she could see that she was winning their respect. She never complained, just got on with it.

At one minute to midnight, they all stood up, drinks in their hands, counting down the seconds, and on the stroke of the clock's chimes, they burst into song warbling out 'Auld Lang Syne' at the top of their voices; even Dougal joined in, glass in hand, ruddy in the face. George would remember this night for the rest of her life. Neither of them recalled how they got to bed that night.

When George woke up in the morning, she was grateful that there was no training. Though she was nursing a bit of a headache, it was nothing as bad as all the others, who did not surface till lunchtime. She spent the day in her room writing letters to everyone; her mother and father, Gracie, Aunt Marlu and Uncle Ted, Connie, Carmelo and last but not least to Evie. She had to be very careful what to write, not to reveal too much information, since she had signed the official Secrets Act, it had become difficult, but at least she put everyone's mind at rest that she was safe and training somewhere in Scotland. When she had finished, she lay down with the intention of having a nap, but later woke up to find she had missed supper. She went downstairs; it was dark and she assumed that everyone had retired. There was a small fire burning and Dougal was sitting on a stool warming his hands and nursing a generous whisky.

'Hello lass, pull up a stool,' Dougal said kindly, indicating one opposite him.

'It looks like everyone has disappeared,' George said chuckling.

'Aye lass they had a bit too much to drink,' Dougal smiled and continued, 'how are you bearing up?'

'Well, I'd like to think I'm doing fine; I certainly feel a lot fitter than when I started and the lads have treated me well, especially Adam.'

'Aye, that Adam's a good sort, that he is!'

'Dougal, very little has been said to us about this whole training thing, I mean what is going to happen from here?' George quizzed Dougal in the hope that in his mellow mood he would disclose some sort of information.

'I canna say much lass except you are all being prepared for whatever the outcome of this war will be,' he replied, not really pacifying George with his answer.

'But lass I have to ask you, what made you volunteer for this? It's a dangerous state of affairs and…' Dougal was about to say more but thought better of it.

'I was a glove maker in a factory called Arnold's in Malta, it was mundane work, I had started to feel like a cabbage,' she said pursing her lips, 'it just wasn't enough for me, I wanted more, I had a good education, but there was very little work and I didn't want to end up married with a husband and children; don't get me wrong there's absolutely nothing wrong with that,' she retracted quickly, 'I just wanted more, and here I am in what seems a million miles away from the simple life I led back home.'

'Well, there's nothing wrong in wanting to better yourself in life, but you're the first lass I've trained and probably won't be the last the way things are going.'

They stayed in silence watching the flames dancing, their shadows flickering over them, till she felt sleep beckoning her to bed. Bidding goodnight to Dougal, George retired to her room.

The next day the rigid routine started again and the day after that, till a week had passed by and they had transitioned from being unfit to running five miles without breaking a sweat. George had never felt healthier and stronger; her physical training had made her gain muscle, which was the whole idea, as their next bout of training was physical combat. She took to it like a duck to water, to the chagrin of Algie, who was finding that his coordination was non-existent. Dougal observed her with a satisfied look on his face, as far as he was concerned, she was turning out to be a star pupil and good material for MI6's plans for her.

The following week they were made to take thirty-mile hikes all over the Highlands with a basic map and compass. This time they were asked to pair up and George and Adam automatically ended up together. They set out after a hearty breakfast, packing their backpack with all the essentials, a small flask of whisky, water, sandwiches, maps and compass. They were dropped off south of Arisaig and left to find their way back to the lodge. The others were taken in different directions. Adam and George trudged through snow for roughly five miles before they stopped for a quick swig of whisky, for although they were invigorated by the brisk pace they were keeping, the cold was still biting through their clothes. They were at the top of a hill and could see the rough terrain they still had to get through. There were no cottages or buildings in sight. George offered Adam a cigarette and they both puffed away pensively.

'What do you reckon George, do you think we will make it by sundown?'

'I hope so, I would hate to be lost out here in the dark.'

'Christ, what a difference from where you come from ay George?' Adam commented.

'To be honest Adam, I still can't believe I'm here and what's in store for us, they haven't been very clear, except that our lives might be in danger.'

'Hmm I think that they are definitely going to send us overseas, my gut feeling is France.'

'What makes you think that?'

'Think about it, George! Hitler has invaded Poland, so the next move is for him to invade the Low Countries and then France, though it's being called a 'phony' war at the moment because nothing is happening, but something tells me that Hitler will be on the move in the next few months!' Adam said.

George mulled over Adam's words, if it was true that she would be sent to France, then she would have to make arrangements to let her family know that she would be out of contact for a while and she supposed she would have to write to Gracie and get her to send her suitcase to her Aunt Marlu.

Adam broke through her thoughts, 'I suppose we ought to make a move.'

'Yes, at least we're on the right track, we just have to head in the direction of those hills in the distance that will cover another fifteen miles' George said as she consulted the map and compass. They set off, George ahead of Adam and him following in her footsteps. It was about one o'clock when they stood at the top of the last hill, they could see Arisaig, a tiny dot in the far distance. There was a thick copse that lay in between, which they would have hike through. They decided to stop and eat their sandwiches. They chose a flattish rock and sat down. Adam munched enthusiastically on his cheese sandwich and George watched him, amused.

'So, what part of London do you come from?'

'Hmm Walthamstow, it's in East London,' Adam replied finishing the last mouthful of his sandwich.

'I've never been, what's it like?'

'It's all right I suppose, I've lived there all my life, the people are a friendly lot and we have a grand greyhound stadium and all.' The last he said rather proudly.

'What's that then, the greyhound stadium?' George asked.

'It's a stadium where greyhound dogs are raced and you place bets on which one you think will be the winner.'

'Gosh that must be exciting to watch!'

'Yes, it is rather, though you can end up with your pockets empty!'

Adam laughed as he said that and lit two cigarettes, giving one to George.

'Goodness is that the time!' she exclaimed as she glanced at her watch, which said one thirty.

'Yes, it certainly is and we had better put our best foot forward so to speak, because I have a horrible sinking feeling that we will arrive in darkness,' Adam said.

Adam wasn't far wrong; it was a nearly five thirty when they saw the lodge come into view. They were looking the worse for wear; the last part of their hard slog was through some very rough terrain and they were both covered in cuts and bruises. The lodge was a welcome sight though, there were no lights showing, they put on their black-out torches to guide them the rest of the way. Once inside they helped themselves to whisky to warm themselves up. The others had not returned yet; they were left to their own devices. Dougal waited pacing the floor, occasionally looking out of one of the bay windows. Eventually Reggie, Hamish and Algie turned up, covered in mud and twigs.

'About time!' Dougal said, not amused.

'Sorry Dougal, we sort of got lost cutting through a meadow we thought would be a shortcut.' Reggie finished off meekly and with a rather embarrassed look on his face, especially when he saw George and Adam standing by the fire obviously pleased with themselves being the first to return.

All of them were by now drinking glasses of whisky, which soon revived their spirits and had them talking animatedly. Dougal broke up the talking, to advise them that in the morning they were to tackle weapons handling and to get an early night; it was going to be intensive and needed full concentration. Algie looked on disinterestedly as if he already knew the subject. He was in fact making a fool of himself because so far, he had failed in the map-reading and compass exercises and was fast losing respect from his fellow companions. George thought the man a pompous arsed idiot! Algie's behaviour did not go unnoticed by Dougal, who was fast losing his patience with the man and that was saying something, because Dougal, though disciplined, was patience incarnate! So, none of the others were surprised when Dougal informed them that Algie had been sent to do some special training, or rather a polite and discreet way of saying he had been kicked out. Nobody saw him leave and nobody was bothered.

CHAPTER 13

It dawned bright with a partially clouded sky but bitterly cold. George and the lads stamped their feet to get some warmth into them. There was a small arsenal of weapons: Sten guns, two carbines on a stand, Webley service revolvers as well as a Welrod silencer gun and two Colt.38 pistols on a small trestle table. Dougal set about quenching their curiosity pointing at each gun, its name, its use and the size of the bullet calibre.

There were targets set up in the field for the hand guns as well as the carbines. After they practiced with the carbines, which gave a solid kick from the butt into their shoulders, they all had to take five minutes to rub the injured spot, which would inevitably have them sporting a good bruise the next day. They were next told to choose a pistol. George went straight for the Colt which was small and fitted the palm of her hand like a glove. Dougal made her shoot first. She missed the stationary figure target as her hand slid sideways upon pulling the trigger. Dougal made her try again, this time she hit the target square in the middle. George grinned, feeling a certain satisfaction and got a slap on the back from Adam. Reggie was next, followed by Hamish and then Adam. They were all good shots especially Reggie, whose Sandhurst training paid off. They shot a number of rounds till they felt confident about pulling the trigger, and Dougal, pleased with their progress, called them to stop for a lunch break. They walked back to the lodge, joking and ribbing each other about who was the best shot.

'Aye lads, you were all good, but you have to watch out for George here,' he winked as he said the words and George beamed. But the training wasn't over yet for the day, a harder course awaited them in the afternoon. They were taken to a different field this time, where a life-sized figure suspended on a winch suddenly came at them from a small wood that they were made to walk through. This was a different kettle of fish, and they found it rather disconcerting. Reggie fell over twice, George missed six targets out of eight, Adam got caught by surprise when walking around a shed and Hamish was the only one to hit almost all targets. Dougal scratched his head in frustration and set them to do the field all over again. This time around they all fared a little better.

'Listen up, you have to do better than this, if you're surprised by the enemy, it's you or them; you won't get a second chance; your reflexes have to be faster, sharper, your life depends on it!' Dougal all but barked at them.

By the time training had finished they had improved considerably, at least enough for Dougal to nod with a hint of satisfaction in his eyes. They were tired and in need of a wash and change of clothes. The truck picked them up and drove them to Garramore Lodge. They were relieved to arrive and when the truck returned to take them back for supper, George refrained and decided to stay in her room. It was just past ten when she heard a knock on her door.

'George it's me Adam, are you awake?' he said in a loud whisper.

George put on her dressing gown and opened the door.

'Come in Adam,' George said, 'is everything all right?'

'Yes, everything's fine, I was just listening to the wireless and it looks like England is to start rationing, can you believe it!'

'Gosh that's not good news is it, I suppose it also means that things are very serious,' George said, 'but is that what you wanted to talk to me about?'

'No there is something else actually; I overheard a conversation between Dougal and this other man I've never seen before, but from what I gathered, we are to be sent over to France for observation purposes.'

'I see, to be honest I have been thinking about where this training here in Scotland is all leading to.'

'Look George, you won't let on, will you? I mean I wasn't supposed to be listening in on the conversation as you might have guessed.'

'Don't be daft Adam, I would never breathe a word, and thank you for telling me because this puts things into perspective for me, I have to put plans I had into action.'

'Well, I just wanted to let you know. Anyway, I will bid you good night and see you in the morning.'

George was calm about the news that Adam had just imparted to her, she was half expecting that her role would involve something to do with

France. After all, in her interviews she was constantly being challenged about her ability to speak French fluently. But having things confirmed for her and the role she was to play in this war, took on a different aspect. She was glad she had written the letters to all her loved ones. She would not need to share a room with Gracie for one, and she would have to write to Evie and tell her in no uncertain terms, that she wasn't sure when they would meet next.

When George woke up the next morning, the lads were already at breakfast. George wasn't hungry, so she settled for some tea. Adam caught her eye and smiled. George was reminded of Adam's conversation the night before. She was determined to excel in her training, she wanted to be prepared as much as possible under the circumstances. They had weapons training again that day and this time they did not fail, hitting ninety percent of their targets. Dougal taught them to tuck the Sten gun into their hip rather than take aim and to fire two simultaneous shots. The next few weeks had them tackling demolition and rail sabotage, silent killing and field craft, but George's *pièce de résistance* came when they started to learn Morse code, she excelled at it, which was just as well, since it was to be one of her main tasks, as she would find out later. They had been in training for 8 weeks when one day Dougal quite simply told them that they had completed their training and were being flown out the next evening to yet another training venue, this time to learn how to parachute. There was much merrymaking and joking on their last night together, even Dougal joined in, for they all knew they would never see him again.

It was dusk, twenty sixth February by the time they reached Altrincham, a town in Trafford, which was some eight miles outside of the centre of Manchester. They were deposited in billets at Dunham House on the Charcoal Road. They were briefed as to their surroundings, this was to be their home for the next four weeks, to learn parachute jumping. They were shown to their rooms and then told to go for some supper. They deposited their kitbags and went to the dining room. George was almost too tired to eat, but the hot beef stew and buttered bread to mop up with, was too inviting to miss out on. After supper they were addressed by staff Sergeant Grimes, who informed them that roll call the next morning would be at 06:00 hours. At this they pulled a face.

Sergeant Grimes asked them if they had any questions.

'Sir is there a phone box nearby?' George asked.

'Nearest one is in town in Manchester,' Sergeant Grimes replied.

'Any more questions?' he asked again.

'Sir, most of us have run out of fags!' Reggie Grenfield stated.

'Right lads, Miss Parker you will be able to go into town tomorrow afternoon, the transport will be leaving at four thirty p.m. sharp. I suggest you get everything you need because you will only be able to go in once a week for your personal things.'

George finally crept into bed, she didn't know what hit her, for she slept soundly till her alarm went off at five a.m. She groaned… getting out of bed to wash and dress was an effort. All the men were already sitting at the dining table tucking into their breakfast. George helped herself to some steaming porridge and placed a small dollop of strawberry jam on the top.

'Want some tea George?' Adam offered whilst getting up to pour some for himself.

'Yes, please Adam.'

'I slept like a log, how about you lot?' Hamish asked in his broad Scottish accent.

'I didn't quite get off to sleep as quickly as I had hoped, too much on my mind,' Reggie answered.

'I'm rather looking forward to this training lark,' Adam chimed in.

'Well, I know I am!' George exclaimed.

'Yes, I think it's all rather exciting,' Reggie added.

No sooner had Reggie finished his sentence than a burly RAF sergeant walked in briskly.

'Good morning gentlemen, Miss Parker, my name is Sergeant Peter Smythe, if you could all follow me please.'

This was met with the scraping of chairs whilst getting up to follow him. He led them to a huge hangar; there were all sorts of planes parked on the airfield, Lysanders, Spitfires, Hurricanes, a de Havilland—the same they arrived on from Scotland, plus a number of vehicles. They came to a halt in front of various pieces of equipment designed for jumping from. George inspected the harnessing hanging from the ceiling she felt anxious at the thought of jumping from such a height, let alone doing it from an aircraft. Adam sensed her apprehension and squeezed her arm reassuringly.

'Right lads,' barked Sergeant Smythe, 'there's your individual harnesses and jumpsuits over there on the trestle table, there's one for each of you, please stand next to your kits and observe carefully as we demonstrate how they are to be worn. Give it your full attention, you want to make sure you get it right first time round if you want to live!' The new recruits looked at each other feigning bravado.

George noticed that this time Sergeant Smythe did not make reference to her as a female, this pleased her immensely. They followed the instructions and put on their parachute harnesses and helmets and followed the instructor to the first rig, where their parachute harness was attached to a rope. They had to swing, which brought much laughter, though George remained grim as the swinging made her feel queasy and was glad when they moved on to the next rig, which had them slide down a chute and fall with their legs tucked in tight on a padded landing. The day was spent repeating the manoeuvres over and over again, till it was second nature to them. It was a relief for everyone when the day came to an end. She was apprehensive about the parachute training; she did not feel confident at all about jumping and got all the more worked up about it the next day when they had to jump from a barrage balloon with planes flying in the background. Tatton Park was noisy and as George found out, it made it difficult to concentrate. They got into the balloon's basket two at a time and as soon as it had reached a thousand feet they jumped. George felt the strange sensation of falling and as her parachute opened, she felt herself being pulled up with a lurch and then started falling rapidly again. She landed with a thump as speed ate up the ground and just like that, it was over. With the initial shock over, George felt a little easier about the rest of the training. Sergeant Smythe called it a day at four o'clock and told them that there was a truck waiting to take them into the town so they could get whatever personal items they needed. They were all looking forward to this little break in their training regime; since Scotland they had not had any time to top up their cigarette stash and personal items. George was especially looking forward to phoning Evie, she hoped that she would find her at home.

The drive into Manchester High Street did not take long and all the recruits were happy to wander among civilisation again after the long weeks of training in Scotland. George spotted a phone box, turning round to Adam, Reggie and Hamish, she informed them that she would meet them outside the Salutation Arms Pub which was just across the road from where she was standing.

They agreed to meet in an hour, which was when the truck would be back to collect them. George opened the telephone box and once inside she lifted the mouth piece off its cradle, she fished out some pennies and pushed them in the slot and dialled Evie's number. The telephone rang a number of times but nobody answered. George was crestfallen, she was so looking forward to speaking to Evie. She left the telephone box and walked to a café nearby and went inside. She ordered a pot of tea and sat drinking it, people-watching at the same time from the window. When she had finished, she paid her bill and went to the tobacconists next door to the café. She bought two cartons of *Craven A* and left the shop walking to the telephone box. She dialled Evie's number and this time she answered.

'Evie its George!' hardly containing her excitement, 'Oh I've missed you terribly, how are you darling?'

'Oh my God! how wonderful, I was going mad not hearing from you, I only received your letter two days ago; I'm missing you too sweetheart, are you OK?'

'Yes, I'm fine, a lot of training for this and that, but now I'm looking forward to a break but I'm not sure when that will be darling, please wait for me; I keep getting worried you will get bored of waiting,' George told her, her voice wavering.

'My sweetheart, my love, please don't worry about anything, I will be here when you get back and we will make up for the time we have not been together,' Evie told her reassuringly.

'Darling I have to go, because I don't have any more coins but I promise I will write to you tonight, and call you again soon, I love you Evie,' she said, all in one breath.

'Goodbye sweetheart, I love you too.'

George heard the click of the receiver ending the telephone call. Elated, she walked over to the *Salutation* and went inside. The lads were all there drinking pints and she joined them.

'You look on top of the world George, who have you been talking to?' Hamish asked winking at the others.

'Yes, George, what have you been up to?' Adam and Reggie said in unison.

George blushed.

'None of your business you wretched lot, now get me a half of bitter please,' George demanded laughing at them.

They carried on ribbing her till the conversation turned to a news item that everyone was talking about: The conscription of able-bodied men aged between nineteen and twenty-seven. There had been a lull in the air since war had been declared on Germany; nothing had happened, not a sound from Hitler, they had been calling it the 'phony' war but the sudden call-up had spread alarm. There was much talk among the youths who were standing next to them laughing at how they would slaughter the 'jerries' and passing patriotic remarks, but all were in agreement about signing up. The others listened in, quietly aware of what their part in the war was to be. Though they were never given any precise details, they were not fools, and by now had gathered enough from their training that they were destined for a secret mission of sorts. George never imparted with the information that Adam had given her, apart from respecting Adam, who had been a good friend to her and had supported her throughout the training they were going through, maintaining silence was a matter of life and death in their line of work.

There had been times where she wanted to tell Adam about Evie, about how she felt, but she knew that she could never breathe a word about her tendencies; she knew it would never be accepted, not by Adam or anyone else, it would be a secret she would have to carry with her for the rest of her life.

Hamish saw the truck driver through the pub bay window pull up by the pavement and hastened the others to finish up their drinks. They left the pub and clambered into the truck.

Chapter 14

The next day the recruits were informed they were to make the first of four daylight jumps. George's heart was in her mouth, she had been dreading this and had hoped it would not be quite so soon. They kitted up and were driven to Ringway Airport where a Whitley was waiting for them. They helped each other into the aircraft and sat opposite one another. George's mouth was dry and she could see that the rest of her colleagues were in a similar state of apprehension. They all lit up a cigarette as the bomber's engines coughed into life. The engines gathered momentum and whined to a sharp pitch. The pilots were given the all clear to taxi the runway and the plane trundled, swaying from side to side as the wings picked up air beneath them. It seemed like an eternity to George till the aircraft lifted, but it did and once up, flew smoothly till it banked to the right. Sergeant Smythe was with them waiting by the hatch on the floor of the aircraft. Over the noise of the engines, he shouted out orders for them to crouch and swing their legs over the hatch. He hooked each one of them to the static line which would rip the parachutes open as they jumped. The aircraft reached a height of ten thousand feet; George was the first in line. She put herself in position; her last thought was 'God help me' the red light turned to green and she jumped. Her parachute opened immediately, hovered for a few seconds, the wind catching it, viciously jerking her up, before floating like a giant kite; the ground below seemed a long way down. For a few seconds she felt weightless, then the ground rushed up to her. She landed with a thump rolling to a stop, the parachute collapsing on top of her, a heap of silk.
The others followed suit and were up rapidly grabbing their parachutes and folding them haphazardly. George got up and carried her chute to where Sergeant Smyth was waiting. They gathered around him.

'Well done lads, not bad for the first jump, four more of these and you will be out of here.'

They finished their training by the eighteenth of March and were glad to learn that they were to be given a week off before their next destination.

George was excited by this prospect, mainly because she had not anticipated the time off so soon and it meant that she was going to see Evie. They were all dropped off at Manchester Piccadilly train station to catch the train to London Euston. The station was packed with a sea of khaki and blue uniforms waiting to be shifted to various barracks. Soon they would all be mobilised and sent off to France, for that was where the war would start in earnest, as speculation grew. George gave an excuse to the others and disappeared to find a telephone box. The telephone box was out of order, so she made her way back to the others on the platform. They lit a cigarette and smoked till the train approached the platform some ten minutes later. When the train stopped, the doors opened and passengers poured out in an endless stream. They waited till most of the crowds abated before getting into a second-class compartment. Adam helped George put her kit bag on the rack and they all settled on the seats.

'Bloody hell I'm glad for this break I'm telling you,' Reggie uttered.

Hamish who was normally the quiet one, looked at all of them in turn and said, 'I know you are all happy for this time off we're getting, but I just want to say how glad I am to have had the chance to get to know you all.'

'Same here Hamish old fellow,' Adam said.

'Hang on Hamish you can't get rid of us that fast, we have the next stage in a week,' Reggie added.

'That's right Hamish and I suppose after spending so much time together, it's going to seem a bit odd not seeing each other.' George understood full well why Hamish had said what he did. Because she knew that he had no family and was going to feel out on a limb without them. That's what camaraderie did to you, you became brothers-in-arms, so to speak. They got into Euston and each went their own way. George found another telephone box and called Evie but there was no reply so she made her way to the Fulham Road to Evie's apartment. When she got there, she rang the bell but there was no answer, so she sat on the doorstep with her kitbag next to her and waited. A few hours had passed when she saw Evie get off the bus and watched her walking towards her,

her heart swelling with love. Evie's eyes beamed when she saw George. They waited till they got inside the door and embraced, hardly daring to believe that they were together again. They climbed the stairs to the sitting room. These days Evie kept all the curtains around the apartment permanently closed. She went around switching the lights on.

'George darling this is such a wonderful surprise,' she said kissing her deeply. George held on to her girlfriend, wanting to savour the feel of her body against her. They remained entwined for a long time. It was George who broke the embrace to look at Evie lovingly.

'I want to see your face,' pausing, 'I've waited so long to see you, I carried your image in my mind, every night I pictured you before I slept.'

'Well then we must do something about it, I can't have you imagining my face, we must get our photo taken,' Evie smiled.

'Yes, I would like that a lot.'

George smiled with pleasure.

Evie disengaged herself to put the wireless on and went back to George holding her hand and leading her to the settee.

'Darling how long have we got?'

'We have just over a week, I have to report back on Monday the 25th March,'

'That's wonderful, we can explore a bit of London then because I know you haven't really seen much since you've been here.'

'No, I haven't seen much at all, I would love it!'

'Shall we make some tea darling? You can then freshen up afterwards if that's OK with you.'

'That would be lovely, I'm really thirsty and the tea on the train was awful, what with the rationing and all, the tea lady only put half a teaspoon of sugar and it was expensive too,' George complained.

'Hmm yes I've been having some problems getting rations myself, just as soon as the public were informed of the rationing everyone went mad and bought out the shops, thank God everything has calmed down now. I'm lucky because my clients have been helping me out, so I have plenty of sugar and I also managed to get four eggs yesterday, it's obvious there is a black market going on, not that I condone it of course, but at least I can get the essentials!' Evie said.

George went quiet at the mention of the word 'clients' and Evie picked up on it straight away.

'Darling I've kept my promise; there have been no extra services, honestly!' Evie reassured her.

George looked at Evie holding both her hands in hers.

'I'm sorry I should not have doubted you, it's just I'm so frightened of losing you, you're the best thing that's ever happened to me and with me being away a lot, well... that worries me,' she ended.

'Sweetheart, I know my work is not conventional to say the least, I'm not happy doing it but as I have explained to you before, it pays the bills and affords me a good life, but that's all; my heart is yours, George, so please don't worry, you have enough on your plate as it is. Just keep in touch with me as much as you can and when it's possible, we will spend time together, these are difficult times and we just have to be here for each other,' she finished off, kissing George on the lips.

'Thank you for reassuring me.'

With that Evie went into the kitchen to brew some tea and George went to the bathroom to freshen up and change.

'George!' shouted Evie from the kitchen, 'I was thinking that you should just get your stuff from Peckham and leave it here at my place, I mean it will save you travelling to get your suitcase, I really don't mind you know.'

George came out of the bathroom with her toothbrush in her mouth.

'Are you sure, I mean if you don't mind, I'd be really happy to do that, I had intended to write to Gracie to forward my suitcase to Aunt Marlu.'

'Really sweetheart it won't inconvenience me; I can just store it under my bed.'

'Well, that's super then, perhaps we can do it one day this week, I will call Peggy and ask her when Gracie will be home, because the last time she wrote to me, Gracie said she was off training with the *ATS* somewhere up country. I'm sure it won't be a problem, I have a key anyway, I will just hand it over to Peggy after I've cleared out my stuff.'

'That's settled then, let's get it over and done with tomorrow, you can call Peggy now if you like.'

George called Peggy, who told her that Gracie was in fact away and had no idea when she was returning, however it was not a problem for her to collect her suitcase. She agreed to picking it up in the afternoon.

'I've sorted the suitcase thing out; we can collect it tomorrow afternoon.'

'That's super; the tea's brewed so come and sit down and talk to me about what you would like to do whilst you're here.'

'Trafalgar Square, Buckingham Palace; I'd like to see Big Ben and the Houses of Parliament and all that kind of stuff really, oh and I wouldn't mind going to see a show,'

'We can do all that and more,' Evie smiled, amused by George's child-like enthusiasm.

A surge of tenderness enveloped George; this woman whom she had known a matter of weeks filled her heart with crazy feelings of fluttering butterflies. There was no doubt about it, she was very much in love with Evie. She just looked at her lovingly and grasped her to her and kissed her deeply, her stomach flipping triple somersaults.

Evie felt George tremble and pulled her head to her neck; George kissed the pulse that was beating fast against her lips. Evie let out a groan of pleasure; hearing her, George moved to her breasts, sucking each nipple in turn feeling them harden in her mouth. Evie was helpless and could not stand the ache between her legs and guided George's hand to enter her. George felt her arch her back feeling her wetness and with slow but deft movements she brought her to an explosive climax. Evie lay quivering in George's arms. George watched her completely awestruck at what had happened. They had made love countless times but this was different, this was deep, an exclusive bonding of two women who were completely immersed in each other. It had begun to rain softly, the raindrops splashing against the window, Evie stirred wanting George, wanting her body, wanting to love this woman in every way possible, she made love to her, every touch, every kiss, permeating her soul to the point that when George reached ecstasy, tears poured down her face and Evie kissed them. They lay in each other's embrace for what seemed like hours, even as the first light of dawn seeped through the miniscule parting in the curtains, neither of them wanted to move. It was around eleven a.m. when they finally stirred, content and sated, they drifted to the kitchen to make a pot of tea, both glancing at one another hardly believing what had passed between them, not willing to be an inch apart, it was as if they were sewn at the seams.

They made their way to Peckham to pick up George's suitcase as planned. Peggy was at home waiting for them, George introduced Evie to Peggy and they sat down at the kitchen table.

'How lovely to see you, it's been a while, where have you been?' Peggy asked as she put the kettle on to make a brew.

'I've been mainly in Scotland and Manchester; they are moving us around a lot at the moment Peggy.'

'Well, that's hardly surprising with the rumours filtering through to us every day; the papers are full of snippets about Poland and Germany,' Peggy said. 'There's talk of a May election, Chamberlain won't win it again, there's very little confidence in him; there's that Winston Churchill chap who is predicted to take over,' Peggy carried on.

'Well, whoever is elected Peggy, he'd better make sure he knows what he's doing, because by the looks of things, everything is going from bad to worse, I mean what with the rationing and all, it's just creating so much hardship for everyone,' George said ruefully.

Evie, who until that point, had remained quiet said, 'The thing is there has to be a change of government, though Chamberlain's intentions have been in the best interest trying to keep Britain out of the war, it still won't keep this war from happening and Hitler has his eye on us.'

The prospect of the future lay heavy on the three women, who drank their tea pensively. Peggy brought over a copy of *The Daily Mirror,* showing a picture of a Heinkel Bomber shot down in East Lothian in Scotland.

'It's definitely started hasn't it?' George exclaimed.

The other two nodded.

After they had finished their tea, George went upstairs and opened Gracie's room, retrieving her suitcase from under the bed and taking it downstairs.

'Peggy, I've got the rent for February and for this month for you because it's only fair I pay my half, at least Gracie can then decide what she wants to do, have you heard from her?' George enquired.

'Yes, she called yesterday; she said she would be arriving here Friday twenty ninth March,' she walked over to check the calendar she had hanging on the wall behind them.

'Oh good, would you mind giving her Evie's number so we can at least meet?'

'Yes of course my dear, just write it down for me.'

George wrote down the number and gave it to her and returned her key.

They left and went back to the apartment. They had decided to do nothing for the rest of the day except to spend time together, listening to music, cooking and eating.

'Darling I wish you could talk to me more about what you are doing at the moment,' Evie said out of the blue.

George looked at her feeling torn, not wanting Evie to feel that she didn't trust her.

'I wish I could darling; all I can say is I'm sworn to secrecy; I was made to sign the official Secrets Act and that leaves me very little that I can talk about. I'm working for the government and I'm just not allowed to part with any information, I'm sorry hon, I feel a bit awkward not being able to tell you anything,' George said reluctantly.

'It's OK, I understand and to be honest it doesn't really matter as long as your life isn't in any danger, I was just being nosey,' Evie said, laughing.

'Well, the only danger I'm in is having fallen for you!' George chuckled, glad that she had averted a most uncomfortable moment.

They kissed after George's remark and ended up making love on the rug by the fireplace. They remained intertwined for what seemed like ages till Evie shifted stiffly and suggested that they go to bed.

CHAPTER 15

The smell of frying bacon wafting into the bedroom woke George up. Evie had made them breakfast and brewed a pot of tea. Whilst drinking their tea Evie suggested they do some sightseeing that day. After they had bathed and changed, they headed towards Trafalgar Square. George was in awe of Nelson's column and the beautiful space it was erected in, with pigeons flying overhead and flocking around them as they fed them with a tuppence bag from an old man who made his living selling the feed to tourists. It was magnificent, so was Buckingham Palace with its changing of the guard in their smart red-and-black uniforms. They explored Soho with its bohemian bars and cafes. They got a tram which took them past Big Ben and the Houses of Parliament and headed to Tower Bridge. George marvelled at the intricate design of the bridge. They walked across watching the murky grey Thames flow rapidly beneath them. Occasionally they looked at each other and smiled knowingly. They stopped at a café and enjoyed a pot of tea before going on to the West End again to watch a show. It was late when the show finished, so they took a taxi home. Evie lit a fire as soon as they got in.

'It's been a lovely day darling, thank you,' George said, feeling content as she sat on the sofa.

Evie sat next to her and cuddled up pushing her arm through George's.

'Hmm I haven't been this happy for a long time,' she murmured.

'Nor I, my love,' George replied, putting her arms around her and pulling her on top as she laid the full length of the sofa. They must have fallen asleep; the fire had died down and the room had gotten cold.

'I'll make some cocoa for us, how about that?'

'Hmm lovely,' George responded sleepily.

George looked at her watch and saw that it was one fifteen a.m. She got up to peep outside and saw that it was raining. She smelt the cocoa wafting from the kitchen and went over to where Evie was standing sipping at her mug of cocoa. George lit them both a cigarette. They were ensconced in a place that offered them shelter from the world outside; acknowledging that their time together was coming to an end.

George especially feared that communicating was going to be difficult, they had said as much in their last training. They were not going to be able to keep in touch with anyone once their training was complete. She wondered how she was going to tell Evie; the fear of losing her was constantly on her mind; how could she explain that her impending covert missions required complete isolation from everyone she loved. Her only communication would be with HQ, whoever they were, for she still did not know. As for Evie, she decided she would cross that bridge when she came to it.

For now, all she wanted to do is lay in bed with her, breathe her smell and feel her soft skin. As if anticipating George's thoughts, Evie took George by the hand and led her to the bedroom. She undressed her tenderly and pulled her to the bed and got in with her. Their lovemaking was soft and sensual, every time it was different and every time George was in awe of the deep emotions she already felt for this woman, her lover, her friend.

The few days they had sped by, Evie took her to art museums, walked the streets of the East End, went to shows on Shaftsbury Avenue as well taking her for jellied eels at Tubby Isaacs' in Aldgate East.

It was Friday afternoon and Evie had to go out to do one of her 'jobs.' George found herself at a loose end and was lazily reading a book and listening to the wireless when the telephone rang. It was Gracie.

She was excited to know that George was in town and asked if they could meet up at *The Gateways* the next evening. George said she would check with Evie to make sure she had nothing on and it was more than likely they would be there. They agreed on a time and finished the conversation. George had missed Gracie, she had been with her from the time she left Malta almost six months ago, and so much had happened since then. Gracie had seen her transition from a confused woman to one who was sure of her direction, sure of what she wanted. Since then, she had not worn her men's clothing but she had still kept everything, just in case. She felt it was not the last time she would be wearing them.

Evie found George dozing on the sofa when she came in. She placed a kiss on her nose, George's eyes opened and she smiled.

'Hmm hello love, I'm so happy you're back.'

'Yes, I'm back and that's it, till you leave on Monday,' she said smiling from ear to ear, 'and now I'm gasping for a cup of tea and I can't wait to get out of this dress.'

'Hmm please do!' George insinuated cheekily.

'Why don't you come and help me then?' Evie taunted with a wanton smile, forgetting all about the tea.

Of course, George could not resist such an invitation and she had just got past undoing the sixth button when the dress slipped off to reveal Evie's delicious curves, making her so very desirable. They ravished each other over and over again till they lay exhausted in each other's arms. Evie got up and brought over her pack of cigarettes and lit one for each of them.

Whilst they were smoking, Evie said, 'Darling, the gentleman I escorted this evening was telling me something rather interesting, he was a bit inebriated to start with and he got worse as the evening wore on, but anyway, he was telling me of this covert operation underway to start a training school for spies, I couldn't help wondering if you are in any way involved in this.'

George looked at her wondering just how much she could actually reveal.

'In all honesty I don't know, all I was told in the beginning was that I had been chosen to go on a mission that meant a fifty percent chance of never coming back, I agreed, had I known you then I would not have volunteered for it, I still don't know what I'm going to be doing, I have been contemplating telling you at the right time, but there never is a right time for this sort of thing is there? But whatever it is or wherever they are sending me, my darling, I will carry you in my heart.'

Evie was silent, George turned over to face her... she could see her eyes were wet.

'Oh sweetheart, please don't cry, I can't bear it!' utterly distressed.

They clung to each other and they stayed that way till the morning. It was George who woke up first for a change. This whole week had been a much-needed rest from the early wake up calls. She slipped out of bed, and put on Evie's dressing gown. She knew where everything was and set about boiling the kettle. She buttered some bread and spread some precious strawberry jam she found in the pantry. She went into the sitting room, put coal from the bucket in the fire and put on the wireless finding Radio Luxembourg. The kettle was boiling; George shifted to the kitchen, poured the hot water into the teapot and put it on the tray. Picking up the tray she shuffled to the bedroom to find Evie sitting up, propped by a pillow behind her, smoking a cigarette.

'You can wake me up every morning this way George,' Evie chuckled.

George beamed with pleasure, placing the laden tray on the bed. She served Evie a cup of tea and then poured one for herself, savouring its hot sweetness sitting opposite her.

'Darling I forgot to tell you, Gracie rang me yesterday evening and asked to meet us at *Gateways*; I said I would check with you first.'

'Hmm I haven't been there since I first met you; yes, I would love to go there, because this time I will be going in with *you*,' Evie said fervently.

That evening they took special care to dress up. They knew they looked good and made a lovely couple, George especially wanted Gracie to see just how happy she was with Evie. She wanted to be stared at when she walked in with her, it was a complete turnaround from the shy George who walked in the first time. She hoped that that Griff woman wouldn't be there, because for the first time, she felt a tinge of jealousy at the thought of anyone making eyes at Evie. Little did George know that Evie felt exactly the same way! They had agreed to meet outside *Gateways* on Brewers Street.

Sure enough, Gracie was there waiting with a cigarette hanging between her lips, which she threw down upon seeing the two women walking towards her.

'George my mate, it's been ages, I've missed you!' she exclaimed as she bear-hugged George, 'Hello Evie love, how are you?'

'Good to see you Gracie,' Evie returned warmly.

'Let's get inside out of this cold!'

Gateways was chock full, since its announcement that it was closing down that evening, the clientele tripled. The bar had a double layer of customers waiting to be served and the atmosphere was a jovial one, with the gramophone playing in the background and couples dancing. Gracie waved a number of times to people she knew as she tried to find a table for them, which was proving to be impossible, since they had all been taken.

'It looks like we're going to have to stand tonight ladies,' Gracie said.

They attempted to get to the bar and order some drinks. Some fifteen minutes later they stood at the corner of the bar — the only empty bit — enjoying their drinks. Evie danced with the grace of a terpsichore... all the women in the club eyed her with envy, and George... her heart swelled with pride echoing her radiant smile whilst looking at her gorgeous girlfriend.

Gracie was happy to just look around and drink her pint of bitter. As more women came in, it got very crowded and very smoky and after a while Evie and George gave up and returned to standing next to Gracie.

'Have you ever seen it crowded like this before?' George asked.

'No mate I haven't, that's because this is the last time it's supposedly opening its doors and there are a lot of new faces here tonight too, quite a few of them in uniform, I see,' Gracie replied.

They stayed late, acknowledging that this would probably also be the last time they would meet all together here in a long time. The bell at the bar rang for last orders.

'I'll get them in,' Evie offered.

'Cheers Evie.'

'George, we haven't had much time to talk, but I just wanted to tell you how happy I am for you both, you've found yourself a keeper there mate, take care of her because I can see she is totally smitten with you and she's a real sweetheart too. Oh, and by the way I wanted to let you know I have to let the room go at Peggy's, especially now that you are staying with Evie!'

'Thanks Gracie, I paid my half of the rent up till the end of this month, so you are OK till then.'

I'm off to start pilot training next week and I will be billeted in close proximity to the barracks, so I don't know when I'm going to see you again, but Evie has given me her address and I will write to you there and let you know where I am.

'Take care of yourself my dearest friend and when this blessed war is over, we will hopefully see each other again,' with a lump in her throat she embraced her, almost reluctant to let go.

Evie returned with their drinks. The place had started to empty, last drinks were downed and punters made their way towards the door. The three women also drank theirs and did the same.

Outside, the air was freezing. They hugged and said goodbye again and waited for a taxi to come by. Since Gracie was on her own and going in the opposite direction, they let her take the first available one. They did not have far to go to the Fulham Road. Another taxi soon came along and they got in, thankful to be out of the cold. In the dark of the vehicle, they held hands discreetly, enjoying the sensation of the illicit gesture. The cabbie exchanged chatter of no real interest to the two women, who were just looking forward to getting home; it had become their sanctuary especially since there were less than forty-eight hours left for them to enjoy. They wanted them to be a lifetime, but they knew that was not going to be anywhere near possible...

The taxi pulled to a stop in front of the front door. They paid and went inside. It was dark but lights in the sitting room soon turned the darkness into a cosy enclosure. They had whisky together to end their lovely evening and went to bed getting as close to each other as possible. They made love desperately, harbouring an ache, a sense of loss, both unable to explain the emotions they were feeling because tomorrow, Sunday, was their last day together. Though Evie never really questioned George's vocation, she knew it would take her away, she knew this could possibly be the last time she would see her. She had never experienced this kind of happiness, this love that grew so quickly with total abandon. She held tightly onto her, who reciprocated, as if reading Evie's thoughts. It had started to rain. George listened to the pattering on the window panes mingling with Evie's gentle breathing. She stretched her arm over to the bedside cupboard and felt for the pack of cigarettes, pulled one out and lit it. The room was very dark, all she could see was the glowing tip of the cigarette. Every time she drew on the cigarette a small red halo lit up the dark, enough to see Evie's profile. Evie shifted and lifted her head and saw that George was smoking. She switched on her bedside lamp, making George shut her eyes at the sudden brightness.

'Shall I light one for you darling?'

'Please.'

George lit one and placed it between her lips. They had an ashtray balanced between them. She stroked Evie's bare arm which was out of the bed covers. According to the little clock on Evie's side of the bed, it was three forty-five in the morning. They said nothing, because there *was* nothing more to say, there were no words to console them. Evie put her cigarette out, she switched off the light and they both slept in each other's arms till way after it had dawned. They had no plans for the day except to spend time with each other, neither of them wanting anything to disturb the last few hours together. They had breakfast, listened to the wireless, talked about the future, as bleak as it looked, both hoping there would be one together. They talked about George's impending departure.

CHAPTER 16

At ten o'clock the telephone rang, it was Aunt Marlu asking George if she wanted to go over to them for lunch. George explained that she had intended spending the day with her best friend Evie, to which her aunt replied that she could bring her along too. George knew she couldn't get out of not going, so she accepted.

'Darling we're invited to lunch at my aunt's; I'm sorry I couldn't get out of it,' George told her.

'It's all right darling, I don't mind going, it will be nice to meet part of your family,'

They washed and dressed and left in three quarters of an hour and made it to Guildford, where they found both her aunt and uncle waiting. They drove the short way to Bramley and were soon settled in the sitting room. Uncle Ted poured sherry into four crystal goblets and gave one to each of them.

'It's lovely to see one of Georgina's friends, how did you meet?' Aunt Marlu asked straight to the point.

'We met through a mutual friend,' Evie answered sweetly, fully aware that George's aunt was trying to extricate information from her.

'Yes, Aunt Marlu, Evie has been an absolute star, showing me around.'

'Well, that's lovely dear and what do you do for a living?' she asked.

George almost choked on her sherry, but Evangeline replied calmly, telling her that she was a secretary for a lawyer's in Kings Cross. Her answer seemed to have satisfied Aunt Marlu, or so she thought. Aunt Marlu asked George to help her with lunch in the kitchen. George followed her meekly.

'I don't mean to interfere with your private life my dear, but please do be careful, there are some people who can be most unkind.'

'I'm not sure what you mean aunty?' George replied, though she knew full well what she was implying.

'Well never mind dear, here, would you mind taking in the vegetables please?'

George took the vegetables into the dining room where they enjoyed a roast chicken with roast potatoes. The rest of the afternoon passed without further incident until it was time for George and Evie to leave. They said their goodbyes and Uncle Ted drove them to Guildford Station.

'Don't take much too much notice of your aunt, she means well,' he said kindly.

George touched her uncle's arm in acknowledgment. They did not speak till they got to the station. It was dark by then. The train arrived at the platform just as they descended the stairs. They quickly got on the train, though both of them remained quiet for the rest of the journey, sensing each other's sadness at George's impending departure. That night, their lovemaking was intense and tinged with a deep sadness.

At four in the morning the alarm rang. George got up and went to wash in the bathroom. She dressed in her uniform and found Evie standing in the bedroom doorway. George went to her and held her tenderly. They remained that way for a long time till George looked at her watch reminding them that their time together had come to an end. They had their tea and George got up to leave.

'Evie, my darling, I have to go,' she said lifting the kitbag on to her shoulder along with the gas mask. She kissed her deeply and they walked down the stairs together to the front door.

'George, I love you, please come back to me safely.'

'I love you too with my entire being, sweetheart, I will be back, I promise you.'

George opened the front door and walked out without looking back, for if she had she would have changed her mind and never have left and that would have had its inevitable consequences.

She made her way to *Baker Street* where she was to join her old comrades.

Adam and Hamish were standing outside number sixty; they were all smiles but Reggie was missing.

'Hello boys, I missed you,' chuckling and giving them a cuffing each.

'Hello George!'

'Where's Reggie?' she asked.

'He won't be with us lass; he's been sent elsewhere apparently.'

'Oh no! Anybody know where? Hmm that's a stupid question isn't it?'

'I'm afraid so George, we haven't a clue as to where he's been sent, but I do know that we are off to Guildford.' As usual Adam was on the ball.

'Let's get inside, there's bound to be some tea and coffee going and if we're lucky even some bikkies.' Hamish was already with one foot in the door.

He was right, there was coffee and tea including a tray of shortbread biscuits. They waited for half an hour before they were met by a staff sergeant who told them there was a truck outside waiting to transport them to their next training station. George grabbed a few biscuits and shoved them in her pocket just in case she got peckish along the way. They went downstairs and the boys hopped on first, helping her up. They weren't alone, there were another six recruits. Once the truck took off they introduced themselves to each other and were soon smoking and laughing, though George's thoughts were with Evie and she kept feeling that familiar tug at her heart, of someone who is totally smitten and in love. Adam caught the look on George's face.

'Someone special lass?' Adam asked.

'Yes, is it that obvious?'

'Hmm, yes, it is, I would be careful if I were you, don't let anybody catch on.'

'Yes, you're right Adam, that was stupid of me,' remorseful and chiding herself for being so carelessly showing her emotions. A mistake like that could cost her her life.

'It's all right, I will look out for you as much as I can. I hope we get sent away together if it comes to it.'

'I hope so too Adam, we make a great team.'

They were heading to Wanborough Manor, at least that's what they had been told. It was to be their last training station. The truck sped along the A3 in a south-westerly direction, they got to the Manor just before twelve, where everyone was glad to get off the army truck and go inside for lunch. The manor was a beautiful Elizabethan house, dating back to the sixteenth century. George felt a certain satisfaction that she had had the opportunity to live and train in these kinds of historical houses. So far, she had enjoyed being put through her paces but she knew that this was the tip of the iceberg and that the real work was to come when her mission was revealed to her. It was impossible not to gather information of why they were training, as tight as security was, something always leaked out and Adam was a perfect detective, because he had a real knack at extricating information and that's what made him so good and ideal for the coming missions. They were the guinea pigs in a way, because nothing as yet had been attempted in the field of sabotage and covert operations, there was talk of setting up spy schools and operations were underway, but as yet nothing was official.

George of course, kept quiet, going as far as to not even discuss or comment on what Adam revealed to her in their secret conversations. She was glad though that he kept her informed; at least nothing was to come as a shock to her when push came to shove. There were rumours that Hitler was going to invade France and MI6 were deeply concerned and needed to have people over there to monitor the situation and to organise underground retaliation and sabotage groups. As yet they had no real significant presence in France. George had picked up from her own sources that preparations were under way; they had already started when she was in the filter plotting rooms. Though they had not seen any real action in the plotting room, just theoretical situations and speculative information; the tension was there, hanging like a storm cloud ready to burst. Together with her colleagues she had sensed that something was going to happen soon. But now George's focus was on finishing her training.

Right after they had lunch, the recruits were taken to their billets and given time to change. George, having brought civilian clothes with her this time changed out of her uniform, freshened up and dressed in casual slacks and blouse with a pullover. At around seven she descended the stairs, hearing women's laughter and on entering the sitting room she was surprised to see two rather gorgeous looking women sitting with Adam and Hamish, as well as the other half a dozen recruits. Wondering where the women had sprung from, she introduced herself to them, 'Hello everyone,' George said as she went round shaking their hands.

One of the women, whose name was Beryl Sykes said, 'Gosh George these lads must have been a handful to work with!'

'Well, I never noticed, to be honest,' George replied with a smile on her face. Beryl carried on laughing and joking along with another woman, Sally Pilkington. The men were lapping up the attention and were drinking copious amounts of whisky. George sat on the windowsill overlooking the garden and the road. She noticed that Adam and Hamish were on the verge of inebriation, getting rather frisky with the women who did nothing to halt their attentions. The other recruits were now surrounding Beryl and Sally, flirting outrageously with them too. George found it strange that the two women were almost encouraging the attentions of all the men… *there was something fishy about these two* she thought. At that moment a rather important looking man walked into the room.

'Enjoying yourselves lads?' he said, 'make the most of it because tomorrow at eight in the morning sharp you will congregate for breakfast in the dining room and straight for your training afterwards.'

The group sobered up feeling somewhat uncomfortable, as if they had been caught out at getting up to no good, which of course they were. George felt just as uncomfortable as they did, except it was more because of the lewd behaviour she had witnessed. She had not seen either Adam or Hamish behave in that way before and started to wonder whether the whisky had been spiked. George didn't wait to find out how the rest of the evening was going to turn out. She went and got her overcoat and went for a walk for some fresh air. She pulled out a cap which she had hidden in her coat pocket and put it on, pulling the brim down and her coat collar up. Under the darkening sky she was a slim chap out for a brisk walk… which was confirmed whilst passing a man on a bike who said, 'Evening sir!' George touched her cap and returned the greeting in as gruff a voice as possible laughing to herself in the process. She picked up her pace turning left out of the drive and headed towards the village of Puttenham, which was a couple of miles away.

She enjoyed the sharp cold which picked up her breath and turned it into miniature clouds of condensation. There was a map she had found hanging on the wall in the hallway of the area surrounding the Manor; she knew that the road led straight over to a place called the Hogsback.

As she neared Puttenham, the night had come on sudden and she was glad she had brought her blackout torch with her; the road was pitch black by the time she reached the Hogsback Pub. She was relieved and went over to the bar where the landlord was serving a couple of old men. George kept her cap and coat on, for one because she was still feeling cold and the other, she wanted to keep her anonymity.

'What can I get you sir?'

'I'll have a pint of bitter please,' she said in a gruff voice.

She paid for her drink and found a corner, next to the fireplace, which had a somewhat meagre fire burning. There was hardly anybody in the pub, which suited George. She wanted to be alone.

'You're not from around here, are you?' a female voice that came out of nowhere took George by surprise.

George was careful not to lift her head and was glad that where she sat there were no lights and what light there was, was subdued.

'No, I'm not from around here,' George replied brusquely, looking at the woman furtively enough to record her face.

'Do you mind if I sit here, only it's very rare that we have company in the pub?'

'Hmm,' George mumbled.

'So what brings you here then?' The woman persisted.

'I'm just passing through,' she replied curtly.

'Oh, come on! At this time of the night?' The woman exclaimed.

George silently drank her bitter, feeling agitated at this new and unwanted interruption.

'Where are you staying?'

'Look to be honest it's none of your business, so would you kindly please leave me alone,' George told her in no uncertain terms.

'All right! All right! I'm just trying to be friendly,' the woman said and moved away.

George finished her bitter and hastily made for the door, noticing that the woman was now chatting to the two old codgers she'd seen when she first came in. She made her way back to the manor, occasionally looking over her shoulder, half expecting the woman to be following her.

She *had*.

George stopped dead in her tracks to confront her.

'What do you want? Why are you following me?'

'Did you honestly think I didn't know that you're not a bloke!'

'I don't care what you think so just bugger off.' George was getting angry by the minute.

'Why should I? You're just like me, aren't you?'

'What do you mean just like you?'

Without a word the woman pulled George to the side of the road where some bushes offered adequate concealment and kissed her passionately on the lips. George, though caught off-guard, responded.

Her thoughts raced *'Where on earth would something like this happen so spontaneously, how did this woman know? What would she tell Evie?* These thoughts did not stop her from taking advantage of this stranger who pulled George to her and craving her to explore her body. In the shadows their bodies were hidden… lust took over, hungrily devouring yielding flesh. As quickly as the incident happened, it ended leaving George to wonder *did that just really happen?* The woman kissed her again and without so much as a backward glance, left in the direction of the pub again.

She was alone the rest of the way and was relieved when the manor house loomed in the dark as one massive shadow. She passed through the wooden gate and opened the front door. It was early still, the grandfather clock in the hallway showed it was a quarter to nine. She could hear the hum of voices in the sitting room. She didn't go there, but climbed up the stairs to her room. In its safety, she doffed her cap and took off her coat and collapsed onto her bed with her arms behind her head. The episode in the pub left her feeling uneasy. That woman had been very persistent and she wondered why. The fact that she had given in so easily to carnal pleasures had left her disconcerted, *Was it a set-up she thought?*

George vowed to avoid an incident like that again, she knew she had compromised her identity and she would not be going back to the Hogsback Pub for the rest of her stay there. She wondered if she should tell Adam about the incident. But then how could she explain why the woman was trying to accost her and how she had succumbed so easily! No, from now on she had to watch out for herself and watch her back.

At breakfast the next day, Beryl and Sally were nowhere to be seen and all of them were quietly either eating or drinking. George pulled a chair next to Adam, who looked up at her and gave her a sheepish smile and said, 'Where did you disappear to last night?'

'Oh, just for a walk, I felt like some fresh air after what you lot were getting up to.'

'Hmm, yes we did get a bit out of hand… look before we get on with training, I want to have a quiet word with you, so let's have a cigarette outside when we finish.'

They went outside ten minutes later and both lit up.

'George, I suspect that last night was a set up.'

'What do you mean Adam?'

'Well didn't you think it was rather odd that on our first night, there are two women who came in unannounced, flirting and literally throwing themselves at us?'

'Yes, to be honest I did think it was a bit unusual, I also thought that your drinks may have been spiked because you seemed to get drunk so quickly!'

'I thought that too, that's why I pretended to drink but in actual fact I fed the whisky to the pot plant,'

George laughed with him.

'So you definitely think it was a set up then?'

'Yes, I definitely do, I think they're testing us, though poor old Hamish and the other lads didn't fare very well, because most of them were too drunk to even go to their rooms on their own, so God knows how they got there and Hamish disappeared with Sally I think and Beryl went off with one of them, but I can't remember which one!'

'But who are those women then?'

'They both work for MI6 though we aren't supposed to know this,'

'Oh Lord, then they walked right in it, poor Hamish!'

George's thoughts went back to the incident at the pub the previous night. She hoped that the woman's appearance was just a one off, a harmless distraction from the boredom of living in a village where nothing happened. What were her chances of meeting another lesbian? She vowed to redouble her efforts in ensuring to not fall victim to MI6's or anyone else's ploys.

CHAPTER 16

The training lasted a week; it was intense but George took it in her stride, she was good at this, it had become a passion. They tackled all sorts of disguises and the one thing the tutors insisted on was being and living, mentally as well as physically, their new role and identity.

George didn't have a problem with that, she embraced the art of disguise wholeheartedly. She passed with flying colours, but the big test was yet to come, they were to be taken into Guildford and had to avoid capture and arrest.

She prepared carefully for the day. She had asked to go into Guildford two days before, under the pretext of running out of cigarettes and personal hygiene items. Adam went with her but had no idea of her plan. She had carefully put on two layers of clothes rolling up her trouser legs under her skirt. She thanked her lucky stars that it was cold so no one would question her and the extra clothing. In her shopping bag she had a cap, scarf and the shoes she had brought from Malta with her. She smiled at the thought of the shoes and what role they were to play all the way from Fredu's shop in Valletta.

She headed to the Sainsburys Grocery store on the High Street and bought a soap and some toothpaste and once she paid for them asked to use the bathroom. The bathroom was small, but there was plenty of room behind the cistern which was high above the toilet bowl. She undressed quickly, taking off the spare shirt and rolled up trousers. She folded them both as tightly as possible and put them in a brown paper bag together with the shoes. She stood on the toilet bowl and carefully tucked them behind the cistern making sure to wipe the bowl off, removing her footprints. One last inspection, standing beneath the cistern showed no one could tell there was anything there unless they actually went looking for the items. George smiled, walked out of the bathroom into the store said thank you to the saleswoman with a smile and left. She saw Adam walk into the tobacconists opposite and followed him in.

He looked up at George as she walked in and smiled.

'All sorted then?'

'Yes, just some cigarettes now,' she replied, worried that he half suspected what she was up to.

'What will you have Madame?' the tobacconist asked her.

'Four packets of Craven A and two boxes of Swan Vestas please.'

When the tobacconist dealt with George's order, she paid him with a ten-shilling note; he gave her the change, which she pocketed.

'And what will you have sir?' The tobacconist asked Adam.

'Six packets of Chesterfields please,'

Adam paid for his cigarettes and walked out with George.

'Fancy a cuppa George?'

'Hmm yes please, I saw a place called the *Woodbridge Café* just up here, let's go there.'

They walked the short distance to the café. It was full with customers, warm and cosy. They settled for a pot of tea with some rock cakes.

'So what do you reckon George? Will we get caught tomorrow?' he asked with a mouthful of rock cake.

'It's hard to tell, I don't want to get caught, I don't think any of us wants to, but I suppose we shall have to wait and see, they are certainly not going to make it easy for us, whoever "they" are. I have to admit I'm a bit nervous…'

'Hmm so am I, believe it or not, as dangerous as what the future is going to be, I don't want to fail George, I just can't, I've never really done much with my life; this is my chance to do something really significant, something I will be remembered for.'

'I know exactly what you mean,' her thoughts turning to that day whilst still in Malta when she decided she wanted to leave the island.

They finished their tea and went in search of the Ford truck they came in. It was parked in front of the *Holy Trinity Church* with the driver leaning against the truck smoking a cigarette. When he saw them approaching, he threw the rest of the cigarette to the ground, stamped it with his foot and climbed inside the cabin. It didn't take them long to get back to the manor and when they did, there were most of the remaining recruits, including Hamish, gathered round the notice board in the hallway.

'Hey up, you two, looks like we're all on our own for tomorrow's cloak and dagger op!' Hamish said. They approached him to inspect the notice board. They were informed that they had to be ready to move out by eight thirty. To where, they had no idea, though it wouldn't be far! How the operation was to work, that was to be left in the hands of each individual recruit. Their objective was to avoid arrest and detention at all costs and find their own way back to the manor.

That night George went over and over her plan, creating every scenario possible and how she would get out of any sticky situations. At midnight she drifted off to sleep. When she woke up, she washed and dressed and took great care with her makeup, something she never wore, but carried with her just in case she needed it. She wanted to make herself conspicuous today of all days especially. She wanted to make sure she was noticed. She applied rouge, darkened her lashes and applied a dark red lipstick that contrasted with her black hair. She inspected herself, she looked very French in her black pencil skirt and crisp white blouse, which she found whilst rummaging around the 'procured disguises' left by MI6. A scarf round her neck and an overcoat, which however didn't look very French, completed her disguise. The last piece of apparel was not very convincing, but it would have to do till she set her plan in action. She knew very well that the others would have scoured and memorised every bit of clothing left at their disposal. She walked into the dining room; all the men looked round, some even wolf whistled her and George's cunning plan was already taking place.

'Bloody hell George you've gone over the top a bit, haven't you?' Adam exclaimed.

'Do you think so? I just wanted to look a bit different,' she replied, inwardly laughing.

'You're supposed to blend in lass, not stand out!'

'He's got a point there George you know,' Hamish said, agreeing with Adam.

The other recruits didn't say a word, not knowing George that well and sniggered instead, as if to imply that she was being a typical woman. She remained calm and sat down and had breakfast with the rest of them. At eight thirty on the dot, they were called outside to climb into the truck which was waiting for them. George, armed with her handbag, climbed on board with the group and they departed. They were all dropped off just outside Guildford at ten-minute intervals, till each one disappeared from the sight of the other. George was the last to go at her insistence; the others took the gesture as one of insecurity and fear, but far from this, it was all part of George's plan. Eventually she got out of the truck which had dropped her on the periphery of Stoke Park and lit up a cigarette. George took her time wanting the others to get way ahead of her. When she finally reached the high street, she made sure she was noticed, especially by a policeman, who seemed to have unexpectedly turned up out of nowhere. George made as if she were window shopping and casually spent time looking at a fashion shop. She went inside and noticed the policeman pretend to inspect a car that was parked just outside, *what an idiot, did he honestly think she hadn't realised that he was a bogus character* she laughed inwardly. She also noticed another man on the opposite side of the road, leaning against the wall, reading a newspaper who also looked decidedly shady. She trusted no one. She bought a beret from the shop, paid and walked out. Her next stop was at the tobacconist's, peering into the window she saw that the man who had been reading the newspaper had crossed to the opposite side of the road. The policeman had also crossed after her, but kept his distance. It was time for George to put her plan into action. She went inside the shop and bought a packet of Camels.

'You were here yesterday weren't you Miss? the tobacconist asked.

'Yes, I was, how silly of me, I left my cigarettes at home,' George replied.

'Happens to the best of us Miss; that will be seven pence please.'

She gave him the money and turned in the direction of the *Woodbridge café*. She entered and sat down and ordered a cup of tea. The man with the newspaper entered the café too and sat three tables away from George. He too ordered something to drink and carried on feigning to read his paper. She smiled slyly. When one of the waitresses came by, she asked her for the bathroom in a loud enough voice to be heard. The man peered over his newspaper; George noticed. The policeman was hovering outside, walking up and down as if he were on the beat. She got up and walked in the direction of the bathroom, which was next to the kitchen. She looked inside the kitchen and it was packed. *Perfect* she thought, as she slipped in and walked unnoticed among the hubbub of preparation going on to the back door. She opened it and checked the coast was clear. She quickly walked in the direction of the Sainsbury's grocery store, passing through the service area. There were a couple of blokes unloading boxes from the back of a Sainsbury's lorry. They looked at her and nodded, thinking she was somebody important to just waltz in like that. It didn't take her long to find the bathroom and quickly set about undressing and changing into the clothes and shoes she had left behind the cistern. She wiped every trace of makeup from her face and pulled out a wine cork from her handbag, lit a match and burnt the end of the cork to give it some charring. She put daubs of the charring on the side of her face, chin and on her upper lip and smudged it to look like a shadow of growth. Finally, she stuck a short moustache to her upper lip and completed her deception with a cap. She looked in the mirror and was satisfied she would easily pass for a bloke. She thought about which way she should leave. After disposing of her handbag and scarf in a bin she pocketed the money from her purse, pulled up the collar of her coat, adjusted her cap and walked out into the store, breathing a sigh of relief that the shop was full of customers queueing up with their ration books. The counter staff didn't give her as much as a second glance, assuming that George was one of the workers from the back. Calmly slipping out of the Sainsbury shop she turned left and walked to the Millbrook Road. At one point she thought she heard footsteps but she carried on walking steadfastly till she reached the road and then turned right in the direction of the train station. George knew that from the train station she just had to keep to the Farnham Road, which would take her to Wanborough. She knew that whatever happened, she had to make it back under her own steam.

It was close on three in the afternoon, there were still a few miles left to walk and George was getting hungry. The hunger thing had escaped her plan but she was happy she had avoided arrest. It was dark by the time the Manor loomed up; she was exhausted. She walked up to the front door and let herself in. It was unusually quiet. She tiptoed to the dining room door and placed her ear to it. There were faint murmurings coming from within. *So some must have made it back* she thought. She opened the door, and there sitting with Hamish and Adam were the newspaper man and the policeman.

'By Jove George is that you?' Adam exclaimed.

'My word lass, you managed to give them the slip then!' Hamish said excitedly.

'You had us fooled completely young lady, well done,' the man with the newspaper said.

George felt flushed and exhilarated, even though she was tired and hungry.

'I'm just going upstairs to wash and change, is there any supper left?' she asked hopefully.

'*Is there*! Of course, there is, the others haven't even come back yet!' Hamish laughed knowing full well that some of them had come a cropper.

George went upstairs, washed and changed and came back down again, by which time, steaming plates of stew with chunks of crusty bread were place on the table in front of them. They tucked in and were soon feeling content after their ordeal.

'Ingenious idea of yours George, to apply a full disguise, I didn't think of it myself,' Adam said as he poured out a generous whisky for himself and George.

'It was the only way… I knew they would be looking for a woman so I thought that's it! I have to change to a man and it worked,' Enjoying the warming sensation as it coated the back of her throat.

'You're rather good at it though George, as if you've done this before!' Adam hinted with a crafty wink.

'Well, I have done it before, just for fun you know, fancy dress competitions and all that.'

'Fancy a ciggie outside for some fresh air?'

'Yes, I don't mind coming out for one,' she replied, suspecting that Adam had something on his mind he wanted to discuss.

The air outside was crisp and the sky was clear for a change; dusk brought with it a canvas of stars which were out in full force. They lit up and puffed at their cigarettes for a while in silence, before Adam broke it.

'George, I don't know quite how to put this, but I've never seen you talking to any blokes, you know, I mean getting close to them, you've never mentioned any boyfriends!'

George felt uncomfortable as usual with this line of conversation. She liked Adam but did not know if she could trust him with anything personal even though he seemed to have got an inkling what her true identity was.

'I'm not sure what you mean Adam, or what you are trying to imply!' she replied with an edge to her voice.

'George I'm not your enemy, I'm just looking out for you, what you do in your private life is your business, but MI6 makes everything their business and I'm just telling you to cover your back.'

'I'm sorry, it's just we both know that we can't trust anybody and it's making me a little bit on edge.'

'No, you're right, it's true, we can't trust anybody, but just watch out for yourself because I know for a fact that they dig deep into our backgrounds and our past.'

'I suppose you're right, but as long as my private life is not in conflict with what I'm doing now, I can't see as it's a problem, and to be honest they're *not* going to find anything,' she sounded far more convincing than she actually was, further validating that Adam knew far more than what he was letting on.

'Let's go inside because we're about to get our instructions for what's to happen next.'

Before Adam went in, she laid her hand on his arm and said, 'Thank you.' And she meant it, because Adam had been her friend from the first day they had met. He smiled at her and patted her hand. There was a hum of conversation going on in the sitting room as they entered. There was a smart man dressed in a fine navy-blue suit. He had a batch of envelopes in his hands.

'Right, everyone, I'm Sergeant Ronald Hughes. Now that everyone's here, may I have your attention please? I have your instructions ready, but first off, I wanted to congratulate you on your training, you all did very well. You are now to be put in accommodation and await further instructions, till then you are to integrate into normal life, but please remember you are bound under the official Secrets Act, you are not to divulge anything you have seen or done in these past months. I wish you good luck and you will be contacted shortly.'

The man handed out manila envelopes according to name, and George, like the rest of them, received hers and opened it. Her instructions were pretty much the same as the man said, apart from an address where she was to live, till she was called up. She was put in a flat in Finchley Road. She had never been there, but she was sure she would find it fairly easily. Her first thoughts were to call Evie as soon as they were dropped off at Guildford Station. She had not been able to contact her even though there was a telephone at the manor and she had had very little time to write. She was looking forward to seeing her though the incident at *The Hogsback* made her feel guilty and question feelings for Evie. *'How was it possible to be in love with someone and yet give in to a moment of lust with another? She loved Evie, she missed her and had counted the days till she saw her again and yet the episode was confusing.'* she thought.

Adam and George exchanged addresses before they left the manor. They were taken to the station by the same Ford truck and all seemed to disappear and blend in with the crowds on the station concourse. They travelled together because they were both going to London Waterloo Station. They bought tickets and wandered over to a small café where they each bought a sandwich and a cup of tea. Adam bought himself a newspaper from next door, intending to read it on the train. They had half an hour before their train left.

'I wonder where they sent Hamish? Did you notice he didn't say a single word to us before he left!' George took a bite out of her sandwich.

'Hmm yes, I did notice but I had a feeling Hamish was not coming with us; a few days ago, he had told me in confidence that he didn't think he was cut out for covert work after all, so I'm assuming he's been sent off elsewhere.'

'Oh well I hope he's going to be happier wherever he's gone, I thought he was a very clever man!'

'Don't worry he'll be fine, I'm more concerned about us; this thing of not knowing when we will be on the 'move' is bothering me, it's like all this training we have had. I don't want to become complacent, not to mention a bag of nerves,' Adam said, laughing at his own statement.

'I know exactly what you mean, it's like life will never be the same again; always looking over your shoulder and the waiting game is going to be the worst, as you say.'

'Anyway, let's just hope we will both get through this in one piece,' Adam ended.

The train had, by that time, pulled into the platform and both of them waited for the crowds to abate before they attempted to board. The platform guard blew his whistle; George and Adam got on in the third carriage and settled their kitbags on the luggage rack above their heads. The train pulled away from the platform, billows of smoke rushing past their window till it gained momentum and then it cleared to show the lovely Surrey countryside unfolding. Adam looked at the front page of the 'Daily Mirror' he had purchased. It boasted the headline *When the Bombs Drop* in large bold letters. George saw it too; they looked at each other. They said little throughout the journey, each lost in thought, wondering when the call would come.

The platforms at Waterloo Station were heaving with passengers. There were mostly soldiers, their sweethearts saying goodbye, guards blowing whistles and porters rushing around, laden with luggage. George and Adam walked with difficulty through the crowds to the station exit, where they got a taxi to their separate addresses. The taxi wound its way through the traffic till it left the station concourse and then it got a little bit easier once they headed towards Waterloo Bridge. The Thames looked exceptionally grey, reflecting the sky.

George let out a sigh; she was missing the blue skies of her island. She hadn't thought of home much, with everything else going on, preoccupying her mind. She hadn't spoken to her parents in a month, nor written; time just seemed to slip by so fast. She would write to them that evening, once she had settled in her new address. She would have preferred to have gone to Evie's but she knew that it would not be possible, at least for the time being, she would just have to commute, there was nothing for it. The taxi came to a halt, 'This is it Miss, Cantley Mansions, 68, Fairhazel Gardens,' the driver said. George paid him and he handed her the kitbag out of the trunk. It looked like a lovely place. The door was imposing, thick and solid. She walked up the six steps. She opened it and walked in and went to the door that said number one and knocked. George heard footsteps and the door opened. A woman in her forties appeared. She looked at George as if she instantly knew her because she said, 'Miss Georgina Parker?'

'Yes, that's me,' George replied.

The woman disappeared for a few seconds and returned with a key. 'It's up the stairs on the left, number three.'

George thanked her and walked up the stairs till she found the door. Slipping in the key, she turned the lock effortlessly and walked in. George let out a low whistle whilst taking in her surroundings. The place was enormous. There were two bedrooms, a large sitting room, a large kitchen and a bathroom, the likes of which she had never seen before. The apartment was very tastefully furnished and even had a phone. It was obvious this place belonged to a very well-to-do person.

She would call her parents later on and she would give them her number which was written on a writing pad by the telephone. She dropped her kitbag on the floor and reread her letter of instructions. She was allowed to have visitors but was to adhere to the Official Secrets Act at all times and she would be called in due course. The latter was becoming a tedious reminder. She was to have a monthly allowance from which all her personal needs were to be taken out of. The telephone could be used for personal calls within reason so that made life easier though she resolved to call Evie from a call box just in case the telephone was tapped. George took her kitbag into the bedroom. There was a large wardrobe on the right-hand side of the door; the large double bed was in the middle of the room with a dressing table and mirror opposite, and two large windows on the right which overlooked a large communal garden with a green lawn that was very well kept. George explored the rest of the apartment, making a mental note to buy some supplies from the nearest grocery shop. She noticed that there was tea and sugar but no milk in the refrigerator, so it meant she had to go out and get some. Grabbing her handbag, she went in search of a call box, first wrecking her brain as to how she was going to explain to Evie that she couldn't stay with her all the time. She found a call box on the Finchley Road.

'Evie darling it's George, I just got in, I'm sorry I haven't been able to call you.'

'Oh, George sweetheart, I'm just glad to hear your voice, where are you, I was getting frantic not hearing from you!' Evie tailed off.

'I'm in Finchley Road, I'll explain a bit later on why I haven't come straight there to you.'

'What time are you coming, love?' Evie asked her, somewhat anxious.

'I will be coming to see you at about four o'clock, is that alright?'

'Yes, yes darling that's wonderful, I can't wait to see you.'

'Me too, see you soon.' George put the receiver back in its cradle. She could tell that Evie was disappointed but she would try and explain things a bit better when she saw her. In the meantime, she went in search of a grocery shop. She had almost walked all the way to Swiss Cottage before she found one. She gave her ration card to the grocer, who set about putting butter, jam, a small loaf of bread, eggs and milk on the counter.

'There you go miss, that should set you up for a few days, is there anything else you might be needing? Some tea perhaps? Or you can have some ham.'

George let Mr Thomas give her the items she was allowed from her ration, there was a substantial pile on the counter and George hadn't thought to bring the shopping basket she saw in the kitchen. He solved the problem by lending her a cloth bag. She paid the bill and headed back to the apartment. Once she had put everything away in the pantry, she boiled some water and made a pot of tea and a ham sandwich and she settled in the sitting room.

There was a wireless in one corner; she got up and switched it on. Music filled the room and she felt herself being lulled into a state of lassitude. After the hectic training of the past three months, this was the first time she had had time to be alone. She must have dozed off, because she looked at her watch and saw that it was past three o'clock. She got up and left the teacup and half eaten sandwich on the coffee table and rushed into the bathroom to freshen up and quickly change. She made it out of the apartment by three thirty and walked the short distance to Finchley Road underground train station. She was going to be late and hoped that Evie would not be worried.

In fact, Evie had been worried; she looked at her watch, which said four thirty. A knock at the door and her worry dissipated knowing it was George. They came together in a suspended embrace not willing to let go of the moment, holding each other tightly, grateful that they were together again. They walked up the stairs to the sitting room and embraced again kissing. They sat down on the sofa.

'Darling,' George began, 'I feel bad about not being able to contact you, it's been hard and it's going to get harder still. I can't tell you much, as you well know, but there's a good chance that you won't hear from me for a long time.'

'Right now, I'm just happy to have you with me, it feels like I've been waiting for an eternity and I can't even think about not seeing you again for a long time, so let's talk about it later, please darling, I just got you, I don't want to think about anything else,' she said despairingly.

'All right my darling, I'm sorry I mentioned it, especially as I have only just got back, but it's playing on my mind, anyway, let's just spend time together and catch up.'

Evie made some tea whilst George fiddled with the wireless.

She now had a job as a secretary; a godsend that came from a recommendation from one of her 'special' clients and recounted to George about it.

'Darling you'll be pleased to know I'm not doing escorting any more, I wanted to surprise you, one of my clients said I deserved better than this, so he had a word with one of his chums in the war ministry and I got a position as a secretary with a law firm called Mills and Darwin, of course *secretary* is a fancy title mind you, because I'm more like a general factotum,' she ended with a chuckle.

'But that's wonderful sweetheart, I can't say I'm not relieved, I know you didn't do 'that' any more but it still played on my mind occasionally,' George replied.

'I know darling, I wasn't happy doing it, but it paid for this,' she said waving her hand in an arc. 'Anyway,' she continued, 'what about you? Tell me what's been happening, or should I say what are you allowed to tell me?' she smiled at George raising her eyebrow in a comical fashion.

George knew that she wasn't stupid and that something was up, she resolved to tell her what she could, without jeopardising the covert parts.

'Well, you were right in thinking that I am being prepared for something, what, I can't tell you, because to be honest, I don't know myself, but I do have an inkling; I'm apprehensive about it all because whatever it is, it's going to be dangerous, I was told as much in the beginning, before I met you. Had I known, I wouldn't have volunteered, but there is no turning back now, I have to go through with whatever is being planned.' George tried to explain as best as possible.

Evie looked at her, alarmed.

'You're scaring me George. What could possibly be so dangerous that you cannot talk about it, is it government work?' she asked her.

'Of sorts yes, I suppose it is, but I have been told nothing, which makes this all the more difficult. I have guessed it's something to do with France and the rest I can only leave to your imagination, as I have done with mine…'

'Oh my God sweetheart if I'm thinking what you're thinking, then this is definitely going to be dangerous. Darling I'm lost for words, I just wish you could get out of this, now that I've found you, I'm going to be constantly worried about losing you!' Evie exclaimed.

They looked at each other in resignation.

'The worst thing is Evie, I can't stay here with you all the time, I have a telephone in the apartment which I won't use to call you on because I'm sure it's tapped and I am being watched like a hawk, I've even risked coming here, but I couldn't not see you. I suppose I can get away with it for the odd night, saying it was too late for me to travel back to Finchley Road.'

'George, I don't care how difficult it becomes for us, I don't want to lose you,' with desperation in her voice.

'Nor I my darling, we will just have to figure out a way of meeting, after all I can't not have any friends, I will see how things go and play it by ear,' George reassured her.

'Anyway, why are we wasting time talking about what might or might not happen?' Evie said pulling George to her and led her to the bedroom.

The bedside light shed a warm glow bathing the room in hues of orange, giving it a mesmerising effect of chiaroscuro. Evie lit two cigarettes and gave one to George, who immediately drew on it, feeling the acrid smoke fill her lungs before exhaling. She watched their smoke float to the ceiling, dancing in whorls.

'You know Evie, this Hitler chap is evil, I can't help thinking about what the bastard is up to; rumour has it that he is persecuting the Jews, he's exterminating the elderly, the sick and anybody that is a threat to his Aryan policies, he's even written a book about it you know!'

Evie shook her head in disbelief.

Honestly, he's a lunatic, he wrote it whilst he spent five years in prison! The man is insane and innocent people will now have to die. I mean, look at what's happening in Europe, he's invaded Poland and soon it will be the rest of the surrounding countries.'

'George what's brought all this on? You've never really spoken to me about this before; I mean it's a stark reality what you've just said, but how come you haven't mentioned it?'

'Since England declared war, I've thought about nothing but the subject, it being the machinations of war and the horrifying consequences, it's not been possible to think anything else, with what I've been going through, these past few months, I just can't help it. Evie, one minute I was leading an insulated life on an island where you don't get to hear about anything and then my mind is exploding with all these things happening. I'm also frightened for my family, because in these last few days it's occurred to me that Malta is strategically positioned in the Mediterranean, which can only mean it will be attacked! Mussolini has his eye on us and you can be sure Hitler is going to capitalise on this!' George exclaimed.

'Whoa George steady on, slow down a bit, who have you been talking to?' Evie asked her.

'Nobody Evie, my mind is like a Pandora's Box, every time I delve inside it, I'm never sure what's coming out, but I must be thinking about things subconsciously.'

'Gosh hon, I had no idea you felt this way,' Evie said, pulling George to her and cradling her.

'It's not your fault, I haven't been forthcoming with my thoughts, because to be honest, since I've been in this hush-hush training, one becomes a bit cautious, perhaps overly so.'

'I know you're not supposed to talk to anyone about what you've been up to George, but you know you can trust me; I would never breathe a word,' she carried on, stroking her hair soothingly.

George felt safe at that moment, lying in her arms, the burden she carried didn't seem so important, though she wished she could tell her everything. But in all honesty, there was nothing she could really add to what she had already said, because when push came to shove, she would only learn what her purpose really was, when 'they' called her up.

'Evie there is nothing else I can add to what I have told you because I don't know anything else.'

'It doesn't matter darling; here and now is more important.'

'Yes, I guess you're right, hon,' she lit two cigarettes, giving one to Evie.

'George love, we can still meet, you know, at least before you get called up, we can go watch a show or two or some other place,' Evie added with a wink, which made George smile.

'You know what? You're absolutely right and I can still come here, as long as I keep the Finchley Road apartment for my purposes only, it should be fine.'

'Well, that's sorted then, let's get some sleep now.'

The next day, George made her way to Finchley Road. She unpacked the rest of her kitbag and made herself some tea. She called Adam and made arrangements to meet him in the West End.

Leicester Square was teeming; George sat quietly in a café with a pot of tea to keep her company. Adam turned up about ten minutes later.

'Hello George, sorry I'm a bit late, hell of a load of traffic on the underground today,' he said apologetically.

'Oh, don't worry about it, Adam, it's just nice to see you, I know it's only been a couple of days, I don't know about you, but I'm already starting to feel alone, if you know what I mean.'

'Actually, I do know exactly what you mean, sort of isolated and indifferent to what's going on around you, with other things which are more important playing on your mind,' he mused.

'I see you've sorted yourself out with some tea; I'm going for a beer.'

'Yes, look there's the waitress, call her over.'

Once Adam had ordered his beer, George carried on with the conversation.

'Going back to what you were saying, yes that's exactly how I feel, things have changed and I feel different; I know I will never be the same again.'

'We are *never* going be the same again, I don't think anybody is, all of us are going to play a part in this war and everyone will be affected by it, one way or another… another mass evacuation of children from London is rumoured in anticipation of aerial attacks…'

'Oh God! I bloody hate this war! There's always going to be the innocent victims isn't there? It's going to scar them for life poor mites!' Her face was a portrait of anger and anguish.

'Look George I've got to tell you something, you may as well know, we are to be summoned in the next few days, the both of us and we're going to be sent to France. I mean it was pretty obvious, *they* made damned sure we spoke fluent French and all this covert training in warfare and sabotage, I mean you would have to be plain stupid not to guess!' he exclaimed.

'Well, I had an inkling Adam, but since I was not told anything concrete, I was reluctant to just make my own assumptions and I certainly never imagined it would be that fast; the situation must be urgent, I suppose this information is through one of your reliable sources is it?' George asked.

'Yes, it is and very reliable indeed too, so I would put your affairs in order,' he added sombrely.

'Damn, I wish there was a bit more time, do you know what we have to take with us?'

'We are to be called into Baker Street HQ and we have to take *all* our personal belongings with us and that's all I know.'

'Well at least I don't have much, I've left most of my stuff at a friend's place and it's safe there.'

'Hmm, this friend of yours… they know about her George, they also know the nature of your friendship,' Adam said, putting it bluntly.

George's jaw dropped in shock and she paled at what he had just told her.

'What are you saying? That I'm being followed? And what exactly do they know?' George demanded.

'George, your friend moved in high circles for a while and now she works at that law firm, they know of her and her movements and they have just done their job where you are concerned. There isn't any cause for alarm because otherwise if there was any, they would have hauled you in a long time ago. Right now, they have a mission they want us to tackle and that's more important, but you can't blame them for checking up on you; this mission is of a very delicate and important nature, so don't take it against 'them''.

George went quiet; she felt totally exposed, her mind was whirling at the bombshell Adam had just dropped on her.

'George,' Adam said laying his hand on hers, 'don't worry we're in this together. I don't have any qualms about your personal life, it's not any of my business, it's just unfortunate that MI6 make it theirs in the interest of National Security and everyone is scrutinised or investigated.'

'Thank you for being so understanding,' she acknowledged quietly.

They finished their drinks and left for the underground to get back to their individual apartments. On the journey home she contemplated the situation… She found a telephone box and called Evie…

It was a heart-wrenching few hours with Evie. George tried to reassuring her that when all this was over, they would be together. She told her she loved her over and over and would contact her as soon as she could. Evie replied with the same depth of emotion. George felt terrible, she felt her heart was breaking, but there was nothing she could do, she did not want to jeopardise Evie's life in any way, nor endanger her. She walked back to her apartment from Finchley Road Station sombrely, hardly realising that it had begun to rain, by the time she got in, she was soaked to the skin. She shivered uncontrollably, quickly shedding all her wet clothes, towelling herself dry and slipping into a pair of slacks and jumper. She switched on the wireless and poured a generous tumbler of whisky from a decanter that stood on a small cabinet. The whisky warmed her through and made her drowsy. She finished it and poured another. George woke with a start at the shrill sound of the telephone ringing. For a moment she forgot where she was and then quickly got up to answer it; the ringing persisted.

'Hello?'

'Miss Parker, this is Michael Cowan calling, you are kindly requested to vacate the apartment the day after tomorrow and make your way with all your belongings to Baker Street HQ by 09:00.'

'Yes, Sir, I will be there, thank you, Sir.'

'Thank you, Miss Parker.' The line went dead.

George wondered who this Michael Cowan was, no doubt she would find out soon enough, but right now all George wanted to do was enjoy her last bit of solitude, for tomorrow she would have to repack all her clothes into her kitbag and write letters to her parents, her aunt and uncle, Gracie and last of all Evie. She had to free her mind and her heart of any damning emotions; if Adam was right, that they were being sent to France, it meant they would be in hostile territory. She wished that her journey to France was going to be under a different set of circumstances; it had always been her dream to go there again someday, but certainly not this way. She mentally thanked her lucky stars that Adam was such a mine of information, how he managed to obtain it was always a mystery; he never divulged his sources, but at least she was able to mentally prepare herself or in part, thereof. That night her dreams were filled with scenes of being chased down dark alleyways and hiding behind doorways. She woke up exhausted and decided to take it easy, with no agenda for the day, except to pack and write the letters, which she did in the afternoon. She had smoked a whole packet of cigarettes and after posting the letters, she stopped at a tobacconist and bought some more. By the time she had packed it was late and this time she fell into a dreamless sleep till the alarm rang at six thirty a.m. She knocked on the same door where she had picked her keys from when she first arrived and informed the woman to help herself to what food was left and made her way to Baker Street. She arrived at eight thirty a.m. and was pleased to see Adam waiting in the annex. They were called into Michael Cowan's office, who was the chief of covert operations and who set about briefing them of their mission.

'As you know you have both been training for one particular reason and that is to go on a mission. Up till now you have not been given any information but I'm pretty much sure you must have some sort of idea.'

Your mission is to go to France and make your way to Paris, where you will be given safe houses to stay in. You, Miss Parker, will assume the name of Marie Colbert, a French teacher from the Gascony and you are on a holiday in Paris. All your papers, ration card and ID card have been prepared for you, study them by heart so your reactions are as sharp and precise as a native would be. Miss Parker, your codename is Chameleon. You, Mr. Potter, shall assume the name of Phillipe Dupont, a businessman from the wine country of Alsace. You will now be kitted out with clothes and personal belongings relative to Parisian lifestyle and fashion. You must submit all your personal clothing and belongings which must include your wallet, money, cigarettes… anything that can incriminate you. From now on you are French citizens. Do you understand? Do you have any questions?'

George could think of a hundred and one questions but asked what she was to do once over there.

'You will carry a wireless set with you and once at your safe house you must make contact with us; you have to be careful at all times, as we do not know the state of the German advancement, which could happen any moment, into France. It's a full moon tonight. You will be taken to Folkestone and from there by boat over to Calais. Then you have to make your way to Paris by train. Here are your maps, study them well; there will be partisans to greet you in Paris and help you on your way. You have been trained for this for the past few months and now it's in your hands. Please pick up your cases and familiarise yourselves with all your equipment; you will have the rest of the day to go over details.' With that Mr. Cowan abruptly left the room.

Adam and George looked at each other, bewildered at how fast things were happening.

'Right, so now we forget our real names and call each other by the new ones, Mademoiselle Marie Colbert!' Adam jested, smiling at George.

'*Naturellement,* Monsieur Philippe Dupont!' she replied.

The door opened and another man walked in, introducing himself as Lt. John Buckley. He led them to another room where they were kitted out. There was an assortment of clothing and specific pieces of equipment; for George and others for Adam, but both were familiar with them. The time had come for them to put their training to use. George was anxious and nervous at the same time, the unknown bringing with it apprehension that left butterflies in the pit of her stomach. They were to leave at nine that night, but in the meantime, they had a few hours to familiarise themselves with where they were to stay in Paris. Adam suggested they go out for a cigarette and a bite to eat before they knuckled down to the nitty gritty details.

'I'm not sure I can eat right now; I'm far too nervous, Adam!'

'You'll be all right lass, I shan't be too far away from you, plus I had a word earlier, before you came in, with that Cowan chap and I suggested that we keep in contact regularly; after all, we are friends too.'

'Well, it does make sense; I'm quite comfortable with your presence, so we won't arouse any suspicion spending time together,' George remarked, feeling happy and relieved that Adam had made the suggestion.

'Well, I'm glad you said that because I was in fact worried you might not take to the idea because of… well… you know!'

'Of course I'm all right with the arrangement, I don't feel so alone now.'

'Besides the fact that it will help, even with the carrying of the wireless… damned heavy I tell you, but I know you're no weakling!'

They finished their cigarette and went to a café nearby, sat down and each ordered a steak and kidney pie.

'I suppose we will have to get changed when we get back; I only gave my clothes a brief look, so I will certainly have to check what they have packed for me,' George disclosed.

'Hmm same here, but I don't suppose there will be that much difference from what I usually wear except all the labels will be French,' he remarked.

When they eventually got back, they were shown to a room where they were able to change. They stowed their belongings in a kitbag that was sealed and taken away for storage. George left the Bible her mother gave her in the kitbag, not wanting to misplace it under any circumstance. She noticed that they had included two pairs of trousers among the skirts, dresses and blouses. She was pleased about that as she did not want to go around wearing skirts and dresses all the time, as they were not that practical to make hasty escapes in. She spotted the shoes: two pairs of sturdy ones, one in black, the other in brown, plus a pair of reasonable heels, also in black. There was also a disguise kit that included false moustaches and beards together with a jar of gum. She had a *portefeuille* stuffed with francs and centimes. There were four packets of French

Gauloise; she made a mental note to stick to the brand. All of the items were in a well-worn case. The other things like soap, toothpaste and toothbrush were put in a separate bag, which also fitted snuggly in the case. She double checked everything, noticing the brand names, till she was able to roll them off the tip of her tongue like a true native. There was a knock at the door; Adam opened.

'George, we have a few hours left, Mr. Cowan has suggested we get some rest; I don't know about you, but I could do with a kip. There's a makeshift room upstairs with a couple of camp beds, shall I see you up there? Or would you like me to wait?'

'Yes Adam, hang on for a minute, I just need to shut the case and I'll be right with you.'

She finished closing the case and left with him. The room was small but comfortable. The camp beds were placed on either side of the wall and they had a thick blanket and pillow. They smoked a cigarette before lying down. George fell instantly to sleep and Adam followed suit.

It hadn't seemed that long that they had fallen asleep, when she was woken up by Adam who had procured steaming cups of coffee.

'Up you get lass, it's time for us to move, we have just over half an hour to grab our stuff and get in the car that's going to drive us. It's downstairs and this is our driver, Private Tom Bertram,' Adam added.

'Oh Lord I feel like I've been out on the town; I'm so groggy!' she said, yawning.

'Never mind, this coffee will get you going.'

George got up off the low camp bed and straightened her clothes, sipped the coffee, feeling revived as it hit her empty stomach.

'I'm actually hungry,' she stated.

'Well then you will be pleased to know we have a packed box with sandwiches and apples, so we can attack those in the car when we get going, which is shortly.'

'Super, well I suppose we ought to make a move then!'

They all left and went down the stairs to pick up their belongings. There was Major Le Petite together with Michael Cowan to see them off; shaking their hands firmly.

'Jolly good show, keep your wits about you and take care,' were Le Petite's last words.

They picked up their bags and walked to the front of the Baker Street HQ, where Private Bertram loaded their luggage onto the boot; George and Adam climbed inside. The car, a Ford, pulled away into the main road with dimmed lights and headed towards the Queen Elizabeth Bridge. The blackout made the journey slow but they chatted and smoked for the best part of the way and later they tucked into their food boxes and drank hot coffee from the thermos provided. As they hit the countryside and rural roads, there wasn't a soul in sight on the roads, which made it easier for Tom to make some headway. Some three hours later, they arrived at the harbour in Folkestone, where a sturdy launch was waiting for them. Tom helped them to store their cases and the wireless on board. The captain, a rugged looking fellow, shook their hands and introduced himself as Alfred Barnes. Alfred started the launch engines which belched clouds of smoke in the process. The propellers churned the water straining at the ropes. They both took a seat on the wooden bench inside the cabin; it was too cold to sit in the open. Alfred slipped the ropes off from their moorings and the launch drifted gently away. He revved the engines up and the launch very sweetly moved off and away in the direction of the open waters of the English Channel. The launch chugged steadily under the light of the full moon, its shadow gliding across the waves. They risked no lights, not even lighting a cigarette, for there had been sightings of German U-boats patrolling the sea between both the coasts. They were nervous about the journey for most of the way, but the crossing was uneventful, so that when they arrived at Calais, it was quiet and dark except for the moonlight, which helped them get off onto the jetty with relative ease. They said their goodbyes to Alfred, grabbed their luggage and walked up to the village, making their way to Rue Royale, where their French contact was to meet them. Though the street was deserted they felt conspicuous and anxious waiting for the person to turn up. They hid in the shadows of a large doorway. A few minutes later they heard someone approach them whistling a tune softly.

'Comment allez vous Madame et Monsieur? C'est un belle nuit!' said a voice.

Adam and George recognised the code of communication and George replied.

'Oui c'est une belle nuit!'

The man came out of the shadows, lighting a cigarette so the three of them could see each other's face. The man, who introduced himself as Pascal, bade them to follow him. He took them through an alleyway not more than five minutes away to a small house. He opened the door and they all entered. Pascal was now able to speak.

'Was your journey a good one?' he asked.

'Yes, it was, it was a good crossing,' Adam replied.

'Bien,' Pascal said and carried on looking at George, 'Madame Colbert would you like some coffee?'

'Oui, yes some coffee would be good,' George answered, taking in her rustic surroundings and lighting a Gauloise.

Pascal set about boiling water to percolate some coffee. George and Adam sat down at the kitchen table. Pascal returned with the steaming coffee, which was extremely bitter.

'Tonight, you will stay here and tomorrow you will go to Arras, someone will take you there by truck. Once you have arrived, you will make your way to the house on *Rue du Des Fours* as instructed; when you are there you will meet with a woman by the name of Albertine, knock four times on the door and she will open. Now shall we eat? I have some fresh bread and goats' cheese and I will make more coffee,' Pascal ended.

They feasted on the simple food till the first rays of dawn peeked through the shuttered window. Pascal blew out the candle that had all but melted away and showed Adam and George to a room, which was a short walk up some flagstone stairs. The room was as simple as the food, two single beds with straw mattresses covered with thick woollen blankets and that was it. They were to rest for the day and move out of Calais by night, not to draw attention to themselves. In the quiet of the room George thought about Evie for the first time since she left England. She thought it strange that she should suddenly think of her now; it was as if she had become another person overnight. She watched Adam sleeping, his rhythmic breathing lulling her into a sleepy stupor. The sun had gone down by the time they both woke up. The house was quiet. Adam lit a cigarette and gave it to George who took it and drew deeply, allowing the acrid smoke to fill her lungs.

They heard the door open downstairs and Adam put his index finger to his lips, telling George to hold her silence; they had to be careful now. It was Pascal; he had brought with him a wicker basket with more fresh bread and cheese and as well as a bottle of red wine. Pascal unpacked the basket on the table and lit a fresh candle. The three of them huddled round the table listening to Pascal's news.

'The British Expeditionary Forces together with the French are no match for the Germans. The bastards are fighting their way through from Belgique towards the town of Arras; in one month they will capture Paris for sure, the Maginot line near Sedan is too weak, we must get this information to London. George didn't think twice about setting up the wireless on her bed in the room upstairs. This is what she had been trained for. After placing the aerial as high as possible outside the window, she switched the wireless on and started to relay her message.

Her finger flew at the Morse button, tapping away furiously sending information; Adam sat on the bed opposite her, watching her and feeling proud that they were both doing what they could for King and country. They waited for a response. Fifteen minutes later she got it, they were to proceed as planned. George packed the wireless away and got ready to move out. There was nowhere to wash or freshen up so George and Adam had to make do with washing their face and hands from a tin bucket that served as a sink, among other things. There was a small brick cubicle at the back of the house, which was rudimentary to say the least, for personal needs, but at least there was one. By eleven p.m., Pascal hastened them out of the front door and led them to the outskirts of Calais where a truck was waiting for them. They hid their luggage under the straw that was in the back of the truck and climbed in the front with their driver, an old man with rheumy eyes, rugged and in his seventies, whose name was Jacques.

'Bonsoir,' Jacques said to both of them, touching his cap and nodding as they climbed in next to him. He started the engine and drove off slowly in the dark, with only the light of the moon to guide him for the first few miles, till they left Calais behind, then Jacques switched on the sidelights of the truck even though it made little difference. The truck rumbled laboriously through country roads where shadows and clumps loomed on either side. They were quiet and not much was said between them, except for the odd proffering of a cigarette, which the old man took without hesitation, even though he was chewing on a cigar stump. They were heading to Arras and would spend the night there before moving on again. Thankfully it was still dark when they arrived at their second safe house. So far everything had gone to plan, they had half expected to meet up with German troops, but nothing like that happened. Pascal had of course warned them that the Germans were approaching and the British forces, together with the French Army, were trying to counterattack, but the outlook was not good.

They arrived in Arras at around three in the morning and it was only the village baker who was awake, hard at work, preparing the day's bread. Nobody noticed them slink into an alleyway under the cover of darkness. They knocked four times on the door and it was opened by a young woman, who bade them enter.

'Monsieur Philippe, je suis, Albertine,' she held out her hand to Adam, who took it and shook it warmly.

'*Mademoiselle* Marie.' Albertine shook George's hand in turn and George nodded and smiled.

'How has your journey been so far?' Albertine asked, directing her question at George.

'It's been uneventful, but I expect that will change, from what we hear!' George replied, noticing that Albertine kept looking at her in an intense manner.

'Some coffee?' she asked.

Both of them nodded, already used to the bitter concoction the French called coffee, which was anything but. They sat at a table on stools and sipped the harsh liquid.

'I have just received word that the Germans are heading in this direction; we have been seeing your troops and our infantry passing through Arras. Tomorrow at around midnight you will continue your journey to Compiègne but till then you must rest here and under no circumstances must you leave this house. The citizens of Arras are very suspicious of any new people passing through, for they too know of the coming war and are of course, with all good reason, afraid,' Albertine said.

George and Adam sat still listening to what Albertine was telling them.

'Yes, I can understand their fears, we won't move from the house and *Mademoiselle* Marie will not use her wireless, as it is too dangerous, we will wait till we get to Compiègne,' Adam said.

This time there was no room to sleep in, everything was where they were. Miniscule kitchen in one corner, tin bucket in another, with no privacy, a hand basin on a metal stand and one bed on the other side. They would have to make do. Albertine left and did not say when she would return.

'George we'll have to take it in turns to sleep, you go first, I'll doze with my head on the table.' Sleeping on the lumpy mattress was easier said than done. George tossed and turned, her thoughts going wild with possible scenarios once they got to Paris. She decided to let Adam have the bed, which he sank onto and fell asleep instantly. George sat at the table smoking and poring over the map they had been given. The candle light flickered as the front door opened; George turned immediately and breathed a sigh of relief watching Albertine walk in.

'I'm sorry Marie; I did not mean to startle you,' she whispered, gently putting down a cloth bag on the table, noticing Adam asleep on the bed.

'It's OK, nothing will wake Philippe up at the moment.' George mused.

'I have some wine, fresh bread, cheese as well as some *jambon,*' Albertine whispered.

She uncorked the wine, found two tin cups and filled them, giving one to George. The villagers outside were going about their business, they could hear people talking and carts with donkeys rumbling outside. They remained in relative darkness except for the candle. The shutters were kept closed to shut out any unnecessary curiosity.

'So Marie is there anything you need to know from me?' Albertine asked.

'Yes, I do, who will take us to the train station tomorrow?'

'Your contact is Jean-Pierre; he is a young man, very handsome and very passionate about his country,' Albertine replied with a smile, placing a hand on George's.

George looked at Albertine, a little taken aback by the tactile act.

She did not move her hand, rather left it there, not sure what she should do. She looked at Albertine, who was looking at George intently. George suddenly understood. Albertine stood up quietly and went around the table to where George was standing and very gently took her hand. She pulled George to the darkest corner of the room, blowing out the candle in the process. Albertine held George's face in her hands and gently kissed her, slowly at first, and then more ardently till she felt her respond to her advances. She pushed her against the wall and let her hands travel over her breasts pressing into her. George felt her body on fire, feeling helpless but to succumb to Albertine's caressing. As soon as she felt Albertine's mouth on her lips and neck, her legs almost buckled and moaned softly. Albertine chastened her to keep quiet, not wanting Adam to wake up. With a swift movement Albertine was on her knees, pushing her face between George's legs, seeking the soft wet flesh with her eager tongue. George was close to reaching ecstasy, she put both her hands, on Albertine's head; her hips undulating to Albertine's rhythm. Suddenly, everything inside her exploded and she felt Albertine's fingers inside her pushing in and out drawing her wetness down her thighs, which Albertine licked and kissed at the same time. George could not believe what had just happened, taking in the surreal image before her. Albertine got up and kissed her, pushing her tongue into George's mouth. George could taste herself, it felt strange but not unpleasant. Albertine grabbed George's hand and placed it between her legs seeking the same gratification she had just given to her. It was over in a few minutes. At that moment it occurred to her that she had not given a thought to Evie; in fact, she had not thought of her since they left London. They sat down at the table after arranging their clothes. They both looked at each other and smiled with a new understanding between them. George lit two cigarettes, offering one of them to Albertine, who took it and dragged on it greedily. They sipped on their wine silently, with Albertine occasionally caressing George's fingers, unaware that Adam had been quietly observing them. He frowned and decided to let them know that he was awake, by coughing. Albertine very slowly withdrew her hand.

'Philippe you are awake! Some wine or coffee?' she asked him.

'I think I will choose the wine and maybe something to eat, I am starving.'

Albertine put plates down in front of George and Adam and bade them help themselves to the crusty bread, cheese and cured ham. They tucked in with relish and drank more wine whilst discussing the details of the rest of the journey to Paris. That night, true to his word, Jean-Pierre took George and Adam to the station.

They boarded the train; within a few hours they were approaching Paris. George got her luggage down from the rack, as did Adam. The train pulled into the platform and they both got off. Gendarmes were everywhere; an air of threat hung like a grey cloud and people walked nervously, as if expecting something to happen. They approached the exit to the station; they parted and went separate ways. George headed to L'Ile St Louis where she was to stay for the first three nights and Adam went to an apartment in the 16th Arrondissement. She would make contact with him in three days. She paid the taxi when it dropped her off at the Pont Marie and crossed it. She was glad she did not have a long way to go. The wireless, together with her other case, was starting to feel heavy; the weight straining her shoulders. She found the apartment on Rue Budé and climbed the steep stairs to an attic apartment. She took up the wireless first and then went down and got her suitcase. As instructed, the key was in the door, she unlocked it and walked into the tiniest space she had ever seen. There was a small window overlooking the street which offered the only natural light there was. A single bed in one corner, a small kitchenette opposite, a round table big enough for two people, and two chairs. Still, George knew this was just a temporary measure, she was to move to the Left Bank on Rue St Germaine in a few days. She was due to make contact with London the next evening, which would give her time to explore Paris. She was famished and went in search of a café, making sure she locked the door, taking the key with her. She walked along the streets as if she belonged and soon came to *Café St Regis*.

Choosing a table next to the window, she ordered coffee and a croissant. She was able to watch people passing by in various states of animation. She started to feel a lot calmer and her nervousness had all but dissipated by the time she finished eating and drinking. She went back to the apartment to change. Her French contact was going to meet her on the Champs Elysees at six o'clock. That gave her two hours to get back and rest.

Once inside the apartment, she laid on the single bed, which was surprisingly comfortable; a luxury after the last few days of lying on lumpy straw mattresses. The warm blankets on the bed brought on a delicious drowsiness that she succumbed to. Her alarm clock woke her rudely; it was five thirty. She quickly got up and refreshed herself at a basin on a metal stand. She dried her face and changed into trousers and a warm jacket, for it was bitterly cold outside. She hurried out of the apartment and made her way over the bridge to the Quai des Célestins, hoping to find a taxi. She had to wait ten minutes before one turned up and by this time, she felt anxious, she didn't want to make a bad impression by being late for her first contact. The taxi sped towards the 8th Arrondissement and they arrived at the Avenue Champs Elysees at ten past six. She paid the taxi and walked to a bench a few minutes down the avenue. It was twilight and the street lamps threw soft shadows on everything. A man dressed in an overcoat and hat sat next to her.

'*Bonsoir* Mademoiselle, it's a beautiful evening is it not?'

'*Bonsoir* Monsieur, yes, it is, but there is a tinge of spring in the air.'

'Indeed. Let us take a walk.'

They left the bench and walked towards Saint Germain des Pres. The man, whose name was Alain, told George that German officers had been spotted around Paris, which meant the rest were not far off. They came to Rue Saint Benoit where the *Café de Flore* was teeming with patrons talking, sipping coffee or drinking an aperitif. Alain found a table and they sat down.

'The thing is there has been much talk of the allies making headway to stop the German advancement, but it's not working. So far there have been a few reconnaissance patrols causing skirmishes, but nothing more than that. Our job is to find out where the Germans propose to attack next, I am keeping my ear to the ground and as soon as I find out, you contact London and tell them.'

'Yes, I understand, I have been hearing talk of the French and Belgians together with the British trying to hold the Maginot Line, but I know that it's a just a matter of time before the Germans break through Sedan and head this way, but since our position here is to observe and report, up to now there has not been much to report on,' George said.

'That's true but the war is near; nearer than we think, the Germans have also pushed through southern France. The Forces are trying to defend the Maginot line but I know for sure it's going to end in tragedy,' Alain said.

'But surely London is aware of all this, are they not?' George queried.

'They have always been aware that the British Expeditionary Force was never ready to attack, but they had no other choice, they had to get the troops over. In their haste the Allies have left part of the Maginot Line unguarded, thinking the Germans would never cross it because of its densely wooded area! But they were wrong — *merde*! They left a weak spot and that was of course Sedan. They will surround the BEF for sure. The Germans are surviving on a drug called Pervitin, it gives them the strength to fight and move forward relentlessly without rest for up to three days!' Alain explained.

'Oh My God! So be it, I will wait for you to send me a message. In the meantime, I am moving to a new address, I will not be far from Philippe, he will also make contact with me in the next few days. I've been ordered to familiarise myself with Paris,' George said.

'*D'accord* Marie I will contact you soon.' Alain put some francs on the table and left.

George remained there for another half an hour before making her way back to L'Ile Saint Louis and the apartment. The air had turned decidedly chillier and she picked up her step. By the time she arrived it had started to rain and she rushed up the stairs. Inside she hurriedly stepped out of her sodden clothes and hung them in whichever space she found, hoping they would not take long to dry. She stepped in dry warm clothing again and sat on the bed. She pored over the Paris map she had been given and mentally made a note of all the places she would visit tomorrow; at least some of them were familiar from her holiday with her family from five years ago.

It was imperative she was able to give directions to the most famous of Parisian monuments and museums without giving it a second thought. She slept deeply and soundly and only woke as she heard a bell ringing from the Notre Dame. It was around seven when she got out of bed. She washed and dressed quickly to go out in search of a hot cup of coffee.

She returned to the Café Regis. It was busy outside, some going to work, the baker's boy with a tray of croissants on his way to the hotel next door, and then her first glance at a German uniform. Her immediate reaction was to shrink back into her chair. She hoped she had not made her aversion too obvious. Her heart was pounding as the officer walked in. George calmed herself by taking a couple of deep breaths. She watched him look around. He sat on the table next to her and ordered a coffee. He turned towards her and smiled. There was something very familiar about him, but she couldn't quite put her finger on it. He touched his cap and said good morning. George replied with a gracious *'bonjour'* and smiled back at him.

'Mademoiselle I have this distinct feeling that we have met before, but where eludes me completely.'

'Monsieur I don't think we have ever met,' George said pleasantly.

'Perhaps not.'

George turned to finish her coffee then placed some change on the table for the *garcon* and left as calmly as possible. She could almost feel the German officer's eyes boring into her back, but perhaps she was being overly cautious, letting her imagination get the better of her. She steadied herself into a brisk walk and decided to go back to her apartment. She stopped to look into the window of a nearby boulangerie just to make sure she was not being followed. She sighed in relief when she noted she was quite alone except for an old woman pushing a small wooden cart with fresh flowers.

It was the first time she had encountered a Nazi officer; at least that's what he looked like, and chided herself for not being more observant of his uniform, badges and epaulettes. Once inside her apartment she made contact with London as she was scheduled to and was given a set of instructions, which had her mind whirling.

There was a person she would have to observe in a place on the Left Bank. George stayed in the apartment occupying herself with preparing a disguise till it grew dark. As had been prearranged before they had left London HQ, she found the clothes she had asked for neatly packaged in a small cupboard. That night she dressed as she hadn't in a long time. She put black trousers on, a white shirt and she tied a black bow around her collar. She finished off with a black jacket and soft black leather shoes. With her hair pomaded back and a black hat, she looked like a young man out for the night with his girlfriend. She was in her element, though the task daunted her; for a moment she wished she could speak to Adam, but she was due to make contact with him the next day. Before she left, she observed herself in the mirror hanging on the door. At that precise moment she thought of her father and the night he had caught her in her dubious clothes, she felt sad, a knot in her throat tightened, but then she wiped all emotion away; she had a job to do. Shutting the door behind her, she stepped out into the quiet evening. Twilight had very quickly turned to a black starless sky. The moist air made haloes around the street lights. She wondered for how long the precarious peace would last, probably not very long. She pulled her coat lapels closed. It was cold. She walked with purpose picturing the route she had studied in her mind. She had a distinct idea which way she was going and met very few people along the way. Most of the boulangerie and charcuterie shops had closed, leaving the odd café with their dull lights lending some sort of warmth to the otherwise dreary streets. The Montparnasse area was dingy, to say the least. She half expected someone to jump her and she was wary of every sound she heard. She stopped on a corner to light a Gauloise. She glanced furtively in all directions and nearly jumped out of her skin when a tabby cat curled its body round her legs. She bent down to pat it and it purred instantly. Footsteps in the distance echoed behind her and she melted into the shadow of an apartment door. The cat sensed her agitation and wandered off whence it came. The footsteps — a man — walked nonchalantly past her. If he had seen her, she did not know, because he carried on walking. She breathed a sigh of relief. Her objective intact, carried on to her destination undisturbed for the rest of the way. She arrived at the Boulevard Edgar Quinet and instantly spotted the place she was instructed to explore and observe: *Le Monocle*, a bar frequented by women only. It was dark. She crossed the street and was greeted by a suited and booted individual who eyed her up like fresh meat from a butcher's shop. George shivered, not so much from the cold, but from the lascivious scrutiny.

'*Entre vous,*' the individual said.

'*Merci bien,*' George replied, surrendering her coat.

The bar was chock full of women in all kinds of attire. The place was gaudy, with nicotine-stained yellowed walls. George swiftly looked around taking in her surroundings before moving to the bar, where a couple was seated and engaging in foreplay, oblivious to George and anyone else for that matter. It occurred to George that London HQ had known all along of her inclination towards women. No wonder they had so readily agreed to her having a pile of alternative clothing for her disguises waiting for her at the apartment. She smiled and looked directly at the bartender. The bar-tender smiled back. George ordered a cognac and quickly gulped it down and ordered another. She had just put a cigarette to her lips, when a thick arm shot out to light it for her. George's heart skipped a beat. Could the task she had been assigned to be turning out easier than expected? She turned around and came face to face with a stocky masculine woman, a cigarette hanging out of her mouth and squinting to avoid the smoke burning her eyes. She had a suit and tie on with cropped hair; her stature was intimidating.

'You are new around here; I have never seen you before, where are you from?' the woman asked, almost suspiciously.

'I am from Lyon originally but I recently moved to Paris,' George answered her calmly.

'I'm Violette Morris,' she said with a certain bravado, holding out her hand.

George took it and shook it firmly, trying to steady her rapidly beating heart. She couldn't believe her luck, meeting up with the one person she was to observe and report back to London on.

'Your name?' Violette demanded.

'It's Marie Colbert,' George answered.

'I am a true Parisian, so I can tell when someone is not from here, but anyway, what brings you here?' Violette asked.

'For the same kind of life you enjoy here in Paris, I suppose, there is nothing like this in Lyons for me.'

'So Marie what are you drinking? Let me get you another,' Violette said.

'A cognac *s'il vous plait*!'

'Are you working?' Violette persisted.

'No, I'm not working at the moment and I'm not going to work just yet, because I have to go back to Lyons for a few weeks before I return permanently,' George answered her, keeping calm outwardly all the time, though her pulse was racing at breakneck speed.

'Then you must allow me to help you when you return, I can get you work, I have friends,' Violette said this with a glint in her eyes, which George was not comfortable with.

'Well thank you, I appreciate it; will you always be here?' George asked.

'Normally yes, you will always find me here at some point or another,' Violette replied.

'So what do *you* do then?'

'I do a lot of things, but mostly I have done a lot of sport, though these days I do business,' she said waving her hand vaguely.

George spent the entire evening gleaning as much information as she could, listening attentively to Violette's very entertaining past. Violette swore a lot and smoked like a chimney, there wasn't a moment when she didn't have a cigarette in her hands or hanging from her mouth. She noticed the other women looking furtively in their direction, this did nothing to remove the qualms she felt. But she had to stay as she was, till she made an excuse about needing to leave. For one moment Violette insisted she come back for a nightcap on her houseboat, *'La Mouette'* but George made sure Violette knew, in no uncertain terms, that she needed to get back to her apartment; however, she did promise to go back the next evening. George put on her overcoat and left briskly, not taking the same route back, for fear of being followed. Thankfully she wasn't and under her disguise, nobody bothered her. When she got back, she sank gratefully onto her bed, feeling emotionally and mentally drained and yet elated that her task had been made easier because Violette Morris had introduced herself. Tomorrow she would contact London. This Violette woman was a threat and a nasty piece of work; HQ had said she was collaborating with the Germans and George's objective was to find out just how deeply involved she was. The next day she had to move to her new apartment, which was not far from Adam's. George had just woken up and was stretching when her doorbell rang, making her jump out of her skin. She wasn't going to answer the door under any circumstances because she wasn't expecting anyone. She got out of bed and slipped her dressing gown on and went to the tiny window overlooking the street.

She didn't touch the curtain but was able to see from the small space between it and the window. Her jaw dropped in shock! It was Violette. She inched away from the window as she saw Violette move back from the front door to get a better view looking up. *How on earth did she find me?* she wondered.

The bell rang again. George ignored it. After a while Violette went away. She must have either followed George or wheedled information from someone… whatever the case, the woman was dangerous, and certainly had collaborative friends. She had to move and fast. She washed and changed into a skirt and jacket and made her face up, hoping she looked totally different from last night. She packed all her stuff, including the package of men's clothes she'd found waiting for her. She decided against contacting London and waited till Adam came to meet her at the allocated time. She nearly threw herself at him when he came up the stairs for her. She literally pulled him inside and related what had happened to her the night before and the incident with Violette in the morning. Adam hugged George because he understood the loneliness of their work.

'George, let's just get away from here, you have a room in a house not far from where I am, you will be safe there and if she is anywhere about, she will probably take you for a mistaken identity.

It was at about lunchtime when they left, George carried her suitcase whilst Adam carried her wireless, it being the heavier of the two. They stepped onto the street cautiously, they passed the *Café Regis*, which only had a couple of people in there and thankfully the German officer she had encountered there was also nowhere to be seen. She breathed a little easier as she linked her arm through Adam's. They caught a taxi crossing the Seine to the 11th Arrondissement. The more distance they put between them and Montparnasse, the easier George breathed. Her encounter with Violette had left her shaken. Adam paid the driver when they arrived at the *Rue de la Roquette*. He led her to a large wide-fronted house which façade had seen better days, but its large heavy door swung noiselessly as Madame Manon, the landlady, opened up for them and led them through the courtyard and up one flight of stairs to where George's room would be. It was a large room and George was pleased that she would be able to operate her wireless without the aerial being seen. It was the perfect location. She thanked Madame Manon and after closing the door set up her wireless immediately to report to HQ. Adam sat on the bed quietly reading a magazine. George's fingers flew at the Morse arm tapping away furiously. She awaited a reply from London, which came some fifteen minutes later.

Her instructions were to get more information from the suspect and to do everything possible to infiltrate. She would have to go back that evening as she said she would and gain Violette's trust in whatever way she could. Adam remained with her till it got dark then he left with the promise of contacting her soon. She unpacked her suitcase. She closed the wireless and hid it under her bed for the time being, till she found a better place. She lit a cigarette and stood by the window blowing out the smoke as she exhaled. She couldn't believe how much she had already been through, hardly giving a thought to her family and Evie with so much else taking over. She knew she had to push those kinds of thoughts out of her mind. Her thoughts turned to her task that evening. Violette scared her, she found her daunting, somehow, she would have to shake off the feeling and just get on with it, whatever 'it' would mean.

CHAPTER 17

She managed to rest for the remaining part of the afternoon and when she got up, she paid particular attention to her appearance. She bound her breasts tight so that they appeared almost flat. She put on a crisp white shirt and a black tie with thin red strips running through it. Her trousers were the same black ones because that is all she had for the time being. She would have to speak to Adam about that, she needed more clothes to add to her disguise collection. She slipped into the soft black leather shoes and then finished with her black jacket. She pomaded her hair back and noticed that she would have to get it cropped. She would see to it tomorrow; she had spotted a barber not too far away. She waited till it got dark and then slipped her overcoat on and made sure she had her money in her pocket. She left her purse behind and carried her identity card with her inside her left breast pocket. She carried a small knife which she tucked into the sock of her right leg. It felt icy cold against her skin but it also gave her comfort. She felt a little more confident about going to *Le Monocle* tonight. The taxi dropped her off outside the bar. The same bruiser of a woman was waiting at the door. She smiled and George walked in. Sure enough, Violette was sitting at a table with another two women. George walked over to the bar and ordered a cognac; she lit a cigarette since there was no arm proffered like the last time and sat at a small table. Violette spotted her and walked over to the table, complete with a *Lanzon* champagne bottle in a cooler and smacked it down.

'I came looking for you yesterday,' Violette said almost menacingly.

'Oh, you did? I don't recall telling you where I was staying,' George replied.

'You did not, but I get to know everything,' Violette looked at her meaningfully.

'You just had to ask, even though I'm not in the habit of giving my personal details to a total stranger!' George made sure her voice had a feisty edge to it.

Violette guffawed whilst eyeing George in the process.

'I like a woman with spirit!'

George relaxed, feeling the tension that had been building up, slip away.

'So, Marie, have some champagne with me!' she said, pouring champagne into a fluted glass.

It was past midnight when George felt that it was time to put her plan into action. Violette had been waxing lyrical about Herr Hitler all night and it was evident that she was enamoured with the whole Nazi concept. She divulged very little though, about her attachment to the Nazi party; George would have to encourage her further. Violette was in an advanced state of inebriation and needed very little persuasion to be accompanied back to her precious *Le Mouette* house boat. They hailed a taxi which drove them the short distance there. As inebriated as she was, Violette walked steadily down the stone stairs that led on to the boat with George in tow. The house boat was in total darkness but Violette found her way comfortably inside and lit a lamp. Its orange glow almost made the atmosphere romantic, but George was far from the feeling. Violette opened another bottle of champagne and bade George to sit down on a comfortable but rather beaten-up old sofa. She sat next to her unceremoniously and took a gulp of the liquid. George tried to appear relaxed and hoped Violette didn't notice as she anticipated her next move. She didn't have to wait long because Violette leaned over to kiss her, George responded mechanically; she did not find this gruff and masculine woman attractive in the least; quite the opposite, she found her repulsive, but to repudiate her now would spoil all the work achieved to that point.

Violette moved closer but her actions were clumsy, rough almost. George decided to get the whole unpleasant business over and done with and removed her clothing. She sat next to Violette again, who by this time, was more intoxicated with the sight of George's naked body than she was with the champagne!

She helped Violette off with her jacket and shirt. She was wearing a vest which did little to hide ugly scars peeping from the sides where her breasts had once been. Violette suddenly became self-conscious and reading George's mind, she said defensively, 'I had them surgically removed to make it easier for me to race cars, or rather I am more comfortable without them, but never mind about me, *ma Cherie*, you look stunning and delicious,' salivating over George's naked body.

George gave herself to Violette, knowing full well that this was her chance to extricate what she needed.

'Violette you are so passionate, you thrill me,' George said softly.

'Yes, and you thrill me, *ma petite fleur*, my friends would adore you.'

This was the opening line George was waiting for.

'I would love to meet your friends,' George murmured seductively.

'Oh, you will meet them soon, they are powerful people,' Violette told her whilst nuzzling George's neck.

'They must really admire you,' George said encouragingly as Violette commenced to fondle her breasts with as much decorum as a farmer milking a cow.

'They *should* admire me, when I am so useful!' Violette replied delirious with passion.

'Useful, how do you mean?' George persisted, pulling Violette's head to her breast, at which the lump of a woman fell to like a bulldog eating its dinner. George grimaced in disgust.

Violette suddenly stopped what she was doing and took a gulp of champagne. George smiled sweetly at her.

'I am useful to them because I give them information to help them with the war, but why do you want to know such things?' Violette said, almost snarling at her.

'I was just curious *mon cher*, this war business is very frightening especially since the British and French are going to win,' George taunted her, scared that she had pushed too much.

'Hah! They will not win, I have given the Germans enough to retaliate, and they are crossing the Maginot line even as we speak!' Violette said with a satisfied smile, and proceeded to ravish George.

George succumbed to the rough physical pawing of Violette, who once sated soon fell asleep. She waited half an hour till she was sure Violette wasn't going to wake up from her drunken stupor and quickly got dressed and left the houseboat. It was freezing cold outside and a fine mist hung in the air. George walked rapidly along the Seine in the hope she would spot a taxi but none came. By the time she had walked all the way to the house it was four in the morning. She fell into bed exhausted, with all her clothes on, thinking of her encounter with Violette and how she would relate all to London when she woke up.

It was one of those rare days when the weak morning sunshine filled the courtyard. It was gone eleven when George woke up. She desperately craved a coffee and a cigarette. Avoiding the *Regis Café*, she found one on the corner of the *Rue de la Roquette* and settled down at one of the tables outside. She was also famished, and ordered a coffee and a croissant. She lit a cigarette and inhaled deeply. A movement to her left caught her eye; a shadow blocked out the sun.

'We meet again *Fraulein*.' The German officer held out his hand to her.

George took it gracefully and shook his hand.

'May I?' he enquired as he indicated to the chair next to her.

'It occurred to me the other day where I knew you; you were on the same train as I when I was arrested and deported back to Germany,' he said.

'Yes, now I remember, what a coincidence to meet you here!'

'My name is Lutz Hoffmann,' he said introducing himself.

'Marie Colbert,' George said, looking at him steadily.

'French?' he asked, raising his eyebrow, 'you do not strike me as a French girl!'

'Well, I am half French, my mother is French and my father English.' It was partly true… She had to think fast to give him a connection as to why she was in Paris.

'Aah I see, but what are you doing here when things are so unstable?' he persisted.

'I was due some time off and I thought I would come to Paris for a short while,' George replied, unconvinced by her own admission.

'I see,' he said, not convinced by her explanation either, 'you have nothing to fear Marie, I am under obligation to wear this uniform; which I would rather not, but choice is not always an option,' he finished off, smiling.

Despite his words, George did not feel comfortable and was

definitely not going to give him encouragement to pursue the course of conversation further.

She smiled back at him and asked, 'So what happened to you that day?'

'Well, I was happily living in England pursuing a career as an artist, which is something my father has always been totally against. He wanted me to follow in his tradition, a career in the Wehrmacht, but I had other plans, and some years ago I absconded to England and travelled all round the country with my paints and easel till this damned war broke out and all aliens were to be apprehended and incarcerated or deported. I would have rather the former but authorities wouldn't have it, so with my tail between my legs, I had to return home, penniless of course. I was given very little choice by my family, who felt I had disgraced them, I couldn't live without an income, my father threatened to leave me penniless and gave me an ultimatum…' Lutz said.

'So you are now an officer in the Wehrmacht?' George queried.

'Yes, I am but it's not a position I have earned; it's one that has been shamefully bought,' he said distastefully.

'I don't know what to say to you, I don't know what I would have done in your position.'

'There is nothing to say except I detest what this uniform stands for,' he said in a low voice.

'How ironic!' she remarked.

'Yes indeed,' Lutz agreed and carried on, 'but enough of this, let me get you another coffee' he said as he called the *garcon* and ordered.

'Since you are on holiday here, may I suggest I accompany you to see some of the lovely sights of Paris?'

George thought very quickly and said, 'Yes I would like that very much.'

'Very well, let us meet tomorrow, say at ten thirty here, would that be convenient?' he asked.

'Yes, that will be fine,' George replied.

'We can start with the Notre Dame and then we can go to Versailles, which will take most of the day, as it is stupendous, French architecture is most beautiful, the palace is a sensational classical building,' Lutz gesticulated animatedly.

They were quietly drinking their coffee and smoking a cigarette when George spotted a familiar figure walking towards them. It immediately made her feel anxious. It was Violette; it felt as if the woman was stalking her. She stopped at their table and brazenly asked her where she had been.

'I don't think it's any of your business, to be honest,' George retorted, wishing instantly she had not been so brusque. Violette knitted her eyebrows, 'Well you weren't so worried about your business last night were you?' finishing off in a threatening manner and completely ignoring Lutz, who was eyeing her abusive body language and 'style' of clothing.

'Is there a problem here?' He directed his question to Violette, who suddenly became aware of the smart officer standing next to her.

'No… no problem Herr…?' Violette said waiting for him to introduce himself.

'It's Herr Hoffmann SS Scharführer in the Wehrmacht,' Lutz said this clicking his heels smartly.

'Violette Morris,' she said shaking his hand tightly just to show him she didn't care less, who he was.

Violette looked as if she was going to say something else but then thought better of it, seeing the determined look on Lutz's face.

'I will be on my way and I hope we shall see each other again Marie,' Violette said, emphasising her name and she walked off.

'You know this woman?' Lutz said incredulous.

'I'm afraid I do,' she said feeling somewhat embarrassed, knowing full well she had to be discreet.

'She looks like a man; how on earth did you get mixed up with her?' he questioned.

'It's a bit difficult for me to tell you and I don't want to talk about it!' she replied almost to the point of rudeness.

'I'm sorry I should not have asked, forgive me,' Lutz said

'I'm sorry, Lutz I don't know you and it's too personal to talk about, one can't be too careful,'

'Yes, you are right,' he said, 'I have to go now but I look forward to seeing you tomorrow.'

'Thank you and yes I look forward to tomorrow too.'

Lutz walked off down the street. George waited till he disappeared. She realised she was trembling from the ordeal. That Violette woman was dangerous, she would have to watch her step. She would go back to her room and stay there for the rest of the day. All she had to do was report to London HQ. She finished her coffee and lit another cigarette before walking back carefully, half expecting to meet Violette, but thankfully she was nowhere to be seen. Once inside, George relaxed. She pulled the wireless from under her bed and went to the window to put the aerial out. She was about to pull the curtains back when she noticed a figure talking to her landlady. It was Violette. George pulled back in time to see the landlady, Madame Manon, shaking her head before letting Violette out of the front door. *How on earth was this woman able to find out where she was?* She would have to find a way of getting rid of her. She did not have long to wait, because the next day, when she met Lutz at the café, he saw that she was agitated.

'Marie are you all right, you are very jumpy!' he remarked.

'Yes, I am feeling nervous, that Violette woman is stalking me.'

'Forgive me, but she must be doing this for a reason, did something happen?' Lutz asked.

George felt trapped, she was going to have to say something to Lutz, maybe just enough to engage his help in getting this woman off her back.

'Let's just walk a little and I will tell you.'

'Let us get a coffee in this place I know on the Champs Elysees.

They walked some way down the street before hailing a cab passing over the Pont de L'Alma before arriving at the Champs Elysees. They found a charming bistro and sat inside as the day was grey and cold, a stark difference to the day before, but the French weather was unpredictable that way. Lutz took off his cap and ordered them both an aperitif before choosing a light lunch. In the meantime, George was trying to work up the courage to explain Violette's behaviour the previous day.

'Lutz, I want to try and explain something to you, something about me and the way I live, I am attracted to women and that is the reason I am here in Paris because of the flamboyant debauchery that is associated with it.' George said this intrepidly.

Lutz looked at her thoughtfully, rubbing his chin and drumming his fingers on the table, a gesture that had her more nervous by the second.

'Marie, you have nothing to fear from me or this uniform, for I too hide a secret not unlike yours, if you get my meaning,' he said smiling indulgently.

'Really Lutz?'

'Yes really, though you must understand, I have to be extremely discreet, but your predicament also explains that disgusting woman's behaviour; you have got yourself into trouble where she is concerned. I made some enquiries and she is much respected by the Gestapo. You have to be careful, but I will try and protect you as much as possible. In the meantime, I am here for another six weeks awaiting the Wehrmacht to reach Paris. I advise you to be away from here before that happens,' he told her with a serious look on his face.

'Oh, my goodness!' George feigned a look of horror on her face. 'When are you expecting them?' she added.

'By all counts they are estimating to be here by mid-June. That's why I have been sent ahead to locate possible buildings for residence. I am also liaising with the Vichy. If anything happens that will be the safest place,' he said.

'I don't anticipate staying that long; I have a passage booked by ferry in three weeks' time, unless anything happens for me to cut short my stay here,' George lied.

'There should be no reason, but in the meantime, before things change forever, we can at least explore Paris together.'

'Change forever?' George queried.

'Yes Marie, the Führer is a formidable man; his rise to power has been meteoric and it scares me; he intends to invade and capture as much of Europe as possible, but the worst is the horrific cruelty I have witnessed towards the Jews, it makes me sick to the hilt and I can't do much about it!'

'It's something I don't understand, why the specific persecution!'

'It's not the Jews only, it's also the weak, the disabled, the old, they are showing no mercy. It has also got something to do with the last war and how it came to an end too soon, when victory was within German grasp. Some feel that had Germany not surrendered; they would have won the war… I am against war, I abhor it and I suffocate in this uniform, but again, as I have told you before, I did not have a choice,' he ended visibly upset and choked.

'I'm sorry Lutz, I wish things had been different for you.'

'Yes, so do I, but in the meantime, I will not waste a moment of enjoying your company; this uniform also has its advantages,' he added smiling.

After lunch they took a taxi to Versailles where they explored the beautiful gardens which spread over 800 hectares. They surrounded The Palace of Versailles, which according to Lutz, dated back to the seventeenth century and was a hunting lodge, a seat of power and now a museum. George now felt comfortable with Lutz especially since his unexpected admission and she marvelled at his historical knowledge about Paris.

He spoke about his life and where he was born, his family, his sisters and George in turn told him her life so far, but she was careful to omit the real reason for being here. The day passed with Lutz dropping her off in a taxi at the Rue de la Roquette and promising to meet the next day. George had enough information to contact London HQ, though she felt guilty because she liked Lutz, and he had delivered information she needed which made her think … he imparted with it far too easily! *Was he on her side? It seemed so but she couldn't be sure and probably never would; her intuition told her she had nothing to be worried about with Lutz.*

She was tired after her day, but pulled out the wireless and placed the aerial outside her window, checking to see if there was anyone lurking outside; the coast was clear.

She quickly coded her message about the German movements. She awaited their reply. She was to remain in Paris till further notice and carry on her observations. She realised that Adam had not been in touch with her for some time and wondered if she had anything to worry about. When she next contacted HQ she would let them know of his absent communication.

That night she slept fitfully with her dreams full of German soldiers running after her with guns, firing in all directions; she could see the sea, tumultuous and heaving like a boiling pot, there were ships broken up and the sea was a bright red. When she woke up, she was drenched in sweat and kicked off the heavy blankets, which she immediately regretted, because the room was cold and she froze within minutes. She had no reason to wake up early; she was meeting Lutz in the afternoon; she would ask Madame Manon for some coffee because she wanted to avoid Violette at all costs hoping that by not going out of the house, she would not encounter her in any way. She poured some water from an urn into a basin on a stand and washed; shivering as she dried herself and changed into a pair of slacks and blue blouse. She finished off dressing with a sleeveless pullover and soft leather shoes. She brushed her hair back put on a beret and woollen jacket and went in search of Madame Manon. She found her in the kitchen, cutting vegetables for a stew.

'Madame Manon, that smells absolutely delicious,'

'Aaaah my child, you are welcome to try some once it's ready, but would you like some coffee?'

'Oh yes, I would love some thanks,' George replied.

Madame Manon went about boiling some water for the coffee, she also tore a piece of baguette and placed it, as well as a wedge of brie, on a plate. George was famished and devoured the bread and cheese, much to Madame Manon's delight. The old woman prepared the coffee and poured it into two porcelain cups. The hot dark coffee, which George had now got used to, travelled down inside her and made her feel warm. It had begun to rain outside and the kitchen seemed all the cosier with its lovely smells from the stew bubbling away in the pot.

'My dear, someone came looking for you yesterday,' Madame Manon said.

'Oh!' George exclaimed.

'I was not sure if it was a man or a woman, till she spoke, but I did not give her any information,' Madame Manon said.

'Thank you, Madame Manon, for not giving her any information, I'm sure she will be back again, if she does could you please tell her the same that you don't have anyone here?'

'Yes of course *ma cherie,* I will, but she looks like she means business and not the type to take no for an answer.'

'Don't worry Madame Manon, she will not be any trouble, I will see to it.'

'By the way, this arrived for you yesterday,' Madame Manon handed her a crumpled envelope.

'Thank you, Madame Manon, I will read it later, I will go to my room as I have some clothes that need washing.'

'Bring them down to me child, I will wash them for you.'

George returned to her room and opened the envelope. It was a note from Adam asking her to meet the next morning at ten a.m. in Place de La Concorde by the Egyptian obelisk. She felt relieved, at least she knew that he was all right. She gathered her clothes and took them down to Madame Manon and returned to her room. By lunchtime the rain had stopped and was replaced by a fine drizzle. George left the house and out of habit, looked left and right to make sure there were no unsavoury characters lurking about. There was no sign of Violette but she still looked over her shoulder, as if she half expected her to appear out of nowhere. She made a mental note to speak to Lutz about her. She walked along the Seine towards the Louvre, which is where she had agreed to meet him. She noticed the appearance of German uniforms on the street for the first time, it made her uneasy. So Lutz was right, the German invasion had begun, she desperately wanted to speak to Adam, but there was nothing for it, she had to wait.

Lutz was waiting for her, looking very smart in his cap and grey overcoat. She noticed that whilst he was with her he never saluted and she was grateful for it. She linked her arm through his as they headed towards the Museum. Lutz patiently explained each and every painting they stopped to examine. By the time they had finished, it was late evening and they left the museum talking animatedly. It was Lutz who spotted Violette lurking on the opposite side of the street.

'Wait here Marie, I will deal with this once and for all.'

George could just about pick up on Violette's accusing voice drifting across.

'I tell you she is a spy!' Violette hissed at Lutz.

'Don't be ridiculous, I'm warning you, don't let me catch you stalking her or us again,' Lutz said threatening her under no uncertain terms.

Lutz watched Violette slink off looking sullen. He made sure she had disappeared before walking over to George.

'She will not bother you again, I will make sure of it, but I do not trust her so I will keep an eye on her. He wrote a number on a note book and ripped the page out and gave it to George.

'Call either of these numbers if you feel threatened in any way, the first one is my apartment, the second my office,' he said.

'Thank you and now I need a cigarette,' relieved that the ghastly woman had left.

They both lit a cigarette and waited for a taxi to turn up.

'Let's go to the *Café Flor*, it's quite a famous place on the Boulevard St Germain in the 8th Arrondissement, there are always some very interesting people there,' he said smiling.

'You know Paris so well, Lutz.'

'Well, this is not my first time here; some years ago, I spent some months painting here.'

'Aah that makes sense now.'

A taxi finally came along and took them to the Boulevard St Germaine. '*The Café Flor*' was teeming with people. They found a vacant table outside and ordered a Pastis. Lutz looked at her intently, his thoughts drifting to Violette's words.

'Marie, I don't know your real reason for being in Paris in such a volatile time, but I urge you to leave Paris as soon as possible; I have been ordered to identify any enemies that might jeopardise the 'master plan' as the Führer says,' Lutz told her.

'I don't understand, what do you mean?' she put on a perplexed look.

'Violette accused you of being a spy!' he exclaimed.

'That's preposterous, why would she say something like that?' George asked incredulously.

'Hmm I don't know I was hoping you could tell me… you know you can talk to me Marie,' Lutz said.

'Yes of course I know that, but there is nothing to tell…'

'Very well then, let's eat, I am quite hungry,' Lutz said, changing the subject. During dinner Lutz said that he was going to be away for a few days and arranged to meet with George the next day at the café at the end of her street.

When George got back to Madame Manon's house and to her room, she sat on her bed contemplating her conversation with Lutz. She felt guilty about lying to him, but there was no other way, duplicity was a part of this job and she hated it, especially when it involved people that she liked. In the quiet of the night all sorts of thoughts were coming to her, thoughts that had not entered her head for some time. She thought of her mother and father, she thought of dear Connie and finally she thought of Evie, who must be at her wits' end, since she had not written to her in weeks now. But George could not allow herself to become sentimental, she was thankful of her natural *savoir faire,* which so far had helped her survive. It was hard enough as it was, concentrating, she wondered if Adam went through the same thing. He was the last thing she thought about before falling asleep.

It was very early when George woke up. She smiled to herself, knowing she was to meet Adam in three hours. She washed and dressed and went in search of Madame Manon. George found her in the confines of the kitchen. She had already placed a pot of water to boil as if in anticipation of George's arrival.

'*Bonjour* Madame Manon,' George went up to her and kissed her on the cheeks.

'Bonjour *ma Cherie,* did you sleep well?' she asked.

'Yes, like a baby,' George replied.

The smell of coffee filled the room. Manon placed a cup of the hot steaming liquid in front of her; she immediately sipped at it, relishing the bitterness that coated her taste buds. How things changed, who would have thought that she would adapt to the French coffee, she couldn't imagine drinking tea now.

'Your clothes are ready Marie, I have left them on the chair in the dining room,' Madame Manon said, breaking George out of her thoughts.

'Thank you, Madame Manon, I will take them now,' she finished the last mouthful of coffee.

She picked up her clothes and took them to her room. She put on her coat and beret and left the house in the direction of Place de La Concorde. There was a smell of spring in the air, flower vendors were making an appearance along the river. George smiled inwardly thinking of how beautiful Malta looked after the rains of winter. The island suddenly burst into green, bringing with it bunches of narcissus flowers, their perfume permeating the air.

Full of nostalgic thoughts, she arrived at the Louvre with its impressive architecture. She waited on the left wing of the palace just as they had agreed. After having been there twenty minutes, Adam hadn't turned up yet. *This was very worrying, what could have happened to him?* she thought. It was time to make a move because she was looking too conspicuous. Her appointment with Lutz albeit a little short, turned into a hasty coffee before she headed back to the house. When she related to London of Adam's absence, her instructions were to make her way in one week's time to the coast of Le Havre and get a ferry across to England. The British Expeditionary Force had failed to protect the Maginot line and the Germans had broken through, which meant that they were closing in. In the meantime, George had to lay low, especially as she did not want to encounter the unsavoury presence of Violette. She spent the week feeling totally frustrated and was close to climbing the walls by the time the week had passed. She was also apprehensive because she had not been able to meet Lutz and tell him she was leaving, she had tried calling his apartment but there had been no answer. There was nothing she could do; HQ had told her to avoid all further contact with anyone.

News had been filtering through via Madame Manon, who was a great source of information, that the Germans were days away. She became nervous and was eager to leave. She decided she would leave Paris under disguise. On that morning, George was up before the sun had risen. She applied her disguise meticulously, careful to dirty her face, hands and grimed her nails. She did not take all her luggage; that she left in the care of Madame Manon, as well as the wireless; instead, she took a cloth bag which Madame Manon had filled with enough bread and cheese to last her a few days. She made sure she had the necessary papers; her identity card and money. Her walk to the station was an apprehensive one, pulling her cap low over her head, ambling in a heavy manner. Her face, which she had expertly made up to look like she had a weeks' growth of beard by putting on a false full moustache and beard, made her unrecognisable. She smiled to herself, pulled out a cigarette and lit it. She quickened her pace leaving a trail of smoke behind her. At the Gare Du Nord station, she purchased a ticket to Le Havre. George was hungry and also craving a hot coffee. She stepped out of the station and found a small nondescript coffee shop, ordered a coffee, drank it fast and returned, not wanting to miss her train. The platform was a mixture of civilians and uniforms complete with German shepherds straining at their leash and snapping at anybody who got too close.

George breathed a sigh of relief when the train finally pulled out of the station, the sight of increased German presence that had been taking place in the last two weeks unnerved her. By late afternoon the train had reached Cambrai where it stopped. George had been fast asleep and awoke with a jolt, hearing explosions in the distance. German officers were barking orders at the station master. Her mouth went dry. They climbed on board, Lugers cocked and ready to fire without hesitation; asking for everyone's documents, they waved their guns in passenger's faces. George handed over her papers to the officer. He scrutinised them meticulously looking at her several times before finally handing them back to her. She almost forgot to breathe. They moved past her swiftly, stopping abruptly to herd a passenger who was sitting just behind her, off the train. She kept her head bowed the whole time the train was stationary. She heard three rapid shots. Then without warning the train jerked forward with a pneumatic hiss, the wheels slipping whilst struggling to grip the track. She peeked out of the window; the poor passenger who was now face down lifeless had been shot in the head. The episode left her shaking violently and only calmed down some half an hour later. She felt drained and hoped that the rest of the journey would be free of any other mishap, but it wasn't to be.

The train pulled into Arras and went no further as rumours of German spearheads breaking through the Perrone—Cambrai Gap had sent the town into a panic. George stepped off the train and headed to the one place she knew: Albertine's house. She walked from the station mingling with the melee of confused passengers. It took her twenty minutes. She knocked on the door. Albertine opened just enough see who it was.

'*Oui puis-je vous aider?*' she asked.

'*Albertine, se moi Marie,*' George replied

'Marie! Oh, *Mon Dieu* what are you doing here, come inside quickly before anyone sees you.'

She quickly stepped inside and took off her beret to reveal her short black hair. Albertine stood looking at George, transfixed for a few seconds.

'I-I, didn't recognise you, your beard and your face all smudged, you look like a labourer!' Albertine exclaimed.

'Yes, I know, that is the whole idea of the disguise isn't it; I was supposed to go all the way to Le Havre hopefully undetected, but the train has been stopped here because the Germans have broken through,' George replied.

'Yes, the rumours are true, I received word from Pascal who has gone underground and now I will have to see how to get you out of here, the British Expeditionary Forces are retreating to Dunkerque and Le Panne, that is your only way out now, but we have to find a way how to get you there,' Albertine furrowed her forehead in concentration.

'If you can somehow get me a bicycle, I will travel at night, though I somehow doubt it will be any safer, I will just have to exercise caution and hope the Germans haven't filtered there yet.'

'Marie, you will have to go tonight, it will take you two days to get to Dunkerque, I will give you food and water. I will also give you a pistol and a knife, you are going to need them.'

'Yes, I left everything behind in Paris, I had to and it's a good thing I did, because we were stopped on the way here and questioned by a group of SS soldiers, with aggressive officers in tow,' George said to a wide-eyed Albertine.

They sat down and planned George's route and course of action along the way.

'You cannot go anywhere near Le Havre or Calais, they have both been compromised, the Luftwaffe are bombing them relentlessly, the best way definitely has to be through Morbecque, you can spend the night there, we have a contact; he will take care of you. You must leave as soon as you are rested and take the route to Bierne and then you are just a short distance from the coast. You have to travel by night and I will give you a compass to keep you in the right direction. You are lucky we have a full moon soon; your journey will be made easier. I also have a torch with a red glass if you need to stop to use it, make sure you are well hidden,' Albertine instructed her.

'Let us make some coffee and something to eat, we can then go over the plans again and get everything you need together.'

George nodded in agreement, pensive and rubbing her beard gently, careful not smudge too much or loosen it. She needed to keep it intact even though she had brought the small repair kit with her sewn into her jacket. The coffee smelt good and she gulped down the scalding liquid, glad of its presence in the pit of her stomach, which was feeling somewhat empty. Albertine poured some more into the cup and proceeded to cut up a crusty baguette, placing chunks of goats' cheese on a plate. They ate in silence, occasionally looking at each other. George felt shy, memories of their last encounter came to mind and it seemed Albertine was echoing her thoughts, for at that precise moment, she caressed the fingers on George's right hand. George did not pull away; human comfort was a welcome affection at that moment. George asked Albertine for a bowl of water and she washed herself unabashed, laying her soiled clothes on the chair. She also gave her a shirt to wear and they both crept into the small bed. Their lovemaking was gentle and sweet, unlike the cold and indifference of the last time. George wallowed in the warmth that Albertine offered her; she took it greedily, she was desperately in need of the warmth of her body. They remained locked in each other's arms for what seemed like an eternity, till the quiescence was broken by loud shouting, hurried marching and heavy machinery rolling past. Albertine shot out of bed and peered through the wooden windows.

'*Merde*! The Germans have penetrated the town.'

George's face went white, seeing her chances of escape disintegrate.

'How am I going to get out of here?' she said desperately.

'Don't worry I will get you out, just get dressed and take the beard and moustache off your face, you will not get past them with it on, I will need to get help,' Albertine said, placating her.

George painstakingly removed the moustache and beard. Her face felt chaffed after the process but she was glad to be rid of it.

Albertine returned about an hour later.

'Listen, as soon as it's dark we will slip out. Most of the German troops are exhausted and resting; it's the perfect opportunity to leave the house. I have someone to take you in his cart but you will have to hide under its cargo of hay. He will take you out of town and then you will have to go the rest of the way on foot.'

George looked worried, this was all alien territory to her, but she knew that this was to be the only way of reaching safety.

'I will get word to London that you are safe and on your way to *Dunkerque*. When you get there, our partisans will help you, they will be looking out for you.'

The raucous noise carried on well into the night. George and Albertine slipped out at around ten p.m.; it was dark except for the soft light of a waxing moon. They walked past the station, avoiding clusters of troops who had gathered to repose at a nearby bar. There was a man waiting by his cart under the pretext of loading it. Albertine pushed George in his direction and without a word she quickly climbed in and the man proceeded to load more bales of hay on top of George. She lay still, hardly daring to breathe. The man finished loading and then sat on the front and urged the donkey on. He was immediately stopped by four soldiers who quizzed him in German. The man pretended not to understand and shrugged his shoulders nonchalantly. One of them pulled a bayonet out and stuck it on his gun. Without any warning he prodded the bales of hay violently in every direction. The tip of the bayonet nicked George's arm, she stifled her cry of pain by biting into her jacket lapel. It was a close call but after a few more prods, the soldier gave up and walked over to his comrades.

'*Weiter Machen,*' he shouted, gesticulating with his hands to make him move along.

The soldiers moved off in the direction of the raucous commotion ahead of them. George breathed a sigh of relief. She pushed her left hand up to her right arm, where she felt a wetness oozing out, the wound did not feel deep; she hoped that it would stop bleeding. As soon as they were outside of Arras, the man, whose name was Arnaud, helped her get out of her hiding place in the hay. She climbed up and sat beside him, he offered her a cigarette, showing her how to smoke and keep the ember hidden by cupping her hand over it. She drew on it deeply, feeling the smoke invade her lungs. She inspected the wound which had already started to congeal and took no more notice of it. They travelled for what seemed like a couple of hours, the road lit sufficiently by the moon before Arnaud dropped her off on the outskirts of the town of Carvin. She found a dense copse on the side of the road and hid there till Arnaud disappeared back whence he had just come, minus the hay. She was now on her own and with the small bag draped over her shoulder, she started to walking in the direction of Premesques — just as Albertine had instructed her. The moon threw soft shadows on the trees lining the road, she kept to the side, occasionally checking her compass. She must have traipsed alone for a good five hours, when a man or rather a soldier, stepped out of the thicket he was hiding in.

'Halt, who goes there?' the soldier said in a cockney accent.

George thought she had died and gone to heaven. The chances of encountering a British soldier after what she had left behind in Arras, had seemed remote.

'It's all right, I'm English,' George replied elated.

'Bloody Nora, what are you doing here lass!' the soldier exclaimed.

'It's a long story, don't ask, but I'm trying to make my way to the coast of Dunkirk.'

'You'd better come with me then,' leading her into the woods.

She followed him through the scrub and trees till they reached a clearing with a large detachment of soldiers and officers, who were sitting all over the place, somewhat subdued. The soldier went to over to his captain.

'Captain Pickering Sir, you had better come and see this' he said.

The captain followed and stopped abruptly.

'Good lord Georgina, what are you doing here?' The captain said stunned at the sight of his niece.

'Uncle Ted!' George exclaimed incredulously.

'Come over here and sit with me,' hugging her and pointing to a pile of ammunition boxes.

After they sat down, George proceeded to explain her presence there.

'Uncle I just don't know where to begin, a lot has changed since we last spoke and I'm here on government business, MI6 to be precise I guess you can call me agent Madeline which my pseudonym.'

'Well, I think I have gathered that you are on some clandestine mission, but I just can't believe you are here, is all, and where are you going?' he asked.

'I had orders to make it to the coast — Le Havre to be precise, but the train couldn't go any further than Arras and I had help to get as far as possible to try and make it on a ship to England.'

'Well Georgina, I can help you get as far as the outskirts of Dunkirk, but we are surrounded, we have orders to hold off the German flanks to the north and we will be on the move again in two hours. There are garrisons in Dunkirk who are going to try to hold off the Germans till the British Expeditionary Force is evacuated, but it's going to be mayhem; the Luftwaffe are strafing the hell out of the troops, so prepare yourself for the worst, my dear.'

'I knew the dangers uncle, it's a risk I was prepared to take and I can't say that the prospect does not terrify me, but I know I just have to do it and once I get over there I will volunteer again, but please whatever happens don't let Mama and Papa know,' George said.

'Child, I'll be lucky if I get out of here alive let alone have the chance to get in contact with them; whatever happens let Aunt Marlu know that I love her,' he said.

'Oh Uncle, don't talk that way, you will get out of here and we will see each other again!' she said, distressed.

'Georgina, I am going to send you with corporal Duffy who will drive you to Bergues, which is just on the periphery of Dunkirk, then it's up to you. Our position at the moment is not far from Armentieres. You have to leave immediately because it's not safe,' her Uncle Ted held her and kissed her forehead.

CHAPTER 18

Corporal John Duffy was the same age as George and was a friendly lad. They talked and smoked cigarettes all the way. As they approached Bergues, the sky was beginning to lighten, the dawn slowly creeping in shooting tongues of orange. George got out of the truck and said goodbye to Duffy. He wished her good luck and was off in a cloud of dust. There was a strange lull in the air which was broken only by the Luftwaffe strafing and bombing the beaches. George stood transfixed as she took in the decimation of buildings around her. Palls of smoke rose and with it a smell of death hung as if in folds. She passed mangled bodies mingling with the debris of what was once their home. George was shocked. Dawn brought with it a destruction she could never have imagined or envisaged. Even as she traipsed through the deserted streets, the drone of aircraft approaching sent chills down her spine. She ran to the side of the road, just in time to see a blockade at the end on the right. Sniper fire reached her, she ran waving her arms in the air, the shooting stopped and a soldier screamed at her to take cover as the Luftwaffe homed in… bullets flying everywhere. One bit deep into her shoulder whilst climbing over the blockade. She fell to the ground in agony, there was chaos all around her, soldiers firing futilely in the direction of the marauding aircraft. She lay there prostrate, traumatised by her injury.

'Get that lad out of here and onto the beach,' a sergeant yelled.

George was roughly picked up and helped by two soldiers to the promenade. They propped her up against a wall. She fainted and remained there for what seemed like an eternity. When she opened her eyes, she felt faint again but drew on all her strength to move onto the beach. Her mind kept telling her to move, but her shoulder, which was bleeding badly, was draining the life out of her. She finally crawled onto the beach and fainted again.

It was close to the end of the day when she woke up again. Blood was still dribbling from the jagged wound in her shoulder, snaking its way down her arm and soaking her sleeve. George watched with morbid fascination; miniscule droplets gathering at the tips of her fingers, which lightly touched the surface of a rock pool, creating graceful whorls of deep red. Her mouth was dry and her lips cracked, but the pain in her shoulder surpassed the temptation to wet her lips with the brackish water. The weak May sunshine did little to warm her cold body, and she flinched whilst trying to readjust herself to a more comfortable position. She lay still, half paralysed, resigning herself to an inevitable ending; a feeling of failure enveloping her; she floated into oblivion. She drifted in and out of consciousness; a brisk wind picking up, making the cloth round the congealing wound flap like a miniature pennant. The sound woke her; as if subconsciously echoing the horrific explosions that had been incessant for the past few hours. A familiar piercing whine suddenly rent the air overhead, her eyes sought and followed in its direction.

A Stuka, which had been giving chase by a super marine Spitfire had its fuselage engulfed in flames after a direct hit. The aircraft stalled and nose-dived into a perilous spin; belching shells from HMS Sabre, lighting the darkening sky and following the aircraft to its doom.

She could just make out the pilot who was struggling to manoeuvre the plane but the action was futile, both crashed into an unforgiving and foreboding sea close to the shore, sending parts of the wreckage scudding across the waves in her direction. They thudded the surface like skimming stones. 'Please! God! Let me die instantly!' The swastikaed wing spun and slapped the surface before plummeting towards her and gouging the sand as it landed literally a few feet away from her. She closed her eyes.

All around her the unbearable putrid stench of bloated corpses hovered like an invisible cloud. Thousands of them in mid animation of escape, poked out of hastily dug trenches and foxholes, tanks and trucks lay inanimate and ghostly. The scene repeated itself. Line upon line of carnage; palls of smoke drifted from the odd vehicle, making the beaches look like a sandy cemetery.

Ships, boats and yachts were dots on the horizon sailing as fast as possible to the beaches; silhouetted shapes frantically foraged for survivors among the dead and the dying. Everything looked almost surreal against the backdrop of the setting sun, bleeding red tongues across a sky, peppered with acrid clouds of smoke.

The tide had crept right up to her, jolting her into painful consciousness. She had to get away, one last effort, HQ was expecting her; she could imagine their stern faces. She spotted the *Mermaid*, it was the closest boat to her, she was but five hundred yards to freedom…escape… *one last effort* she thought as she struggled to move her numb and useless body.

'Allez! Allez! 'Elle est ici, nous l'avons trouvée.'

The beaches and promenade of Dunkirk were one continuous line of blazing buildings and burning equipment; a high wall of fire, roaring and darting in tongues of flame, with the smoke pouring upwards, disappearing into the dusky sky above the roof-tops. The shore was now a lurid canvas of red and black; flames, smoke, and the night itself, all mingling together to compose a terrible panorama of death and destruction. The smoke offered a small reprieve from the relentless Luftwaffe who were unable to navigate through the thick curtain obscuring the vulnerable vessels desperately evacuating the thousands of stranded troops.

It was a perfect beacon for Ron Pegg, whose cabin cruiser *The Mermaid,* made haste towards the beach of Malo Les Bains, among a fleet of every known vessel available. The Luftwaffe circling above in droves pounded them relentlessly with their bombs, and strafing anybody and anything in their paths.

Impervious to this, Ron brought his vessel close to the gooseberry of tanks and trucks all lined up next to each other like ugly apparitions poking out of a dull and murky sea, making an easier approach to the shore. The mole had thousands of troops waiting to be evacuated. He watched, distressed; wounded soldiers clambering over the gooseberry, shortening the distance they had to run or to swim, in a desperate bid for freedom.

Figures in civilian clothing scrambling swiftly across the dunes briefly caught Ron's attention, they seemed to be searching for someone in particular and there was a sense of urgency about them. They gathered around the lifeless form, picked it up and spirited it towards the gooseberry.

Helpless in the arms of her rescuers; they carried her up and over the dunes, George saw her chance of escape renewed. *The Mermaid* pulled away. She watched the sea around the small cruiser heave and bounce as it took a single direct hit, sprawling what was left of it and its passengers to mingle with the cacophonic mess and debris that had accumulated over the past few days.

George succumbed to her perpetrators, who rushed to the edge of the beach and carried her over the gooseberry. Another boat, *The Swan* came in fast through the floating debris, signalling to the Frenchmen to bring the limp body onto the boat. Several soldiers, who were making their way to the *Swan*, endeavoured to assist them and lifted the body above their heads so as not to wet it.

They lifted her over the boat railings and she fell unceremoniously with a thump and a groan on the deck. Soldiers climbed on from what seemed everywhere and the boat was full to the brim before it started to pull away among the brutal aerial attacks. One soldier looked intently at her. He moved towards her and slid down on the deck, taking her head and resting it on his lap.

'It's OK, miss, I've got you,' the soldier said… with a concerned look on his face. She looked up at him… he was covered in grime; his face looked familiar and a brief look of recognition crossed her eyes. It was young Toby Lewis from the village of Bramley. She felt a sense of relief knowing she was with someone she knew. They were halfway across the Channel before she gave way to exhaustion and pain and fell unconscious; Toby didn't let her go for a second, worrying about the blood still flowing out of her wound.

'Captain, Sir, I think it's best you have a look at this one,' Toby said, calling the medic over.

'*Madonna Santissima*, what is a woman doing here?' Captain Tommy Warrington exclaimed.

George instantly opened her eyes as she heard the captain talking.

'Are you Maltese? Are you from Malta?' she asked in a weak voice.

'Yes, how do you know?' the captain asked her.

George never answered because she fell unconscious again, waking up only to catch a glimpse of the white cliffs of Dover. By that time her wound had been dressed and the bleeding stemmed, though she felt incredibly weak. She still lay in Toby's arms and the friendly Captain

Warrington was sitting close by smiling at her.

'How are you feeling?' he asked.

'Weak but relieved to have made it this far,' she replied wanly.

'You are a long way from home,' he commented.

'Yes, I am,' a sadness creeping into her heart.

'Where do you come from?'

'Valletta,'

'Aah our capital; me, I'm from Isla,' he offered.

'You're a long way from home too,' smiling at him weakly.

'True but I'm a medic and I *should* be here as opposed to you dressed in man's clothing and badly injured, you must have quite a story to tell,' he surmised.

'Yes, there is, but under the circumstances too long to tell.'

'Some other time then perhaps,' he said, ending the conversation with a smile.

The *Swan* was approaching land; George could hear the lap of the waves smacking the jetty as they pulled in. There were hundreds of people cheering and clapping; soldiers — able bodied and wounded — disembarked with the help of the civilians lining the jetty. Tin mugs of tea and bread and jam were being handed out to those who were able to stand, the rest, like George, were carried on stretchers to waiting army trucks and transferred to Buckland Workhouse in Dover, which had been turned into a casualty hospital.

CHAPTER 19

Col. Maurice Buckmaster of the Special Operations Executive observed civilian life out of the window of his office. For a moment he almost resented their blissful ignorance of the machinations of war. 'No word from Parker then?' he said despondently to a smart looking woman sitting at the front of his desk.

Vera Atkins' face was impassive, 'I'm afraid not, Sir.'

'Pity!'

'We're still waiting to hear from her, Sir,' Atkins replied.

'Tell me, have we got any more news from Dunkirk yet?'

'According to our last communication, Sir, 'Operation Dynamo' is going to plan and Maj. Alexander will be the last to leave Dunkirk; Vice Admiral Ramsey will be reporting shortly on the progress.'

'Thank you, Vera.'

'Will that be all, Sir?'

'Yes, but keep me posted on Parker.'

'Yes, Sir,' she acknowledged as she left his office.

Vera Atkins summoned, her assistant.

'Hargreaves, I want you to contact Adam Shilling and find out any information on Parker, tell him we lost contact three days ago. I just hope to God she made it to Dunkirk.'

'I'll get onto it right away, Briggs is operating the wireless today.'

Vera Atkin's face remained impassive. Hargreaves left the room; she was a formidable woman who had come a long way from her humble Romanian background. Vera Maria Rosenberg had come with her parents to London in 1933, subsequently changing her surname. It hadn't taken her long to start carving a career in the WAAFS. As head of the section, Buckmaster had spotted her flair and made her an Intelligence Officer and his deputy.

Vera was worried, not just about Parker's safety, but more importantly, her silence, which posed a problem. Chameleon had information that SOE needed urgently. The last contact made in Paris was affirmative; Parker should have made the first evacuation. There was no sign of her yet. Vera's face mellowed at the thought of SOE's most precious protégée… Parker had shown great courage and intelligence, the first female recruit and a harbinger to the future of female spies under the newly formed Special Operations Executive; she allowed a split second of emotion to show on her face, before she masked it again, impenetrable to the world outside.

The last reports that had come in were not good; the casualties were high. Though the Panzer groups, for some odd reason, were holding back, the Luftwaffe however remained relentless; the report made no bones about the thousands lying dead on the beaches. She pulled a file out of a cabinet near her desk and perused it intently, immersing herself in Parker's last known movements. At that moment the phone rang and a smile gradually spread across her face. Parker had been found in Dunkirk and was in Dover Buckland Workhouse. Vera hurriedly went to find Buckmaster to give him the news.

When George regained consciousness, she was in a clean and comfortable bed. There were hundreds of others, some were moaning, others swathed in bandages whilst others slept. She was aware of her own wound aching. She could hardly move and had no idea how long she had been there. There were nurses bustling about the patients and she just waited her turn quietly. Eventually a nurse came to her bedside trying her temperature and taking her pulse.

'You all right Miss? Your wound is healing nicely; you've been asleep for nigh on three days now, want a cup of tea?' she asked.

'Hmmm,' George nodded a 'yes' and mumbled with the thermometer still in her mouth.

As if by premeditated agreement, the tea ladies turned up with a trolly laden with tin mugs, milk, sugar, tea and biscuits.

George realised she was not only thirsty but hungry too. The nurse helped to prop her up, she winced. With a mug of tea in her hand, George took her first sip and thought she was in heaven after all the bitter coffee she had drank in France. She nibbled on a digestive biscuit, her thoughts trying to take in all she had been through in the last seventy-two hours. *Who on earth would believe her back home, all the adventures she had*

254

been part of? And what about the Maltese doctor? What a coincidence that was, she thought! She wondered if the evacuation — Operation Dynamo — had been a success. She asked some nurses for information but no one seemed to know. She also wondered if Uncle Ted had made it back, there was no knowing; she had to get word to Aunt Marlu somehow, but she knew she wasn't going anywhere yet. George had been in hospital for a week; she was reading the Daily Mail which printed Winston Churchill's inspirational speech, she felt his words go to the core of her heart absorbing every part...

"We shall go on to the end," Churchill said. "We shall fight in France, we shall fight on the seas and oceans, we shall fight with growing confidence and growing strength in the air, we shall defend our Island, whatever the cost may be, we shall fight on the beaches, we shall fight on the landing grounds, we shall fight in the fields and in the streets, we shall fight in the hills; we shall never surrender."

His words were imprinted in her soul, an indelible gospel of hope and courage.

She was told she was being transferred, along with another twenty patients, to convalesce at Fulham Military Hospital in London.

On her second day at Fulham, George asked for a fountain pen and paper; the nurse laughed, citing 'she should be so lucky' but returned sometime later with a small stub and brown paper. George began writing to her parents first and foremost, though what to write despite what she had just been through, was a dilemma. She could not tell a word of what she had been up to and instead she told them how she had been coping in London and how her work was going and how she was enjoying it, the general stuff that would placate them and stop them from worrying. She next wanted to write to her aunt but stopped as she thought better of telling her about her meeting with Uncle Ted. Aunt Marlu had no idea what she had been up to and she had no idea how to put into words without causing her aunt grief or jeopardising her secret. She decided to wait till she could get more information. It was at the end of July that she was discharged, with orders to report to HQ F section at Baker Street. They sent a car for her, the journey from Fulham to Baker Street lasted all of three quarters of an hour. She was escorted to Major Le Petite's office, where he stood by the window looking out. When the door opened, he turned and gave George a delighted smile.

'Agent Parker, you have no idea how glad we all are to see that you made it back to British soil!' the major said, walking up to her and shaking her hand.

There was also a smart and tall woman in a tailored uniform.

'Me too Sir,' George replied saluting smartly in the process of the warm greeting and also swelling with pride with her new title.

'Agent Parker, this is Miss Vera Atkins, who will now be working closely with you,' the major said.

Vera Atkins shook her hand warmly.

'Cigarette?' the major asked, offering the cigarette box.

'Yes Sir, thank you Sir,' she said, taking a cigarette and accepting the light from the major.

He lit one himself and dragged on it pensively, not taking his eyes off George.

'How's the injury?' he asked.

'Getting better but still a bit sore Sir.'

'You did a fine job out there, especially on the Morris woman, she is positively dangerous and we are keeping a close an eye on her,' the major commented.

'Thank you, Sir, she is a formidable character.'

'Yes, I can imagine' the major murmured. 'We will expect you to go over again as soon as you are well enough, however we will of course make sure your training is extended, as things have changed since you were last here, there have been certain alterations to the way we will expect you to react in certain situations.'

'Sir?' she looked at the major inquisitively.

'Well as you know, your lot were the first to undergo such a training and of course some of it was a little bit of trial and error, you know sort of guinea pigs, as unpleasant as it may sound, however we have now set up proper schools and have recruited a lot more men and women to strengthen our programmes.'

'I see, and am I expected to undergo more training then, Sir?'

'Yes, not much unlike what you have already done, but we will polish you up, more towards what we want you to do,' the major said.

'Very well Sir, when am I to begin?' George asked.

'Not just yet, you have to be fully recovered before you can start the rigorous training, so let's just say you will take a two months' sojourn, you will occupy the flat you had in Finchley Road and keep in touch with us regularly. You will have to come here to collect your wages each month and call us once a week. Once you are fully recovered, we will more than likely call you up in September. In the meantime, keep yourself updated with current affairs. You will have all the newspapers delivered to your apartment.'

'Thank you, Sir.' With that she stood up, shook his hand, saluted and left. Just as she was going to leave, she turned around again.

'Agent Parker is there something you wished to ask me?

'Sir I was just wondering what happened to Adam, I mean Mr Shilling?' she asked.

'We have heard nothing from Adam Shilling since the Germans entered Paris, our guess is that he is laying low for a while till it's relatively safe to send us word, besides he does not have a wireless operator, however we are dealing with that issue, will that be all?' he asked.

'Yes Sir, thank you very much Sir.'

The belongings she had left behind were already in the car that was to take her to Finchley Road. She settled back on the comfortable seat and lit a cigarette, watching the scenery of London brick houses go by. She felt tired since her injury and now all she was looking forward to was a nap. The driver came to a halt outside the apartment and took her luggage up the stairs to the front door. George thanked him and found the key under the doormat. She opened the door and went inside, everything was as she had left it, except there was quite a pile of letters on the table by the telephone. She grabbed the letters and took them with her to the bedroom and lay down on the bed. She fell asleep instantly. The sun had long gone down when George opened her eyes.

The room was pitch black. She waited for her eyes to adjust to the darkness before getting up to put the light on. She cringed at the sudden brightness and looked at the bed where she had left the letters still unopened. The kitchen was calling her; she was gasping for something hot to drink. To her relief they had stocked the refrigerator. There was a pint of fresh milk, half a dozen eggs, a small paper package of sliced bacon. She also checked the cupboards; there was porridge and jam and two tins of baked beans; well, she had breakfast sorted, that was for sure. She found the tea in the caddy as well as sugar. She filled the small kettle with water and lit the stove. In the meantime, she went around making sure all the windows were blacked out so she could switch on the lights in the sitting room. She switched on the wireless, keeping it on low in the background. The kettle boiled and she made some tea and put all the other things on a tray and took it over to the coffee table. She was about to sit down when she remembered the letters again. She fetched them from the bed and sifted through them. There were three letters from her parents, three from Connie, two from Aunt Marlu and four from Evie.

George stroked her fingers over Evie's letters. She felt bad, she had hardly given a thought to her these last few months. She checked the dates on the envelopes and put them in chronological order and opened the first one, a heart-rending letter whereby Evie told her how lost she was, not knowing where she was or if she was all right. By the time she had read the last one, she resolved to contact her the next day, to at least straighten things out with her. The ones from her parents were frantic and fraught with worry for her, she would have to call them and explain as best she could that she was not always able to make contact with them. She picked up Connie's letter. She recognised the writing, neat and leaning to the right. It was dated 10th of May 1940; according to her calculations that was around six weeks ago, today being the 27th July. Connie's letter was full of foreboding, the war was at Malta's doorstep: Mussolini had bombed the Island on the 11th June, the Italian Aereo Nautica had attacked the three airfields; but casualties were thankfully low. Connie was frightened; both her brothers had joined the army. She went on to say how much she missed George and ended it with 'I love you,' George was taken aback by the last sentence and found that the words 'I love you' struck a chord deep in her heart lodging in the back of her mind. She found some writing paper and a fountain pen and a bottle of blue ink. She spent the entire evening writing letters and prepared them for posting the next day. She hadn't realised it was so late until she looked at her watch and instantly yawned. The bed beckoned her, not even bothering to undress or brush her teeth, she was asleep in seconds.

She was woken up by a loud banging on the door. She looked at her clock, it was nine thirty a.m. She got up and opened the door. There was a postman with a telegram, she signed for it and went inside. She opened the telegram; it was from her Aunt Marlu and it simply said. Please call.'

She picked up the telephone and called her aunt.

'Hello Aunty, its George.'

'Georgina, oh thank God you're all right, I've had such a difficult time trying to locate you, the WAAFS directed me to the MoD who didn't want to give me any information, they told me to send them a telegram and they would forward it to you, so I'm assuming you've got it then?' Aunt Marlu said.

'Yes, I just got it not more than a few minutes ago, I did know about Malta though I only just found out, I haven't been able to keep abreast of the news,' George replied.

'They started bombing Malta on the eleventh of June, I managed to speak to your father, they are safe; Frances is living in the shelter beneath the house, but that Mussolini is not letting up, the Italian Airforce is bombing Valletta and the harbour incessantly,' Aunt Marlu told her.

'Oh God, they must be so terrified, I will try calling Papa after I hang up with you though I imagine it's going to be near impossible getting through,' George said.

'I haven't heard anything from your uncle,' Aunt Marlu said worriedly.

'Aunty, I'm sure he is fine, have the MOD not given you any information?' George asked feeling frustrated at not being able to tell her anything.

'Only that he is still in France laying low, but that's about it, since the evacuation I've heard nothing,' Aunt Marlu replied.

'Oh, well that's not much to go on, but at least they know where he is,' George said.

'Yes, I suppose that's something, anyway dear, best to make that telephone call to your parents and let them know you are well, goodbye George, we'll talk again soon.'

'Yes of course, thank you Aunty, goodbye,' George ended, putting down the telephone in its cradle.

George was worried, she felt terribly guilty at not telling her aunt that she had seen Uncle Ted, but she couldn't jeopardise her position.

When she had agreed to her uncle Ted's request, she had done so with complete conviction and honesty, with love and compassion, but when push came to shove, she could not fulfil her promise. She just hoped that her uncle was unharmed, holed up in France. She knew she would soon be sent back. She placed a call to Malta. It took forever to establish a connection; the operator said that a lot of the lines were down, but she eventually managed to get through. After reassuring her father that she was all right, she tried pacifying his relentless questions by telling him she was doing some government work and was bound over by the official Secrets Act. It made him more anxious but he finally relented and made George promise not to mention any of this in her letters. George gladly promised. With the telephone call out of the way, George bathed and got dressed. She had to go and find Evie. She felt apprehensive, she had been through so much since the last time she saw her.

She made her way to Epple Road. She hesitated twice before knocking on the door. She half expected Evie to come rushing out of the door.

'Hello, miss, she ain't there,' said a mystery voice to her right.

'Pardon me?', turning in the direction of the voice.

'She ain't there, hasn't been for a long time,' a woman, her hair in curlers, said.

'Oh,' was all George could utter and was about to walk away.

'She went off to the country; are you George by any chance love?' the woman asked.

'Yes I am.' Wondering why and how this woman knew her name.

'She left something for you, she told me to give this to you if you turned up,' the woman said as she went inside and returned with her suitcase and a letter.

The woman handed over the suitcase and letter to George.

'Thank you,' she said, not know what else to say.

'S' all right love, you take care now,' the woman said, and went back inside.

George left and headed back to the underground station trying to formulate some sort of plan as what to do next. Once she was sitting down, she opened the letter and read it. Her eyes welled up whilst reading Evie's agonising words of love and how she missed her and how she hoped she would get the letter. She had moved to Looe in Cornwall 'away from the dangers London would face in the coming months' she had written. There was an address but no telephone number. George decided she would go to Cornwall, but she would let Headquarters know that she was going away for a few days to the fresh sea air.

Back at the flat George made herself a pot of tea and sat down on the sofa. She noticed a small pile of newspapers under the coffee table. She pulled the pile out and started to read. Immediately her eyes fell on an article on how Malta, the little Mediterranean island, had been attacked and bombed by the *Aeronautico Italiano*. A lump came to her throat, she could just imagine her mother, terrified and on her own; for her father would certainly be down at Kalafrana maintaining the only three seaplanes the island had. She missed Connie, dear sweet Connie, her friend and soulmate, who had always been by her side and supported her every whim. All these thoughts brought a longing in her heart to be there with them all, to be part of the island's survival, she almost wished she had not been so reckless, wanting to leave her tiny island, but her heart had wanted more, seeking adventure, seeking... *something*. She finished reading the newspaper and placed it back on the pile, there would be enough sadness and death for her to deal with soon enough. She put a call through to HQ and advised them of her trip to Cornwall. She went to the bedroom and opened her suitcase. Her clothes she had brought from Malta were still as she had left them. She found the small Bible her mother had given her and put it to her lips and kissed it as if she were kissing her mother's cheek. She leafed through it; the photo that Evie had placed among the pages fell out. She held the photo staring at it, wanting to feel that tight feeling of love in her chest, but nothing happened. Perhaps it was because she was still traumatised by all that had happened. Without another thought she put the photo and the Bible on her bedside cabinet. She emptied the case except for the man's clothes, those she left in the bottom. She packed enough to last her a week, all that was left was for her to go to Barclays in the morning and withdraw some money. She had grown sombre with her thoughts, but the idea of spending time by the sea cheered her up. George decided to leave early the next morning and take pot luck at finding Evie, because by the time she would have written a letter telling her she was coming, it would have taken too long. When she got to Paddington, she checked for train times and saw there was a train leaving in half an hour, which left her just enough time to get a cup of tea and a rock bun. She finished up and walked to the platform, where the train was just coming in. People poured out of the doors like scurrying ants, George smiled and made her way to the second-class carriage. She bought a newspaper to read on the journey, which was a long one, with a few changes along the way, but the train passed through some wonderful countryside and the weather was fine, with sunshine most of the way. She read her newspaper and dozed for most of the way. Occasionally her shoulder twinged but nothing that she couldn't put up with. The train finally pulled into Looe Station. There was a large number of passengers waiting to board the train; most, George supposed, were holidaymakers returning home. Looe was a pretty little seaside village with houses built into the hillside. It had a lovely golden beach and the bay was crammed with fishing boats. George felt very light-hearted, the same sort of feeling she used to have when she was a child and her mother used to take her to Mellieha Bay. George smiled to herself making her way up a steep lane leading to the address that Evie had given her. It was a pretty little cottage, the kind that one found in fairy tales. It had a small front garden bursting with hollyhocks and roses. A clematis framed the red door and two windows. George stepped up to the door and banged the knocker. She waited, but nobody answered, she sat down on the front step and lapped up the warm sun, listening to the buzzing of the bees and watched the odd butterfly flapping in short swoops over the flowers.

'Geooorge,' shrieked Evie and literally threw herself at George, who lost her balance and toppled on to the grassy path laughing.

'George I can't believe you're here, I thought I would never see you again, where have you been? When did you get back?' Evie bombarded her.

'Steady on, let me get my breath back,' George said, laughing as Evie led her into the cottage.

'Oh, George this is wonderful, I wondered if Mrs Leatherby would hand over the letter and the suitcase to you for that matter,' Evie said breathlessly.

'Well yes she did and that's how I'm here,' George replied, feeling a little awkward.

'Oh, darling, come here, let me hold you,' Evie said, as she went over to George and held her tight, kissing her.

George winced at the tight embrace, her wound was still tender and she also felt a bit indifferent.

'What's the matter George?' Evie asked her, alarmed.

'It's nothing, love, just a small injury.'

'How silly of me, come and sit down, you must be exhausted, let me make us a pot of tea and I have some fresh scones, strawberry jam *and* some clotted cream, believe it or not!' Evie said triumphantly.

'Clotted cream! What's that then?' George enquired curiously.

'Just wait till you taste it,' Evie said, winking at her and busied herself in the kitchen preparing the tea and scones.

By the time they had finished tea, George was feeling exhausted. Evie noticed this, she had dark circles under her eyes, but she also noticed something was different. She decided not to mention anything; she would let George tell her when she was ready. It was still bright outside and Evie suggested they go for a short walk to enjoy the sea air. They didn't have far to go; the beach was ten minutes away. George felt the soft crunch of the sand beneath her feet which immediately brought back memories of Mellieha Bay. She closed her eyes for a moment imagining she was there, watching the children play in the bay's shallow waters. Her eyes misted over. The reaction wasn't missed by Evie. She linked her arm through hers. They both took their shoes off and walked along the water's edge, enjoying the sharp coldness of the water and the sand between their toes. Evie sensed that George wanted to talk but was hesitant, as if she had something heavy, weighing on her soul. Evie said nothing and kept her silence, concentrating instead on the glorious sunset before them. George too took in the orange tongues of the sun's dying rays and breathed in deeply.

'Evie, I'm sorry I'm so quiet, it's just that I have been through so much in these last few months and the words are there but I'm finding it hard to just let go,' she said quietly.

'I know darling, I know you are finding it hard, talk to me when you're ready,' Evie told her lovingly.

George squeezed her arm and they carried on walking the length of the beach till the air grew chilly and then they returned to the cottage. Though it was the height of summer, the evenings were cold, cold enough for Evie to light a small fire. The glow lit the cosy sitting room. After they had finished a supper of boiled ham and boiled potatoes — for food had become scarce and the ration book was not always of any use, the black market was better and Evie had her ways — they sat together watching the embers of coal with the little tongues of flames dancing, mesmerising them, lulling them into a sense of drunken lethargy. George felt as though she were floating, it had been a long time since she felt that way, content and quiescent with not a care in the world, at least not for the time being.

Evie gathered George in her arms letting her head rest on her bosom. She stroked her hair and caressed her face. George felt loved and everything was perfect. They stayed that way till the embers died down. Coal was scarce so they did not put any more on the fire, they saved what little there was for another day.

'I'm going to make some tea hon, would you like a cup?' Evie asked

'I would love some.'

She joined George back on the sofa with the tea.

'I drank so much coffee in France you know, it was very bitter, but you get used to it, drinking tea now is like a luxury,' George chuckled.

'I can imagine, though no one can get their hands on coffee over here, so it's a good job you like tea, or at least missed it,' Evie remarked laughing.

'It's a different world I was in, you sort of adapt to your surroundings, you have to be that way to survive, I felt very vulnerable the first few days, you're in a strange place, you don't know anybody, and you feel as if everyone is watching you.'

Evie just listened and nodded.

'Evie, the thing is there is something I want to tell you and there is no other way of putting it except to tell you the truth.

Evie went very quiet not knowing what George was going to come out with.

I… I met someone whilst I was there; it just happened,' George

264

blurted out.

'You mean you slept with this this person? Was it a man or a woman?' Evie asked, her face ashen.

'It was a woman, it was nothing Evie, it just happened, it took me by surprise, I mean, I never imagined something like that would happen.' George was looking crestfallen; she didn't want to lie to her.

'Evie, a lot of things happened in the line of my work, stuff I can't talk about, not all of it; look, I will understand if you don't want to see me anymore, I can just leave first thing tomorrow.'

Evie remained quiet, not hiding the fact that she was crying. George went to her and put her arms around her. Evie let her head rest on her shoulder.

'I can't let you go; I love you too much, at least you're here with me now,' Evie mumbled.

'Evie, I can't make any promises, I'm going back again, I don't want to hurt you,' George said, with a lump in her throat.

'I understand, George, let's just enjoy what time we have together.'

Later when they were in bed, Evie lay in the crook of George's arm, listening to her breathing. She had noticed the healing wound on her shoulder. It was a reddish-purple colour with a noticeable dent in the middle. She touched the wound gently, George winced.

'Does it still hurt very much hon?' Evie asked softly.

'It's a bit tender, but it's the memory of it that hurts the most, I ran like mad to try and get to the beach in Dunkirk, there were bodies everywhere, young men barely eighteen, I heard the sound of a machine gun, then it felt like something searing biting me in the shoulder. I was shocked and numb at first, then the pain came, it was unbearable, I remember lying on the sand, there were a couple of rock pools, I was thirsty but I couldn't drink of course and I had lost so much blood. I kept drifting in and out of consciousness, wondering if I was going to make it or die there, just another victim left to rot on the beach.' George's voice trailed off as if she had already said too much.

'Oh George, my darling you certainly have been in the wars, I'm sorry you had to face this, so you made it over with the soldiers from Dunkirk?' Evie said.

'Yes, that's where I escaped from; I chose this Evie, I chose this because I wanted to do my bit, I never anticipated all this happening or being involved in espionage, because this is what it is,' George said.

'I know, I've always known, but it doesn't stop me from loving you.'

'I can't hurt you Evie, I can't be selfish, I don't know what's going to happen, nobody does, but especially me, I know you are aware of what I'm doing, but you can't breathe a word to anyone Evie, promise me!' George said with urgency in her voice.

'George, I won't; surely you know you can trust me by now?' Evie almost pleaded with her.

'I'm sorry, I didn't mean to doubt you, it's just that this is meant to be top secret,' George told her, pulling her close and kissing her forehead.

No more was said, and they fell asleep entwined, listening to each other's rhythmic breathing.

George woke up in a wonderful mood. She had no idea what time it was, except that it must be morning. Evie was not in bed next to her, she suspected that from the sounds coming from the kitchen, Evie was busying herself with breakfast, at least that's what she hoped, because she was famished. She got up and poured some water from a jug into a ceramic basin on a stand and splashed her face. Whilst towelling her face, she walked into the kitchen and watched Evie frying bacon and eggs.

'How on earth did you manage to find eggs, let alone bacon?' George asked Evie incredulously.

'Believe it or not it's easier than getting them in London, I made friends, on one of my jaunts, with a farmer's wife, Mrs Chellew; she's lovely, she lets me have an egg a day, I buy them at above average price of course, but I'm grateful. I've been saving them for baking and the odd boiled egg in the mornings,' Evie laughed playfully.

'Well, the smell is wonderful and I'm starving,' she enthused, helping Evie take the breakfast things to the dining table.

There was a veritable feast; half a loaf of bread, a small pat of butter and strawberry jam as well as the bacon and eggs and tea.

'Well darling, I feel I can take on the world after that lot, I can't remember when I last had a breakfast like that!' she laughed.

'Actually, it was in London when you were still living with Gracie,' Evie said as a matter of fact.

'Oh my gosh! Gracie, I'd forgotten all about her, I wonder how she's doing, I haven't heard from her in a long time, I wouldn't even know where to write to her, to be honest.'

'I haven't seen or heard from her either, I hope she's all right.'

'I'm sure she is; a chip off the old block, nothing puts her out of joint; I wonder if she made it to flying planes,' George ended, chuckling.

'George, the weather doesn't look too good outside, in fact it's threatening to rain, there's no wireless here, but we can take a walk to The Jolly Sailor Inn for a pint if you like?' Evie suggested.

'You know what, I really don't mind, I don't have a care in the world! In fact, I also feel on top of the world,' George laughed.

'Right then, let me just change and I will be right with you.'

George looked out of the window in the sitting room, as she craned her neck, she could just about make out the beach in the distance, for a moment she wished she could stay here forever, but that wasn't going to happen, so whilst she was here, she was determined to enjoy herself and spend time with Evie.

The Jolly Sailor Inn was a hodge-podge of buildings that seemed to be attached to each other haphazardly and connected by a large chimney stack in the middle. When they entered, they saw that there were wooden beams everywhere, with intermittent whitewashed walls. They bought their drinks from the bar, which according to the publican, boasted a central beam in the bar from a shipwrecked French ship that was part of the battle of Trafalgar. They chose to sit at a table that had seen better days and God knows how many drunken brawls in its heyday.

George imagined how travellers and seafarers must have come to this pub; it certainly looked old and had a plethora of antique maritime objects hanging on its walls.

Whilst hoping to escape the machinations of war, George had to endure the conversation in the pub which was all about the evacuation and how over 300,000 of their lads managed to escape in any manner of boat available, from the British coast. Evie looked at George, who's face revealed nothing, but Evie knew, she knew how she suffered inside from the gruesome images that would live with her forever. She lay her hand on George's leg, which was obscured by the table. George smiled gratefully. It was at that moment that they heard the sound of aircraft flying in overhead, followed by eleven huge explosions that shook the seaside village of Looe.

The whole pub shuddered. Huge patches of plaster rained down on punters, who a minute ago were enjoying a pint. A few seconds of inertia was followed by a surge of everyone in panic, running haphazardly out of the door. In the distance, palls of smoke drifted upwards into the sky, blending in with the greyness. As news filtered in, they heard that the bombs had caused devastation, but no casualties.

'So much for escaping the war!' Evie exclaimed angrily, both hurrying back to the fragile safety of the cottage.

'Well, that's that then, nowhere is safe,' George commented, sinking into the sofa, 'Evie, I think you should come back to London with me,' she carried on.

'You took the words right out of my mouth, let's just leave tomorrow, I'm due back at work soon anyway, so we may as well enjoy a bit of London life before the changes are permanent, there are some shows still going on and a couple of other pubs I wanted to show you, other than *The Gateways*,'

'That sounds good to me,' George nodded in agreement.

They went to the train station early, bought tickets and headed to London. They arrived late afternoon and were relieved to be back in Evie's flat. George helped Evie pull back the curtains to take advantage of the light that was left outside before they had to close them again. There were barrage balloons as far as the eye could see, it brought a chill to her spine. Evie came and stood next to her.

'It's odd isn't it, seeing all those balloons?'

'Hmmm' George murmured.

She turned to Evie and wrapped her arms around her.

George suddenly felt vulnerable and needed Evie's warmth. At that moment life felt precarious and fragile. Away from her mother and father, away from her little island, away from all the people she knew and loved. She wished she had not taken everything for granted, like it would be there forever. Nothing was forever, not since she had left the devastation of Dunkirk behind, the thousands of soldiers, dead, half buried in the sand in mid-animation.

It brought a sickly feeling to her soul and a furious anger in her heart. The Germans would pay, they would get retribution, all of them, when this war was over, they would pay for what they had done and what they were about to do, for in her mind, George knew that this war was not going to be won in a matter of months, unlike what politicians had speculated; no — they had underestimated Hitler; the short little man with the signature moustache, whom many had ridiculed back in the day when he was no one important, had failed to see that his meteoric rise had been built on his ability to exploit social unrest and instil a sense of Aryan patriotism in every German citizen to the detriment of the much hated and mistrusted Jews. There was no mistake about it, Hitler was going to make his mark in history.

George pushed away any sentimental thoughts she had and replaced them with a deep hatred for anything German; she resolved to continue with her vocation, no matter the cost.

That night George relinquished herself to the kind of love-making that was tender and sweet, almost to the point of healing. Evie, sensing George's intense need to be loved, gave herself, mind, body and soul; there was nothing else she could do, she loved George with an intensity. She did not want the night to end, she knew this deep emotional feeling would never be repeated again, but she was grateful, for everything now hung in the balance; the war would see to that.

The next day, after spending most of it in the flat, Evie suggested they go to a pub in the East End on the Columbia Road to see a drag artist called Diamond Lil. George was all for it, she was feeling a bit cooped up. After they had washed and dressed, made their way to The Royal Oak. Though it was only six in the evening, the pub was full of drinkers and revellers talking loudly and shouting out at Diamond Lil, dressed in her full regalia, together with her sidekick Maisie.

She swaggered and sashayed among the punters; a wink here, a wink there, imagining she could pull any bloke she wanted and the punters loved it, they loved Diamond Lil with her bawdy jokes and her pick-up lines, cheekily flirting with all and sundry. She even flirted with George, which made Evie crease up with laughter. They listened to Diamond Lil sing her rendition of 'I Want a Boy', which had everyone clapping and cheering and joining in.

George went to the bar and eventually came back with two halves of ale.

'Fancy a ciggie?' George asked Evie above the noise, holding out a packet of cigarettes.

Evie helped herself to a cigarette and they both lit up.

'You know, tonight is not unlike the bars in Straight Street in Valletta, we have drag artists called Guzi and Bobby and a couple of others, and the sailors love them, the *street* is quite amazing you know.'

'Really? I could never imagine anything like this on such a Catholic island!' Evie exclaimed.

'You'd be surprised Evie, what goes on in those narrow streets, especially Strait Street, I mean you should see the Maltese girls, they are real beauties! The navy and army can't keep their hands off them. The girls ply them with drinks and make a hefty penny out of it too,' she said chuckling, 'You never know, one day you might just see it.'

'I would love that darling.'

The evening wore on and nobody seemed to want to go home. The landlord called the last round and everyone groaned in unison. By eleven most had left the pub in very high spirits and quite drunk. George and Evie feeling merry themselves, headed back to the flat. They hailed a passing taxi. It was dark outside, no street lights lit. The taxi, with its lights dimmed, could see only a few feet in front of him. They arrived in Epple Road, paid the driver a hefty price, before opening the door and climbing the stairs.

'Oh gosh, I feel a bit giddy, I think a hot cup of tea will sort me out.'

'One for me too!'

George went over to the wireless, turned it on and returned to sit on the sofa. She lit a Player's and drew in deep, letting out a stream of smoke. Whilst she smoked, she wondered what her mother and father would say about it, her mother would not approve for sure, her father would probably turn a blind eye and Connie would want to try it out herself. Dearest Connie, she hoped that she was being brave. The Italian Airforce was sending frequent sorties to the island, she also hoped her mother and father were safe, at least they had the shelter beneath the house. The very thought of the shelter reminded her of that awful moment her father had caught her out in her disguise. George swallowed hard, it broke her heart to have hurt her father, it was something that would remain with her for the rest of her life, she felt guilt and shame wash over her. Evie noticed George had gone very quiet. She sat next to her, putting the tea tray on the coffee table.

'Hon, you're very quiet, are you, all right? Is something bothering you?'

'I was just thinking about the time my father discovered me in the shelter beneath our house, dressed in my man's clothes, I mean the look of hurt and confusion shreds me raw, every time I think about it; I can never forgive myself for being so damned careless…'

'Darling don't be so hard on yourself, I know it's not something that can be done in public, being free to wear gentleman's clothing; the thing is, it's not accepted anywhere is it? We have to do everything covertly, there is no way around it, we have to hide who we are and I would think you would have had to be that way, especially in Malta,' Evie replied.

'Oh gosh, yes of course, I only got away with it in Strait Street, everybody gets away with it there, especially the transvestites, they do a rip-roaring trade with the military; but for me it was different, I never saw anyone like me there. I was accepted you know, they used to call me Mr George, and the bar girls used to flirt something chronic with me, but that's as far as it went. I was too frightened of pursuing anything more than the odd flirtation, I had conflicting feelings, part if me wanted more but didn't know how to,' George said contritely.

'Well darling, you have me now and behind closed doors you can be anybody you like with me.'

'Let's go to bed Evie, I'm knackered.'

They both fell asleep instantly and did not wake till ten a.m. After they had breakfast, George told Evie that she had to go to her flat in Finchley Road, she needed a change of clothes and also suggested to Evie that she stay with her for a couple of days, before she went back to work. Life seemed to settle for them both, George spent most of the month of August going for walks on Primrose hill, visiting museums, commuting back and forth between apartments, sometimes at Evie's and sometimes at hers. It was whilst they were at George's flat on the morning of the 24th August, that gave the first indication of what London was to expect. A flight of misguided German bombers dropped clusters of bombs in the West End. The Thames Haven Oil Terminal suffered the worst, the bombs setting ablaze and damaging St Giles's church in the process. The explosions woke London up rudely, sending those lucky enough, scuttling to the nearest underground for shelter.

George and Evie sat upright in shock.

'For Christ's sake, we have only just escaped from Cornwall, I can't believe it's started with no bloody warning!' George muttered.

They waited, hearing the barrage of bombs renting the night. When the wave of bombers passed, they almost expected a second onslaught, but nothing happened. More was to come; the following morning George received a telephone call from Headquarters that she was to report for training immediately. There was nothing for it, George packed her kitbag, kissed Evie goodbye and they both left to go their separate ways. By the time George reached headquarters, it was lunchtime, the journey by bus had been laborious. She went straight to Major Le Petite's office, where he was waiting with a very smart looking Vera Atkins dressed in her WAAF uniform.

'Aaah, Agent Parker, it's good to see you and you are looking better than I thought after your escapade. Miss Atkins made sure you returned safely by sending partisans to look out for you,' Le Petite said gesturing towards Miss Atkins.

'Thank you, Ma'am, I'm grateful.'

'We're just happy to have you back.'

At that very moment there was a knock at the door.

'Aaah, we have a surprise for you Agent Parker. Come in!' Major Le Petite called out.

The door opened and to George's joy, Agent Adam Shilling walked in, as cool as a cucumber, with a very wide grin on his face. He quickly went over to George and shook her hand warmly.

'It's good to see you both together; you will be going to Scotland again for some more intensive training, you leave tomorrow, but in the meantime, Miss Atkins here will brief you as to what is expected of you this time round. There have been some changes, for the better of course, and things are now a little more professional and official too. I will leave you in her good hands. Miss Atkins?' Major Le Petite said.

'Right then, if you will follow me to my office, I will brief you,' she said leading them out.

Miss Atkins wasted no time once they were in her office. She spelt it out very clearly, that this time around, the missions would be dangerous, as the Nazis now occupied most of Paris, except for the Vichy, which she informed them harboured the Free French and government by mutual agreement. The Vichy officials were just as dangerous as the Germans, since they were collaborating. George and Adam would be in direct danger and had to be a hundred times more vigilant. The Gestapo were out in full force to expose any spies. George was to go in as a wireless operator again, but she also had to hone her prowess in using weapons of stealth, as she would not be able to carry a gun, so it would only be a knife and garrotte at her disposal.

Adam on the other hand, would be working closely with the French Underground and would be passing on information to George to relay back to Col. Buckmaster at London HQ. George and Adam were trying to absorb all the new information. A thrill ran through her in anticipation of getting back into the thick of things. They were to leave immediately and were driven to RAF Hendon and board a Lysander which was already on the tarmac, awaiting orders to fire up its engines. They climbed on board with another six passengers. Two women and four men; they found a place to sit and with no time to waste, the engines hissed and spat to life, making the whole plane judder and vibrate. They taxied to the runway, the pilot thrust the throttle forward and they were off, slow at first, then as it gained momentum, the Lysander left the runway and into the sky drawing up its landing gear. George breathed a sigh of relief, she hated the flying part and pulled out a cigarette, smoking it to steady her nerves. Adam smiled at her and introduced himself to the rest of the passengers as best he could, over the noise of the engines. George did the same. The co-pilot brought out three thermoses of hot coffee and poured everyone a cup. Soon they were all laughing and shouting out conversation. They arrived late in the afternoon; George and Adam were familiar with the routine and were soon showing the others the way, climbing into a lorry waiting for them.

At least this time it wasn't so cold, it being September. In fact, the whole countryside was in bloom, with purple, pink and white heather as far as the eye could see; it was a magnificent sight. George breathed in the pristine country air and Adam watched her with delight. The two colleagues had missed each other. At Airisag House two very familiar figures stood waiting for them. LT James Kerrigan and Dougal Mc Donald, ruddy faced and with a big grin, stepped forward to shake George's hand.

'Welcome back lass, I didn't think I was going to be seeing you again!' he said smiling broadly.

'Thanks Dougal, it's good to be back.' She genuinely meant it.

The rest of the crew were led inside for a hearty supper of roast venison with all the trimmings. There were appreciative gasps all round the table. They all tucked in with relish, it had been a long journey. As usual there was free-flowing whisky and George, feeling relaxed, even managed a couple of glasses herself. Feeling a bit more familiar with each other, they were all engrossed in conversation, when Dougal stood up and clinked a knife on his glass.

'Now then, I'm glad to see you are all enjoying yourselves, make it last lads and lasses, your wakeup call is at seven in the morning sharp, breakfast is at seven thirty and at eight you will be on the heath for your first bit of training. All will be revealed tomorrow. In the meantime, Captain Kerrigan will take you to Garramore Cottage; some of you have already been there,' he indicated with his hand to George and Adam, which made them feel important and singled out. 'Make sure you get some sleep, you've a long day ahead of you,' he mused, knocking back the last bit of whisky from his glass. He smiled at everyone and then left. Charlie Dobbs and Harry Kite, who were from the East End, were the jokers of the group, and kept the others, Sid Armitage, Andy Camp, Pauline Hughes and June Bishop, creased up with their antics. George and Adam left them to it and walked outside to smoke a cigarette and get some fresh air at the same time.

'It doesn't seem that long ago that we were here, does it…' Adam reminisced.

'No not really, in fact I feel sort of like an old hand next to them, if you know what I mean.'

He gave a grunt of agreement.

'Adam, what happened to you in Paris? I mean you just disappeared!'

'I was being followed by this unsavoury masculine woman and she had a bad habit of turning up in some very unlikely places, in the end I had to lay low as the Gestapo started to filter into Paris. I was near the Arc de Triomphe when Hitler drove past with thousands of German soldiers marching past in their dreaded goose-step, hundreds of tanks rumbled by… the noise was deafening, most of the French bystanders were devastated, especially the older ones. I watched them sob… it was heart-breaking.

Very soon Paris was swarming with the Gestapo; the German high command moved into the Majestic Hotel, the Abwehr — German intelligence — are in the Hotel Lutetia, the German Air Force in the Ritz and the Kriegsmarine — the German navy — have taken over the very aptly named Hotel de la Marine. You got out in the nick of time, I can tell you, so you have to keep an eye on these building and steer clear of them!' Adam warned.

'Oh God, I hope it's not the same woman that I met, she is a nasty piece of work and collaborating with the Gestapo, I suppose you heard what happened to me then?'

'Well news filtered through to me eventually, but it's become very dangerous, the Gestapo have already started rounding up members of the French Resistance. Most have gone underground, awaiting orders from us.'

'Well, I suppose it won't be long before we go back then!'

'No, not long at all, they are in desperate need of agents to start organising disruptive missions, like blowing up munitions factories and train lines, but I doubt you will be involved in these kinds of missions, you are more likely to go back as a wireless operator again; incidentally I managed to get your wireless from Mrs Manon, that woman is a darling,' Adam ended.

'Does that mean I don't have to carry one back with me?' George asked.

'I'm afraid not, George you are still going to have to carry another one, we need as many spare wirelesses as possible.'

'Oh well that's that then…' resigning herself to carrying the cumbersome contraption.

They went inside and picked up their kitbags and loaded them back on the lorry for them to go to Garramore Cottage. They waited in the lorry for the others, who took their time, acting as if this was some sort of holiday. This did not go unnoticed by Captain Kerrigan.

'Come on you lot, get yourselves into the lorry!'

George and Adam looked at each other and laughed as they heard him shout at the rest of the group inside. They came rushing out and sobered up before climbing onto the lorry. The cottage was warm and cosy; a blazing fire had been lit in the sitting room.

'See you back down here then Adam?'

'Yes, I'm not quite ready for bed just yet, I wouldn't mind another whisky and a ciggy,' Adam replied.

They had been assigned the same rooms they had before. It gave George comfort, being in the familiar space. So much had happened since the last time she had been here, it seemed like a dream. She left her kitbag by the bed and went back down the stairs to where Adam was in the sitting room. The others hadn't come down yet.

'Want a dram George?'.

'Yes, just a small one, I don't want to wake up the worse for wear in the morning,' she chuckled.

They sat sipping their whisky and smoking one of Adam's Players.

'God these cigs are strong, how can you smoke them?' George asked, coughing her lungs out.

'I don't know, I suppose I'm just used to them now; been smoking them for years.'

They were quiet for a while, enjoying the warmth from the fire. The whole room glowed, there was no electricity at the cottage, instead there were paraffin lamps hanging on the walls. Even their bedrooms had paraffin lamps as well as candles. It reminded George of home, because although they had electricity, her mother preferred the paraffin lamps. She could just imagine her filling the base of the lamp and trimming the wick before placing the glass shade back on. Her mother did that religiously every week and every week when the paraffin hawker Giuseppi came knocking on the door, George would go down with a tin can and get it filled. She could see Peppi (for that was what he was called by those who knew him) very clearly pulling his donkey to a halt, tying it to a ring in the wall and proceeding to the back of a large drum on the back of a cart and opening the tap. George smiled.

'Penny for your thoughts?'

'I was thinking of our paraffin hawker back home; oh Lord don't ask how I got there!' she laughed.

'I won't, but what I do want to ask you is about this woman who was stalking me back in Paris, she was a nightmare and at times I just couldn't seem to shake her off.'

'Where do I start?' she said, letting out a huge breath in resignation.

She told him about how HQ wanted her to tail the notorious Violette Morris, her background, and her very persistent nature. She told him of what she had done to get information from her for HQ and how it almost cost her her life. Adam let out a low whistle when George had got to the part where she had led Violette to her barge on the Seine and the scene that followed.

'My word lass, I admire your courage, I can't say I understand that kind of life and I don't want to, but it can't be easy for you!' he exclaimed.

'Adam it's not, far from it, it's not something I embrace, but I can't help it, I love women… certainly not Violette Morris's type, she scares me to death, there is something not quite right about her, you know, she even had her breasts removed to make it easier to race cars, can you believe it!' George said incredulously.

'It certainly is bizarre, let's put it this way, I will have no problem in dealing with her next time I encounter her, woman or not, or whatever she has turned herself into,' Adam replied.

'Be careful Adam, she is as strong as a man and she can box too, there's nothing she can't do and she can drink you under the table too, I have never seen anyone put away bottles of champagne like she can, and she smokes like a trooper as well, I thought I was bad enough!' she exclaimed.

'Hmm well I'm glad we've had this conversation though; she won't be the only thing I have to watch out for when we go over. The Gestapo are all over the place and from what I hear, they are now trailing the streets with detection equipment to detect wireless communications and capture them, which means you have to keep your wits about you.'

'Shhhh, the others are coming down!' George hushed Adam, as the others all walked in.

'So… what can we expect tomorrow Adam?' Charlie Dobbs asked.

'Well first off Charlie, you certainly can't all take this training with a nonchalant attitude, because they don't take to kindly to that. This is a serious business and you have to take things with a certain amount of responsibility,' he replied sternly.

'All well and good Adam, but we haven't really been told anything, except that it's government work and we are just to keep our traps shut and do what we're told,' Harry Kite piped up.

'In that case I suggest you do just that then!' Adam retorted,

'Oh… come on Adam, surely you know more than that?' Sid Armitage goaded.

'Look everyone, I'm not here to give out information, just bloody well take your training seriously and get on with it.' Adam clammed up after that.

He drank the rest of the whisky and mumbled some excuse to George and left.

'What's up with him?' Pauline Hughes asked.

'You wouldn't understand,' George said, wishing them all a good night and followed in Adam's footsteps.

She heard them mumbling, disgruntled that they did not get the response they wanted, but she didn't really care, they would find out soon enough.

At seven o'clock sharp they were all carted off to Airisag House for breakfast. They were quiet at the table, except for the chink of cups and the clink of cutlery. George helped herself to porridge, knowing full well it was perfect for the day ahead. Adam drank copious amounts of coffee and ate toast and jam. The others fell on the kippers and scrambled eggs, like there was no tomorrow. George understood their behaviour, since rationing had come into effect, the plentiful food at Airisag House was like a feast compared to London and the surrounding counties, where the rationing left people without their normal commodities. Butter, eggs, cheese, flour were all scarce and almost considered a luxury.

The door opened and Dougal walked in, looking ruddier than usual. He had obviously been talking to Captain Kerrigan, because he had this determined stance and looked at the new recruits steadfastly, making them most uncomfortable. Dougal wasn't one to mess with. Both George and Adam had great respect for him, he was a hardened and seasoned soldier. Dougal barked at them to get outside. There was a small table with maps and compasses. Both George and Adam knew this part well.

'Right, you lot, shape up, you have a twenty-mile-long slog ahead of you. You will split into two groups; Georgina Parker will take one group and Adam Shilling the other. Be back before sundown or no supper for the lot of you. There's a haversack each with a canteen of water and a packed lunch to get you through the day. Grab your surveillance gear and get onto the lorry. You'll be dropped off in two separate locations and you will make your way back here.' Dougal walked off with a merciless grin on his face, knowing full well that this latest bunch of recruits was going to have a difficult time adapting to the training regime.

They wouldn't last long. George and Adam would get them back, but Dougal was confident they wouldn't make it through the rest of it. He would have to have a word with Baker Street HQ about the lousy recruitment. Both groups were back before sundown, George's lot were the last in. They were exhausted and looked forlorn and glum as they sat to a supper of steamed salmon and boiled potatoes. They ate in silence, a big difference to the night before. Dougal walked in halfway through.

'Your day tomorrow will be a little easier, we have arms and weapons practice followed by explosives in the afternoon. Eat up and cheer up!' Dougal said, walking out with a sadistic grin on his face. The others grumbled as he walked out.

'Bloody tyrant,' Charlie mumbled.

Charlie's comment broke the silence and everyone started laughing, including George and Adam.

'You'll get used to him, he's all right you know, he's a decent bloke and a tough Scotsman, his heart's in the right place,' Adam remarked.

'Yes sure, but God knows what he's got up his sleeve for us,' Pauline retorted.

'He's just following orders you know Pauline, after all we are all here for a purpose,' George interjected.

'And what's that Georgina? Because nobody is telling us anything, there's a war on, surely someone knows what all this is about,' June Bishop, who had hardly said a word, commented.

'For goodness sake, you are obviously being trained for some sort of mission, just do your training and you will be told later on, just stop asking stupid questions!' Adam interjected visibly annoyed.

'Blimey Adam you're being a bit cross aren't you, what's up old chap?' Andy Camp remarked, noticing Adam's obvious irritation.

'Nothing Andy, just a waste of time asking all these questions, when everything will fall into place later!' he replied.

'I think we should go back to the cottage and get a good night's rest,' George suggested.

With the state of exhaustion they were in, nobody argued and left the table making for the waiting lorry outside. Once at the cottage they all disappeared, but George and Adam remained downstairs smoking a cigarette.

'Gosh they're a sorry lot, aren't they?'

'They're pathetic; remember that bloke Algie who was with us in the beginning? I thought he was bad enough, well they soon got rid of him and I suppose they will do the same with the others, although I rather like that June Bishop, she seems to have a good head on her shoulders, she hardly said a word on the hike and just trudged on like a trooper,' Adam made it obvious he had a crush on her.

'Well, I don't know any of them, I suppose when a bit more time passes, we shall see, Adam,' she said, dragging on her cigarette.

'I suppose you're right. Dougal will soon put them in their place, though I can't see Charlie Dobbs lasting long and that's de facto!' Adam concluded.

'Hmm you may be right.'

'Anyway, I'm ready for bed, see you in the morning George.'

'Righto, good night.'

For the first time since she was shot, George dreamt she was back at Dunkirk, stuck in the sand, unable to move and she could see herself covered in blood, trying to scream for help, but nothing came out of her mouth. She woke up covered in sweat and gasping for air. Even though the window in her room was open, she felt stifled. She foraged around for a cigarette and lit it, inhaling deeply till the smoke burned her lungs. She was shaken, she thought it strange she should dream about the episode now and not before.

It was three in the morning, the night air smelt fresh and as she stuck her head out of the window it reminded her of when she used to do the same thing from her balcony window in Valletta. It was in the midst of her thoughts, she noticed a movement down below. She pulled in fast and hid sufficiently to observe what was happening. It was Charlie Dobbs and he had a torch which he kept switching on and off as if signalling to someone or something. He was acting suspiciously and moved furtively in between some trees to the left of the cottage. George quickly got dressed and took a torch with her and crept downstairs. She opened the door and waited with bated breath. Charlie had disappeared. She waited quietly till her eyes adjusted to the darkness and followed in the direction she had seen him. She heard voices, very low and barely audible just by the slope at the back. It was pitch black but she knew where Charlie was because she saw his face as he drew on a cigarette. *Very careless, Charlie,'* she thought to herself. She moved closer, thankful that the grass beneath her feet muffled her footsteps. The other person who was also smoking, spoke in a very strange accent. *What the devil is he up to?* George wondered. She heard them mention Loch Nan Uamh a place she knew to be not more than an hour and a half away, she had seen it on her map. She had to get back and tell Adam, he would know what to do. She crept back to the cottage and into her room. Her mind was racing, Charlie was up to something and her instinct told her that he was up to no good. Though sleep was far from her mind, she drifted off and woke up groggily when her alarm rang at six fifteen. Remembering the events from earlier on, she shook herself and went to the basin stand, splashing cold water on her face. She was dressed in minutes and went over to Adam's door.

'Adam,' she hissed and knocked.

She heard footsteps and Adam opened the door, he wasn't quite dressed yet but invited her in unperturbed. He saw that she was agitated. She related everything that had happened.

'That swine! He's definitely up to no good, I vote we speak to Dougal about this and better still, I will ask him if we can tail him for the next few days; it will be good practice for us.'

After breakfast they went and found Dougal and pulled him aside in a quiet corner. George repeated everything to Dougal.

'The slimy bastard, I knew it! I just didn't like him from day one. Let me talk to Captain Kerrigan about this.' Dougal was livid.

After that, they carried on as normal and went to their firearms practice, which was followed by silent killing and demolition. Dougal was especially keen for George to learn the silent killing technique perfectly, teaching her how to overcome a man twice her size with simple but effective manoeuvres. She learnt how to use the garrotte and how to retain the hold on her victim till death ensued.

'That's good lass,' Dougal praised George, 'now go gather the others, let's get a wee spot of lunch.'

They gathered at the dining table, each looking forward to a delicious lunch cooked by Mrs Robertson, who appeared from the kitchen, laden with a pot of Scotch broth. She put it on the table and left them to help themselves, she returned with a large plate of warm oat bread and some butter. They fell to and left nothing in their plates.

It was Sunday the eighth September, the recruits were taking it easy, it was their day off from training; it was a date they would never forget. Dougal and Captain Kerrigan walked into the sitting room and everyone turned to look at them.

'We have some bad news, I'm afraid. London was bombed by the Luftwaffe yesterday afternoon, it suffered extensive damage in many parts, so if any of you want to place a call to find out as far as possible, if your families are OK, we will run you into the nearest village tomorrow morning. This state of affairs of course makes your training all the more important. Those of you who get through the next three weeks will be briefed with further information at the end. With that they both walked out.

'Well, that's that then, I bet now it's started it's not going to stop,' Harry said.

'That's stating the obvious Harry! Without a shadow of a doubt the Germans are not going to stop here, they are swallowing up most of Europe, it wouldn't surprise me if Russia is in the pipeline too,' Adam predicted.

'Give over Adam, they don't have the resources to go that far surely?' Andy retorted.

'You mark my words, that Hitler wants it all!' Adam added.

'He's going to have a huge fight on his hands, we may have failed in the Dunkirk affair but at least we saved most of our men to fight another day,' Charlie said.

Both Adam and George looked darkly at him, loathing this duplicitous character who just sat there making patriotic statements and yet was possibly involved in counter intelligence! They had been given the go-ahead to tail Dobbs. They would take it in turns to keep an eye on his movements. If he was a traitor to his country, they vowed to catch him red-handed. They did not have long to wait. It was obvious that Charlie knew his way around the area of Lochaber and Adam could have kicked himself for not seeing this when they had gone on the day-long hike. Charlie — Adam now realised — had been very confident when they had set off and at one point, when Adam had misread a particular path, Charlie had waited, totally unflustered, as opposed to the others who were worried.

At exactly three in the morning, Adam who had stayed in George's room to take the first watch, saw Charlie's form sneak out of the front door. Adam woke George, who had slept fully clothed and was wide awake in seconds.

'Hurry, he's walking towards the hedgerow again,' Adam whispered to her.

They snuck out of the front door and waited till their eyes adjusted to the darkness; the sky was cloudy but a waning moon peeped out from between them and when it did, it's silvery light made it easier to walk without a torch. They caught sight of Charlie lighting a cigarette by an old shed. They waited with bated breath. Sure enough, the other man turned up. Adam and George crept close to the shed keeping it between them and the two men. Adam gesticulated to her to go around the back.

He struck first, walloping the foreigner on his head with a cosh. He sank to the ground, but Charlie, taken completely by surprise, had not anticipated George coming up behind him, striking him a blow at the back of his knees, which made him collapse on his knees, yelping. She gave him no time to recover, throwing her weight on him and twisted his arm to the back, making him grunt in pain. Adam was soon upon both of them and helped George tie Charlie's wrists behind his back whilst he shouted and cursed. Adam tied the wrists of the prostrate foreigner too, who was now regaining consciousness from Adam's resounding blow. He too started cursing. The fracas brought Dougal and Captain Kerrigan, who had been waiting in the cottage.

'Well, well, what have we here? Charlie Dobbs I'm placing you under arrest!' Dougal said, lifting Charlie with one hand by the collar.

'Bugger off Dougal you can't arrest me, you've nothing to arrest me on!' Charlie said, smirking.

'We'll see about that!' Dougal responded.

Captain Kerrigan and Adam apprehended the foreigner who struggled violently in their grasp. They frogmarched the captives back to the cottage. In the meantime, the others, who had heard the commotion came down from their rooms in various state of clothing.

'What's going on here?' Andy asked, looking confused as he stared at Charlie's bound wrists and the strange man next to him.

'This, ladies and gentlemen, is what you are being trained for; to detain weasels like Charlie here and his shady counterpart,' Dougal shook them both viciously.

'What do you mean Dougal?' June questioned.

'Charlie here has been caught collaborating with the enemy, and in this case sometimes you will have to apprehend or even kill the enemy!' Dougal said.

The others had now got the gist of what had happened and were solemn and silent as they took in the gravity of the situation. Captain Kerrigan had gone to the wireless in his office and communicated the situation to the policeman in the village. There was one cell there and both of them would be spending the rest of their time there under arrest till they were transported to London for questioning.

Within an hour they were shoved onto a police van and driven away. Now that the fuss had died down, the others went back upstairs to get the last few hours of sleep.

Captain Kerrigan and Dougal turned to George and Adam.

'Well done you two, though it was a relatively easy operation however, you can expect much worse in the future, but it was a good example of what you have to face.'

'Thanks Dougal, we'll see you in the morning then.'

After the incident of the morning the others seemed to sober up and take their training more seriously. Nobody talked about Charlie any more, he had disgraced them. None of them wanted to fail and as soon as their three weeks were up, they were all sent to separate schools to finish off their training. The new unit at Baker Street, was formed by the Minister of Economic Warfare, Hugh Dalton, under direct orders from Winston Churchill. The Special Operations Executive was in its infancy and had started to organise finishing schools dedicated to sabotage and espionage, for potential agents who were to be sent mainly to France.

George and Adam were proud that they had been the first to start the initial unit transforming it to what it was now, the SOE.

CHAPTER 20

Back in London, George and Adam were sent to get their briefing from HQ at Baker Street. Again, George encountered Vera Atkins.

'Agent Parker, a pleasure to see you again,' Vera Atkins said, taking her hand and shaking it firmly.

Vera did the same with Adam.

'As you have probably already deduced, you will be going back to France, this time you will parachute on the outskirts of Paris, giving you just a day's journey to get into the centre. There are a number of French resistance units being gathered but they — the partisans — need leadership. This will be in your hands agent Shilling, to start the first one and agent Parker will be your wireless operator, but she will also be assisting you in a number of sabotage missions,' Vera Atkins briefed them.

At that moment, a smart, middle-aged man stepped into the room and introduced himself as Col. Colin Gubbins.

'Sir!' George saluted him as he shook her hand.

Col Gubbins turned to Adam and did the same. He looked at them both and said, 'I heard about the incident in Arisaig, jolly good show the both of you. The two men in question have been brought to London, they are still under arrest, the foreign fellow is of German descent and had been living in Inverness for some time, our sources told us that he is an agent and had been spying for the Germans for quite a few months with intent of guiding U-Boats to the coast. He won't be going anywhere except to a prisoner-of-war camp of course,' he finished off.

'Thank you, Sir, and do we know when we are leaving Sir?' Adam asked.

'We haven't got a firm date as yet, but all I can tell you is that it's soon; by the way agent Parker, how's that shoulder of yours, I heard of your escapade at Dunkirk,' the colonel said.

'I'm well Sir, just a bit tender is all, but I'm well on the mend,'

George said, amazed that he knew.

The Col. left the room and left Miss Atkins to deal with the rest. After discussing other matters on their personal affairs, which Miss Atkins indicated should be, so to speak 'put in order', she advised them to be ready to leave at a moment's notice. To George this spelt excitement, albeit a dangerous excitement, which she felt ready for more than ever. She resolved to spend as much time as possible with Evie. She felt it would be some time before she would see her again, or anybody else for that matter; perhaps it was a sixth sense that made her feel that way. She would write to everyone back home: her parents, Connie, Aunt Marlu and even Carmelo, though she hadn't heard a word from him since she left. They left Headquarters at around three in the afternoon. George headed to her apartment in Finchley Road and Adam went his way. They had made no plans to meet since their departure to France was imminent. George took a bus and, on the way, smoked a couple of cigarettes, contemplating over the afternoon's events. Her mind was awash with many thoughts, each tumbling into the other, trying to put them into some semblance of order.

There was a lot to do, this time she decided she would leave her personal belongings with HQ and should anything happen to her they would forward them to her parents, praying to God that it would not be necessary and that they, like herself would survive this wretched war, for she had been keeping abreast of what was happening on her island. Though air raids had been frequent, so far, the casualty list had been low and the Italian Aero Nautica had more misses than hits. For however long this would last, she did not know; but she did have fears that once Hitler decided to involve the Luftwaffe, things would be much more serious. Malta was a strategically positioned island in the Mediterranean and many marauders over the centuries had recognised its potential safety as a harbour and stepping stone to other countries. She wondered how life had become now under the hardships of war; *did people still go to bathe in the island's blue waters? Did they still walk the promenade of Sliema to enjoy the balmy evening breeze? Were they still going to the Chalet to dance under the stars?* she thought. How she missed all that and so much more; she missed the juicy summer peaches and purple plums, the sweet grapes that she sometimes went and cut from the vines herself, and then for a moment she wondered if she would ever do all that again, she wondered if she would survive, if she would live to tell her story when she got back to the island.

George hadn't realised that tears had been trickling down her face, until a passenger sitting on the other side of her asked her if she was all right. She felt embarrassed yet grateful that there was someone who cared. She had not felt alone like this before. Her thoughts had made her feel emotional. She was glad when she got off the bus at Swiss Cottage. She walked the rest of the way to clear her head. It was cloudy, so the light that evening was waning a little faster than usual. The street lights no longer came on and by the time she got to her flat in Cantley Mansions, it was twilight. Once inside, after switching on all the lights, she was glad to just collapse on the sofa. Her mail had been left on the coffee table. There were three letters. One from her parents, one from Evie and wonder of wonders there was one from Gracie. She read Gracie's letter first. As usual her letter was full of humour and excitement at finally making it as an ATS pilot and also at meeting Amy Johnson, a top female pilot who was famous for flying all the way to Australia; it sounded like Gracie was enamoured, but Amy had a husband so Gracie had to make do with a friendship.

Gracie's letter made George laugh; she missed her and wished she could meet up with her, like old times. She put Gracie's letter away and read Evie's next. Evie's was a short note to let her know that she was back into the swing of things after her sojourn and that she was looking forward to seeing her soon. When she read her parent's letter however, her heart felt heavy. There had been casualties around the Three Cities. Isla had taken hits, so had Valletta and Floriana and some people she knew had even lost their lives. Her parents were now living permanently in the shelter beneath the house, it was far easier that way rather than run helter-skelter every time there was an air raid warning. *Her mother must be terrified*, she thought; the guilt ate at her more times than she liked to admit. It hovered at the back of her mind constantly; she chided herself for having left her mother's side, and to make matters worse, she also carried the guilt of having disappointed her father, the scene in the cellar never left her.

She sighed and carried on reading the letter. It left her depressed.

She put it on the coffee table and was about to go to the kitchen to make some tea, when she heard a series of muffled explosions reverberating around the apartment. She ran to the window and saw what looked like a dark cloud flying overhead, lit by searchlights, row upon row of German aircraft, over a thousand of them, she knew they were German because she saw the unmistakeable cross beneath the wings. She heard the bombs whistling down, exploding on impact and according to her calculations, they must be in East London and the docks. The *Blitz,* as everyone was calling it, was relentless night after night claiming hundreds of victims.

She saw people below her window running into the street, heading towards the underground station. George grabbed her coat and did exactly the same. She ran without stopping, hundreds were pushing their way into Finchley Road Station. George managed to squeeze in. Rumours were flying around that the German Luftwaffe had blasted their way over the Thames. The RAF was, at that moment, engaging them in a ferocious battle. George stayed by the entrance, watching the dog fights, when they came into view. So far, no bombs had landed close, but the whining of crashing aircraft sounded nearby. The bombing went on for what seemed like over an hour; the pounding was unyielding and horrific. She watched loose barrage balloons floating untethered and on fire. The air outside the entrance was permeated with the smell of hot oil and choking smoke; the dog fights continued well into the night lighting up the sky and the merciless bombing claimed building after building and its countless victims — those who did not make it in time to seek shelter. George remained at the underground station till it grew dark. Then and only then, did she consider walking back to the apartment. She sped up the stairs and opened the door. She switched on the sitting room light and very quickly shoved her clothes into her kitbag, she grabbed the half a loaf of bread she had left and shoved that into her kitbag too and went back to the station. Most of the people were still there, crammed next to each other. There was no food or anything to drink and most were too frightened to move and do something about the situation. It was dreadfully uncomfortable; everyone tried to grab a space as best they could on the platforms. Children cried and the air became stifling. She felt suffocated in the confined space of bodies and left the station to return to the apartment. Once there she tried placing a call to Baker

Street, but the phone line was dead. She would have to wait till the morning. She gathered the rest of her things and put them into her kitbag ready for the next day. The next thing she did was move the kitchen table into the middle of the sitting room. She grabbed the pillows and blankets from the bedroom and made a makeshift bed for the night, not that she was going to get any sleep, for the sound of explosions told her it was going to be a long one. She filled a jug with water from the tap and took a glass with her and placed it next to the table on the floor. So far, no bombs had reached Finchley Road and Swiss Cottage but she was sure that would soon change. Her thoughts turned to Evie; she hadn't called her to let her know she was back. That went out of the window with the telephone line dead, she would try and get to her tomorrow. She got up countless times in the night to look out of the sitting room window from her darkened apartment, watching the glowing fires that looked like a fireworks' display in the distance. By three in the morning the bombing abated, she fell into a restless sleep, dreaming she was back on the beach of Dunkirk. When she finally woke, it was seven. She was drenched in sweat and shivering. She got up, washed and changed her clothes, putting on her uniform. She hadn't worn her uniform for some time and there was no real reason why she chose today to wear it, she just knew she had to. She made a cup of tea, literally gulped it down, before she locked the apartment door and left the building. She had no idea how she was going to get to Evie's; she walked in the direction of Swiss Cottage hoping that the underground trains were running. There was a very limited service and the platforms were packed. She was able to get on twenty minutes later and headed towards Baker Street Station, eventually getting to Earl's Court. Getting a bus to Fulham was a near impossibility. She walked the rest of the way to Epple Road. Her last few paces slowed down completely when she saw Air Raid personnel standing by what was once Evie's apartment. It was completely obliterated. George's legs collapsed beneath her and she fell to her knees covering her face. The Air Raid personnel rushed over to her and tried to lift her from her armpits. George remained crumpled sobbing her heart out.

'I'm sorry miss, it was a direct hit, apparently there were no survivors; two women were pulled out of the rubble and taken to the hospital morgue,' he said sombrely.

George finally stood up and walked closer to the rubble. She tried to comprehend that Evie was gone, she had never lost anyone close to her; her heart was exploding with a pain that almost stopped her breathing.

'I didn't get the time to say goodbye, I didn't get the time to say goodbye,' she lamented and sobbed uncontrollably.

The Air Raid worker put his arm around her, trying to comfort her. The gesture did not register with her. She felt as if she had stepped into a cocoon and heard nothing but silence as she walked off back whence she came. Everything was a blur: streets, faces, trees, houses; the tears kept rolling down her face the accumulation of the last few months seemed to culminate into an implosion of undealt with emotions, she was crying for everything and everyone.

She had no idea that she had passed Earl's Court Road, she just kept walking, oblivious to the air-raid sirens blaring out and the people out in the street rushing to safety. The sky, filled with the hum and whine of hundreds of aircraft overhead which hung in the air with dread. George was completely numbed. Bombs fell everywhere, crashing into the ground with ear-splitting explosions of brilliant white and red lights. A piece of brick hit George squarely on her brow and knocked her out.

As the doctor said at the hospital, it was probably the best thing that happened to her, because she was found in a heap with her kitbag strapped over her shoulder beneath a church archway, some kind soul had pulled her out of harms' way.

George was nursing a prize headache; she was disorientated and for a moment had no idea who she was and where she was supposed to have gone.

'You're very lucky young lady, no concussion, just a superficial wound,' a kindly doctor told her.

'Where am I?'

'You're in Fulham Hospital, once the nurse has changed your dressing, you can leave,' he told her, as he left to see the other patients on the ward.

George put her hand to her head and felt the thick bandage. She suddenly remembered the ugly scene in Epple Road and started to cry again.

'There now what's all this? Here, have a nice cup of tea, it will make you feel better.' An attractive nurse stood over her with a cup.

'I just lost my best friend,' George lamented with a trembling bottom lip.

'I'm sorry love; there's been a lot of that in the last couple of days; the world's gone mad since that Hitler bloke started this blessed war, we've not stopped, we still have some soldiers left over from the Dunkirk operation,' the nurse said.

George sipped her tea whilst watching the nurse move off to deal with the other patients. She took in her surroundings for the first time. There was a row of beds opposite her, where the patients were so wrapped up in bandages, they looked mummified; these must be the Dunkirk soldiers the nurse was talking about. They were in various states of body slings, mostly the legs from what she could see. She felt sorry for them; their injuries seemed so much graver than hers had been. The nurse came back to her bedside.

'The doctor says you can leave if you are feeling up to it.'

'Yes, I am feeling better actually,' George replied lying.

She got up and picked up her kitbag and walked out of the ward. It was dull and grey outside and passers-by walked hunched, whilst a cold wind blew down the street, taking with it anything it could pick up. George picked her way through the debris, choosing most accessible streets to Baker Street Headquarters; she wanted to make contact with Adam but had not asked him if he was still staying in the same apartment. HQ would know, she would go in search of Miss Atkins. It seemed to take forever, there were so many passengers on the underground trains and it made it all the more difficult moving about, because the majority carried their cumbersome gas masks. George walked the short distance to HQ. After signing in at the reception, she climbed the stairs to Miss Atkins's office. She knocked on the door and waited. There was no answer.

'Aaaah, agent Parker, there you are, we've been calling you at your apartment, we were getting a bit concerned when you had not answered… my word, that's quite a bandage you have around your head, what happened?' Miss Atkins asked her.

George told her about Evie and how she ended up in Fulham Hospital.

'I'm very sorry, that's a terrible thing to happen; we had in fact been in the process of making enquiries, you're being called up for your next mission. Agent Shilling is on his way up at this very moment, he seemed very anxious when we told him you had been out of contact for the past forty-eight hours,' Miss Atkins said.

'I'm sorry Ma'am; there was no way of contacting you especially with the telephone lines being down,' George replied.

'I totally understand, we will also have you accommodated elsewhere as it's not safe to remain in London,' Miss Atkins told her.

There was a knock at the door and Adam walked in.

'Aaaah, there you are lass, I'm jolly glad to see you, it looks like you've been through the wars though,' Adam said, eyeing her bandage.

'I'm happy to see you too Adam and the bandage makes it look worse than it is,' she replied, smiling affectionately at him.

'Seeing as you are now both here, we have planned your next mission. You will leave in five days, weather permitting; in the meantime, I think its best you stay with Adam, I believe you have a spare bedroom in your apartment?' Miss Atkins turned to Adam.

'Yes, Ma'am I do and it will be a pleasure to have George stay, we can go over details together and prepare for the jump, I'm assuming it's going to be a parachute job?'

'You assume correctly, you can pick up your details from the Operations Room two doors down and they will brief you accordingly; by the way, agent Parker, you will assume the same code name Chameleon,' Miss Atkins stated.

'Yes Miss Atkins, thank you,' George replied smartly.

'Thank you, Ma'am,' Adam said and they walked out of the door and turned to their right towards the Ops Room.

'Oh, Adam I'm so glad to see you, I've had a terrible time these last couple of days.'

'Tell you what lass, let's get our orders and get out of here and you can tell me all about it.'

George grabbed her kitbag and followed Adam into the Ops Room. There were two large manila envelopes, one for each of them. They thanked the dispatcher and left. As it turned out, Adam's apartment was in Stanmore, in Middlesex, which was the same underground train that

George used to take to get to her apartment in Finchley Road. At least Stanmore was a bit safer in comparison to Finchley Road. So far, the town had not suffered any attacks. She sat with Adam, her arm linked through his, feeling a degree of comfort. Adam was the closest person she had now that Evie was gone. He squeezed her arm gently as if anticipating her thoughts. He pulled out a packet of cigarettes and offered it to George, who took one and lit up.

'Are you all right George, I mean, are you up for this mission?' he asked her quietly; their carriage was empty except for one old man nodding off at the top.

'Yes, I want to do it Adam, I'm so bloody angry; I can't believe that Evie's gone, the war has only just started and she had to be a victim of it straight away. I couldn't believe it when I got to her street Adam; it was just awful, there was nothing left except a pile of rubble strewn all over. The policeman and Air Raid warden told me that it was instant, thank God. Her neighbour died too, I spoke to her once you know…' George said, her voice trailing off.

'I'm sorry lass, you must be devastated.'

George nodded and felt tears welling up. He gave her his handkerchief; she took it gratefully. Homesickness mixed with grief crept up on her, she wished she could talk to her mother but even then, what she wanted to say she could never utter a word about. How could she tell her about Evie, about the anguish and loss she felt? Instead, she leant her head on Adam's shoulder and wallowed in her thoughts till they arrived.

'We're here lass, it's only a short walk to the flat; I can carry your kitbag if you like?' he offered.

'It's all right, I can manage, thanks, I can't wait to take this blessed bandage off, I've got more dressings in my bag so I will change it once inside,' George said.

It didn't take them long before they were inside the flat. Adam showed George her bedroom, which was nothing special, but adequate with a single bed, a bedside cabinet, a small wardrobe and a chest of drawers. The curtains were drawn so it was relatively dark.

'I keep the curtains constantly drawn; I've been out most of the day so just in case I forget when I come in and switch on the lights,' he said.

Which is what he did as soon as they entered!

George smiled, it was a neat flat, or rather Adam was a tidy bloke, she was surprised. She half expected to find pile of clothes everywhere and dirty dishes.

Anticipating her thoughts Adam said, 'As I said I'm not here much and I have a cleaning lady come in and tidy up twice a week.'

'That explains it then,' George said, laughing, 'I appreciate you letting me stay Adam.'

'I wouldn't have it any other way and now what can I get you to drink, you can have tea or coffee or maybe a beer, I have a couple of them in the refrigerator if you like?' he asked.

"Hmm a beer please, I haven't had one in ages.'

Adam went into the kitchen. George heard him pull out two beers chinking the bottles as he took the caps off. He came out with the bottles of India pale ale and two glasses and placed them on the coffee table. He pulled out two cigarettes and lit them, handing one over to George. It reminded her instantly of when she had done the same gesture for Evie after they had made love one evening. She felt tearful again and chided herself inwardly; it was dangerous for her to feel emotional, especially with what lay ahead, God knows how much more death she would have to face. Adam took a long draught from his glass and pulled on his cigarette, looking pensively at George.

'What is it Adam, why are you looking at me that way?'

'I just worry about you George, you know how fond of you I am, I know you are strong and have proved yourself just as good as any man in the field, but you have been through an awful lot in the last few months and I'm just making sure you are ready for all this!' he exclaimed.

She went quiet for a few seconds and then said, 'I'm not feeling as strong as I should do, but I will be ready by the time we leave and as long as I have you watching out for me, I feel safe.'

'George lass that's the problem, what if I have to disappear like the last time, I can't be around to take care of you or watch your back.'

'I know but at least you are here now and this has to be my worst moment, I'm just in shock over Evie is all, I will get over it,' she concluded.

Adam got up to put the wireless on and kept it on low in the background. It was just after five in the afternoon when they heard RAF fighter planes flying overhead towards the south, they jumped up and went to the window.

'There must be another raid! This is what it's going to be like George, we may as well get used to it. It's not just going to be here, it's going to be the same in France,' Adam said gloomily.

'I knew that much from a couple of days ago; I mean I thought that Dunkirk was the epitome of death and destruction, but this war has many facets and each one brings on new atrocities and more pain and more death and I just want to have a part in stopping it,' she said passionately.

'I have a feeling it's not going to be over for a long time, after witnessing the strength of the German Wehrmacht and Luftwaffe at Dunkirk and the rest of Europe I doubt this war is going to be over just yet, so I've prepared myself for the worst, and like you I want to be a part of the fight.'

George went quiet and just sat next to him, eventually nodding off, her head sliding onto his shoulder. Adam readjusted himself to make her comfortable and held her with a tenderness that exposed his true feelings for her. For the fact was he had loved George from the first time he saw her. He had never showed her of course, especially when he found out George's inclination towards women. He remembered so clearly when they had been in France, he had pretended to be asleep in Albertine's house and had caught them in the act of lovemaking. He had felt a surge of jealousy but his honour kept him in check, especially since George was his friend and did not want to lose that with her, so he portrayed himself like a brother, almost.

Adam wasn't like other men; he was a gentle fellow, good at what he did, which was a little of everything clandestine. It was the main reason Baker Street had taken him on; he was perfect for the job of disrupting German Operations. He had no problem with executing anything, be it a mission or a human; he was as cold and calculating as he was gentle and affectionate, especially towards George. He knew George admired him and loved him in her own way, he did not want to do something stupid and spoil everything by displaying unwanted advances towards her. George stirred and yawned and opened her eyes, pulling him out of his deep thoughts. She realised he was holding her and remained that way in the warmth of his embrace, listening to the wireless, which was still playing, but not music, it was the news broadcasting that the RAF boys had warded off a strike on London by the Luftwaffe. George sat up and straightened herself and turned to Adam.

'Let's make some tea, I'm spitting feathers.'

He made a pot of tea and brought the tray to the coffee table. They did not say much, but it felt it was all right to be that way; it wasn't necessary to talk, they had that kind of relationship between them, understanding each other's right to solitude and yet being next to each other. When they had finished, Adam got up and put out his hand to George, she took it and he led her to her room. It was as if there was a new kind of understanding between them, it was as if George understood his affection for her but that he would never act on it or take advantage. She closed the door, undressed and got into bed. She fell asleep fitfully and then awoke, trembling from a dream. She couldn't remember what she was dreaming about, but she needed a cigarette. She crept out of the room, hoping to find Adam's cigarette packet on the coffee table, but it wasn't there. She wondered if she should knock on Adam's door. She saw a light from under it. She put her ear to it. It was quiet. She knocked and called Adam's name at the same time. He opened the door and let her in, he was wearing pyjamas whereas George was in a nightdress, but she was so comfortable around him, she thought nothing of it.

'I'm sorry I didn't mean to wake you up; I had a bad dream or at least it felt like it and I needed a cigarette.'

Adam said nothing and lit two, one for each of them. He sat on the bed and patted the space next to him. George went to the bed. After she had finished the cigarette George asked, 'can I stay?'

Adam said nothing but pulled the blanket back, inviting her in. He switched off the light and gathered George in his arms. In her mind George had never imagined that she would lay in bed with a man, but Adam was no ordinary man, he was her best friend, her protector and when he turned to kiss her, she did not stop him; rather, she wanted to experience the difference of kissing between him and Evie. She felt safe with him, she felt he would not violate her and she was right. Adam was gentle with her and caressed her with tenderness. When he entered her, there were no explosions of ecstasy but a sweet sensation of togetherness. It wasn't like what she felt with Ginny or Albertine or Evie, with them it had been much more intense, much more emotional… deeper, but she was glad it had been Adam to show her the difference. They stayed locked in embrace all night long and in the morning, when they got up, everything was as usual, like the night before had never happened. The only evidence of the night before was when Adam went up to her and kissed her affectionately on the forehead, for he knew that George would never be his, but he was grateful for the one night he had with her. He knew that last night would never be spoken of, but they would forever be bonded because of it.

They spent the next few days holed up in the apartment because the Luftwaffe were relentless, every night hundreds of bombers wreaked havoc, death, destruction and there was only some respite after the weather had made it impossible for them to perform any sorties.

They played cards; they listened to the wireless; made copious amounts of tea, ate mostly sandwiches and slept. George had recuperated marvellously, so much so, that as the five days passed, she was more than ready to leave on the mission.

The next day a car came to pick them up to drive them to Baker Street for their last briefing. They were to leave at midnight of the following day, the seventeenth of September. The moon was at its third quarter and there was a low cloud hanging over most of the Channel, but according to their contacts in France, there was interspersed clouds south of Paris. The conditions weren't perfect, but with the coordinates, the pilot would drop them over the designated point.

They got their kit together and were driven for two hours or so to the airfield. They parked near a huge hanger some distance on the outskirts of London and were led to a makeshift office, where they were able to wait in comfort. A shot of whisky to steady their nerves was placed in front of them. It was still only one thirty, they weren't due to leave till midnight. They were offered lunch, which Adam accepted, but George couldn't eat a morsel, at least not just yet. After some hours going over the drop map, which was to be in Giverny, they were told to try and get some sleep. George thought that there was no way she could shut her eyes, but to her surprise she must have dozed off, because their pilot woke both of them up with some hot strong coffee. It was nine thirty and the sky was mostly clear and the moon shone through sparse clouds.

CHAPTER 21

'It's a go, we leave in half an hour, so I suggest you go over your kits one last time and put your jumpsuits on as well as your parachutes,' the pilot said.

George's nerves returned in an instant; she realised that the time of reckoning had arrived. For one small moment, she contemplated pulling out, but then she looked at Adam, whom it seemed, was reading her mind yet again and smiled at her reassuringly and went over to help her with her parachute. Their cases were loaded on an old-looking Halifax bomber, along with George's wireless, which weighed a ton, but thanks to her physical training, George could lift it without much visible effort. The Halifax's four engines sputtered into life; its blades gaining momentum. The pilot, from his wind screened window gave the thumbs up and both of them were helped on board through the hatch. They settled in the hold, which was dark and dank and smelt of fuel. They waited for the juddering aircraft to taxi the runway. Its engines whined with the pilot accelerating to full throttle, pushing the plane forward. Gathering speed, it lifted off the ground and into the air with a suddenness that made George's stomach lurch. Adam saw her grimace and put out a reassuring hand on her arm. She looked at him, showing her appreciation. He could see she was nervous.

'George, don't worry, everything will be fine,' he shouted over the noise of the engine. The plane jolted as they climbed high through the clouds. George could smell the fuel in the hold and it was making her queasy to the point that her face became ashen. The pilot looked back to check on his passengers and noticed Adam gesturing him. He sent the navigator to the hold with a bag which had thermoses of coffee and sandwiches. The navigator pulled one of the thermoses out and expertly poured two cups without spilling a drop despite the juddering aircraft. He passed the cups one at a time to both Adam and George. George sipped hers gratefully, feeling better as the coffee hit her stomach. After a while they tried to doze but it was seemingly impossible because the aircraft continued to jolt even more whilst approaching the coast of England, where a bracing wind had whipped up. They flew for another three hours before the pilot shouted out something inaudible, as the aircraft suddenly pitched and nose-dived and then steadied itself. After what felt like an eternity, the red light came on in the hold and the pilot signalled George and Adam with a thumbs-up to move to the open hatch. Adam clipped his parachute to the zip line and made sure George did the same. There was no time to think, the light went green and Adam jumped, followed by George. The cases followed suit. For a while they dropped into an inky black nothing, except for a line of lights, which were being extinguished. They floated down; the dark shape of trees looming. Suddenly the ground rushed up at them and they fell with a thud some five hundred yards apart. Both of them very quickly unstrapped the parachute and rolled the billowing silk material into a manageable bale as fast as possible.

The reception committee made up of four armed partisans crept out of the shadow of the trees to greet them and retrieve the three cases that Adam and George had brought with them. They kept the silk parachutes, it was a useful commodity since their wives and sweethearts made the parachutes into lingerie. The party began to walk through the trees rapidly, till they came to a truck. They all climbed in and drove away to a safe house in the village of Giverny; it was not far from Paris, which was their objective. They were silent; they had to be for they had no idea if they would meet any German troops along the way. They were apprehensive but alert, rifles gripped tight, ready for any skirmish. One of the partisans whose name was Philippe, pulled out a packet of cigarettes and offered it to them, they obliged, took one each and lit up. Philippe lit one himself and held it between his forefinger and thumb with the ember pointing into his palm. George and Adam did the same. The truck suddenly braked. They had just come to a fork in the road and there was a roadblock guarded by two gendarmes. They approached the driver's window and questioned him asking for his papers. The passengers in the back could hear everything and prepared themselves for the worst. The driver then pulled out a small wad of francs and handed them over, placating the gendarme, who eventually waved the truck along. Everyone breathed a sigh of relief and settled back to finish the journey. Giverny was in deep slumber when they arrived. The four partisans melted into the shadows of the darkened streets and the driver dropped Adam and George at the safe house, which lay on the periphery of the village. It was far enough from prying eyes. They hauled the cases from the truck and before they even had time to knock on the door, it was opened by a ruddy looking man. He had obviously been waiting for signs of them. With as little fuss as possible, the party entered into a cosy kitchen where a fire was burning in the hearth. A cast iron pot was giving off an amazing smell of stew. The table had been laid with a three-foot-long baguette, goat's cheese and pork pate. George was ravenous and needed no encouragement to sit and eat. The patron, Pierre, beckoned Adam to sit at the table and he poured them all a glass of red wine. They talked about the advance of the Germans and how the underground resistances were growing eager to sabotage train lines and factories that were being used by the Nazi regime. They talked well into the early hours of the morning till they heard cocks crowing, heralding the dawn. Pierre suggested they get some sleep, as they were to leave Giverny that same evening for Paris. It was Pierre who had to wake them both up from the toll of their long journey, which had rendered them out for the count. Their spirits were high, having rested and eaten Pierre's food. They waited till seven o'clock before leaving the safe house and boarding the truck once more. This time Philippe was driving them and they sat up front with him, leaving their luggage and wireless at the back. Philippe drove them as far as Aubergenville, which left them halfway to Paris. George and Adam made their way to the train station; they bought tickets to Paris and waited for the train to arrive. There was no German presence, instead a group of gendarmes was checking passengers' documents, which did not necessarily alarm them, but they kept an eye on them whilst sitting on a bench. It was their turn to have their papers checked. George gave them hers and after a few minutes they gave them back to her. They then requested Adam's and seemed to be taking an extraordinarily long time to check his. One of the gendarmes asked Adam to follow him. George outwardly remained calm even though she was anxious. They were taking a long time and she became concerned when she saw the train approaching in the distance. Just as the train pulled into the platform, Adam came back with a smile on his face, reassuring George with a wink. He picked up the wireless case and beckoned George to follow him with the other luggage. They climbed aboard. Most of the carriages were empty, so they chose one midway and settled inside. George waited till the train left before plying Adam with questions.

'What the bloody hell happened? I thought you weren't going to make it.

'They were looking for a pilot whose plane had apparently crashed in the vicinity, well I put their nose out of joint when I told them that I didn't know how to fly a plane let alone crash one!' he said, laughing.

The rest of the journey was uneventful, even though German presence was visible at a couple of stations, the closer they got to Paris.

Gare Du Nord Station was heaving; there was a confusion of people all in a hurry to board trains out of Paris and into the Vichy area, better known as the free area of Paris. George had her first glimpse of the Gestapo in large numbers. It was overwhelming and almost made her stop in her tracks, but Adam, anticipating her reaction, grabbed her arm and made her pick up her case and walk firmly out of the station concourse. To others they looked like an ordinary couple, which thankfully, did not draw any unwanted attention. Adam led them to a café nearby and they ordered coffees and croissants. The weak October sun was enough to make them relax, smile and enjoy the moment. Being back in Paris made George think about Lutz and she wondered if he was still based here; it also made her think of that ghastly woman, Violette. She would have to be vigilant this time, it was going to be more difficult. After they finished eating and drinking, they walked a short distance away from the station and parted ways, as they had been instructed to do, in London. She hailed a taxi and told the driver the address. She noticed how things had changed dramatically since she was last there. Buildings brazenly draped in swastikas, troops patrolling, officers occupying all the cafés drinking beer, armoured trucks coming and going, even street signage was in German. It made her feel uncomfortable, almost like she wasn't in Paris at all, if it weren't for places like the Eiffel Tower in the distance as a stark reminder. George was in an apartment in the 4th Arrondissement. It was a large place on the third floor and it had everything she needed. It was quiet except for a piano playing somewhere in the block. She unpacked her case and looked around for a safe place to hide her wireless. She found it in the most unlikely place. An old soot-covered fireplace, which hadn't been used in a while. It had a recessed box in the floor, which was meant to catch spent ashes. She removed the grate and then scooped out the dank smelling ashes into a copper bucket; the wireless fitted in with a squeeze. She covered the case with ashes and replaced the grate, putting the copper bucket on top to add to the disguise. She would make contact that night; meanwhile she stayed in the apartment, going over her first assignment, which was to ride a bicycle past the Nazi headquarters in Avenue Foch with a camera hidden in the front basket. The bicycle was to be delivered in the morning and left parked just inside the apartment courtyard. The cine camera she had to pick up from the boulangerie downstairs, it would be covered by an assortment of bread. For the time being, even though George was back in her beloved Paris, she decided to lay low. The notion that Violette Morris might be hanging around left her with a bad taste in her mouth, for if she encountered her, it would be a foregone conclusion: the evil woman would see her incarcerated in the hands of the Nazis. She brushed away the nasty feeling her thoughts had brought on. She would get some sleep and be fresh for the morning.

The heavenly smell of fresh bread wafting through the window woke George up. By the time she had washed and dressed, she was salivating. She rushed down the stairs to the bakery and bought a crusty baguette. Running back up to her apartment, she managed to brew some coffee and fell to devouring chunks of the baguette, dipping it in her coffee. Sated, George prepared a small handbag and draped it over her shoulder leaving the apartment to collect the bicycle. She wheeled it to the boulangerie and left it resting outside.

'*Bonjour Monsieur Armand, comment allez vous?*' George asked politely.

'*Je suis bien Mademoiselle, que puis-je vous obtenir?*' Armand, asked.

'*J'ai mon panier dehors, peux-tu m'aider?*' George asked.

'*Bien sûr Mademoiselle,*' Armand replied again.

Satisfied that the code had been affected satisfactorily, the baker removed the basket from the front of the bike and disappeared at the back of the shop. Five minutes later he came back and gave the basket loaded with baguettes and a loaf of bread to George, who thanked him and walked out. She slipped the basket over the handlebars. She mounted it and rode towards her intended destination. Along the way she nodded to passers-by and smiled and at the same time studied the string that had been attached loosely to the basket but was long enough to be draped inconspicuously under the left handlebar. As the morning wore on, more and more people appeared walking along the streets and boulevards and among them mingled the dreaded grey Nazi uniforms. George kept going, following the traffic of cars till she came to the beginning of Avenue Foch. She pulled the string with one discreet deft movement and instantly heard the whirring of the camera. She cycled slow enough to capture the length of the wide residential tree-lined street. Along the way the Swastikas flapped on impressive and grandiose buildings. The concentration of uniforms was at its highest in two places. At the end of Avenue Foch, she turned left and carried on cycling, passing the Prunier Restaurant. It took her an hour to reach the apartment. She took the basket of bread upstairs and locked herself inside. George removed the bread and pulled out the cine camera, an 8mm Kodak, which she was familiar with. As a precaution, she closed the curtains and proceeded to wind the film up to the end as she had been taught, and then removed the film from inside, careful to keep the film in complete darkness to avoid exposing it, she wrapped it in a square of black cloth and placed it in a Manila envelope, sealed it and put it on the mantelpiece. When it got dark, she slipped down to the boulangerie with the basket and handed over everything to the Armand, who she knew would pass it on to Adam.

That night she made contact with London. She painstakingly removed the wireless from the fireplace, careful to move all the ashes to one side. The wireless was set up on the table which she had pushed under the window and all that was left was the antenna. The apartment had been chosen with the window facing the courtyard to avoid any unwanted attention from the street. She carefully secured the antenna to an iron water pipe on the outside and arranged the wire to run along the side of the window. She switched on the wireless and it leapt to life. Within seconds George was tapping away furiously in the Morse code of dots and dashes, sending information of her endeavours of the day.

Satisfied that she had understood their instructions, she switched the wireless off and returned it to its hiding place and repeated the camouflage. She would be meeting Adam soon to send new information but meanwhile she was to mingle in everyday Parisian life.

She understood exactly what was wanted from her. It was time for her to change clothes and assume her usual disguise, though she would not go out in daylight. The night was her cloak, one that shielded her from prying eyes. Her mission was a dangerous one. She would traverse the place called the Nazi triangle, which was an area that was favoured by the Nazis for recreation. Her disguise would have to be faultless, but that didn't bother her, for she was now an old hand and they had supplied her with an extensive kit of false moustaches and beards, as well as the clothing, tailored to enhance her shoulders. She looked the epitome of French fashion and this made her confident. No detail was spared, from the label sewn on her jacket, to the expensive Caron eau de cologne. She now smoked Gitanes and with her disguise, completely blended into the Parisian way of life.

The next few weeks George spent sitting at cafés, drinking Pastis aperitifs and smoking, watching black and grey uniforms mingle. Paris was the Nazi's favourite playground and indeed things seemed to be uncomplicated, that is, until orders from Hitler, made the presence of the black uniforms a thing to be reckoned with, for suddenly there was an air of danger and threat hanging over the city. George had been sitting in the 122 Club on Rue De Provence, a fancy brothel run by a woman called Fabienne Jamet.

Jamet loved entertaining the young Aryans dressed in their smart black uniforms, who showered her girls with flowers and gifts. The champagne flowed freely, all the while George sat quietly in a corner, observing everything. When everyone was drunk and at a stage of oblivion, she slipped out quietly and made her way to the apartment. It was late; the street lamps did little to light up the narrow alleyways. She had walked for not more than ten minutes when she thought she felt a presence behind her. She stopped to pretend to look at a darkened shop window and furtively looked over her shoulder, in time to see a man in a trench coat disappear up an alley. George kept her pace and as soon as she could, slipped up a narrow unlit street herself and hid in the shadows of a large doorway. She was right, she was being followed!

Her hand closed around the garrotte wire she had in her pocket and waited. The man turned up her street. George could get a clearer view of him; he was a few inches taller than her and of slight build. Her heart crashed over and over against her ribcage; she readied the garrotte in her hands; he was almost upon her. He never anticipated her! With one swift movement, she had the garrotte round his neck and pulled it with a superhuman strength. The man collapsed to his knees; the element of surprise helped George get a firm grip. The garrotte cut into his throat, bulging veins spurting blood as the garrotte severed them. She heard him gasping and gurgling; his hands were flailing at his neck, George held tight pushing her right knee in between his shoulder blades, in a desperate attempt, the man managed to pull out a knife and stabbed wildly, catching George in her right thigh. Still, she held on till his body fell limp against her, a dead weight. She collapsed on top of him, the ordeal exhausting her. But she had to move fast. She removed the bloodied garrotte and put it back in her pocket. She propped the body up against the doorway she had been standing in and quickly left the scene. One thing was for certain, the man had been looking for her; it was obvious, he had probably been tailing her, George cursed herself for being so careless, she clearly had not seen the man observing her.

Suddenly she heard voices and footsteps rushing towards her. George took off; shouting and gunshots fired in her direction. She dodged into an alleyway, where a pile of boxes filled with garbage gave off a horrific stench of rotting fish; it was her only chance of escape. She quickly hid herself among the pile and pulled some of the boxes over her. There were three Gestapo officers wielding guns. George held her breath as one of them came so close she could almost touch his shiny boots.

'Ach,' one of them exclaimed, 'we've lost him, we will deal with this in the morning, the bastards will pay, let's get back and report to headquarters.'

They left, walking back the way they came. George did not move for another half an hour. She extricated herself from the rubbish heap and kept to the shadows till she got back to the apartment.

George gradually limped back; she felt strangely elated and any fears she had had, subsided into oblivion. Once inside and only then, did she breathe a sigh of intense relief. She lit a cigarette and drew deeply before exhaling; her hand was shaking. She checked the tear in her trousers and removed them. The wound was a thin deep gash where the knife had struck. Blood had already congealed around it. She found a bandage from her first aid kit, applied iodine and put a piece of gauze over the wound then bound it. When she finished, she pulled out the garrotte from her jacket and washed it clean. Her jacket and trousers were ruined. She would dispose of them by giving them to the baker, he would burn them in his wood oven. The SS would be investigating the killing and there would be no let up till someone's head rolled. Someone would pay and be gruesomely tortured and executed.

She would have to make contact with Adam and let him know what happened. George realised how frightened she had been as she played the incident over in her mind, but at the same time she was thrilled she had managed to escape capture. She finally lay down and fell asleep. The next morning George woke late. She half expected a knock on her door, but it remained quiet. She was in dire need of a coffee but it was cold, so she huddled under the blankets till hunger forced her to get dressed. She inspected what was left of the provisions that had been left for her. There was a hunk of goat's cheese and the last of the baguette. She breakfasted on the food and hot bitter coffee, making a note of what supplies she needed, on a piece of paper. When she finished, she noticed that she had written the list in English and chided herself for being negligent; she rewrote it in French and destroyed the other note. All that was left was to leave the list with Armand, which she would do later when it was dark; she would slip it under the bakery door. With that out of the way, she settled back on her bed and dozed throughout the day till it grew dark. At a quarter past seven, she crept downstairs to push the note under the bakery door and then returned back to the apartment. She locked the door and proceeded to pull the wireless from its hiding place. She fixed the antenna outside the window. The contraption sputtered to life as she switched on the dials. She transmitted her message, letting London know of all that happened and asking them to get Adam to make contact with her. She was to radio again the next evening when her next assignment would be revealed. George dismantled everything and returned the wireless to the fireplace, repeating the same camouflage and hid the antenna behind the cistern.

George received a message from Adam to meet him by the Synagogue of Versailles on Rue Albert Joly at four p.m. The day seemed to drag for George, who wanted to see Adam badly, but the time finally arrived for her to leave. It was twenty past three when she left the apartment and walked in the direction of Versailles, till she could hail a taxi. At ten to four she bade the taxi stop her on the Rue Berthier. She then doubled back and walked to the Rue Albert Joly, slipped through the heavy double doors of the synagogue, climbed up the stairs to the gallery and sat in the back pew. It was so quiet you could hear a pin drop. A beautiful silver menorah was lit, sending graceful halos of light flickering over the altar it stood on. The wooden gallery on either side of the walls supported by intermittent ornate columns, stood high on the walls, as if ready for an audience. Stained glass windows reflected the last rays of the day and leant to the glorious aura of the synagogue. Whilst George was revelling in her peaceful surroundings, Adam had crept up behind her and placed his hand on her shoulder, making her jump out of her skin.

'Steady on there, it's just me,' Adam said, calming her down.

'Am I pleased to see *you*!' George exclaimed.

'I'm not surprised, since I got word from London about the whole incident, I've been frantic with worry, it's too soon for anything like this to happen now, the only positive thing about all this is the Gestapo are looking for a man. They have rounded up several Parisians and beaten the shit out of them,' Adam finished off.

'Oh Christ! There was nothing else I could do, he followed me and it was the only way to get rid of him, though I nearly came a cropper after. There was a group of officers who must have seen him collapsed and just caught sight of me leaving the scene, well I tell you I was at my wits' end. I ran into a cul de sac and found a mound of fishy smelling boxes and garbage and I just dove into them, only in the nick of time, because one of the officers stood so close to me, I could have touched his boots,' George recounted.

'I think you should lie low for a while, I will get word to London, when's your next broadcast?' Adam asked.

'It's supposed to be in three days' time, I wasn't going anywhere anyway.'

'Just as well then, because there are some very strange things going on; I've been watching the SS and Gestapo rounding up hundreds of Jews and questioning them,' Adam commented.

"Really? They are doing that here too! Bastards! I thought that was only happening in Germany!' she spat out with pure hatred.

'There seems to be an enormous hatred towards them and I've heard rumours that there's a programme to incarcerate them in purpose-built camps with the aim to exterminate them, heaven help us all,' Adam finished with a disturbed look on his face.

'Oh my God Adam that's awful, what's being done about it?' George asked.

'At the moment nothing can be done, we're just gathering information and sending it on. We have bigger problems George, the German forces have swallowed up everywhere: Holland, Poland, Belgium, Norway… the advance never stops, Russia is next!'

'Is London sending more of us over here?' George asked.

'Yes, they are, but they're still training the new recruits and they will be posted all over France.'

'Well, that's a relief!'

'Anyway George, we have to get moving because this is not a safe area, I will be in contact again soon, Armand will let you know.'

'Right, you go first, I want to remain here for a short while.'

'All right then, watch your back George and don't stay too long.' He left the synagogue.

After Adam's departure, the quiet enveloped George again, leaving her feeling peaceful yet vulnerable, because it was at that moment that she thought of home; it would be olive picking season now; she smiled to herself remembering the first time her mother and father had taken her to watch the olive harvest in Wardija. It was October with the summer waning and the fresher *Majjistral* northwest wind blowing in. They had feasted on *hobz biz-zejt*, a traditional Maltese bread filled with tuna, olives, capers and mint and everyone was happy eating and drinking homemade red wine. A tear trickled down her face, her heart was heavy with homesickness, a feeling she had shut out for a long time. She wished she could hug her parents, talk to them even, but she knew it wasn't possible. Her thoughts were broken by the sound of footsteps coming towards her from the direction of the altar.

'What are you doing here so late child? It's almost eight, don't get caught after the curfew it's very dangerous,' he said.

'I came to pray,' she lied.

'Then I hope Yahweh has heard you,' The rabbi said with a smile and waited for George to leave, locking the doors behind her.

George left the synagogue and walked to the Rue Berthier and hailed a taxi. Back in the apartment she noticed that Armand had brought the supplies she had requested; he must have good connections on the black market, she supposed. She put them away in the small food cupboard hanging on the wall in the tiny kitchen area. There was not much else for her to do. She could not write letters to send back home or read a book; she had none. They were the longest three days she had had to wait. But then things moved fast. Adam had sent word that they were going to blow up a Nazi troop train just outside of Paris. However, before George could take part in the sabotage plan, something happened that forced her to flee from her apartment. The Gestapo had surveillance trucks scouring the streets of Paris. One such truck had been dangerously close to the boulangerie. Armand had just about enough time to warn her. She had to move, and fast. Armand arranged for a female resistance fighter by the name of Fleur Petrus to move George to an abandoned apartment at the Square Le Bruyere in the 9th Arrondissement, close to the red-light district and the opera Garnier. Fleur helped George move her things under cover of the night. When Fleur opened the door, George was in awe and asked Fleur who the place belonged to.

'It belongs to Madame de Florian, but she died last year. Her son normally lives here but he is away for a short while and we obtained a key, but don't worry he is not coming back, at least not for the time being.'

The apartment was massive and filled with luxurious furniture. It seemed suspended in time. Gold-leafed armoires and mirrors adorned most of the rooms and it had been left in a state of hasty departure. George took the main bedroom, which had a heavy ornate wardrobe — one of the doors had been left open to reveal beautiful dresses — a vanity table equally ornate lined with bottles of scent and silver brushes and combs; George had little use for the luxury, but was grateful for the comfort. The sitting room had an enormous mirror hanging on the wall. Heavy yellow damask curtains adorned the windows which complemented the chaise longue and ladies' chairs by the fire place. There was a wooden trolley laden with books—all in French of course and a taxidermised ostrich, stood by the window, finishing the exotic and decadent feel the place exuded. The dining room was an elegant wooden beamed affair with porcelain plates and cups spread across a table. A French dresser boasted a collection of a finely painted dinner service and the walls showed off a plethora of paintings. George carried on exploring the grand apartment and came across a painting of a beautiful woman in pink; next to it lay a stack of what looked like love letters, tied in coloured ribbon. She took one out, curiosity getting the better of her. The letter was an intimate affair and signed by Giovanni, she imagined the rest of the pile belonged to the same Giovanni. George replaced the letter not wanting to disturb a memory that felt somehow sacred to her. After she finished exploring her surroundings, she hid the wireless among a heap of boxes and papers lying on the carpeted floor in the sitting room. It looked inconspicuous. Her thoughts turned to the mission she was to be part of the next day. She went to the bedroom where she had left her suitcase. Fleur had also given her a duffle bag which had a pair of trousers, a sweater and black wool coat; she also found a small automatic pistol with a spare magazine. She checked both of them, they were fully loaded; a shiver of excitement ran up her spine.

At three the next morning, a canopied truck picked her up. Adam was in the back waiting with another four men and Fleur. They were all smoking. Adam lit a cigarette for George. The truck made its way through the streets of Paris till it reached the outskirts. They stopped close to a wooded embankment and hid the truck on a concealed path among the trees. They all got off the truck and crept into the woods, till they reached a railway line. Adam handed out haversacks with explosives and detonators to two of the men and kept the third one himself. He gave out instructions and they separated, going in different directions along the track. About two hundred yards along Adam stopped.

'Here you go George, you know what to do.'

She nodded and took the satchel from Adam. She pulled out the explosives gingerly and bent down on her knees next to a sleeper. It was very dark with very little light from a quarter moon, but it was enough to see its reflection on the metal rail. She placed the explosive between the sleeper and the rail and inserted the detonation wires. She walked with the detonator towards a clump of bushes that hid them both. The others signalled by torch that their explosives were also in place. The train was due in twenty minutes, according to Adam's calculations. The twenty minutes passed but no train appeared. They carried on waiting and finally they heard the sound of the train's wheels echoing whipping sounds along the track as it approached. They waited, tensed, for the right moment.

The explosives went off with an almighty flash of light, lifting and destroying three carriages which toppled off the track. Confusion reigned among the German troops, who shouted, as injured survivors clambered over the wreckage. The partisans opened fire, downing them like skittles. George emptied her pistol, picking out the troops by the light of the burning and smoking carriages. She reached for the machine gun that Adam had at his feet. She swung it round and opened fire at the Germans, who were now pouring out of the train like angry ants.

'George, fall back, run to the truck, I'll be right behind you!'

George didn't hesitate; she ran as fast her legs could carry her towards the truck. She could hear Adam crashing through the undergrowth behind her. The remaining Germans followed in hot pursuit. They hastily climbed into the truck and pulled away; a hail of bullets tore through the side of it, one of which struck George in her side. She keeled over and collapsed. Fleur slid to the floor and held George, to cushion her from the bumping of the truck, which hurtled through the darkened roads. Adam too had been injured, a wound in his arm was bleeding profusely, but he took no notice, he was more concerned about George. She was thankfully unconscious. He quickly slipped off his seat and took off his vest, which he gave to Fleur to stem the flow of blood from the open flesh in George's side. They were not going to Paris but to a safe house on the outskirts; they would all then split up and gradually make their way back. Adam and George would have to wait, their injuries were too conspicuous. Once at the safe house Adam had his arm bound, but George's injury was more serious. She had lost a lot of blood. They couldn't risk taking her to a doctor; instead, one would have to be brought to the safe house.

One of the *resistantes*, Pierre, went to an American doctor who practised from his home on Avenue Foch. It was a tremendous risk; the doctor was an ally sympathiser and had frequently helped the French resistance since the war had started.

CHAPTER 22

Doctor Sumner Jackson bade his wife goodbye and left with Pierre. When Sumner, all six feet of him, arrived at the safe house, George was deathly white. She had lost a lot of blood.

'She needs a transfusion,' Dr Jackson declared.

'It's impossible, we can't move her; she won't make the journey,' Adam retorted, worry written all over his forehead.

'I've done the best I can, I've sutured the wound, but it has to be kept clean and your surroundings here are unhygienic, you have to get her to our hospital.'

'Doctor Jackson, Paris is crawling with the Gestapo, I don't see how the hell we are going to get her in without being seen!'

'Look, I will make an appearance at the hospital at around midnight tonight under the pretence of an emergency, I will send an ambulance to you but don't come with her; there will be a couple of nurses who, if stopped and questioned, will say she has an infectious disease. I will get word to you when she's ready to be discharged, but it won't be for a while yet.'

'Thank you, Doctor Jackson, I'm grateful.'

That night George was transferred to the American Hospital in Paris. The Boulevard Victor Hugo was thankfully quiet. When the ambulance arrived, two orderlies, together with two nurses, spirited George away on a stretcher through the back of the premises. There were concealed wards where 'special patients' were attended to. Doctor Sumner Jackson played a pivotal role in taking care of them. He was waiting for her and directed them into an operating theatre where he administered George with nearly four bottles of blood. Satisfied that he had done all he could, he had her transferred to a room, which door was obscured by a huge medical supplies' cabinet. The only way in was to move the cabinet each time. George had a nurse with her twenty-four hours a day for a week, before she started showing signs of recuperation.

Sumner realised the importance of saving every possible agitator, allied spy and French *resistante*, even if it was to his detriment. George would not be his last. It was another two weeks before she was moved to a safe house just outside of Paris, where she stayed for a month. There had been no contact from London or Adam for that matter. She was now ready to get back to Paris and carry on what she came to do. She had become impatient and was eagerly waiting for news. Her hosts, simple peasant farmers, had fed her well and she had become strong under the watchful eye of Paulette, a ruddy woman in her fifties, who always seemed to have a scarf on her head day and night and her husband Baptiste brought her a fresh egg each day to go with the copious amounts of pork pate, the wonderful *chevre* goat's cheese and crusty bread that Paulette baked each day.

George had been grateful, but the cossetting was suffocating her; she had to get out. Three days later, without warning, she was picked up and driven back to Paris to the apartment she had been staying in. Everything was as she had left it except that fresh food had been left on the sideboard. George smiled, happy to be back. She had been told to await orders and that she did for nearly ten days, during which she occupied herself exploring the massive apartment and sifting through the many books she found. She read all day and well into the night, stopping only to eat and drink copious cups of coffee. Her thoughts inevitably turned to Malta and her family and Connie. Bits of news filtered through to her by Adam were horrific. The island was being bombarded relentlessly, the devastation indescribable and the death toll unimaginable. The whole island was going through immense hardship and suffering and yet the worst was still to come. Hearing all this, George had been engulfed with sadness and grief; she felt helpless, useless even. She had no idea what had become of her mother and father or anyone else for that matter and she could not get word out to them either. She had wanted to cry out of frustration but nothing happened, instead she bottled everything up inside and channelled her emotions through her covert work. It was whilst she was reading that she heard a slight noise outside her apartment door. George crept to the door and noticed a folded piece of paper had been pushed under it.

She did not open the door to see who had posted it. The note was from Adam asking her to meet him that evening at seven. George calculated that it gave them a couple of hours before curfew, it did not give them much time but it would have to do. George was still aware that the Gestapo was still searching for the killer of one of their officers. There had been no word of the victim's identity. The one thing that helped George was the fact that they thought they were searching for a man. She smiled to herself. George felt a twinge of pain in her side and gasped, though her wound had healed completely, she still felt a little tender when she made a sudden movement. She went to rest for a couple of hours and then got up and dressed, preparing to meet Adam. She arrived at Champs Elysees Boulevard in front of the Café de Flore and spotted Adam immediately, who got up from where he was sitting and embraced her like he would a lover. George returned the embrace affectionately. Adam ordered her a coffee and a *pastis*. There were a few tables with German officers mingling with French patrons. George was surprised to see the Germans there; it was not one of their haunts. She raised her eyebrow questioningly at Adam, who anticipated it with a smile and the wave of a hand. He placed his hand on hers and squeezed it reassuringly.

'I'm glad to see you're much better.'

'I'm more than that, I'm bored,' she replied, smiling at him all the while.

'Well, I have some good news for you, you're going home.'

'Really?' George's face showed only the slightest disappointment.

'Yes, in four days you will be transferred to a landing site outside of Paris and you will be flown back, you will make one last broadcast to London the day before, just to let them know you are ready,' Adam told her.

'Who will replace me?' she asked.

'Another female agent especially chosen by Vera Atkins; she's the one taking care of recruiting the women now; she is the one who has ordered you back.'

'But I'm fine; I don't understand why I can't carry on!' George said, this time not hiding the disappointment.

'I know you're fine but maybe they just want you to take it easy, you've done your part and now it's time for others to take over,' Adam replied.

'Well, that's that then!' she exclaimed.

They finished their coffee and left together, arm in arm, walking the length of the Champs Elysees before separating. George caught a taxi to the 9th Arrondissement. She asked the driver to stop her by the Church of the Trinity. She had half an hour before curfew; she walked the short distance to the church, went up the stairs and seeing the massive door to the church was partially open, slipped inside. She sat on a pew nearest to the door. It was peaceful, with the flickering candle on the altar throwing playful shadows across the Norman shaped windows, the effect was mesmerising. She looked at the crucifix and suddenly felt sad. *If God really exists, how could he let all this suffering go on?* she wondered. Her Catholic upbringing was, of late, fighting a battle of conflict in her heart. There was a noise behind her, she turned around slowly. Her heart filled with an icy fear. Violette Morris walked up to her.

'Finally, I have found you!' Violette hissed with a sadistic look on her face.

In a matter of seconds George was surrounded by the Gestapo and a couple of other sinister looking men who were from the German Intelligence Service. They escorted her swiftly out of the church and into a waiting sleek black car. The silence in the car was unbearable, she could hear them breathing next to her. Her heart was beating so fast she could feel it on every breath she took. Fear shot through her faster than the blood pumping through her veins. She had an idea where they were taking her and a sense of foreboding enveloped her like a sheet of darkness. The car finally pulled up just as she had suspected, in front of 84 Avenue Foch: the Gestapo headquarters. George's heart sank when she saw SS guards standing smartly outside. Long red banners with the swastika on them flapped as if waving at her menacingly. She tried to prepare herself mentally for what was to come; her mind was in a whirl of possible scenarios. It was obvious that either Violette Morris had been stalking her or someone had betrayed her. The anger welled up inside her; how could she have been so stupid as to think that bitch had given up on her? They got out of the car. She was pulled roughly making her fall to the ground. She picked herself up and was frogmarched up the imposing stairs. Guards stood to attention, stony-faced, at each door they passed. They went up five flights of stairs; George counted them mentally whilst climbing them and then they came to a stop at the far end of a corridor in front of a door. It was opened and George was thrown in. The room was bare; a small window overlooked the street. George could hear the distinct sound of motor vehicles passing. It was dark except for the faint light from the moon, but even that disappeared behind a cloud. She calculated that it was about eight at night. She hoped she would be left alone to gather her thoughts and prepare for the onslaught that was to come. She had been prepared for such a situation as this, but they had taken her handbag where, hidden in her lipstick, she had the dreaded vial that would end her misery if the worst came to the worst. Tired and despite her fears, she fell asleep fitfully sitting up, her back against the wall.

Halfway through the night, George awoke with a start. The door to her cell opened and banged against the wall, shattering the silence. She was escorted to the sixth floor where an interrogator stood sullenly with his hands folded behind his back. Ernst Vogt was a ruthless man. His perverse methods of extricating information from his victims were superseded by the smile he portrayed on his face, instilling a false sense of calm before he began the process of interrogation. He made her sit in a chair and bound her arms behind her. George watched Vogt pace slowly, circling her like a tiger ready to pounce. In a split-second Vogt punched her hard in the face; an explosion of pain engulfed her. Her lip split on impact and bled in a rivulet down the front of her chest. Vogt stood back with a cruel smile on his face and watched the left side of George's face start to swell. George, still reeling from the assault, spat out the blood that had accumulated in her mouth. She faced Vogt and looked at him in defiance.

'What is your name?' he asked.

George did not reply.

'What is your name?' Vogt asked again calmly.

Again, she did not answer. Vogt punched her in the stomach, making her almost retch. She coughed and spluttered, doubling up in agony.

'What is your name?' Vogt repeated.

'Marie Colbert,' George answered, barely able to talk.

'You are lying, that is not your real name!' Vogt replied. The questioning went on for what seemed like hours.

Vogt gestured to another interrogator, who had so far remained silent, standing by the door, observing Vogt's actions. The interrogator, a burly man, pulled out a small roll of canvas. He placed it on a table in front of George and proceeded to open it purposely. Inside was an array of shiny surgical instruments. He selected a pair of pliers. Vogt nodded at him. George watched him approach her with the pliers.

The interrogator grabbed George's left ankle and took her shoe off. He clamped the pliers on her big toe nail and tugged at it enough to make George moan.

'Tell me your real name?' Vogt ordered, punching her squarely in her left eye.

George remained silent. The interrogator ripped her toenail out, making her scream and sob. After that the torture and interrogation went on for two hours till George lost consciousness. Vogt had her removed to her cell, leaving her in a heap. The return to consciousness was excruciating. Her toes were congealed with blood, as were her lip and mouth. Her stomach felt like a herd of cows had trodden all over it and her eye throbbed. She pissed herself and lay helpless in the warm puddle; she was unable to move; she was afraid to move, as each time she did, it brought on waves of pain. Tears slid down her face, not out of self-pity, more out of indignant anger and wishing her mother could be there to hold her, to alleviate the fear and pain. She silently called to her, telling her she loved her. George fell asleep exhausted. Her sleep, fraught with dark dreams, was cut short. The door opened and swung against the wall; two SS guards slung buckets of icy water over her. She awoke with a jolt, stiff and shaking from the rude awakening. She remained in a heap in the corner, unable to move. She stank of her own piss. They picked her up with little decorum, the guards wrinkled their nose and uttered derogatory remarks. They dragged her to the interrogation room she had been in a couple of hours previously. They dumped her unceremoniously on the chair. George found herself in front of Vogt again. This time he wasn't smiling. He gave her a glass of water and George drank from it greedily.

'It is pointless for you to remain silent; you will only make things worse for yourself.' Vogt said.

She remained silent. For one, she did not have the strength to reply and secondly, she was not going to give the bastard in front of her the satisfaction of seeing her cave in; she would rather die. This last thought, though brave, frightened her.

'Who were your compatriots in the train incident? We know that you were part of the sabotage,' he said.

'I have no idea what you are talking about,' George mumbled, just about coherent.

Vogt, hearing her reply for the first time, was encouraged to carry on grilling her, bombarding her with question after question and each time George replied with the same sentence. They did not beat her this time or inflict any torturous wounds, instead they took her back to the cell and left her with a crust of bread on the floor. George moaned like an injured animal and cried softly for hours, sobbing at times, which came as a relief. She felt empty, but strangely better when the tears stopped flowing. She chewed gingerly on the bread, careful not to touch her split lip, which hadn't stopped throbbing, along with her swollen face. She endured a further two weeks at the hands of Vogt and then for a whole twenty-four hours she was left alone. She had not been allowed to wash for the entire time. She lived in the cell among her own faeces and piss, surviving only on bread and water; her clothes were badly soiled. She lost all track of time because the cell was dark except for a very small skylight; her wristwatch had been removed a few days after she had been arrested. She tried to keep her morale intact but despite her training, she understood only too well now, how one had to be in the situation to understand and acknowledge the gravity of being caught, arrested and tortured. George glanced at her big toes; both were swollen and bloodied. She tried to stand up but her legs gave way; she remained prostrate in the corner of the room resting her back against the cold wall, shutting her eyes tight. George heard voices outside the door. She tensed instinctively, waiting. The voices stopped and the door to her cell opened. Two SS guards walked up to her and pulled her up from under her arms. She hobbled between them down the long corridor. Negotiating the same stairs she had climbed three weeks ago, a complete wreck, holding her breath, with each step curling her injured toes upward so as not to have contact with the ground.

CHAPTER 23

It was bitterly cold; her clothes gave little respite from it. The front door to the Gestapo headquarters loomed. They dragged her down the steps and shoved her in the back of what looked like a cattle truck. At least it was partially covered by an awning. One of the guards got in with her. They both huddled underneath the awning. There was little relief from the biting December wind outside. The truck sped off the Avenue Foch. The SS guard held his rifle tightly but then relaxed enough to pull out a packet of cigarettes. They turned off to the right. It must have been quite late, there was no one on the streets. The guard lit his cigarette and to George's surprise he handed it to her. For one moment she wondered suspiciously if there was some ulterior motive to this charitable gesture... *was he going to rape her*? But he didn't make any other move. She took it and sucked greedily at it. It was a sheer luxury after three weeks without a single one and she enjoyed every drag. The guard smiled, nodding at her. He next offered her some water from his canteen. She drank from it and handed it back, returning the smile as best she could; her face was still badly bruised and her split lip had not healed yet. The guard pulled out two bandages from his haversack and gave them to George, pointing at her feet. She took them gratefully and bandaged both of them; at least the bandages offered some sort of protection against the cold and the painful wounds on her toes; she was grateful for the kindness which was definitely not reflected by any other soldier she had come into contact with.

The journey was spent in silence with the odd cigarette being smoked. George hadn't a clue where they were going but a deep feeling of foreboding had settled on her. Once outside of Paris she had lost all sense of direction. They came to a halt outside a train station. On the platform stood an army of uniforms of different ranks with ferocious Alsatians.

A whole row of cattle wagons, most of them locked and windowless, waited. Puffs of steam escaped from the engine at the front. Fog haloed the subdued platform lamps, making for an eerie and macabre milieu. The scene before her sent a shiver down her spine. One of the cattle wagon's doors was open. What George saw whilst pushing her in that direction had her in utter shock. Faces, white with fear and hollow eyes, loomed at her. She clambered up to join them. There was no room to sit down, all remained standing. The stench of piss and faeces made her gag. The smell of unwashed bodies hung like a gruesome cloud. Nobody said a word. The door to the wagon was closed shut and a lock put in place decisively. George could hear breathing, some rapid, some convulsive and a few weren't breathing at all. Those who were not breathing were in a corner, their bodies already swollen and putrid. She recalled her conversations with Adam, how Hitler had created a programme called I4, to eliminate the sick, the vulnerable, the disabled, but none on this cattle wagon were either of them. She felt sick with fear, she knew what these cattle trucks were for; these were the Jews whom Hitler wanted eliminated to create the perfect Aryan race. This train was bound for a concentration camp where they would all be exterminated; its passengers did not know this; they thought they were being relocated but George knew…

The train jolted violently. Hissing and sputtering it pulled away from the platform among shouts and orders from the Gestapo. The Alsatians barked, straining at their leash as if waiting for escapees. But there were none and as full as the station was just a few seconds ago, now it emptied rapidly and its ghostly appearance looked just as undisturbed as before the German intrusion of two hours ago.

The wagon was so tightly packed that there was no room to manoeuvre. They all stood, sleeping by leaning onto each other. George could not sleep; her feet kept being trod on making them bleed over and over again. They had been on the train for what seemed like days, with no food and no water, the air was dank; body waste was all over the floor of the wagon. Somewhere in the midst of the appalling conditions came a voice, low, lamenting, uttering words George did not understand.

Eliy, Eliy, lamah azaf'Tanaiy rachoq miyshuatiy Div'rey shaagatiy
(My God, my God, why hast thou forsaken me? Why art thou so far, from helping me and from the words of my roaring.')

Her eyes welled up and her heart felt it would explode from sadness; she felt the sudden change of mood among those she stood with. Some sighed, some cried and others hung their head dejectedly, murmuring the prayer asking God for salvation. George then understood that these Jews, persecuted, hounded and hated for who they were, were God fearing. Adam's words rang in her ears: *Hitler's victims of his hatred.*

Then she cried, letting the tears fall for all the strife, the pain, the cruelty, all their predicament. The sadness overwhelming her, she sobbed, her body heaving. She felt a comforting arm on her shoulders, holding her, sharing her grief. She thought of her mother, her father, Evie and dear Connie. If she were there at that moment, she would have held on to her for dear life, telling her how much she loved her. The arm on her shoulders held her tight. She had no idea if it was a man or a woman, but right at that moment she didn't care, for that very action of endearment held her from falling apart. Her sobs had subsided and she became quiet. Just as suddenly as the arm had appeared to console her, it disappeared. The train was slowing down. It stopped, its wheels screeching in the process. A familiar noise of shouting and dogs barking greeted the filthy passengers; the cattle wagon doors were flung open. Bedraggled, hungry and thirsty, they were herded like animals. They had left in the dark and they had arrived in the dark. George could just make out the name of *Furstenberg* on the platform. Her knowledge of constant poring over surveillance maps told her that they were north of Berlin. What was there, she was still to find out with the rest of the prisoners; for that's what they were, nothing but prisoners. The soldiers wore a handkerchief obscuring their faces from the wretched smell of death permeating the air. Hundreds of prisoners, most of them women, poured out like ants, gasping and gulping in the harsh cold air. The prisoners themselves were made to pull out the bloated dead onto horse-drawn wagons. George watched with horror... limbs falling limply. She retched but nothing came out, leaving an intense hollow pain in the pit of her stomach. The German soldiers prodded them roughly with their rifles and led them towards cattle trucks that were waiting in a line.

George found herself sitting next to a young woman, not more than her age. She looked emaciated, her eyes were sunken and her arms pitifully covered in sores. Despite her obvious condition, she looked at

George and smiled saying something incomprehensible. George just nodded and then looked down at her feet. The bandages were black and congealed. She put her hand down to touch them and winced. George heard the word Ravensbrück for the first time from a female guard, who sat menacingly near the tailgate talking to another guard who was making sure the tailgate was secure. The convoy of trucks moved off in unison and headed deep into the forest of Mecklenburg, coming out near the shimmering Lake Schwedtsee.

On the far side was the village of Furstenberg where they had come from, George could just make out a church steeple. Ahead of them lay a grey wall at least sixteen feet high, topped with vicious curled barbed wire and signs saying, 'Trespassers Keep Out'. The forest track led the convoy up to the daunting steel gate. George's heart sank. The trucks emptied their contents like a mass disembowelment. Waiting for them was an army of female guards — *Aufseherin* in grey uniforms, complete with whips and formidable Alsatians who snarled at the newcomers as they staggered and hobbled in to the *Appellplatz*, a sandy square the size of a football pitch. The interior perimeter wall had an electric fence all around it. Grey barracks in neat blocks stood in a grid and dominated the compound. In a moment of bizarre hysteria, George giggled as she thought of what her father and mother would say if they saw her predicament. One of the female guards heard her and quickly wiped the smile off her face by hitting her several times with her whip. George fell, cowering to the ground, covering her head. She felt the hot salivating breath of the guard's Alsatian as it snarled and snapped near her neck. The guard kicked her and told her to get up. She did, with great difficulty. George felt the welts on her back throb. She didn't dare move for fear of bringing on another onslaught.

George learnt her first German words at the camp.

'Schnell! Schnell!' Hurry! Hurry!

They were marched to a building to the right of the gate and herded inside. A line of tables where guards waited with piles of striped clothing next to them. They ordered the women to strip off all their clothes and place them and their belongings into brown paper bags. They stood shivering, stark naked and humiliated. Almost all looked down at their feet and those who didn't, shrieked with indignity when they realised that male SS guards had been present throughout the process. George watched the guards laughing and hurling insults at the women, who tried to hide their shame, but she remained indifferent. From now on it was going to be a matter of survival.

They headed to the showers where icy cold water gushed out of shower heads. George welcomed the freezing water on her skin and scrubbed herself with the nondescript vile-smelling bar of soap. The water ran grey off her body. She discarded the foetid bandages from her feet, seeing her butchered toes clearly for the first time since she left Avenue Foch. They were still purple with the gouges visible where her nails once were. The water stopped and all the women were given towels to dry themselves. They were checked for lice and then the shavers were called in. George had her head shaved down to the skin. Her hand went up instinctively to feel her bristly head. Her pubic hair was also shaved before she was led to pick up her new camp clothing: Blue and white striped dresses with a jacket and a white headscarf, socks and rough wooden clog-like shoes. She was given a white piece of cloth with her camp number as well as a needle and thread to sew a black triangle onto her jacket, which, she eventually found out, labelled her as an asocial and a lesbian.

A siren screamed across from one of the tannoys spread around the camp, and they all lined up again in the Appellplatz before being marched by category to separate blocks. Each block had a Blockführer — block guard. George noticed that the women with a yellow triangle were led off to a separate area of the blocks.

The woman walking next to George whispered, *'Jehuden.'*

George nodded and carried on following the line in front of her to a block. There were bunkbeds three high running all along the length of the hut inside. Each bunkbed had a mattress filled with wood shavings, a pillow and a blue-and-white checked blanket. George was exhausted and, as uncomfortable as the bedding arrangements looked, she longed to lie down and sleep. She was allocated a bottom bunkbed towards the middle of the hut. A bowl, a plate, an aluminium cup, a knife, fork and spoon as well as a small cloth to dry and polish them with was given to her and all the other women. There was a toothbrush, toothmug, a small piece of soap and a small towel on her bed. At least she would be able to keep clean and for one moment allowed herself to think that perhaps things weren't so bad. Life in the camp started with an early roll call by their Blockova — the block leader, after which they were served a horrible swill that was supposed to be coffee and a lump of dry bread. Later those who were physically able were escorted outside of the gates to do hard labour, digging sand. George adapted to the gruelling work and kept to the rules, it was her only survival. Beatings were frequent and most of the time done for no reason at all. The guards' dogs were set upon them and George was a victim of a nasty bite on the leg many a time, which generally festered, leaving gaping sores.

When this happened, she went to the camp doctor, who administered a smelly ointment to her wounds. When they healed, further bites from the vicious dogs meant the process was repeated constantly. The guards kept the dogs starving; George frequently witnessed an inmate being savaged to death and the dogs fed off the corpse. The food they were fed was barely enough to keep them alive and the gruelling hard labour was back-breaking. If there was any resilience left in either of them, they soon resigned themselves to their fate. She watched many die; political prisoners were locked up in solitary confinement for weeks on end, left to starve and wallow in their own excrement and urine and others were taken away to be experimented on. These last never returned. Occasionally inmates would receive a letter; George received nothing. It had been two months since Christmas had come and gone in Ravensbrück, with little celebration. The new year of 1942 brought changes to the camp. It was March and though the camp was still covered in a light dusting of snow, the fierce cold of the past two months had subsided a little. George had grown thin and sinewy and constantly wondered when it was her turn to be fed to the crematoriums which belched smoke and soot constantly. She was summoned one day by a guard and pushed in the direction of the camp's chief female guard, Johanna Langfeld's office. It was with trepidation she climbed the three steps. Langfeld's headquarters was in a perfect position. From her desk she had a view that looked out over the Appellplatz. Langfeld watched as George made her way in her direction. waiting for her to enter the room. She gestured for her to come to her desk. She handed George a paper that was typewritten. She couldn't make head or tale out of it and

326

she supposed she wasn't meant to either, since it was in German and her understanding of the language was just enough to get her by. Langfeld saw her confusion and got up and summoned one of the guards outside. She spoke a few words to the guard who quickly dragged George down the steps and pushed her brusquely towards the kitchen block. At first George thought she was being taken to the mess kitchen, but a sharp detour meant they were in fact heading to the crematorium. George was numbed with shock. When they entered there were dead bodies lined up, ready to be shoved into the ovens. The guard sniggered at George's expression and pushed her towards one of the bodies, indicating her to help another woman to place a decaying body in the oven opposite to where she was standing. George grabbed another emaciated body which was skin and bones and full of sores. She gagged and nearly lost her grip of the corpse. The guard whipped her soundly across her back, but George, now used to these beatings, carried on with the process till the whole body was in the oven. She closed the heavy iron doors with the help of the other woman and moved on to the next oven. This went on the whole day. The smell of death had permeated her skin, her hair and her breath. When back at her block, the meagre piece of stale bread and watery soup lay untouched and eyed hungrily by the other inmates. George knew that she had to eat to keep up her strength—what was left of it. She ate her portion of food and cleaned her plate. That night as she slept on her sawdust-filled mattress covered by her thin blanket, she dreamt of home, of the first spring blossoms on orange and lemon trees, the red poppies mingling with green wheat fields, the prickly pear palms lining the country roads, the smell of minestrone wafting from her mother's kitchen and her father poring over his model planes. She awoke to the tannoy's wakeup call with her face saturated in tears and her chest aching. She was herded with other women to the crematorium again, and ordered to do the same gruesome task as before. It became as natural as eating, shoving dead bodies in the ovens to be cremated. It went on for weeks and months. George lost all sense of time, the day dawned and the night came and each day was the same, a struggle to just survive. The only thing that George looked forward to, were the summer months. At least the warm climate was more bearable than the harsh winter. July came and one day a truck drove through the gates and six new guards climbed out.

One in particular was a beautiful blonde-haired woman who couldn't have been more than eighteen. The new guards were being given a tour of the camp; the crematorium was left till last. The six guards marched into the interior and were hit by a foul smell of decomposing flesh. One of them vomited, the rest covered their face with a handkerchief, except one. Her name was Irma Grese, she looked on indifferent, observing every move and motion that went on. George caught Grese's eye, not that she had intended to, but the woman was beautiful. Compared to the sallow and white faces she saw every day, Grese looked like an angel, with her long curls under the peaked guards' cap. If Grese had noticed George looking at her, she did not show it; her face remained impassive. With the tour over, the guards were led away to their quarters. The next day it was Grese who came to wake them up; she had been assigned to George's block.

'Raus! Raus!' Out! Out! came a loud voice.

Grese stood in high black leather boots, skirt and shirt with a tie and peaked cap and a whip dangling at her side. In an instant she grabbed her whip and started to walk along the bunk beds, thrashing each and every inmate, who climbed down from their beds, terrified and moaning. One inmate Danka, a Polish Jew, lay still in her bed. Grese went for her like a rabid dog, screaming at her to get up and whipping her till she drew blood. Danka still did not move. George approached Grese.

'I think she is dead *Aufseherin,*' George volunteered in broken German.

'Nobody asked you, you bitch!' Grese sputtered, spinning round, beating George viciously, each lash biting into her thin dress. George huddled up, drawing her knees up to her chin and gritting her teeth in the process. Each lash left a searing pain in its wake. The others looked on helplessly, unable to help George, for fear of retribution. As suddenly as Grese flew into a rage, she stopped. Rearranging her clothing, she left the hut, kicking George in the ribs on the way out, making her yelp. The others waited till Grese left and rushed to George's aid. They helped her up. Crippled with pain, George sat on the edge of her bunk, but not for long. Their Blockova rushed over to where George was sitting and slapped her soundly on the face.

'Get up stupid woman and make your bed, and that goes for the rest of you too, hurry! You have five minutes to roll call.'

She hobbled out with the rest of the block and held herself up as straight as possible, whilst the camp Blockovas counted the women in rows of five. Grese stood in the distance tapping her cellophane whip against the right side of her leg. The roll-call over, the women were sent to their various jobs, including George, who walked in the direction of the crematorium. Before she could enter the building, she was stopped by Grese. George lowered her head and kept her eyes to the ground.

'*Sieh nach oben,*' Grese said with a commanding voice.

George understood the order to look up and for a moment her eyes caught Grese looking at her intently.

'*Du gehst morgen nach Auschwitz,*' You are going to Auschwitz tomorrow night, Grese said, one corner of her mouth giving a hint of a sardonic smile.

George's heart sank at the word 'Auschwitz'. Grese saw the impact she had had with her words and walked away. George spent the rest of the day burning corpses. She had gotten used to the deathly smell that emitted from them as had the rest of the women who worked at the crematorium. In a way, it prepared George, who was convinced she would one day suffer the same fate, even more so now she knew she was going to the place that all of the inmates feared. Rumours had long spread among them that being sent to Auschwitz was the end of the line.

CHAPTER 24

True to Grese's word, George, together with twenty inmates, boarded a bus just after roll-call. Grese watched them and then turned away.

The bus took them all the way to Berlin train station. It was the early hours of the morning when they arrived. There were no civilians in sight, just SS uniforms with the usual rabid Alsatians constantly growling and barking. They were herded on to the cattle wagon ramps which were already full to bursting. Deja vu enveloped George; the same wistful and frightened faces watched her as she clambered after the others. She resigned herself to the hellish journey they were all to embark on, and a hellish journey it was, they stopped only twice and were given morsels of dry bread, which did little to quell the hunger pangs gnawing at her belly. When the train finally slowed down for a third time, George knew that they had reached their destination, she could smell it, that putrid stench of burning corpses, it clung to her like a second skin. When they had been allowed to bathe in Ravensbrück, George would scrub her flesh till it was almost raw, but it was futile, she could never get rid of it, instead any sores that she had, she aggravated and made them worse, but it didn't matter any more, certainly not now.

The train pulled the carriages on a straight track through an arched tower and onto a long 'ramp'. From a gap in the wagon George could make out an iron sign *'Arbeit Mach Frei'* (work sets you free). The wagons were opened and its contents emptied onto the 'ramp' where SS officers were waiting at mobile desks to select where they were to be placed. George felt powdery flakes float onto her arms and head and she looked up, it almost resembled snow, but she knew it wasn't, the flakes were grey and smoky human ash. She shivered. There were five chimneys bellowing the remains of God knows how many bodies from the gas chambers. A feeling of dread enveloped her; she wished she could conjure up something from the past to give her a moment's reprieve from the heavy and dark sadness living within her like a canker, but she couldn't, the only strength she had left, she mustered to keep her going. She didn't know if Grese had anything to do with her deportation. George felt a brief flash of anger at Grese, which dissipated instantly when the selection process started. The *ramp* was littered with prisoners' belongings, the sick were shot, and thrown on lorries like sacks of wheat and children who had lost their mothers were spirited away in the direction of the chimneys, as were thousands of others. George found that she had been spared the gas chamber for the time being and assigned to latrine work; she was tattooed on her left arm and became camp serial number 221142. A roll-call went on for two hours and then she was placed in a block of emaciated Jewish women, most of whom were too weak to work. The next day they were selected again and the number of women in her block was reduced. The weak were there no more. George was numb inside, not caring if she lived or died. Every day she cleaned the shit out of the latrines, the smell was even worse than the crematoriums, the stench resembled rotten flesh and clung to her like a dense cloud of disease. But as time went by, she realised that cleaning the latrines wasn't such a bad job after all; none of the guards came near her on account of the fact that she smelt like a latrine herself, she was left to her own devices. This gave her some respite from the daily beatings of the guards. The inmates she shared the block with gave her a wide berth, the others did not trust her and were wary of her wearing a black triangle and the other reason was the unbearable smell she carried around with her. This did not bother George in the least, her only instinct was to survive as best she could, every inmate for themselves, food was scarce and any of it that there was, she ate, sometimes having to fight for it. When a cockroach made its way into the latrines, George didn't think twice, with a resounding slap the insect was knocked out and went straight into her mouth, chewing on it like it was a roast dinner. She had been at Auschwitz two months when the cruel hand of fate struck. The gates opened and a truck, carrying female guards drove in.

Irma Grese stepped down from the truck, her blonde curls obscured only by a peaked cap. Her whip by her side and suitcase in her hand, she walked away in the direction of the guards' quarters. George hid to make sure she was not seen, she watched miserably as Grese faded into the distance. For weeks Grese was not seen, till one day she walked up to the latrines and wrinkling her nose, ordered George to the showers. She was given a small block of rough soap and ordered to scrub herself. Grese then made her discard her dress and gave her a new striped one and ordered her to sew on a black triangle. George was wary of all these new happenings. She wondered what Grese was up to. She soon found out. She had been assigned to Canada Barracks, where all the sorting of inmates' belongings went on. The barracks were piled high with every imaginable object; jewellery, money, pots, pans, cutlery, gold teeth, you name it, it was there in macabre piles. Everything had to be sorted. In Canada Barracks, life was as good as it got. They were allowed to keep any food they found, they were allowed to wear civilian clothes instead of the striped rags and best of all they were able to wash and keep clean. This new position, George found, had a price. Her new status meant that she also was to be Grese's personal servant at her beck and call. Every day George had to be at Grese's quarters to make her bed and clean the cabin, which she shared with another guard. Grese was particular about everything and if she did not make the bed correctly or if an imaginary speck of dust was found, Grese would beat George black and blue with her cellophane whip. The only good thing to come out of her position was the fact that sometimes Grese would bring her scraps of food back from the canteen, which was a luxury compared to the small piece of dried bread and muddy liquid that passed for coffee, she was accustomed to. The increase of her food intake meant that George went from emaciated to a semblance of normal. Her block inmates resented George; they jealously watched her living better than they, but there was nothing they would dare do and risk the wrath of Grese, for she was an evil bitch and the whole camp feared her. She beat and kicked inmates to death for no reason at all; she also built a reputation for her unorthodox sexual appetite. She frequently made totally unwanted advances on both the male and female prisoners, who dared not oppose her, for fear of their lives. Anyone who did, ended up dead. She struck a mean and cruel figure whilst she strutted the camp with her Alsatian and dreaded whip hanging at her side.

One afternoon George had been assigned by Grese to fold all her uniforms neatly and place them in a small pile in a chest of drawers. Whilst placing them in the top drawer, George saw a tube that said the word *Pervitin*. She quickly opened the tube and inspected its contents; it was full of white tablets. George removed two of them, took her shoe off and hid them between her toes and put her shoe back on. When she had finished her chores, Grese came back and made her sit down on a small wooden seat. George kept her eyes lowered. She felt Grese move close to her and lift her chin with her whip. She had no choice but to lift her eyes. Grese had no expression on her face, she just looked at her and started to caress her breasts with her whip. She froze in shock; she could hear Grese's breath quicken; she became excited and then, without warning, struck her across her neck and face, drawing blood from a deep welt on her cheek. George remained still, her face impassive, even though the wound smarted.

'Get out!' She all but screamed.

George ran out as fast as her legs could carry her and she did not stop till she got to her block. It was empty inside, there was another hour before the inmates returned from whatever hard labour they were doing. It was the first time in two years that she found herself alone, with no smelling bodies squashed next to her. Since she had to keep herself clean to work in the barracks and for Grese, the once putrid smells that had become a part of her, now suffocated her. She had moved to the bunk bed at the far end of the block, wanting to hide, almost become inconspicuous, from the others who regarded her with suspicion since becoming Grese's personal servant. They resented the fact that she got more to eat than they did and she had lost the gaunt look from her face as the food that Grese gave her to eat had allowed her to put on weight, making her look better off than the other inmates, who were weak, emaciated and ridden with disease and sores from starvation. George was also suspicious as to why she had been singled out by Grese and treaded carefully around her and her latest physical advances, which repulsed her. Grese was the last woman on earth she would touch. George remembered the *Pervitin* tablets she had stolen and carefully removed them from between her big toe and hid them in a crack in her bunk bed. At roll-call that evening they all stood in the Appel as inmates were counted and recounted. For two hours they stood, they heard the dreaded train of death approach the ramp with squealing wheels as it came to a halt. The crematoriums belched smoke constantly, almost unable to keep up with the thousands of Jews being gassed and transported to the ovens. George shuddered and rapidly thanked her lucky stars at the turn of events that now afforded her a small glimpse of survival. She was walking with the other inmates back to the block when Grese crossed her path. George stopped dead in her tracks, keeping her head down.

'Come with me!' Grese commanded.

George followed Grese in the direction of the guards' barracks. She pushed George roughly inside the door. The other female guard was nowhere to be seen.

'You are nothing but a Jewish dog,' Grese spat and kicked George in the legs.

George mumbled something under her breath.

'What is that you said?' Grese all but growled back.

As if out of nowhere George threw caution to the wind and replied, '*Ich bin kein Jude!*'

'What do you mean you are not Jewish?' Grese repeated.

'I'm not Jewish! I'm half Maltese and half British,' George reiterated.

Grese looked confused for a few seconds, 'Maltese? What kind of a language is that?' she mocked.

'It's a place called Malta, it's an island near Sicily, very near Italy,' George explained.

'Ach yes, I now I remember, I read about it in the *Völkischer Beobachter* last year when the Luftwaffe bombed the Grand Harbour,' Grese grinned with satisfaction as she said this.

For a very short moment Grese forgot that George was an inmate speaking to her with less harshness. From that day on Grese did not beat George any more. Occasionally when George was cleaning Grese's room, Grese would talk to her, just a few sentences, enquiring as to how she liked her job in the Canada Barracks or if she was being treated well. This behaviour left George feeling uneasy, she was not sure how to deal with this side of Grese, a side that probably only she saw, for outside in the camp every day, Grese was an evil woman, beating and even killing some poor innocent inmate with complete ruthlessness. George saw all this and inwardly hated Grese, for what she saw was her complete abuse of power, but at the same time George's instinct now was to survive, survive the day, avoid the gassing and maybe even escape. If Grese had decided to favour her, she would have to play it to her advantage.

George had been routinely cleaning Irma Grese's barracks for about two months, when one day, she walked in carrying a letter. Grese said it was from her sister.

'My sister Helene has sent news from home,' Grese said with a rare smile on her face.

George did not reply, just nodded her head.

'I have two brothers too and another sister but I never hear from them and I don't hear from my father; we are not on speaking terms, he never accepted me working for the Nazi regime,' she said.

George noted she didn't mention her mother. As if Grese read her mind, she said, 'My mother, her name was Berta, died; she killed herself because my father was having an affair with a younger girl from the village,' showing a slight hint of emotion as she spoke.

'I'm sorry,' George said, meaning it, thinking of her own mother, something she had stopped herself from doing because it was too painful to think of anyone close to her.

'It doesn't matter,' Grese replied.

Grese locked the door and sat on her bed and patted the space next to her. George was taken aback. It was a gesture that she never expected from Grese and it frightened her. She knew the punishment of fraternising with any German official, it meant certain death. But she couldn't refuse. She walked warily towards the bed and sat next to her.

'You do not have to be afraid of me, I will not hurt you.' She stroked George's short hair.

George shrank from her touch as it grew bolder. Grese entwined her fingers at the back of George's short hair and drew her to her face and started to kiss George full on the lips. George froze, but knew the consequences for refusal. The time had come for her to take advantage of the situation. She engaged in Grese's sexual advances and when it was over, Grese lay spent on the bed with George lying next to her.

'Get dressed quickly,' Grese ordered her; any softness she had showed earlier completely gone.

George dressed and was about to leave when Grese came to her and stroked her face.

'I will see you tomorrow' Grese said, her face impassive.

CHAPTER 25

George left quickly but the ritual repeated itself every day. Grese's sexual appetite was voracious. George found out that she was also having several affairs with other German officers. She was also aware of her increasing association with a new camp doctor called Josef Mengele, who was conducting horrific and maiming experiments on the camp's children, especially twin children.

George absorbed as much information as she could, if she ever made it out of Auschwitz, she would make sure she would be the downfall of as many of the camp guards and officers as she could, with Grese being at the top of her list, but for the time being she took care not to jeopardise her position. She did not want to be one of the thousands coming to the camp and straight into the gas chambers. George shuddered at the thought as she spent long hours sifting through the new arrivals' belongings.

They had sent her countless times to the ramp to help load all the piles of things onto carts whilst men, women and children were being selected before her eyes. The children cried as they were separated. One time a guard grabbed a child who could not have been more than a year old and shook it hard because it wouldn't stop crying, this only made the child scream in fear and the guard swung it hard against a cattle wagon, splitting its head open, trailing its brains as he threw it to the ground. The action put a hush over the remaining crowd of women who sobbed quietly, resigning themselves to their fate. George turned her face away and bit hard on her lip; if she had had a gun in her hands at that moment, she would have emptied it into the guard without even thinking about it or the consequences. Instead, she hardened her resolve and pushed the cart back to Canada Barracks and got on with her work.

Life at the camp went on, it was December 1943, the Germans celebrated raucously as the rest of the wretched suffered. When the New Year, heralding 1944, came a week later, it was a bitterly cold one. The meagre clothing that most of the inmates wore wasn't enough to keep them from dying of their miserable predicament, life didn't change much. George did not notice immediately that Grese's attentions were waning. It began when one day, as George had finished her usual chores in Grese's barracks, she walked in and whipped her out of the blue, leaving George badly bruised with welts all over her body. George had remained curled up on the stone floor, not daring to move. Before walking out Grese said 'I have made sure you have a map of scars all over your body so you will never forget me.' Grese then walked out. Alarmed by this latest behaviour, George got up with difficulty and hobbled back to Canada Barracks. From that incident on, Grese ignored her and even stopped her from cleaning her quarters. This left George feeling anxious with good reason. Whilst in Grese's favour, George was 'safe' from being eliminated, but now things were different.

For a few weeks George carried on her usual work in the sorting barracks, till one morning, after roll-call, she was summoned to join a group of women. The group was escorted by guards towards gas chamber one and she watched them carry two cans of *Cyclon B*. George was terrified, she knew what the walk and the direction meant; her end had finally come, no one knew where she was, she hadn't heard from the outside, no contact was ever made with her, this was it, she looked up to the grey sky and told her mother and father she loved them, her heart beat faster and faster; the door to the gas chamber came into view. Some women started to cry, others seemed to accept their fate as if this end was better than the suffering they were enduring. One woman tried to escape and was immediately shot. They were at the stairs leading into the bunker.

'Alt!' came a loud voice from behind them.

George, along with the others, stopped dead in their tracks. She heard voices behind her; she found herself being dragged away from the group and was brought to attention in front of a German officer.

'Yes, this is the one, have her brought to the transport, I have all the necessary papers, she is to be taken back to Berlin,' the voice said.

George was frogmarched to the sentry post, where a shiny black Mercedes car was waiting. She looked up perplexed and saw the German officer walk towards the car. She was gestured by the sentry guard to get inside. The German officer got in next to her.

'Drive please,' he barked.

The sentry lifted the barrier and the car sped off, leaving a trail of dust and chippings; the tyres biting the ground. The German officer removed his hat and reached out for George's hand. George recoiled in shock and looked at him. Surprise and confusion spread across her face; it was Lutz.

'It's all right don't be afraid, I know you are wondering what on earth is going on, I have been searching for you for months,' he said with a smile, waiting for his words to register.

'I don't understand,' George said, even more confused than ever.

'Let me explain, I work for the Special Operations Executive, not unlike what you had been trained for. That day when you saw me on the train, I was going to be deported as an illegal alien, an enemy of the State, so to speak, but I said I did not want to go back to Germany and instead I persuaded them to give me the opportunity to become a double agent, which is why you saw me in Paris and I befriended you to watch out for you,' he said with a smile. 'SOE have had me on your case all these months and frankly I'm surprised you are still alive, since most of our female SOE agents have been executed; you slipped through the net.'

'But how have you managed to deceive the Nazis? I mean surely they have had their suspicions?' George asked, still incredulous at the turn of events.

'There have been times when I thought I was going to come to a sticky end, but thank God my German ancestry has been my saviour; so far I have managed and now we are getting out, I have a change of clothes for you. Once we have reached the borders of Spain, Catalonia to be precise, we have a hard journey over the Pyrenees but we have partisans waiting for us to take us across,' Lutz informed her.

'I can't believe this is happening!' George said.

'Well believe it, we just have to keep going as far as we can out of Poland, we still have a long way to go and it's not going to be easy, but as soon as we cross Czechoslovakia, we then have to go through Austria, Switzerland and France and finally the Pyrenees. When we get there, we can at least breathe a little easier,' he said reassuringly.

'So how did the SOE know I was alive?' George asked.

'We didn't until Adam got word to us after a lot of careful

digging.'

'Dear Adam,' George murmured affectionately.

'I suggest you get some rest; I will wake you when we get to our first safe house, you can get changed there.

They were to take the *Chem De La Liberte* escape route into Spain. The journey had been arduous, and had proved a challenge, George put the Pervitin she had stolen from Grese to good use on a couple of occasions when she felt she could no longer go further. At the border to Spain, they crossed into the Pyrenees, passed on from helper to helper and safe house to safe house, avoiding all possible German contact. Finally, they made it to a fishing boat to freedom.

Dawn broke, George and Lutz, who never left her side, caught sight of the White Cliffs of Dover. She allowed herself a smile; a feeling of freedom enveloped her. In the afternoon of the next day, they found themselves at Baker Street HQ. Vera Atkins was there, so were Major Le Petite and Col Buckmaster.

'Welcome back Agent Parker, Agent Lutz!' They all said shaking their hands in turn.

'Thank you, Sir, any news of Adam Shilling Sir?' George enquired.

It was Buckmaster who answered her.

'Parker, I'm afraid I'm the bearer of bad news; Adam Shilling has been arrested on charges of treason, it was he who betrayed you to that Morris woman!' Buckmaster concluded.

'*What?* That's impossible, I don't believe it!' George uttered, incredulous.

'I'm afraid it's the truth George,' Lutz reiterated.

George felt drained and sat down almost losing her balance. She mulled over what she had just heard and now the words made perfect sense; he was the only one who knew her movements. She couldn't believe it, Adam, she had slept with him, trusted him and would have given her life for him. How could he have so cleverly duped her?

Vera Atkins came up to her and put her hand on her shoulder. George looked up.

'It's time for you to go home agent Parker,' Vera said with a smile.

Home George thought, *was a word I would never hear again; yes, I am ready to go home, but I know it will not be for long, I have old scores to settle!*

Printed by Amazon Italia Logistica S.r.l.
Torrazza Piemonte (TO), Italy